PENGUIN BOOKS

This Secret We're Keeping

Rebecca Done lives in Norwich and works as a copywriter.
This Secret We're Keeping is her first novel.

This Secret We're Keeping

REBECCA DONE

PENGUIN BOOKS

PENGUIN BOOKS

UK | USA | Canada | Ireland | Australia
India | New Zealand | South Africa

Penguin Books is part of the Penguin Random House group of companies
whose addresses can be found at global.penguinrandomhouse.com.

First published 2016
003

Text copyright © Amderley Books Ltd, 2016

The moral right of the author has been asserted

Set in 12/14.25 pt Garamond MT Std
Typeset by Jouve (UK), Milton Keynes
Printed in Great Britain by Clays Ltd, St Ives plc

A CIP catalogue record for this book is available from the British Library

B FORMAT ISBN: 978-1-405-92394-1

www.greenpenguin.co.uk

MIX
Paper from
responsible sources
FSC www.fsc.org FSC® C018179

Penguin Random House is committed to a
sustainable future for our business, our readers
and our planet. This book is made from Forest
Stewardship Council® certified paper.

To Mark

The second time Matthew Landley entered Jessica's life, he nearly killed her.

Only minutes earlier, she had glanced up from where she was caught inside the closed fist of a crowd to see that he was standing with his back to her, just a few feet away. Incredibly, after more than seventeen years apart, he was now so near that if she had opened her mouth and uttered his name, he would have turned round.

She simply froze. Perhaps she was waiting for the sight of him to dissipate as she tried to work out why her mind seemed so determined to trick her. She had been seeing his ghost for weeks now, a haunting of her peripheral vision that kept disappearing before she could properly perceive it, like a shadow being chased by cats.

But then he smiled at something – and, instantly, she knew that he was real.

Undetected, Jess watched as he began to move off through the crowd. He was taller than most so was easy to pick out, and was graced too with the distinctive shadowy stubble and angled jawline of someone who always looked good in pictures. A pair of sunglasses was pushed up on top of his shaved head – but in another life, Jess knew his hair would have been wild and dark.

After all this time, he was as familiar to her as a favourite photograph.

*

Jess was a caterer, and had agreed several months ago to cook for an audience at a food fair in the grounds of a nearby stately home in North Norfolk. It was the first really warm day of the year, and the lack of free-flowing air, gently sweating grass and scent of fermenting microbrew inside the main marquee felt oddly reminiscent of waking up half suffocated and hung-over under canvas at a music festival.

As she tried to locate the Cookery Theatre, a thick, slow-moving crowd surrounded her, an impenetrable mass of damp T-shirts and craning necks. From what Jess could make out, she had arrived at the tail end of a crush following unsubstantiated reports of a celebrity chef being spotted somewhere near the antipasti stand – though it eventually turned out to just be someone with an uncannily similar taste in spectacle frames. Collectively disgruntled, the crowd was now attempting to disperse, but all the stallholders had seized upon the extra footfall as a good opportunity to make up for the disappointment by peddling free samples, so moving anywhere at speed was becoming about as achievable as pushing to the front at a Justin Bieber concert.

Strains of intermittent feedback emanating from a malfunctioning microphone headset at least meant the Cookery Theatre was easy to find, though it sounded more like a half-arsed soundcheck than something people would pull up a seat for. Jess was on next, with Asian Fusion Food, but she'd already begun to wonder if it was too late to make a dash for home and claim an eleventh-hour outbreak of gallstones or similar.

It was then, as she casually pondered her escape, that she saw him.

A few seconds elapsed before he started to walk away. Feeling her heart rate notch up slightly, Jess mirrored his direction left, though reacting was made awkward by the stack of boxed ingredients she was carrying and the bag slung over her shoulder. As he emerged from behind a family buying armfuls of artisan bread, she saw that he was talking to a slender brunette – presumably his wife – in vertiginous heels and a coral dress that showed off to perfection her impeccable tan. A small dark-haired girl wearing shorts and a yellow smock top clung happily to his left hand.

They paused for a moment to look at a stall, and Jess saw him reach over to pick something out, turning his head to hear what his daughter was saying. Each movement he made was as deliberate as ever – careful, considered. For a few agonizing seconds, Jess thought she might have the chance to call his name. But by the time she was nearly upon them, they had already started to move again, his wife and daughter working hard to keep up with the long, purposeful stride Jess knew so well.

Beginning to feel as if a piston was going berserk back and forth in her chest, she strained to keep him in view as he made his way towards the marquee's exit. A path opened up unexpectedly through the crowd in front of her and she caught her breath, breaking into a sort of improvised quickstep to keep pace. But then, from out of nowhere, she found herself boxed in by three carers who were patiently angling wheelchairs round the back of the queue for the specialist vinegars.

Jess gasped audibly in panic as she was forced to wait. The crowd converged, and she lost sight of him. Sensing her impatience, the carers attempted a coordinated manoeuvre to let her past, but the surrounding throng was now too thick and there was nowhere for any of them to go. She met their helpless apologies with tears in her eyes. 'It's okay, don't worry, don't worry,' she managed, ashamed of her

3

rudeness, flooded with embarrassment and dismay. The humidity in the tent was becoming almost unbearable.

By the time she could move again, he had disappeared. Jess's hands were so damp that her boxes kept nearly slipping from her grasp. Too nervous to dump them – she'd convinced herself somehow that in less than fifteen minutes she would be tracked down and frogmarched on stage by someone very strict with a clipboard and set jaw – she began to push shoulders and elbows aside like swing doors as she made for the tent's exit. She was strangely aware that this might not bode well for audience appreciation later on: a middle-aged woman swore as she passed, and a young father exclaimed as her knee caught the arm of his toddler. *Sorry*, she tried to gasp, pushing on. *Sorry*.

She spotted the three of them instantly, halfway down the sloping field that led back to the car park. As her feet hit the grass and her lungs finally drew fresh air, she wanted to call his name, but internal hysteria had decimated her capacity for speech. She was running clumsily after him now, like a child trying to catch up with a pissed-off parent, her chef's clogs slapping awkwardly as she moved, slowing her down.

Eventually she was forced to stop and bend over, heaving and helpless, as she watched him climb into a black estate car. Strapping their child into the rear seat before joining him up front, his wife laughed loudly as she slammed the door. It was as if, having spotted Jess sweating and struggling to catch her breath above them on the hill, she had decided to taunt her with a triumphant display of family unity.

For just a few precious minutes Jess had found him again – yet far too soon he was slipping away from her. She had to move now.

The car began to reverse. Jess felt a simmer of panic in her chest as she watched it swing smoothly round to join the bottleneck at the exit gates. The driveway leading to the main road was long and single track with no passing places: it was one in, one out. The car's brake lights gleamed, the engine humming as it idled.

She saw then that she had a chance, a window of perhaps thirty seconds or less. So she finally ditched the boxes and her bag and ran, cutting across the lawn to meet the drive-way where it made a sharp elbow of ninety degrees beyond the line of cars. She had only intended to perhaps memorize his number plate or catch his eye – but as she approached the edge of the gravel, he reached the front of the queue and a space opened up on the single track. He accelerated, pos-sibly with impatience.

He was about to disappear for ever. The impulse to step out and stop him was so instinctive, it was barely a decision.

Right at the last moment, he must have seen her – because the car came to a screeching halt at exactly the same time as it knocked her off her feet. The impact in the end was more like a sharp nudge, which left her sitting down in the middle of the gravel as if she had simply decided to take a break from walking across it.

Her half-trance was interrupted by the strange orchestra of a car door slamming, a child crying and a woman swear-ing, accompanied by the first stab of pain somewhere in the area of her right thigh. And then he was squatting down next to her, putting his hand against her back, asking her if she was okay.

He hadn't yet seen her face.

'Oh my God,' his wife was exclaiming, each word a con-vulsion of shock as if she was the one who'd just been hit by one-and-a-half tonnes of German engineering, 'oh my God, oh my God, oh my God.'

'Don't move. Are you okay?' he asked Jess again. 'Don't move.' To anyone else, he would have sounded calm, but Jess could detect the panic in his voice.

And then she turned to look at him at the same time as he pushed his sunglasses on to the top of his head, and her tears came instantly.

At half the speed, half the volume, he echoed the words of his wife. 'Oh my God.'

His eyes were exactly the same. Green. Penetrating. He looked older, browner, more self-assured, as if the previous version of him had been in draft.

They stared at each other for a full five seconds, during which time her legs began to compute the impact of what had taken place – or perhaps they were processing the enormity of the real drama, unfolding now – and they began to twitch slightly. In the cherry trees flanking the driveway, a flock of chaffinches was chattering merrily amongst the blossom like nothing had happened.

'Are you okay, are you okay, are you okay,' his wife was gabbling now, but it was coming out like more of a shrill imperative than a question.

He let his head hang, and Jess moved a shaking hand from her mouth to cover her eyes, and they sat there like that on the gravel for a few moments as if this was the conclusion of everything that had come before, like they'd both just exhaled a breath they'd been holding for a very long time.

As all the sound around them seemed to fade they became their own island in the middle of the driveway, bunched up and motionless against one another. Jess was aware of nothing beyond the anaesthetic warmth of him breathing by her

6

side, the comforting span of his hand on her back, the sliver of distorted joy she could feel from them being – in the smallest of ways – together again. All the commotion appeared by now to have been suspended somewhere far away. The seconds stretched. She felt oddly calm.

But then came the brutal blast of a car horn ripping between them, forcing Jess to finally raise her head. She could see his wife angling her manicure against a mobile phone – nine, nine, nine – as a queue formed in both directions, the cars taking turns to circumvent the awkwardly positioned vehicle. Some people thought it was important to rev their engines very loudly as they passed, presumably to make a point about the inconvenience of unforeseen queueing on a three-day weekend. Others simply stared out at Jess from behind their windows with the same sort of blank indifference they probably reserved for the mentally ill or mortally drunk.

'Jesus *Christ*, Will!' his wife barked then, at which the child's cries made a sharp crescendo.

Jess's eyes met his. 'Will?' she whispered, to check she'd heard it right.

'Please,' was all he said. The fear was scrawled across his face like bad handwriting. He didn't need to say anything else.

Jess looked down. Her jeans were intact and as such there was no visible damage, like protruding fibulas or kneecaps pointing in the wrong direction. She could fake it, for now. Trying to ignore the pain, she said, as loudly as she could manage, 'I'm fine.'

He hung his head again with what could have been anything between relief and grim despair while his wife began to project-manage the accident scene, barking orders for Jess to stay where she was, for Will to give her his jacket, for

7

their daughter (who was frozen with fear) not to move – 'Do not move, Charlotte!' Then she turned her attention back to her phone: 'He's run someone over, Sheri, fucking hell, Sheri, he's run someone over.' It was unclear if she was already on first-name terms with the emergency dispatcher or if she'd redialled a friend in the time it took Jess to grab on to the car bumper and haul herself to her feet. Either way, she felt an unexpected stab of pity for whoever was on the other end of the line.

'Are you okay? Can you move your leg?' He still had one hand at her back, and was using the other to grip her elbow and steady her.

Jess stuck her foot out and jiggled her leg gently. It hurt like ████. She felt his fingers tense against her as she winced.

'Oh my God Will Jesus Christ,' his wife kept repeating, though she was keeping her distance, shielding herself with the car door as if she was afraid of getting blood on her shoes. 'Fuck. Is there any damage?'

Jess realized she might be talking about the car.

He turned round and regarded her then like he had no idea who she was, this meddlesome stranger with the high-end motor and untouchable footwear. 'No,' he said, though his voice was wavering, 'she's okay.' He gestured gently at Jess with an open palm as if she was an animal at a petting farm he thought his daughter might want to come and stroke.

From somewhere to their left, Jess noticed a female steward wearing a luminous tabard and determined expression striding towards them, preparing to vault a stationary hatchback and organize the chaos. Unwittingly, though, she only really added to it by starting to shout bossily around for witnesses, most of whom were pushing ninety with failing eyesight.

He looked across at her one last time, but just as he began to speak, Jess found herself being rugby-tackled from behind into a fold-out wheelchair by someone from the first aid tent clearly desperate to break up the monotony of a day on OAP-watch. And as she was wheeled briskly from the scene with a sheet of tinfoil over her knees, she could hear his wife still breathlessly exclaiming, 'Oh my God Will Jesus fucking Christ,' like he was giving her the best orgasm of her life.

2

Jess spent her afternoon and early evening in the confines of a vastly complex, digitally ticketed queueing system at A & E, where the doctor's eventual offhand diagnosis of bruising felt strangely anticlimactic after the initial promise of all the high-tech crowd management. The whole experience led her to crave alcohol in a way she knew should never be combined with painkillers, but she called her oldest friend, Anna, anyway, imparting just enough information to give her chest pains and suggesting they meet for a bottle of Merlot and some calm, objective analysis of the day's events. Anna got things off to a promising start by swearing loudly down the phone for a few seconds and then bursting into tears on Jess's behalf.

The village's delicatessen-cum-wine-bar, Carafe, was their favoured haunt. Run by Philippe, an expat from Bordeaux with a genetically faultless palate and a nose for an interesting cheese, the converted barn was a beautiful jumble of upturned oak barrels, chatter, clatter, and the mournful strain of Léo Marjane songs grinding away in the background.

When it started out, Carafe had been unexpectedly successful in recreating the ambience of rural France in semi-suburban England, but that was before the *Guardian* did a big reveal in an ironically titled *Hidden Norfolk* supplement and the place became overrun with quilted gilets and second-homeowners clamouring for New World wines, better lighting and a broader variety of E-numbers on the food menu. Only last week Jess had listened, fist in mouth, to a hysterical mother demanding orange squash, fish fingers and spaghetti hoops for her three (equally hysterical) under-fives.

Tonight, the place was full. It was warm and steamy inside and out, like something was brewing. Philippe had thrown all the windows open, letting in the close heat of the evening and the faint sound of rehearsing bell-ringers. Even more thoughtfully, he'd reserved a table in the window for Jess and Anna, topping it off with a Saint-Émilion claret and a plate of Carafe's best Camembert.

Jess made slow progress through the bar, exchanging pleasantries with neighbours and acquaintances as if she hadn't just had the strangest day of her life. On reaching their table she took a seat and poured the wine, allowing her gaze to drift to the courtyard outside and her mind to journey back to the driver of the car crouching next to her in the gravel only a few hours earlier. The expression on his face had been one of bewildered defeat, like he'd just received an unexpected knee to the groin from somebody six inches taller than him, his unspoken anguish a painful reminder of the last time they had met. It made her heart flinch even thinking about it.

Swallowing the thought away with the aid of the wine, she helped herself to some Camembert. She really should do more with soft cheese, she thought, as its stickiness clung to her fingers. She'd read somewhere that it was a winner paired with raspberries and black pepper.

And then, like always, there was Anna, raising a hand to Philippe as she elbowed her way through the crowd spilling out from the bar. Joining Jess at their table, she wordlessly took up her wine glass, like the weight of its full bowl against her palm offered a grade of reassurance that the medium of speech, for the moment, could not.

She looked beautiful tonight, Jess thought, with her kinks of dark hair tumbling softly down in tendrils, skin slightly flushed from the power walk and possibly the prospect of alcohol. Anna had been trying for the past year to conceive, so she wasn't really supposed to be drinking, but she generally made exceptions for significant occasions, such as weddings, birthdays and unforeseen road-traffic accidents.

'So, your hit-and-run . . .' Anna began, and then waited, presumably for Jess to explain how she was not half in plaster and getting her oxygen from a pump.

So far, Anna only knew what Jess had told her over the phone, which was that a car had driven into her leg but no real harm had been done. She had stopped well short of revealing the driver's identity. That sort of news could only be delivered face-to-face.

'It wasn't exactly a hit-and-run,' Jess said carefully. 'As in . . . he hit, but he didn't run.'

'Probably because you were wedged underneath his front bumper at the time,' Anna suggested, before softening slightly and taking Jess's hand. 'Jesus, Jess. Are you sure you're okay?'

In the hours since the accident and arriving at Carafe, Jess's leg had turned a surprisingly violent shade of purple and had started to gently pulsate like something slowly dying – but she'd been moderately reassured by her clear results from X-ray and the remarkable indifference of the consultant, who had popped his head round the curtain to diagnose soft-tissue bruising before promptly disappearing again. The extent of his advice had been to go home and self-medicate – by which he'd obviously meant it was nothing a fistful of painkillers and a glass or two of wine couldn't fix.

'I think so,' she said, nodding slowly. 'I mean, it's sore, but it could have been a lot worse.'

'Well, he must have been speeding,' Anna decided, her face so furrowed up with concern that Jess wanted to reach over and smooth it all out for her.

Jess shook her head, thinking it might be wise to start by pleading mitigating circumstances on the driver's behalf. 'No, it was completely my fault. I ran out in front of the car.'

'Really? Why?' Anna looked sceptical – which was reasonable enough, given that Jess, like most people, was normally sufficiently level-headed not to jump voluntarily in front of moving traffic.

As Jess fumbled for the right way to break the news, Anna's predisposition towards logical analysis began to system-overload with a flurry of diagnostic questions.

'What sort of car was he driving?'

'An expensive one.'

'Was he old? Like, too old to be driving?'

'No.'

'Too young?'

'No, no.' She thought about it. 'Middling.'

'Any passengers?'

Jess nodded. 'Two.'

'What about his registration?'

'The stewards got it.'

'Are you going to press charges?'

'No,' Jess said quickly, frowning. 'It's just bruising.'

But the two of them had been friends for so long now that they both knew this agitated probing to barely be necessary. All Anna really needed to do was lean back in her chair and look Jess in the eye – so she did. 'Okay. Why do I get the feeling there's something you're not telling me, Jess?'

Jess swilled the Merlot gently around the bottom of her

glass, admiring its viscosity, watching the wine legs appear. For so many years she had thought that 'wine legs' was just another term for pissed (it was Philippe who had eventually, discreetly, put her straight – possibly to prevent Jess from further embarrassment at his distinctly well-to-do wine-tasting evenings).

Jess exhaled sharply and met Anna's eye. 'This has to stay between you and me.'

Fortunately, Carafe wasn't the sort of place where people paid too much attention to neighbouring tables – but Jess leaned in anyway, letting her blonde hair create a little screen over one side of her face, as if it would somehow help her to get the words out.

'It was Matthew. Matthew Landley was driving the car.'

'Oh my God.' Anna put a hand across her mouth and they sat in silence for a moment, the sounds of the bar washing over them like water over someone drowning.

After a couple of seconds, Anna seemed to remember how to breathe, though she was still gripping the edge of the table with one hand like she was afraid it might be about to take off. 'But it was . . . it *was* an accident?'

'Yes . . . sort of. I mean, it was my fault. I ran out . . . I was trying to stop him.'

Anna stared at her. 'What?'

'I panicked.'

Anna failed to blink. 'About what?'

Given that she was neither police officer, security guard nor stuntwoman, Jess could see that flagging down traffic by throwing herself in front of it was always going to be tough to justify. 'He was driving away,' she said lamely. 'I wanted to stop him.'

'Enough to kill yourself?'

Jess swigged away the reality of the risk she'd taken with

some more wine. 'It wasn't like that. I didn't even think it through. There was no time – I just . . . stepped out.'

'How many people saw?'

'Too many,' Jess said, feeling a small twist of dread in her stomach. 'And he was with a woman and a little girl. I mean, his wife. He was with his wife and daughter.'

'Jesus ~~fucking~~ Christ.'

Ordinarily, a man in his forties being married with a daughter could hardly be described as breaking news. *Well, tonight it is,* Jess thought darkly, taking another long swig from her glass.

'And he definitely recognized you?'

Jess tilted her head at Anna like, *Come on.*

'Sorry,' Anna said quickly, pausing to remove temptation by sloshing the remainder of the wine from the bottle into Jess's glass with the sort of vigour that implied she would have quite liked to be necking it herself.

'So what did he say, Jess? When he saw it was you, I mean.'

'Not much. Hardly anything. There were people around . . . we were both in shock.' She hesitated. 'But – his wife kept calling him Will.'

A flicker of confusion crossed Anna's face before she caught on. 'He changed his name,' she breathed. 'So that's how he managed to disappear off the face of the planet.'

'Makes sense,' Jess mumbled through another mouthful of ripe cheese, deciding to keep to herself for the time being her immense relief on having seen first-hand that Matthew Landley wasn't dead.

Anna paused. Her thoughts seemed to be cascading so quickly that Jess wouldn't have been surprised to see her head begin to vibrate. 'Maybe it wasn't an accident.'

'No, it definitely was. I saw the car, and I –'

Anna shook her head and leaned forward. 'No, I mean, him being there in the first place. You said yourself you've been seeing him everywhere. Maybe you were right. Maybe he's been following you.'

Choosing not to challenge Anna over this rather interesting departure from her previous assertions that Jess simply needed to swap alcohol for tap water and insomnia for a good night's sleep, she just shrugged, all out of ideas. 'Maybe. I don't know. I don't *know*.'

Anna frowned. 'Okay. Okay.' Unlike Jess, Anna had been an excellent mathematician at school, and she generally dealt with problems by trying to out-logic them. 'Let's look at the facts. Even if he has been stalking you, I doubt he'll carry on now. Not if the police are involved.'

Jess swallowed. 'But I need to talk to him, Anna.'

Anna leaned forward so that Jess couldn't ignore what she was about to say, her voice gently insistent. 'There's nothing either of you need to talk about. Seriously – there's no words for what went on. It's best for both of you if you never have contact again.'

Jess didn't voice agreement but she didn't protest either.

'You know I'm right, Jess,' Anna pressed softly.

Even as their eyes met, Jess couldn't respond.

'So what's his wife like?' Anna asked, after a brief silence.

Jess was surprised to find she could recall details she didn't remember registering at the time, and struggled for a moment to articulate what they all represented in her mind. Silver statement jewellery. Glossy chestnut hair, spirit-level straight, and an excellent fringe. Gym-honed, with enviable muscle tone. The kind of implied authority that commanded careful handling.

'Not his type,' she informed Anna eventually.

'You don't know what his type is.'

'I know she's not it,' Jess replied, a little too briskly.

'Do you think she realized who you were?'

Jess shook her head. 'I don't see how she could have done. She just stood next to the car bellowing at him. I think she was a bit worried about the paintwork.'

'This is ▓▓▓▓ ▓▓▓,' Anna declared, like it needed saying.

As Anna finished her glass and Jess the rest of the bottle, their conversation eventually moved on to braking distances, the intricacies of Anna's online ovulation calendar, and the merits – or otherwise – of veganism (polishing off the Camembert, Jess was not altogether surprised to find herself coming down firmly on the side of foodstuffs-deemed-more-likely-to-give-one-a-heart-attack).

The Merlot was gone by the time Philippe arrived at her shoulder a short while later, bearing two toasting flutes and a bottle of Laurent-Perrier champagne in a bucket. 'From the gentleman near the bar,' he declared with a soft smile, raising an eyebrow. He unfolded a stand from beneath his arm and set the bucket in it.

Jess whipped round and straight away through the crowd locked eyes with Dr Zak Foster. She'd had no idea he was even in Norfolk.

He simply looked back at her, motionless, waiting.

Tonight was the one-year anniversary of their first meeting beneath the portico of the temple in Holkham park woods, where they'd been strangers at the wedding of a mutual friend. Zak had been enthralling a small audience with a medical story when she'd first encountered him, but of course it was the sort of anecdote she couldn't hope to start following halfway through after two glasses of wine. So instead of guffawing along with the others Jess found herself scuffing around behind a pillar like some sort of tragic walk-on part in an outdoor production of *Othello*, listening to him talk and wondering if he was perhaps famous, or at least related to someone who was. He had that air about him, somehow – or maybe it was just because he was devastatingly handsome and by far the most captivating of all the guests in attendance. She didn't normally go for men who attracted attention in that way, and for this reason alone, she knew he had the potential to be definitively Not Suitable. But by then, of course, he'd spotted her drunkenly gazing at him and – understandably perhaps – interpreted it as a massive come-on.

They'd ended up kissing on the temple steps at midnight, fireworks exploding in the background, and Jess remembered smiling inside at the time and thinking, *This is pretty perfect*. She still bore the scar from the burn she had acquired in the small of her back just a couple of hours later from a particularly rough patch of oak bark.

After that they'd spent a heady and intoxicating forty-eight hours together, though Jess had been disappointed to discover that Zak was in fact only an occasional visitor to Norfolk. His parents had recently moved to Dersingham but he himself was resident in Belsize Park in London, working as an A & E consultant. His erratic shift pattern and frequent hours on call combined with Jess's catering commitments should have equated to a relationship that was finished before it had even begun – not to mention Zak's highly acrimonious divorce that had only just arrived at its bitter conclusion after months of protracted wrangling over an assortment of financial assets.

But as it turned out, they were both committed to making it work. Jess would visit Zak in London on her days off, with Zak travelling back to Norfolk on his. She'd met his parents. He'd shaken her sister's hand at a christening.

Things had progressed more healthily than she'd ever expected at the outset.

To date, Jess had only seen pictures of his ex-wife hidden away in various albums on his Facebook page – tall and blonde, with an aristocratic chin and a pout that only dermal fillers could achieve. As far as Jess could tell, Octavia was a part-time everything – jewellery designer, society magazine columnist, raving lunatic. The sort of woman who wore shorts with wellingtons and liked to shoot ducks at the weekend.

In most of the ways that mattered, Jess was Octavia's complete opposite, which she knew was part of the reason Zak had liked her in the first place. He had admitted as much – to being charmed by the novelty of her – but as time passed it worried her more, because novelty value had a conversely predictable habit of wearing off.

Of course, he had his faults – he was hot-headed and had a foul temper; he could be controlling and more than a little patronizing. Jess had always quietly wondered what role these qualities had eventually played in his divorce, mostly because Zak liked to sidestep the topic of why he and Octavia had split up and, if pushed, would only repeat the phrase 'irreconcilable differences' without ever remaining calm enough to elaborate.

But Jess had recently discovered that Zak's definition of irreconcilable differences varied slightly from hers, in that his seemed to encompass rampant infidelity – something she in fact considered significant enough to warrant its own category of marital breakdown, since it was hardly the same as bickering over household chores or not getting on with the in-laws.

Anna had already started busily decanting the Laurent-Perrier into the champagne flutes. 'Just a taste won't hurt,' she murmured, almost under her breath, making Jess feel slightly guilty because Anna was usually such a paragon of self-control.

Averting her eyes temporarily from Zak, stalling while she sought reassurance, Jess leaned in towards Anna. 'I found out the real reason that Octavia and Zak divorced, as opposed to the Zak Foster edited highlights.'

'Ooh,' said Anna, like they were discussing a local celebrity and not Jess's actual boyfriend. 'Go on – surprise me. Secret fetishist? Gambling addict? Reptile fanatic?'

Jess wasn't sure if Anna was referring to Octavia or Zak, though she couldn't resist a smile at her friend's proclivity for turning everything into a Friday night in with reality television. She shook her head. 'None of the above. Zak caught Octavia in the toilets at the theatre. She was shagging his *brother*.'

'Jesus ████████ Christ,' intoned Anna, digesting the news with the aid of a lengthy swig of Laurent-Perrier.

'Yep,' Jess said with a nod. This particular development in the Zak Foster divorce court saga she had not yet had the opportunity to discuss with the man himself, having only discovered it last night. It had been a throwaway comment made as part of a group conversation, with Jess forced to virtually interrogate her unwitting informant afterwards in order to get the full picture.

'His *brother*? At the *theatre*?' Anna said, like she was trying to decide which was worse – keeping it in the family, or the crime against performing arts.

Jess shook her head. 'I know.'

Apparently Zak had turned up late to a weeknight performance of *La Bohème*, by which time Octavia and the brother had got sozzled in the bar and assumed he wasn't coming at all. The ensuing showdown in the toilets was, according to reports, nothing short of an operatic spectacle in itself. Six weeks later, Zak had filed for divorce, the brother having already fled to San Francisco to make it big in the world of online gaming.

'Bloody hell,' Anna breathed. 'Poor Zak.'

Anna was a big fan of Zak's, stemming mainly from the fact that he represented a change from Jess's previous boyfriend, who although very sweet had a creative interpretation of full-time employment involving round-the-clock Xbox, Domino's pizza and Jess's credit card. In Anna's eyes, the fact that Zak had not only an actual paying job, but the staying power to have completed a medical degree before climbing the ranks to become a consultant was more than enough to override his various faults (although she was no doubt also slightly dazzled by his brooding charm, shiny white teeth and the fact that he was half Andalucían on his mother's side, which had genetically predisposed him to Hispanic good looks more befitting a film star than a doctor).

'Why would he keep something like that from me?' Jess said now. 'She cheated on him, and he never told me.'

Anna looked uncertain. 'Male pride?' She frowned. 'How reliable's your source?'

'Solid. His brother's best friend.'

'▓▓▓▓.'

'I don't know – maybe it doesn't matter,' Jess murmured, half to herself, repeating what had been whirring around her head since discovering Zak's lack of honesty the previous night. 'I mean, it was before we'd even met. He's definitely going to say it's completely irrelevant.'

'*Yes*,' Anna cut in, slicing her index finger through the air in the manner of a Westminster spin doctor knee-deep in damage limitation. 'Exactly. Irrelevant.'

Jess took a contemplative swig from the glass Anna had passed her, but she couldn't shake the thought of such a gaping omission in Zak's account of his marriage. 'I just . . . I really think he should have told me.'

Anna opened her mouth to reply, then appeared to change her mind in favour of clearing her throat and nodding subtly in Zak's direction. 'Just to clarify, I take it you don't want to discuss Mr Landley and his bad driving within earshot of Zak?'

'Actually,' Jess mumbled, 'Mr Landley does do a very good emergency stop.'

'Well, Zak's coming over,' Anna said, switching on a sparkling smile and talking through her teeth, 'so you need to tell me fast.'

'Not here,' Jess said urgently, her bad leg performing a reflexive little throb against the thought of Zak finding out and losing his rag about it all in the middle of a busy bar.

A couple of moments later, she felt a palm against her back.

'I was going to send over wine, but champagne suits you so much better.' Zak's voice was creamy smooth, a cool announcement of himself like they'd been waiting all night for him to come over. He smelt vaguely of something lovely in musk by Calvin Klein, and his eyes twinkled darkly, as if in anticipation of an effusive reception – though until he'd explained himself about Octavia, Jess was reluctant to oblige. She shot a look in Anna's direction designed to elicit solidarity, which promptly went ignored as Anna twittered something small-talky about his journey up from London and thanked him for the Laurent-Perrier.

'You're welcome,' Zak told her. 'I must say, I love your hair that colour, Anna. It suits you.'

Apparently not thinking this strange, given that she'd never in her life changed her hair colour, Anna simpered. 'Oh, thanks.'

Zak turned to Jess, his hand still flat against her back as he bent down and delivered a kiss to the top of her head. 'Managed to swap my shift. Happy anniversary, baby.'

'How long are you in Norfolk for, Zak?' Anna asked him brightly, saving Jess the trouble of having to cold-shoulder him out loud.

Cradling a glass of red, Zak took a seat next to Jess, flexing his jaw and running a hand over his dark graze of stubble as he sensed her coolness towards him. 'Bank holiday. I'm here all weekend.' He took a chance and slid his hand on to Jess's left knee. 'So, tell me. What have you two girls been talking about all this time?'

Forcing herself to nudge Matthew Landley from her mind, Jess met Anna's eye, upon which Anna started gabbling across multiple fertility-related topics, from the benefits of acupuncture to her husband Simon's sperm count. Jess remained quiet, happy for Anna to do the talking as she tried to ignore the intermittent squeezes Zak was applying to her thigh, though admittedly she was grateful he'd selected the leg without the automotive injury.

By the time Anna's soliloquy had arrived at a natural pause some minutes later, Jess's glass was empty. 'Good girl,' Zak murmured approvingly, grabbing the champagne and topping Jess back up before moving the bottle across to Anna, who shook her head.

'Thanks, Zak, but I should go,' she said, swigging back the last of her drink. 'Told Simon I'd be back by ten. I'm literally ovulating as we speak.'

'Good for you,' Zak said encouragingly, like she'd just

announced she was off to scale Everest, but Jess caught him glancing slightly reproachfully at the array of empty glassware on the table.

'Nice to see you, Zak,' Anna said. 'Make sure Jess gets home safely.'

Zak squeezed Jess's leg again. 'Oh, I will.'

Jess only just held back from smacking his hand away like a secretary from the sixties being groped by her boss.

'Call me tomorrow,' Anna said to Jess, then got up and click-clacked past them, blowing a kiss in the direction of Philippe on her way out.

Zak swivelled instantly round to face Jess before leaning in and kissing her. It was a slightly insistent kiss, the sort that suggested he really thought they should be heading off to locate the nearest mattress. 'So am I a good surprise?'

Without really meaning to, Jess turned her gaze away from him to the row of cherry trees outside the window, their blossom turned dusky pink in the gathering gloom. For some reason, an image of Matthew floated gently into her mind. With some effort, she blinked it away.

'Baby, what's up?' Zak was whispering, his hand against the back of her neck, his mouth close to her ear. 'You literally haven't said one word since I sat down.'

Jess swallowed and attempted to focus, reluctant to spoil their anniversary with an argument but too upset to discount what she'd heard. She looked across at him properly for the first time that evening. 'I found out what really happened with Octavia,' she stated flatly.

Zak frowned and sharply exited her personal space by leaning back in his chair and crossing his arms. 'What?' he snorted, to buy himself some time.

'They weren't irreconcilable differences. She cheated on you with your brother. That's why you divorced her.'

There was a short pause, during which Zak appeared to waver over continuing the pretence or saving himself the trouble and dropping it. Never one to make unnecessary work for himself, he opted for the latter by trying to evade the issue entirely. 'Really? We're doing this on our anniversary?' He glared meaningfully at the champagne bottle, as if to suggest that Jess was not being sufficiently respectful of the occasion. Zak took celebrating seriously, and tended to become indignant when people chucked curveballs at his forward planning.

'Zak, how could you have not told me this?'

Zak hesitated, his expression betraying nothing, before shrugging defensively. 'I didn't want the sympathy vote. *Oh, poor guy – wife shagged his brother. Maybe I'll go over and cheer him up.*' He made what Jess had come to think of as his horseradish face, the one he usually pulled over beef wellington in gastropubs. 'No thanks.'

'But we've been together a year,' Jess reminded him quietly. 'You could have told me at any time.'

Zak shrugged again, arms still folded to defend him against low-flying pity missiles. 'Well, we reached that point, Jess . . . where it was too bloody late to say anything.'

'So that's why you don't speak to your brother,' Jess concluded. Zak rarely even made reference to him, something she'd naively attributed to sibling rivalry. 'I thought you just didn't get on.'

Zak's face clouded over slightly. 'Yeah. We don't.'

A tension hung between them now, a palpable patch of cool air in the corner of the crowded bar. 'So the real story is, Octavia broke your heart,' Jess said quietly.

Zak arched his back uncomfortably and looked away from her. 'Yes, Jessica, she broke my heart. Can we talk about something else now please? It doesn't matter how it ended with me and her if the outcome was exactly the same.'

'It does matter,' she countered.

'Why? What I told you was true,' Zak clipped, throwing back another slug of wine. 'There were irreconcilable differences.'

'You mean adultery,' she corrected him.

He lowered his glass. 'Is that not the same thing?'

Jess swallowed. 'So . . . do you still love her?'

Zak's expression of distaste quickly darkened to become deep offence. 'Is that a serious question?'

'Yes,' she said hesitantly, though the chill of his stare was making her suddenly doubt herself.

'Wow,' he said then, leaning back again in his chair and running a hand through his mop of brown hair like a Wall Street trader being caught red-handed with his fingers in the Forex. 'I did not see this coming. So much for the champagne.'

Zak's scant reserves of patience rarely held firm under pressure, so Jess decided not to push him on the love issue. 'I just can't believe you would hide something like that from me,' she said, a final attempt to dismantle his obstinacy.

'Okay, Jess,' Zak countered in a tone of mounting exasperation that implied there was something she was failing fundamentally to grasp, 'if you really want to know, I never considered it to be that relevant, okay? I still don't. It's in the past.'

Punctuating this by slinging back the last of his wine and setting down the glass with only slightly less force than he'd have needed to smash it, Zak chose to close their debate with a form of ultimatum.

'Look, are we going to forget this now and celebrate our anniversary? Because, if not, I'll piss off back to the beach house. It's been a long week, Jess, and I was sick enough of discussing Octavia when we were getting divorced, let alone twelve sodding months later.'

Though still unsettled by his deception, there was a tiny part of Jess that was beginning to wonder if perhaps he was right. Maybe it wasn't relevant. Hadn't everyone had their heart broken, in one way or another? Did it mean he loved her any less?

But by the time she'd remembered that Zak had a particular talent for making her question herself, he was on his feet and waiting for her to choose: traditional anniversary as observed by functional couples or sullen celebratory stand-off?

So with some effort – given that her leg felt like it had been force-fed through a meat grinder – Jess got to her feet and made her way through the bar towards the door, Zak at her shoulder. But she'd only managed to take two steps on to the gravel outside before he reached for her arm and pulled her to a halt.

'Jess, what the fuck is up with your leg? How pissed are you?'

For a brief moment, she felt relieved. Clearly he had not yet been privy to any local gossip about the accident and, with a bit of luck, it wouldn't be long before her ageing collection of witnesses began to confuse it with something they'd seen on *Midsomer Murders*.

'It's fine,' she said, wincing as she took the weight off it, though the pain was actually starting to feel worse.

Zak frowned and stared down at her thigh like he had X-ray vision. 'Hang on, you're not fine. What have you done?'

She hesitated, but the thought of his reaction if she told him exactly how it had happened deterred her. 'Just bruised it,' she mumbled eventually. 'Nothing serious.'

'Baby,' he said, more softly then, 'I'm a doctor, remember? I can tell when something's wrong.'

This was true, and was one of the arguable downsides to dating a medical professional. (Another was the impromptu requests for medical advice Zak often received from friends-of-friends while out and about. They'd been at lunch a fortnight earlier when a middle-aged female acquaintance of his former best man had approached their table and virtually moonied him to get a second opinion on an arse boil that had gone septic.)

'I'll be fine,' she insisted, praying he wasn't overly adept in hands-off diagnoses.

He slid an arm round her ribcage to support her, putting up a hand to sweep the hair from her face with a tenderness that made her shiver. Clearly thinking they had reached that point of the night where he could attempt to disguise contentious issues as seduction, he put his mouth close to her ear. 'Have you had any more thoughts,' he murmured, letting his voice go gruff, 'about moving to London with me?'

For a moment, she didn't attempt to speak, just allowed herself to feel the heat of his breath on her skin as his lips moved down to gently graze her neck.

'I'm sorry about all that Octavia stuff. I've thought about you all week,' he whispered. 'You keep me going when things get shitty. *Tú me alegras el día.*'

He did this occasionally – swapped over to Spanish when he thought he might need a little help in winning her over. His success rate with it to date was fairly low, in ratio terms of smile to shrug; but tonight Jess was particularly tired, in addition to which she appreciated the fact that he was holding her up and taking the weight off her bad leg.

'I'm sorry I never told you about Octavia,' he insisted then, lowering his head to kiss her. 'I want to be with you, *cariño*. I want you to move to London with me. Happy anniversary, baby.'

Then his lips were on hers and, just like always, the taste of him shot straight to her groin, a sort of erogenous equivalent to mainlining class-A drugs. And as she found herself pressed up against a patch of nearby brickwork, Zak's hands running all over her and their kissing becoming more and more urgent, Jess resolved – as she did every time – that tomorrow she would make her mind up about London once and for all.

3

Matthew

Wednesday, 22 September 1993

It was the start of a new school year and, to mark the occasion, I'd been entrusted with teaching the first year of the GCSE maths syllabus to a portion of the lower fifth. Admittedly it was the portion at the base end of the ability spectrum, but that didn't faze me – I loved a challenge and didn't feel in the least bit intimidated. In fact, if you set aside the fact that the sadist in a boiler suit whom some people referred to as the school caretaker had cranked up the central heating to a temperature formerly unique to the equatorial tropics, I was about as cool and collected as it was possible to be when autumn blew in.

At the end of last term, my ageing predecessor had been sacked for creative expense claiming, so it was now my job to turn this sorry ship around. I was determined to succeed, promising myself that in two summers' time my class would ace their GCSEs and prove to the Hadley Hall staffroom that being sour, middle-aged and a big fan of diarrhoea-coloured knitwear were not, in fact, prerequisites for being a good teacher.

Oh, I was well aware that my habit of dressing for work like I was heading to a rock concert wasn't exactly popular among my colleagues. I wore my dark hair long, cultivated my stubble and never tucked in my shirt; sometimes I'd even

30

team my cords (no jeans allowed) with cowboy boots to really stir things up and get them talking. I saw it as doing them a favour, in a sense, because they needed something to gossip about other than the growing non-attendance at the sixth-form choir rehearsals or the German exchange student who'd been caught dealing weed when she was supposed to be playing rounders.

But in my quest to work hard, I'd somehow, conversely, become lazy. Too tunnel-vision. Obsessed with grades and neglecting to observe behaviour.

We were only two weeks in, and halfway through simultaneous equations, I realized someone was crying. At first the sound came at me like the intermittent buzz of an insect, a mild irritation. This was the start of the GCSE syllabus – important stuff. *Why can't they just pack it in?*

Eventually my eyes followed the noise towards the back of the room, where the Witches sat. (That was my own private term for them, not something I would be sharing around the staffroom over coffee and Dundee cake any time soon. In the year since I'd started at Hadley Hall, I'd worked out that you were allowed to moan about bad behaviour, pierced ears or unfulfilled academic potential, but you weren't allowed to take the piss out of them. That, apparently, was taboo in the manner of mentioning periods or hormones, or commenting on their legs.)

The crying girl wasn't one of the Witches, I knew that much. She was new to the school this term, and I was annoyed with myself for not being able to instantly recall her name. (I'd not taught this year group before, but that didn't mean I was planning on walking around with a register permanently appended to one hand like most of my colleagues. I was happy with my own personal system – individual pupil ability mapped out on a mental seating plan – but admittedly I probably did need to expedite the addition of other identifying features, such as their names.)

'Get on with your work,' I barked at the rest of the gawping class. The Witches obediently and predictably lowered their heads too, a cheap trick to demonstrate their innocence: clearly, the crying was nothing to do with *them*. It was the oldest, most transparent ploy going, which on the plus side made it relatively easy to sidestep.

'What's going on?' I strode purposefully forward, mainly because a bit of well-timed striding was sometimes all it took to get them to shut up.

The Witches twittered. The girl shook her head.

It was then that I noticed a clump of auburn hair lying on the desk behind her. One of the Witches tried too late to brush it away, and my gaze travelled down to the polished parquet floor, where an entire ponytail – a good eight inches of hair – had been shorn clean away from the girl's scalp with a pair of craft scissors.

Actually, my first reaction was one of dented pride: I couldn't believe they had been so fearless as to do this in *my* class. I could have understood if it had happened under the watch of Mrs Witts (English literature, walking stick, virtually deaf – great combination, the girls got away with murder) or Miss Gooch (Latin, nervous, blushed way too easily and over-sweated). But I hadn't been expecting them to behave so brazenly in this class, *my* class – and to realize that the bullying had been going on under my nose came as a humiliating shock.

There were five Witches in total, and four of them were laughing, hard. The fifth one looked slightly pale and sick: it was perhaps not a testament to my fair-handed approach that I decided to start with her. I was furious, my supervisory competence was hanging in the balance and I wanted to get to the truth as quickly as possible. She looked like she would be the easiest one to break.

'*Out*,' I told the five of them. They scuttled past me like cockroaches, all still twittering except the fifth, who paused as she reached the discarded ponytail but appeared to decide against saying anything when she came under the heat of my glare.

'Aimee,' I said, addressing the desk partner of the crying girl, who looked about as stunned as if someone had taken a brick to her head, 'would you two please go together to Mr Mackenzie's office and wait for me there.' And then I strode from the classroom.

As Aimee and her shorn friend made their way past us down the staircase, I turned to face the offending rabble, who had lined themselves up against the thick brick walls of the corridor, all short skirts and sardonic expressions. The blonde girl, the quiet one, still looked like the easiest target, so I pulled her aside into an empty classroom and barked at the others not to move.

She blinked at me as I shut the door behind us. 'It wasn't me,' was the first thing she said.

'Oh, come on,' I snorted. 'You're going to have to do better than that. I've been a teacher long enough to know when someone's lying.'

(That wasn't strictly true. I'd only started teaching three years ago, but I was well aware that in the eyes of a fifteen-year-old, three years probably counted as a lifetime.)

'I didn't want her to do that. I told her not to. I tried to take the scissors.' She opened her right hand then and my jaw dropped. It was an absolute bloody mess, quite literally: a deep red gash had been sliced across the pale flesh of her palm. She was holding a pool of blood in her fist and, as she

33

unfolded her hand, it began to drip horrifically through her fingers, turning the carpet crimson at our feet.

I wasn't great with blood at the best of times. 'Jesus Christ.'

'Don't say anything!' she said, her eyes wide with fear. It was only then that I registered how white she'd become. 'Don't say anything, Mr Langley, please.'

'Go to the nurse,' I told her. 'I'll deal with the others.'

She started to cry then. 'Please don't say anything.' She put her hand over her mouth, a sort of instinctive reaction to try and disguise the fact she was crying, and ended up smearing the whole lower half of her face with blood.

The feeling of everything spiralling rapidly out of control fell somewhere between a test I had to pass and a wind-up. 'Jesus . . . just stay here, okay? Don't move.' I exited the room and strode sharply back out into the corridor.

'Come on. Who did it? I don't have time for this, and neither do any of you. In fact, I'd go as far as to say, I'm fucking pissed off. You've got GCSEs coming up. Do you *want* to fail your exams?'

None of the other teachers ever used the f-word. This wasn't the sort of school where the f-word was acceptable. Parents weren't paying four grand a term to hear their daughters' maths teachers throwing expletives around the minute things got a bit heated.

When I'd applied for the post at Hadley Hall, I'd put on my application form that I *'thrived under pressure'*. I guessed that was one of the things the head, Mr Mackenzie, had liked about me (along with the fact that with my ponytail, facial hair, relative youth and refusal to wear cardigans, I had represented what he had termed a 'well-needed breath of fresh air' for Hadley. Mackenzie had always been happy to take risks in that way, championing the benefits of

34

pushing one envelope or another, a fact for which I remained entirely grateful).

But the problem with claiming to thrive under pressure was that I had never before really found myself under any. In fact, it could be said that my life was generally pressure-free: no real responsibilities, no stresses, a select handful of friends and no girlfriend to speak of. And apart from occasionally giving me the sense of being stuck in a bit of a rut, that was all fine – except now it wasn't, because the shit was hitting the fan, and the sole onus for dealing with it was firmly on me.

I made a quick mental tally. So far I had the girl with the unscheduled haircut downstairs, the one with a stab wound in the room behind me, and a defiant group of delinquents sloping sulkily against a wall, facing me down. Double maths, it was fair to say, was not going too well.

At this point I had no other option than to remain doggedly convinced that I could claw it back, have them all rearranging formulas with their eyes shut by lunchtime – and my first move was to take a hard line. 'Detention, every night next week. And I'll be contacting your parents, you can be sure of that,' I declared, slamming down my emergency hand of behavioural management ace cards. 'Now get back inside, and I don't want to hear another word from any of you. For the rest of the year.'

As they shuffled back past me into the classroom, heads down and grim-faced like they were moving up the bread queue in Marxist Russia, I glanced through the glass panel of the door to my left. The injured girl was sitting down – not yet passed out, that was good – gripping her hand and biting her lip. She looked okay; but then again, maybe that was how schoolgirls always looked when they were bleeding to death. Impelled to hurry, I ran down the stairs two at a time to finally deliver the crying girl and her friend with a brief précis to Mackenzie – he'd seen it all before and would no doubt have something helpful to say. It would be more productive than talking to me, we all knew that: I had no words of wisdom to impart that didn't relate in some way to mean, mode or median.

Then I legged it upstairs again and opened the door to where I had left the fifteen-year-old with the blood-smeared face and slashed hand. I was starting to wonder how I was going to explain all this at the next parents' evening.

'Let's get you to the nurse,' I said. 'You might need to go to hospital. It looks deep.'

Seeming to accept this, she nodded. I held out my hand and helped her up. The blood from her palm smeared all over mine, wet and bright like the poster paint from a primary school art class. I could have used it to do something creative on A3 with handprints and taken it home to stick on my fridge.

'I know why they do it,' she informed me as we faced one another.

'Huh?' I couldn't take my eyes off all that blood around her mouth. Flecks of it had dripped on to her shirt. She looked like an extra from a horror film. And now that I had touched her, so did I.

'I know why they do it,' she repeated quietly.

I frowned. 'You know why they do what?'

'Stuff like that.' She made a scissoring motion with her left hand.

'Oh,' I said, wondering what explanation she could possibly offer me to disprove my less-than-complex theory that they did it because they were misbehaving little shits.

'They're bored.' She wouldn't look at me as she said it.

'Bored?' I repeated, like she'd invented a new word.

36

Just as I was about to inform her that only boring people get bored (and, for good measure, that there was no such word as *can't*), she elaborated. 'It's because they don't understand. None of us do. You're going too fast, you're only interested in Laura and you're forgetting about the rest of us.'

Laura Marks was the star of my class, a girl who had already shown herself to be an entirely competent mathematician – so far ahead of the others in terms of ability that I had started to wonder recently if she was in fact some sort of departmental plant, sent in by the other teachers to spy on the rookie.

'Too fast?' This still wasn't making sense. I'd been praised on my pacing ever since my first day of teacher training. For a moment, I felt like telling her that, then decided against it. It would have seemed a bit petty. I could rise above these baseless allegations, for God's sake.

'Yeah, like . . . you moved on to quadratic equations, and we still don't get . . .'

'Equations?' I supplied with a sinking feeling.

She shrugged. 'Yeah.'

Though I could sense there was an opportunity here to delve deeper, I decided it might be prudent to revisit this unsolicited feedback on a day when things were slightly less fraught. 'I still don't think that's an excuse for poor behaviour though, do you?' I said, my way of reminding her that there was a girl downstairs who by late morning had succeeded in retaining only half the head of hair she'd woken up with.

Another shrug. They could shrug instead of speak for days at a time, these girls. 'Maybe not. I'm just telling you what I think.'

As she said this I noticed that blood was beginning to trickle between her fingers again. 'Don't ball your fist,' I told her. 'Come on, we'd better get you to the nurse.'

Please don't pass out. Please.

'You know,' I said to her as we walked, drawing a few strange looks and the odd question from stray pupils and teachers on the way (with her blood-smeared jaw and my bright red hand it could easily have looked to the casual observer, I realized afterwards, like I'd punched her in the mouth), 'I do run a maths club. After school on Tuesdays.'

She wrinkled her nose. 'Maths club? That's not cool, Mr Landley.'

Well, you've got to admire her honesty. I smiled. 'I know it might not seem cool now, but don't you think you'll feel cool when you ace your GCSE and get a really great job after university?'

'Yeah,' she said, deadpan, 'but I've heard maths club's really dross.'

For some reason, that made me laugh. I didn't bother to ask her what dross meant – it clearly wasn't a compliment.

'Tuesdays,' I said as we reached the nurse's office. 'Check with your mum first.'

'I might do,' she said.

'Tuesdays,' I repeated.

A few days later, she caught up with me after school. As I was unlocking my car I sensed someone standing behind me, and when I turned round, there she was – with significantly more colour in her face than the last time I had seen her. 'I bought you a present, Mr L.'

'A present?' I repeated, slightly confused. In my experience, pupil–teacher presents only really featured at Christmas, Easter and (when the parents were feeling flush, which at Hadley was always), the end of term. I regarded her with a bemused expression as she fished around in her bag,

38

admittedly slightly intrigued to see what she was going to pull out of there.

'Here you go.' She held it aloft, triumphant.

It was . . . a can of Diet Coke.

She looked so excited to give it to me that the smile I shot her was genuine. In fact, I probably seemed a lot happier to receive it than I should have been. 'Wow, thank you. What have I done to deserve that?'

She thrust it towards me, and I took it. The scar from her scissor wound was still a mess of stitching across her palm.

'To say thanks for looking after me the other day. And you work so hard,' she added, her expression steady, as I gave the can a jaunty little toss without thinking. 'I thought you could maybe do with a Diet Coke break.'

Of course, I completely missed what she was saying – mostly because I was wondering if this could be an opportunity to renew her interest in solving basic formulae.

'Well, that was very thoughtful of you, but you really shouldn't be spending your money on me,' I told her. 'And you know, fizzy drinks aren't good for your teeth.' I wiggled the can at her like a twat and she started laughing.

'Oh, by the way, Mr L,' she said then, brushing her hair back from her face, 'my mum said it's okay.'

I smiled at her. 'Your mum said what's okay?'

'Maths club,' she said, as if there could only be one thing in the world that a fifteen-year-old would be begging her mother permission to do after school (ironically enough, such a scenario was indeed the stuff of my teaching fantasies). 'I'm coming to maths club.'

I didn't know it then, of course, but the simple act of signing her up that afternoon was the moment the tide began to rise.

4

'Fuck,' Zak growled. 'Late.'

Zak had a habit of restricting his sentences to single syllables when he was tired or stressed – something Jess assumed had come straight from his hospital A & E department, where such efficiencies probably meant the difference between life and death. Hung-over and sour-tempered, he was supposed to be dashing off to meet his father, a retired architect who was redesigning the roof of Zak's new weekend bolthole to let more light in. Zak always referred to it as a beach house but, in fact, it was of that industrial style of architecture that made it look more like a misplaced storage facility. There was steel involved, and talk of tensile forces, and given that Zak's neighbours already considered him to be a crass city-dweller with no respect for surrounding sand dunes, Jess could envisage raised voices, which she didn't foresee doing much for her headache. So she opted to quietly nurse her hangover solo with the aid of some fresh coffee – a free sample from Colombia via Philippe, which was very generous of him, given that he usually sold the stuff for five quid a cup.

Unable to sleep, she'd risen early this morning, creeping down the staircase and on to her mother's old Shaker-style chair next to the Aga in the kitchen. Smudge, her border collie, had loyally migrated from his basket to lie on top of her feet, squeezing his eyes shut and keeping her toes warm while they'd waited together for the sun to rise.

One year with Zak, yet all she could think about when she closed her eyes was Matthew.

'Where are my fucking keys?' Zak was raging now, his neck going pink as he turned over the contents of Jess's living room with escalating frustration like a drug addict in urgent need of items to sell for cash. 'Jesus, Jessica. If you actually chucked out some of this junk then maybe you wouldn't lose things so often.'

The junk he referred to – her trinkets made from driftwood, collection of vintage postcards, half-burnt candles, old photographs and miniature glass milk bottles – was scattered lovingly across her stuffed, creaking bookcases, mantelpiece, mismatched furniture and upright piano that still had the book of Christmas carols open on 'Joy to the World'. She knew that it was ramshackle and tumbledown, and that it all probably could have done with a squirt of furniture polish, but it was her.

'I like my junk,' Jess replied, feeling a little bit riled that Zak was criticizing her for losing things while he looked for something he'd lost.

Finally he located his keys within the folds of her cotton paisley scarf, which he'd hastily unwound on her behalf last night before discarding it on the sideboard. 'Okay,' he said, shaking his head and bending down to kiss her where she was curled up on the sofa, 'I'll see you tonight. I'll pick you up at seven, okay? Be ready.'

She nodded up at him, hands wrapped round the coffee cup. He'd surprised her with a dinner reservation at Burnham Manor, where apparently there was no leeway for being late as they served the food in a single sitting, shouting out the Michelin-starred menu to a room full of salivating food fanatics.

'Dress up,' he threw over his shoulder as he exited the cottage. 'Wear your new shoes.'

She glanced over to where her anniversary present – a pale brown paper bag bearing the famous scrawling logo of Christian Louboutin – was resting by the fireplace. Inside, a matching cardboard box stuffed with folds of creamy tissue paper, and nestled down amongst it all, a pair of shoes – flawless black patent with distinctive scarlet soles, heels not much sturdier than chopsticks.

Her stomach had churned when she'd opened the box, partly because she suspected Zak was still basing all his gift choices on the things that had made Octavia happy, but partly because the shoes were two sizes too small, and she hadn't had the heart to tell him.

As lunchtime approached, Jess took a shower, soaping her skin in something vanilla-scented and finishing with a blast of cold water for her damaged leg – admittedly not the ice she'd been advised to use, but the sole item currently in her freezer was an oversized portion of home-made beef lasagne, and she could only think that combining it with compression and elevation would result in half-thawed beef and marinara sauce becoming inconveniently smeared across her sofa and thighs.

She finally chased away the stubborn dregs of her hangover with a late lunch, caramelizing some cauliflower in the Aga with olive oil and coarse sea salt before devouring it greedily from a soup bowl with loosely scrambled yellow eggs, her thoughts rotating steadily between Zak, Octavia and Matthew. Finishing off with a damp slab of banana bread, she exchanged a couple of texts with Anna as she ate, although she was currently unable to say much about last night without wanting to caramelize her own head.

While the air was still warm, she popped several ibuprofen,

eased on her wellies and headed for the beach with Smudge at her side.

Walking extra slowly, they made their way on to the perfect expanse of empty marsh, transected at its horizon by a dense block of clouded sky. Jess took time to savour the salty breeze, allowing it to whip her bob of blonde hair across her face.

The southern edge of the marsh closest to the village was where children came to play on the hot summer mornings of their school holidays, to cake themselves in mud the colour and texture of treacle and hunt for slim, silver fish in the creeks and pools with bright, cheap fishing nets purchased from Wells-next-the-Sea. It was where dogs could charge freely and parents could stand idly chatting, collecting plump strands of electric-green samphire from the damp ground, getting clay between their toes and salt spray in their hair.

The tide was going out, so the mud was still wet and the creeks half full. Together Jess and Smudge picked their way expertly across the thick carpet of sea lavender and fleshy crops of sea purslane, Smudge bounding along his favourite well-worn route over the winding channels, the white patches of his coat quickly turning grey. Jess favoured her own path across the uneven ground, averting her eyes as she always did from the small wooden cross planted near the bridge.

Sunk deep into its own little patch of wiry sea lavender, nobody else would even have known it was there, but Jess did. It stared her down every single time she passed it, but she never stopped and she never looked. *Just keep walking.*

The roar of the outgoing tide crescendoed and the breeze became a stiff wind as they approached the beach. Smudge picked up speed, jumping and delighting in the vast stretch of deserted sand ahead of him. They crossed it together to the shoreline, where Jess stared out at the horizon and thought – as she had almost every day for as long as she could remember – about Matthew. She threw Smudge's tennis ball into the edge of the surf over and over again, while he cantered around in delight like an overexcited pony. Then the sun dipped down behind a bank of solid cloud, so they turned back and headed for home.

The knock on the door came as Jess was mixing up Smudge's tea. Setting his bowl on the floor, she rinsed her hands and hobbled through to the living room, Smudge at her ankles, too curious to ignore a visitor in favour of eating.

And just like that, Matthew Landley was on her doorstep, locking eyes with her properly for the first time in seventeen years.

For a few moments, he didn't speak, seemingly needing to absorb the sight of her. Then, eventually, he found his voice. 'Hello,' was all he said.

As she moved silently aside to let him past, she caught the scent of him, still deliciously familiar. He was an attractive combination of muscular and brown that suggested he worked outside shifting things for a living, his back and shoulders far broader than she remembered. Suddenly he became the only man she could think of who could carry off a grey T-shirt and jeans quite so impressively. Tattoos that hadn't been there before covered his upper arms, and she couldn't help noticing that his biceps had bulked up too. But the most significant difference was his shaved head and jawline.

He's aged so well he's barely aged at all.

She shut the door, and they turned to face one another.

Trying to speak, she realized there was a lump in her throat she needed to bypass first, and it was proving problematic.

Eventually she succeeded. 'I can't believe it. How are you?' She knew it was a question so vast that he wouldn't have a hope of answering it, but she thought it might at least buy her some time to try and remember how to behave normally.

He laughed softly, and scratched the back of his neck. 'Er, a bit head-fucked.' His voice, unbelievably, sounded just the same. 'But very relieved to see you're still in one piece.'

Smiling nervously at one another, they could have been teenagers on a first date. Smudge, who had positioned himself at a neat equidistance between them, kept looking from Jess to Matthew and back to Jess again, as if to say, *Hello? What the hell is going on here? Can someone fill me in? Guys? Guys?*

'This is great,' Matthew said then, his gaze conducting a tour of her living room, of all the things Zak had been flinging around and swearing about only hours earlier. 'It really suits you.'

'I collect trinkets,' she said apologetically. 'I'm not very of-the-moment.'

He shook his head to disagree. 'My house has hand sanitizer where all the ornaments should be. Trust me, this is much better.'

She smiled. And then, because she couldn't quite believe he was standing in front of her and she'd been waiting to say it for seventeen years, she said quickly, 'I'm sorry, Matthew.'

This seemed to catch him off guard, and for a couple of moments he remained motionless, just looking at her. Eventually he spoke, his words tumbling out on a tightly coiled snatch of breath. 'Jess . . . don't be crazy. You're not the one who should apologize.'

Absurdly, she disagreed by nodding fiercely. 'I am. I am. I'm so sorry for what happened to you.'

He stepped forward then and grabbed her hand, finger-tips grazing the scar that crossed her palm. His grip dwarfed hers as it always had, the warm clasp of it enough to send her heartbeat into full pelt.

'It's me who should apologize. I've been trying to find you so I could say it. I'm so sorry – for everything. I know I was the one in the wrong. I know that, Jess.' He was squeezing her hand on every second word.

'No,' she managed, working her fingers against his in return, aware somehow that this might be her only chance to rediscover him. 'You weren't.'

'You don't have to say that.'

'I know I don't. But I never blamed you. Never.'

Matthew seemed surprised enough by this to gently relinquish her grasp. 'Fuck,' he said, rubbing a hand across his face in apparent confusion. 'None of this is making sense in my head.'

'Did you come here expecting me to hate you?'

'Yes,' he said simply, and then became quite still. They were both now staring helplessly into the eyes of their past, unable to change a thing.

'I don't hate you,' she said. It was only a half-sentence, and she wanted to finish it, but she swallowed back the words just in time.

Matthew moved forward then and pulled her into an unexpected hug. She slipped her arms round his waist in return, burying her head against his shoulder with the same quiet ease as she used to. His body felt almost exactly the same as it had all those years ago – more muscular, perhaps, but otherwise just the same.

'Sorry,' he mumbled into her hair. 'Just tell me to get off.'

46

She shook her head against his chest and they stayed like that for maybe thirty seconds, breathing in sync, before he finally pulled away.

He took her hand and they sat down next to each other on the sofa, knees almost but not quite touching. Smudge trotted over from his usual spot next to the hearth and positioned himself with satisfaction on top of Matthew's feet, claiming him for the duration of his visit, however long that should happen to be.

'Yesterday, Jess,' Matthew said, 'when I saw it was you . . .' He ran a hand backwards over his head, a gesture of lingering disbelief. 'I'm so sorry I let them cart you off like that. I have never wanted anyone to be carted off less in my entire life.'

She waited, sensing there was more to come.

'But Natalie . . . my girlfriend . . . she doesn't know. She doesn't know about my past. And neither does my daughter, obviously.' He winced, like it pained him to admit it. 'I was planning on being at the food fair alone yesterday because I wanted to see you. But then at the last minute Natalie said she'd join me.' He shot her a half-smile of resignation. 'She normally hates things like that.'

'How can she not know about us?' Jess whispered, like she was afraid Natalie might somehow be able to hear them.

'She was out of the country at the time it all happened, working in New York. She completely missed the whole thing. And I just . . . never got round to telling her. So now I inhabit this weird little world where I'm half normal person, half paranoid wreck. I regret not telling her, obviously, but now it's too late. If she found out . . . well, I'd never see my daughter again, for one.'

'You really can't . . . ?'

'No,' he said quickly. 'I've come close to telling her,

sometimes. But that kind of thing . . . it's not Natalie's bag, if you know what I mean.'

Not Natalie's bag. Like they were discussing gangsta rap or anti-establishment rallies.

'You don't have to explain anything to me,' she said.

'Well, I think an explanation's the least you deserve, Jess. Not that I'm doing a particularly great job at it.'

She wanted to take his hand again, to reassure him if that was even possible, but as she looked down she noticed that he was wearing a bracelet, woven in black leather and fitting snugly round his tanned wrist.

The sight of it coursed through her chest like electricity.

Attempting and failing to swallow, she began to produce words at a previously unvisited pitch. 'Do you wear that all the time,' she asked him, nodding down towards his wrist, 'or is today a special occasion?'

Following her gaze, he paused for a couple of seconds, like he was trying to work out what to say. 'Both,' he replied eventually. 'I've worn it every day for the last seventeen years. But, yes – today feels . . .' He paused. 'Slightly extraordinary.'

'I can't believe it's lasted all this time.'

He cleared his throat before lowering his voice in confession. 'Between you and me . . . I have been known to wax it.'

She broke into a smile. 'That's very diligent of you.'

'Well, you know. It's the only one I've got.'

Their eyes met with a mutual memory. She wanted to lean in and hug him again but resisted as a fleeting image of Natalie crossed her conscience.

'So . . . does Natalie know you're here?'

He nodded. 'Actually, she asked me to come.'

Jess felt her heart sink a little.

'She thought I should probably check you weren't briefing

48

your legal team or something. And,' he added, shifting slightly and digging into the pocket of his jeans, 'she wanted me to give you this.' He extracted his wallet and, from it, a wad of notes that he passed to her. Jess swallowed as their fingers brushed. 'Just . . . think of it as compensation,' he said, though she knew he could sense her doubt. 'For you missing your slot yesterday, and everything.'

'How did you know I had a slot?'

'I picked up a flyer in the deli on Friday. And I just thought . . . maybe it would be a good chance to speak to you. With the aid of some crowd cover, obviously, in case it went horribly wrong.'

She watched him for a moment while she took this all in. 'Honestly, you don't need to do that,' she said eventually, holding out the money.

'Please keep it,' he said with a shake of the head. 'I'll only have to launder it if you don't.'

She relented with a smile; but as she set the notes aside, a thought occurred to her. 'You're not being charged with anything, are you?' she asked him, suddenly fearful. 'I told them it was my fault.'

'I know. I called in at the police station yesterday. And no – they're not charging me. Thanks mainly to you, obviously, for so evidently having never read the Highway Code.' He released a breath. 'Ah. It's been an interesting twenty-four hours.'

By his side, Jess experienced her own small hiatus of quiet relief.

'But look, never mind me.' He turned to her. 'What about you – are you okay? What happened at the hospital?'

Involuntarily, she shifted, her thigh muscle twinging painfully in protest. 'I'm fine,' she reassured him. 'Soft tissue bruising and swelling. No lasting damage.'

49

Visibly relaxing, he nodded slowly. 'Thank fuck for that.'

'It wasn't your fault.'

His expression became thoughtful. 'No, I mean, listen – at the end of the day, I think we should all just be grateful that you never decided to become a lollipop lady.' He shot her a smile and ran a hand over his jaw. 'Imagine the carnage.'

Jess covered her mouth with renewed mortification. 'I'm so sorry. You must think I'm insane.'

He shrugged lightly, but his eyes were twinkling. 'Just assumed you were bored, or something.'

She attempted to explain. 'I'd been seeing you everywhere. Or I thought I had. In the end I managed to convince myself that I was imagining you. Until yesterday, obviously, and then . . .'

He laughed. 'Oh, you definitely get points for the most creative way to ID someone.'

She laughed back. 'Thanks. I think.' A pause. 'So I was right? It has been you these last few weeks? I wasn't imagining it?'

He hesitated, meeting her eye with a smile. 'You might have to bear with me on this. It involves an amount of stalking I'm not quite comfortable with.'

She smiled back, pretending to mull it over. 'I'll try.'

'Okay, well . . .' He rubbed his chin. 'We got here a few weeks ago, and I'd been sort of working up the nerve to contact you. I wanted to say sorry, for everything that happened between us, but the moment never quite seemed right. Either I was with Natalie or you were with . . . someone else or you were out when I knocked. I thought about putting a note through your door, but I didn't know your situation. And I really wanted to see you face-to-face, anyway.'

Her mind was racing, attempting to process all the facts. 'So, you actually live here now – in Norfolk?'

'Not really,' he said. 'I mean, temporarily. Natalie's always had this . . . fantasy of a second home by the sea. We came up here for a long weekend last summer, and she ended up having an unexpected love affair with the place. Anyway, after we got back she started looking for houses, found one she liked and put in an offer – all without telling me.' He shook his head. 'And she's spent the past year trying to convince me it would be a fantastic idea to move here for a few months while we do it up, so . . . here we are. She's taken some time off work to project-manage.'

Jess struggled to imagine a job so high-powered that sabbaticals for property development were factored into the remuneration package. 'What does she do?'

'Management consultant,' he said in a way that made Jess think he'd been forced to listen to one too many anecdotes about efficiency bottlenecks and profit margins. 'So . . . anyway. That's why I'm here. I thought maybe enough time had passed for me to be able to risk coming back to Norfolk for a few months, what with my false name and everything.' He met her eye, then looked down.

She swallowed. 'So . . . Natalie doesn't know your real name?'

'No,' he said, speaking carefully as if he appreciated it might sound odd. 'She knows me as Will. Will Greene.'

Jess nodded. 'You changed it officially?'

He nodded back. 'Before I met her. I needed to start again.'

'I know the feeling.' And she did – she knew it better than anyone. There had been many times over the past seventeen years when she'd been tempted to wipe clean her own identity and start afresh. 'So would you rather I called you Will?' She didn't want to, of course: the man sitting next to her was Matthew Landley, and she couldn't really imagine thinking of him as anyone else.

'Well, why don't you try it?' His eyes were fixed on hers.

Jess hesitated for just a moment. 'Hi, Will. Pleased to meet you.'

'There you go,' he said softly. 'How does it feel?'

'A bit strange. I liked Matthew.'

'Yeah, me too,' he said. His eyes had crinkled up at the corners but his smile was one of deep sadness.

'Well, I'll give it a go,' she said.

'I appreciate it.'

'And you shaved your head,' she said, motioning to where his hair had once been.

He touched it like he'd forgotten. 'Oh, yeah. What do you think?'

'I mean, you look different. But it really suits you.' She smiled. 'Though isn't it normally the other way around? You grow a beard . . .'

'Yeah, but that's so obvious, isn't it? Like wearing a false nose.'

'Or sunglasses,' she said, nodding at the pair he'd set down on her coffee table.

He laughed. 'Never without them.'

'Well, they're nice ones. Clearly you didn't find them in the false nose shop.'

'No, although I do spend a lot of time in false nose shops. I've found them to offer an unrivalled browsing experience.'

By now their knees were touching, but neither of them made a move to draw away.

'So, anyway – how have you been?' he asked her. 'Before yesterday, I mean.'

She exhaled. Where should she start? 'Well, I run my own catering business.' She caught his eye. 'No restaurant yet, but . . .'

His eyes glistened with apparent admiration. 'Wow. I'm so pleased for you, Jess.'

To anyone else, her career choice might have sounded pedestrian, but she knew that to Matthew – Will – it meant everything.

'Is it going well?'

Jess nodded, trying not to think about the raft of bills that had landed on her doorstep only this morning. She'd been wondering more and more recently if self-employment was invariably the road to financial ruin – but, as yet, her love of the work had managed to make up for all the worry. 'I mean, there's a lot of competition, and I have overheads, but . . . yes. I really enjoy it.'

'And . . .' He cleared his throat. 'Are you seeing anyone?'

There was the lightest of pauses, and she realized that he had probably seen her with Zak at some point. 'Yes,' she said, but then hesitated.

She tried to read his expression as he waited patiently for her to elaborate. Could she detect a shred of disappointment in his face?

Why could she think of nothing else to say?

'What does he do?' Will prompted her.

'Oh, he's a bit different to me. Actually, he's very different to me. He's an A & E doctor in London.'

'Long commute.'

'Oh, we don't live together. I mean . . .' She paused. 'You know. He has a place in London. I'm here.'

'No kids?'

She exhaled through her nose with what she realized too late might have sounded like derision. 'No.'

He was waiting again, perhaps expecting more detail, but having none she felt able to offer him, instead she said, 'So what do you do now?' She paused cautiously. 'For a living, I mean.'

The question hung uncomfortably in the air as it left her mouth.

'I homeschool Charlotte,' he said, meeting her eye. 'Not a huge fan of the British education system myself.'

Jess had expected, of course, that he would no longer be a school teacher, but somehow to hear it still felt unjust – shocking, even. 'You were . . . *such* a good teacher.'

'Well. I was good at the maths.'

She shook her head. 'I'm really sorry.'

'Thank you.' After a beat, he appeared to swallow the thought away. 'Okay – can I say something completely naff and crap?'

She nudged him with her knee. 'Always.'

He laughed. 'What?'

'No! I don't mean . . . you're always naff and crap.' She smiled. 'I just meant, you can say anything you like. Of course.'

He looked down at his hands. 'You're exactly how I imagined you to be, all these years later.' He winced. 'There you go.'

'That's not crap,' she reassured him.

He made a face. 'Naff?'

She smiled. 'That depends. How did you imagine me to be?'

'Oh, it gets naffer. We should stop there.' He shook his head and looked across at her then as if she fascinated him, the same way he used to all those years ago. 'This is crazy. I thought I was going to come round here and quite possibly make everything ten times worse, and then I see you and it's . . .' He paused. 'Just how it always was.'

She smiled. 'Well, that's a good thing.'

'I don't know about that,' he mumbled.

A short silence fell between them, like something decompressing.

'Jess,' he said then, his voice low. 'I wanted to say as well . . . I heard about your mum. I'm really sorry.'

She shook her head. 'Don't be. I mean, it feels like a long time ago now.'

A couple of moments passed. 'Really? I bet it doesn't.'

Glancing down into her lap, she said nothing. He was right, of course. It was just a line she trotted out, little more than a pleasantry, like discussing a milestone birthday or the worsening dementia of a distant relative.

Matthew shook his head, as if he was trying to dislodge any ancient memories that may have been lurking there. 'Sorry. Change of subject?'

Jess nodded quickly and, with some effort, got to her feet. 'So now that you're here . . .'

'. . . like you've been expecting me.'

She crossed the room. 'Well, you know.' She leaned over and flicked the wheel on her iPod, parked in its dock above the inglenook. 'You'll never guess what's on my playlist.'

'Hang on. Let me think. Enya? Kenny Rogers? Richard Marx?'

She caught his eye and smiled. 'Yep, all of those – but also this. Trust me, you'll like it.' She pressed 'play'. The sound of Morrissey filled the room.

Will snorted. 'Holy shit, Jess. I can't believe forcing The Smiths on you actually worked. Although you are aware that you're starting to show your age?'

'You've got ten years on me.'

He looked at her for a moment like he wasn't quite sure how to respond. 'Yeah,' he said eventually, his voice slightly heavier. 'Funny, isn't it, how no one would bat an eyelid about that now.'

A slow, sorry pause descended.

'Would you like a drink?' she asked him gently. 'Sorry. I'm normally a much more competent host, but ... you threw me off a bit.'

He hesitated. 'I would love to, Jess, but –' Reluctantly, he checked his watch. 'I should probably get going.'

Jess tried to arrange her face in a way she hoped would hide the hard thump of disappointment she felt. Not in a million years when she woke up this morning would she have predicted this scenario: being face-to-face with Matthew Landley in her living room, getting to know him all over again. She didn't want it to end.

'You finally got your tattoos,' she said as he stood up.

He looked down at his arms. 'Oh, yeah.'

'Let's see.' Stepping forward, Jess had to make a conscious effort to concentrate on the artwork, given that Will had tanned skin and muscles not dissimilar to a *Men's Health* cover shot. His left arm bore the image of an elaborate, ancient tree with an inscription inked across its branches; around the other was wrapped an intricate labyrinth in an Aztec design.

'What does it say?' she asked, gesturing to the lettering around the tree on his left arm. She couldn't quite make it out.

He glanced down and paused.

'It can't be night for ever.'

She swallowed, surprised by how suddenly the tears rose in her eyes. She blinked them back. 'That's lovely,' she managed, but then, without warning, her bad leg gave way, taking her sharply back down on to the sofa.

Will squatted in front of her and gripped both her hands with his. 'Jess . . .' For a few seconds it almost looked as if he might cry too.

Smudge chose this moment to stuff his head between their linked arms so that just his face was showing, his wet nose quivering and tail wagging optimistically. Will started laughing and dropped Jess's left hand to fondle Smudge's head. The other held on to her. 'He's lovely.'

'He's a rescue. I think he had a bad start. Mind you, I think I'm pretty lucky. Most collies have a screw loose somewhere or other, but Smudge is near-enough perfect.' She smiled. 'Although . . .' She started laughing.

His eyes crinkled at the edges again, his face angled up towards hers. 'What?' he smiled.

She took a breath. 'When I first got him, I thought he was deaf.'

Will laughed. 'What? How come?'

'Because he wouldn't sit or do anything I asked him to! I actually took him to the vet's and asked them to test his hearing.' She smiled and covered her face with her free hand, embarrassed at the memory. 'They thought it was hilarious.'

He looked at her for a couple of seconds before reaching up and peeling her fingers from her face. 'It is. But that's what makes you so lovely.' She swallowed and for a moment he held her gaze; then he seemed to check himself. 'Sorry. I should go.' He let her hands drop gently and stood up. Smudge looked up at Will, tail wagging, clearly convinced that some sort of outdoor-based activity was about to begin.

'Can I say something weird and annoying?' Will said, pausing by the front door.

'Is it to do with not telling anyone?'

He smiled grimly. 'Oh God. Was I always this predictable?'

'Well, back in the mists of time –'

He held up a hand. 'Don't answer that. I don't need to be reminded of how much I've aged.'

'Don't worry,' she said, gesturing towards the iPod, 'I'm right there with you now.'

He started laughing then. 'Remember that time you thought Morrissey was Neil Morrissey out of *Men Behaving Badly*?'

She smiled. 'No.'

'Oh, come on. Don't be embarrassed.' And as he spoke he took her into a hug again, this one tighter and much sadder than the last because they both knew it was the one before they would have to say goodbye. 'Sorry,' he murmured eventually, reluctantly pulling away. 'Highly inappropriate. You see, nothing changes.'

'I think after everything that's happened, we've probably earned ourselves a hug at least. Don't feel too guilty.'

'Yeah, you're right.'

She looked up at him. 'So, maybe we could go for a drink or . . . ?'

He allowed his eyes to rest against hers for a couple of seconds. 'You know how I said before I was feeling a bit head-fucked?'

She nodded.

'Sort of doesn't really cover it now.'

'Well, if it helps – me too.'

He took a moment to gather himself. 'Right. I need to go home and try to remember how to cook fish fingers, chips and beans for my seven-year-old.'

And then, without warning, there it was: that familiar little glimmer of grief and shame. She swallowed it quickly, before it could snag in her throat and take hold. 'Of course,' she managed with a weak smile.

'Well,' he said, looking down at her again, and now he

really appeared to be fighting off tears, 'it's been great to see you again, Jess.'

Then he walked through the door and down the front path, away from the cottage and out of her life once more.

5

Tuesday morning, and Jess was returning from a dog walk at the beach with a friend. They parted ways at the gate to the car park, whereupon Jess hesitated momentarily before cutting right along the line of trees whispering gently against the subtle morning breeze.

Breathing in the heady and familiar scent of the surrounding greenery transported her back seventeen-and-a-half years: breath freezing, teeth chattering, watching for headlights, stomach turning over and over in excitement.

It took her twenty minutes or so to reach the bird hide. She had forgotten how far it was and her bad leg was slowing her down, so by the time she got there a faint film of sweat clung to her skin. Looping Smudge's lead over a fence post, she paused to steady herself, took a breath and reached for the door. Her anticipation was so intense that she almost collided with someone coming out, a grey-haired man in a green birder's waistcoat. He looked her up and down. 'Few redshank. Couple of lapwing,' he grunted.

'Thanks,' she murmured.

Once inside, ensconced there in the gloom, she was alone. That garden shed smell was so familiar and took her so keenly back that she felt tears spring to her eyes.

She reached out and lifted a shutter, fastening it at the top, and took a breath as she surveyed the grazing marsh in front of her. She ran her hand along the bench she was sitting on, fingering the grain of the wood. Through the sharp slice of daylight in the darkness came the faint call of birds from the marsh as they bobbed their way across the sun-baked ground. The air was warm.

Suddenly, a thought occurred to her that made her heart pound. She got to her feet and stood on tiptoe, extending an arm and groping around in the rafters above her head. To her delight, her fingers soon closed around something hard, wedged into the space at the rafters' footing where the roof joined the wall. With some effort, she hauled herself up on to the bench to get a better grip on the object, tugging to loosen it.

Eventually it sprang free, though the force of her pull nearly sent her spiralling backwards. Her leg pounding, she grabbed on to a rafter to steady herself before looking down to inspect her prize, sitting comfortably against the thick white scar transecting her palm.

It was an ordinary torch of black plastic that had remained hidden up there in the rafters for nearly eighteen years.

She half smiled and flicked the switch, but the battery had long since died.

Her phone rang as she reached the car.

'Jessica? It's Natalie – Natalie White.'

A brief pause followed, and for a moment Jess thought Natalie might qualify her opener by saying, *You know – Natalie from the car accident?* Her inflection was smooth like butter, the sort of tone she probably used to introduce herself before going in for the kill over unpaid invoices. Jess felt her stomach contract with something halfway between fight and flight as she braced herself to be strongly warned against enlisting legal expertise, and most specifically the sort that did a good line in fake cricked neck claims.

They had exchanged telephone numbers in the aftermath of the accident, though not face-to-face. The food fair's

61

stewards, having been issued with bumper packs of craft beers in lieu of sterling for their time, had found themselves able to agree at lightning speed that Jess was unequivocally at fault and Natalie not a woman to be crossed. For the purposes of the accident book, they had dithered temporarily at the end of their shift to ensure that party details were swapped, after which they had all legged it out of the first aid tent and back across the grass to their cars, roaring off in convoy down the driveway without so much as handing in their tabards or swerving to avoid no-waiting cones.

So Jess had received a folded piece of paper headed *Will Greene*, which she'd propped up next to her bedside lamp. Only last night, unable to sleep, she'd struck a soft line through his name in pencil and written *Matthew Landley* instead.

Finally, squinting against the sunlight, she found her voice. 'Natalie, hello. How are you?'

Natalie sounded as if she was forcing a smile down the phone. 'Wanting to see how *you* are, of course.'

Jess flushed momentarily with guilt as she considered replying with the truth: *Thinking non-stop about your boyfriend*. But she opted to go with a slightly less confrontational response by offering Natalie an update on her wounded thigh tissue instead.

Natalie, however – clearly a woman for whom rhetorical questions were a mark of social competence – simply rattled on across the top of her. 'We're having a bit of a party on Saturday. Nothing fancy, just a get-together so we can meet some other people in the village. Convince them we're not ghastly second homeowners.' She spoke airily, without a trace of irony. 'Anyway, we're looking for a caterer.'

Jess wondered perhaps if Natalie had forgotten the car accident after all. There followed an expectant pause, during which Jess felt sure she could discern the impatient tapping of fingernails on the other end of the line.

Natalie finally made an intake of breath that was verging on brusque, as if she was rarely expected to qualify her demands. 'I've been asking around, and you come highly recommended. Your friend Philippe assures me there's no one better. Short notice, I know, but would you be up to it?'

Jess hesitated. She had a christening already planned for Sunday, and had earmarked Saturday for prepping. But it seemed ungracious to decline off the back of glowing recommendations – and, right now, she needed all the work she could get. 'What time?' she asked doubtfully.

'Seven? You'd be doing us a huge favour. With all this building work to coordinate I simply don't have the time to be messing around with canapés.'

Forced to assume that Will's input to this decision had either been declined or overruled, Jess knew that either scenario made accepting unwise. But her desperation to see him again was too strong for logic to prevail. 'Yes, okay,' she said impulsively, making a quick mental timetable of how she'd fit it all in.

She realized the offer was probably just a hasty appendage to the money Natalie had already persuaded Will to give her – another way to try and soften the blow of a bumper to the leg. In negotiations of a difficult nature, Jess suspected that Natalie was always firmly in the driving seat.

'Wonderful. I'll text you some ideas. Right, must dash – Charlotte's late for horse riding. And where's her father been for the past half an hour? Standing in the power shower singing at the top of his lungs like he's sodding Pavarotti!'

Lucky you, Jess couldn't help thinking – not that she had a particular weakness for operatic tenors. But the pang of envy she felt was quickly replaced by the reassuring thought that she was, at least, going to see Will again.

6

'Don't do it, Jess.'

Jess and Anna were in Anna's flat above Beelings, the four-star hotel she owned with her husband, Simon. Jess had been slightly thrown on her arrival to find the living room aglow with candles and whale song reverberating off the walls, with Anna's ancient fish tank restocked and re-positioned in front of the dormant fireplace. There was incense burning and someone had even popped back to the 1990s to dust off a Lava Lamp. The room now resembled the sort of shop that peddled crystals, tarot cards and cotton skirts embroidered with mirrors – all Anna needed was to swap her cashmere pyjamas for a kaftan and she probably could have started inviting guests to pop up for impromptu palm readings before their à la carte.

But Anna, appearing conversely studious and deter-mined in Buddy Holly glasses with her hair scraped back into a practical topknot, had justified this bizarre home décor refresh by claiming it was all for the benefit of her fallopian tubes. Jess suspected this to mean she was experi-encing mild internal hysteria about the fact that, as they spoke, a fertilized egg was quite possibly embarking on the slow and perilous journey towards her womb, where it would then be required to find a suitable toehold before clinging doggedly to the cliff face of her uterus for the next nine months.

Anna had donated her sofa to the cause of Jess's bad leg, which was now elevated at forty-five degrees by an armrest and several cushions. The arrangement kept making her dress slip up along her angled thigh, inducing sympathetic flinching from Anna every time the injury became exposed. By now it was so swollen and black, it could have passed for gangrenous.

Anna was sitting cross-legged in front of the fish tank, its silver light bestowing her with a sort of watery halo. She had cracked open a bottle of sparkling grape juice, which they were sharing now along with some tart tangerines and a difference of opinion.

'It's work,' Jess was insisting, wincing through a mouthful of too-sharp citrus flesh. 'I'm hardly in a position to turn it down at the moment. And it's an opportunity to make contacts.' Smaller jobs like private parties and the occasional house-warming kept her ticking over in late autumn and the first few months of every year, when work for larger events tended to dry up.

'Er, you turned down catering for that crazy lady with seven dogs,' Anna pointed out.

'There's a clue in there somewhere.'

'I thought you had a christening Sunday.'

'Well, this is Saturday. I can do both.'

'Putting yourself out for Mr Landley already, I see,' Anna remarked with a smile, though the tone of her rebuke wasn't entirely jovial.

'It's just a good opportunity,' Jess reiterated.

'Don't you think it'll be a bit weird though? You know — being at his house with his wife and daughter, surrounded by people?' Anna scratched her nose and popped a tangerine segment into her mouth, wide-eyed as if to pretend she wasn't asking leading questions.

'Actually, they're not married.'

Anna appeared to consider this for a moment or two.

'Well,' she said eventually, 'they have a daughter. So they're as good as. And what about Zak – have you told him?'

'No. As far as Zak's concerned, this is just another catering job.' Jess slid Anna a meaningful glance. 'As far as *you're* concerned, this is just another catering job.'

'And you? Let me guess – just another catering job?'

'Yep,' Jess said quickly, ignoring the urge to hesitate.

Anna's face disagreed, but she let it go. 'So Matthew really is back then? For good?'

Jess shook her head. 'Just for a few months. They bought a holiday home down the road. They're doing it up.'

Anna smiled then like she had some positivity to impart, and began attempting to steer Jess's thoughts firmly away from Will by enthusing about Zak. 'For what it's worth, I think Zak is perfect for you, Jess. I know he has his faults, but who doesn't? He's devoted to you, and he likes all the same things you do. He's committed. What more could you want?'

Admittedly Anna had always been fond of Zak – but Jess couldn't help wondering if this gushing endorsement would have been *quite* so urgently delivered had Matthew not made his recent reappearance. 'Why are you telling me this now?' she asked her, though she suspected she knew what the answer would be.

'I thought you might need reminding. Ahead of – oh, I don't know – Saturday night.'

Jess looked down at her hands. 'Seriously. It's not a date, Anna, it's business.'

Anna narrowed her eyes like she was trying really hard to pick out a path through Jess's impenetrable bullshit, before suddenly brightening. 'Ooh, speaking of dates. Tell me all about Burnham Manor,' she said excitedly, presumably to flag Zak's appreciation of fine food as another of his many plus points. 'I'm jealous.'

'It was . . . nice,' Jess conceded. 'We had a nice time. Very posh, but . . . it gave me lots of ideas.'

'Got any soppy photos for me?'

'They don't like it when you whip your phone out in places like that. They think you're doing food porn.'

'It's so perfect for an anniversary,' Anna murmured dreamily.

Jess nodded. 'They wrote "Happy Anniversary" on our dessert plates in coulis.'

Anna made a melting face. 'Romantic. So when's he next over?'

'Sunday,' Jess replied through a mouthful of tangerine. 'We're going to dinner with his parents at the White Horse.'

'Which one?'

'Brancaster.'

'And when he asks what you got up to the night before, you're going to say . . . ?'

'*Catering*,' Jess insisted firmly. Matthew Landley was one subject she and Anna were never going to agree on, but that was nothing new: they'd been arguing about him for nearly eighteen years. 'Let's talk about you,' she suggested instead, taking another sip of grape juice and imagining it was Prosecco, which was made slightly easier by the fact that Anna had decanted it into champagne flutes.

Anna gave a short sigh. 'Well, let's just say if one more person advises me to "let fate take its course", I shall be striking them over the head very forcefully with this bottle.'

Jess smiled. 'You, let fate take its course? Who are these people?' Telling Anna to stop worrying was like telling a camel to stop stockpiling fluid. Some things were just down to DNA.

'Do you remember Claire Bartlett, from school?' Anna

asked Jess, absent-mindedly constructing a mini-Jenga tower on her knee with the tangerine peel. 'I bumped into her by the pool yesterday.'

Jess attempted to recall. 'I think so. Was she a goth?'

'Ha! Not any more. She was doing Aqua Zumba in full make-up and a Boden tankini. Anyway, she couldn't wait to tell me she's had triplets.'

'What's a Boden tankini?' Jess wondered, bemused.

'Never mind. The point is, Claire said having the triplets was all down to yoga. She'd been trying to get pregnant for two years, then she started the yoga, and –'

'Three came along at once?'

'Yes! Apparently it's all about opening and toning the pelvis, reducing stress and providing inner balance for a calm and detached mind. And cleansing the system, obviously. Hence the fruit and . . .' She cast a slightly resentful glance the grape juice bottle. 'Anyway, Claire put us in touch with her yoga teacher. She's a fertility guru, and she's only in Thornham, so we popped round last night for a chat.'

'What's she like?' Jess asked, trying to pretend that she didn't feel a niggle of suspicion towards anyone without a medical qualification declaring themselves to be a world authority on the inner mechanics of somebody else's reproductive system.

Anna made a little grimace that fell somewhere between excitement and trepidation. 'Quite strict, actually. She gave us a list of rules.'

'Rules?'

Anna nodded. 'Yep. Like – we can't drink any alcohol at all, and we have to eat properly and take the yoga really seriously. And Simon's got to do it all with me. She even made us sign a disclaimer.'

'What's she disclaiming?' Jess asked, suddenly envisaging

69

an ill-tempered female Buddha being fanned by servants with palm leaves as she beckoned desperate couples over one at a time to be assessed then slapped round the jowls with a yogic rule book.

'Liability for us failing to get pregnant if we don't follow the regime?' Anna suggested with a shrug, like such a thing would be perfectly reasonable. 'She is *amazing*, Jess. Even if she wasn't already a fertility goddess, she has a body to *die* for.'

'So have you,' Jess pointed out. Anna was long-limbed and elegant, like a ballerina.

'You should see Rasleen,' Anna said meaningfully.

Jess shaved a few stone off her imaginary Buddha. 'Is she Indian?'

Anna shook her head and frowned. 'No, she's from Clacton. Her real name's Linda.'

Jess suppressed a smile. 'Oh.'

'I don't know, Jess. I've got to do *something*,' Anna said desperately. 'I can't wait another eight months before they add us to the list for IVF. And Simon's already drawn the line at going private.'

Jess was personally of the opinion that Anna was already doing all she could. As she saw it, the monthly stress and expectation of trying for a baby was enough to drive anyone to stick their head in a vat of cut-price Merlot and stay there – yet Anna refused to allow herself any slack, punishing herself by agonizing over whether she'd ruined everything with that takeaway last Tuesday or the lager she'd indulged in two Saturdays ago.

'You spend your whole life assuming that having babies is as simple as just having sex,' Anna said wistfully, finally demolishing her little peel high-rise with a thumb. 'God – just imagine if I'd got pregnant when we first started trying, like most people do. We'd have an actual *baby* by now. A son or a daughter. Or twins.'

Jess caught her eye and they regarded one another for a few seconds. 'Yeah,' Jess whispered. 'Imagine that.'

Anna looked away, and a silence fell between them as they allowed themselves to be briefly submerged in the howls and clicks of North Pacific whale song.

'Simon thinks Rasleen's too expensive,' Anna said eventually. 'He keeps telling me I'm "bound" to fall pregnant, just because my stupid sisters are all super-fertile. He says I'm being too control-freakish about everything.'

Though Anna's two youngest sisters (she had three) were definitely not stupid, no one could deny that they were super-fertile – and to make matters worse, they'd both ended up having twins. Anna loved her nieces and nephews, but the sudden proliferation of young babies in the Baxter family meant that get-togethers and celebratory occasions were slowly turning into breeding grounds for unspoken resentments and frustration.

'Do *you* think I'm a control freak?' Anna asked Jess. Surrounded by the empty champagne flutes, an abundance of tangerine peel and a glow from the fish tank that could easily have passed as festive, Anna suddenly had an air of the Boxing Day blues about her.

'Yes,' Jess said firmly, 'but that's because you're a Baxter female. Control-freakery runs in your blood.' This was true, and (she'd recently discovered) the sole reason behind Anna's father's new shed, which he cryptically referred to as a 'garden room' and made routinely available for use by any male as an emergency bolthole during Baxter family gatherings.

'Sorry I made you drink grape juice,' Anna said eventually with a rueful smile.

'No problem. Sorry I made you drink all that wine and champagne on Saturday. Don't tell Linda.'

Anna lifted an eyebrow. 'Oh, I think we can lay the blame for that one firmly at Matthew Landley's door.'

There followed a pause that seemed oddly heavy.

'Jess?'

'Mmm?'

'About Matthew. I know you'll end up going to his stupid party. Be careful, won't you?'

'What do you mean?'

Several seconds passed before Anna said quietly, 'You know what I mean.'

7

Matthew

It was high tide.

I was renting a cottage just outside Holt at the time, a brick-and-flint end terrace which had come furnished, with space for the car. It wasn't exactly cool – unless you were a particular fan of condemned 1970s gas fires and textured ceilings – but the landlord hadn't yet cottoned on to the principle of economic inflation and he didn't seem to care if his tenants stained the carpets either, both of which were plus points.

Sometimes, I hung out with the other teachers at the weekends. They weren't a bad crowd. We'd divide our hours of freedom fairly evenly between Josh's Super Nintendo, drinking at Salthouse and games of five-aside in Fakenham.

Hadley Hall's home economics teacher, Sonia Laird, often came along to watch our football games, or to share a drink in the pub. I didn't have a girlfriend at the time, but Sonia had a boyfriend she'd been seeing on-and-off for five years.

For someone who had a boyfriend, Sonia was incredibly flirtatious when she got pissed. She would sling one of her legs across my thigh, all eyelashes and lipstick, and purr, 'So come on. How come a gorgeous guy like you doesn't have a girlfriend?'

I could never really think up a good answer to that.

Sonia was big into fifties style – halterneck dresses that skimmed her knees, hair with bouncing curls she'd fashioned with enormous rollers and stunned into place with hairspray, lipstick so red it made her teeth look yellow – and when she was really pissed, she'd lean over and slur what I could only assume to be further seductions into my ear.

I didn't mind too much: listening to Sonia when she got like this rarely required me to do anything but nod and occasionally shift out from beneath her wandering hand, but I felt a bit sorry for her boyfriend.

Looking back, she seemed so intent on me fancying her that it was almost inevitable we would soon find ourselves alone together. If there was something she wanted, Sonia was as determined as bindweed.

It had started out innocently enough on a Saturday night in Salthouse, where I'd arranged to meet Josh and Steve for a drink. But I was surprised to see on arriving at the pub that the only person at our usual table was a wide-eyed Sonia in a low-cut top, who straight away began fluttering and making out like bumping into me was the most outrageous coincidence.

It soon became obvious that the others weren't going to show, but Sonia – probably sensing my strong desire to flee – worked hard to convince me they were just running late. (They weren't: Steve's defence the following morning was that he'd been struck down by chronic food poisoning, with Josh claiming he'd been prevented from going anywhere by a sugar-beet lorry that had jackknifed at the end of his road. At first I thought the whole thing might have been a set-up, but Steve had lost almost a stone by the next time I saw him, and over a similar timescale Josh had become embroiled in a sort of bitter turf war with the sugar-beet farmer. Plus, I had never shown the slightest bit of interest in Sonia Laird, even when she was flinging her legs around, so what pleasure Steve and Josh might have hoped to derive from me continuing to show no interest, I couldn't really imagine.)

As soon as enough time had passed for my friends' poor time-keeping to become implausible, Sonia changed tack by insisting that her boyfriend would be joining us shortly, and would I mind waiting until he got there? I was reluctant to just get up and walk out, leaving her on her own, but whenever I asked her what time he was likely to turn up, her response was to raise a finger to her lips and wink. Three rounds of that unnerved me enough to shut up about him, so for another hour or so I indulged her with some company and stilted conversation, which mostly consisted of Sonia laughing uproariously at everything I said.

By nine o'clock, I decided to call time on our little tête-à-tête. This was partly because Sonia had started slurring her words and I could no longer be bothered to try and decipher what she was saying, and partly because I judged there still to be a small risk of her boyfriend showing up, and I didn't really fancy the idea of him taking issue with all his girlfriend's empty wine glasses and using them as weaponry.

Sonia lived in a village halfway between Holt and Sheringham, so it made sense for us to share a taxi. So far, I hadn't been paying too much attention to her repeated complaints that she was hungry, but I did as soon as our taxi driver pulled up outside the address she'd given me – which turned out to be a terraced house masquerading as a Lebanese restaurant – and attempted to charge me a tenner for the pleasure.

At first I tried to stand my ground, but taxi drivers in the

75

rural counties aren't known for their equanimity, a reputation he was more than happy to uphold by immediately switching the meter back on. With Sonia still flirtatiously refusing to tell me her real address and the fare racking up, I had no choice but to take her inside for a quick salad, whereupon I hoped I could sober her up and possibly ask the owners if I could borrow their BT book so I could track down this nomadic boyfriend of hers and bribe him into taking her back.

The restaurant was essentially a converted living room, and we were the only customers. An elderly woman gave us a bowl of withered olives to share that I hoped were complimentary, along with a side plate for spitting stones on to. I ended up ordering a lamb kebab on Sonia's behalf and nothing for myself in the hope of hurrying things along, which turned out to be ironic because the food took so long to arrive that I was tempted to politely enquire if they were shipping it in across the Med. The wait had given Sonia more time too to get off her face on house wine and become staunchly resident in my personal space – but fortunately she'd also let slip that she lived opposite the church, so I asked for the bill before she'd even started eating and didn't argue when she suggested we got out of there about ten minutes later.

The whole disastrous evening culminated in Sonia threatening to be sick on the walk home before almost passing out in her own front garden. As tempting as it was to leave her there, I managed to haul her up and fit the door key into the lock for her, upon which she took advantage of the one-and-a-half seconds I was standing still to try and stick her tongue down my throat.

When I finally made it back to the safety of my own cottage, I was greeted by a series of six fairly abusive

76

answerphone messages, each one demanding with escalating outrage to know why I had resisted.

After that, Sonia seemed determined to make me feel like I'd done something heinous by refusing to manhandle her on demand, so I resolved to try and avoid her as far as possible. I was wary of unwittingly giving her the wrong impression – as she'd informed me via my answerphone that I had done already – and of somehow finding myself held hostage in a restaurant again while she masticated olive stones. So if I got the heads-up that she was coming to the pub, or to watch us play football, I'd cancel at short notice. It was simply less complicated to spend an evening at home by myself with a Pot Noodle than be made to feel like failing to kiss her had been a crime akin to punching her in the face.

That Saturday evening in November was one such occasion. Five of us had arranged to see a film in Norwich – sci-fi action starring Sly Stallone – but then Craig informed me that Sonia was coming, so I cancelled. I was pretty pissed off about that. It wasn't as if I was a die-hard Sly fan or anything – unlike my slightly weird brother, Richard, who secretly believed he was Rocky in disguise and had spent much of our childhood petulantly begging our dad for boxing lessons – but still, I wanted to see the film. Even more irritating, I'd overheard Sonia earlier in the day saying she thought Hollywood action films were sexist claptrap appealing only to nerds who would never have the balls to throw a punch in real life. I was now regretting the missed opportunity to tell her there'd been a last-minute change of plans and we were meeting at the cinema in Lowestoft instead – or even better, Hull.

The upshot of all this was that I would either have to go and see the film alone (loser) or take Richard along (ditto). I was fairly sure too that a viewing with Richard would come complete with some sort of skills-of-Sly running commentary, which wasn't exactly the cinematic experience I had been hoping for. Sod it: I would just have to write tonight off and borrow the video from Richard in a few months' time.

I stretched out on my sofa (black leather and wipe-clean, it neatly fulfilled my landlord's bad-taste criteria of being both ugly and practical), sank a beer and came up with a brief but satisfying revenge fantasy in which Sonia was caught in the back row of the cinema giving head to someone who wasn't her boyfriend.

The doorbell went at about eight. Over the past two hours I hadn't really moved from my position on the sofa except to put on a Smiths tape and crack open some more beer – an unbeatable combination.

I thought perhaps my elderly neighbour, Mrs Parker, was going to be on the other side of the door with an objection to music and an order for me to get out more (both conversations we'd had previously in some depth), but when I opened it I was surprised to see Jessica Hart, the girl from my maths club, standing in front of me.

'Can I help?' I said politely, which was pretty stupid. I knew who she was. Obviously the way to approach this *wasn't* to pretend I thought she was a Girl Guide trying to recycle my tinfoil or sell me strange flavours of home-made jam, or whatever it was they did.

'Mr Landley, it's me – Jess.' She laughed slightly nervously and pushed a glossy sheath of straight blonde hair back over her shoulder. 'Don't you recognize me out of school uniform?'

I slapped a hand to my forehead. 'Oh, *Jess*. Sorry.' I realized then that I had a beer in my other hand. Inappropriate.

'You caught me . . .' I floundered for a cool activity I could be in the middle of. No teacher wants to be unmasked as a loner or a nerd, however close to the bone that might be. I wished then that I'd spied something interesting to pick up en route to answering the door, but the only prop I had was the beer can, so I raised it lamely. 'I'm a bit busy.'

She peered past me then, presumably to try and spot all the trendy people I was doing my drinking with. I shifted sideways to block her view, then cleared my throat. 'So, er, Jess – what can I do for you?' Had I not been a beer-and-a-half down, I might have told her straight away she could catch me on Monday if she needed to ask me anything, and shut the door firmly in her face. But instead I just stood there, the beer can dangling at my side, waiting for her answer.

To my surprise, she fished around in her bag and produced her battered old maths textbook, flicked to a page marked with a piece of folded notepaper and pointed to it. 'I know I'm probably being really stupid, but I just don't *get* why x equals . . .'

At that moment I was distracted by a passing car and a young female face staring out of the passenger window. It looked a bit like my star pupil, Laura Marks, watching me with my beer and the girl from my maths class.

I took a sideways glance at the street. There were probably people peering at us from behind their living-room curtains at this very moment. I needed to take this inside, not conduct it out on my doorstep for everyone to gawp at.

'Come in,' I said gruffly, promising myself I would quickly tell her what x equalled and then show her out – possibly through the back garden, just to be on the safe side.

She followed me into the living room, where I gestured for her to sit down on the sofa. It occurred to me that her weekend clothes – jeans and a Nirvana T-shirt – made her appear older than she did at school.

Her eyes met mine then, which was the part where one of us was supposed to establish exactly what she was doing in my living room on a Saturday night. I had been expecting her to be completely self-assured, entirely unfazed by the fact that she was here – but now that we were looking at one another, she actually appeared slightly hesitant, as if someone had just dropped her off and she'd never met me before in her life.

I had to ask. 'Jess, how did you know where I live?'

She frowned. 'Your car's parked outside.'

'Yes, but I mean – how did you know I live here? In this village?'

Her hesitancy melted a little. 'Your house is on the bus route to Norwich, Mr Landley,' she said gently, like she thought she might be breaking bad news.

I shook my head and took another swig of beer. 'Sorry. I'm a bit –'

'Drunk?' she supplied, a teasing smile creeping over her face.

'No,' I said firmly, as if to pretend there was orange squash in my beer can and I only ever drank at weddings. And then I just sort of stood there, which was probably force of habit, given that standing up while my pupils sat was how I spent most of my working days. All I needed to complete the picture was a board rubber in my hand and a pained expression on my face.

'I like your house,' Jess said then, seeming strangely enchanted by its distinct lack of charm, and I wondered at first if she was taking the piss before remembering that most teenagers thought any house not belonging to their parents or parents' friends was the epitome of cool. I hadn't been sure before now where maths teachers happened to fall on that particular spectrum but I'd suspected towards the lower end of the scoring system. Clearly things were looking up.

From her seat on the sofa, she tipped her head at the music. 'What's this?'

I cleared my throat. 'The Smiths.'

Her face remained blank.

'*The Queen is Dead?* Lead singer's Morrissey?' I prompted.

She frowned. 'The guy out of *Men Behaving Badly*?'

That earnest little juxtaposition of Morrissey and Neil Morrissey was so beautifully innocent it was almost the funniest thing I had heard all year. (Almost. The actual funniest thing I'd heard all year was the real story behind Josh's broken hand last summer, which did not involve a love triangle as Josh had claimed but a mere low score on a fruit machine, one too many pints of lager and the idea that the screen might apologize if he punched it hard enough.)

I smiled at her. 'No. Close – but not the same guy.'

She smiled back. 'Well, I like it. Sounds like good music for chilling out to.' I couldn't work out if she meant it as an observation or a suggestion, but either way it made me start to wonder if she really was here for the free maths.

'Look, Jess. You know you shouldn't be here, don't you?'

She frowned. 'Why not?'

'Come on, Jess.' The girl wasn't stupid (though admittedly her ability to grasp Pythagoras still needed some work), so I just waited for her to drop the pretence.

She did, more quickly than I had been expecting. 'Okay, I know. But you weren't at maths club on Tuesday and then Miss Wecks took our class on Wednesday, and I thought maybe . . . well, I thought you might have left or something. And then I started to panic because you're the only one who knows how to explain things to me.'

81

I watched her for a couple of moments. She was right in a way: I did know how to explain things to her. I wouldn't have gone as far as to call it a bond, but we'd definitely developed something of an understanding. She was still arithmetically useless — completely terrible — but in maths club, without the Witches to distract her, she tried bloody hard and wrote down everything I said to her, word for word. And then, if I could hit on just the right way of phrasing it, there would be this little light-bulb moment of comprehension, and she would quite literally gleam. As a teacher, those were the moments I lived for.

Maybe I should have had loftier goals than running a half-decent after-school club for my D-grade students. But I liked the idea that, many years down the line, one of them might remark as they climbed the corporate ladder at KPMG or made waves at Credit Suisse, *It all started with Mr Landley. He was the best teacher I ever had.*

'I haven't left, Jess,' I told her now. 'I just had a funeral to attend this week in Southend.' (An ancient great-uncle from my mother's side. I had discovered to my mortification when I convened with the others outside the church that I had momentarily forgotten the poor sod's name.)

Jess looked relieved. 'Excellent.' And then horrified. 'Shit. Sorry.' She covered her mouth with her hand. 'Sorry.'

Smiling, I shook my head. 'Don't be. It's fine. I know what you meant.' By now I was actively suppressing the urge to take another swig of beer, because it suddenly seemed wrong to carry on drinking in front of her. 'Would you like a drink?' I asked her, mostly to distract myself.

I swear, I meant tea, coffee, cola, juice. Part of me thought she wouldn't have the nerve to ask her maths teacher for a can of beer.

'I'll have what you're having.'

I stared at her. 'Oh, I meant . . . I meant something soft. Non-alcoholic.'

She shot me a smile that punched two perfect dimples into her cheeks, before appearing to hesitate – I assumed to deliberate on her choice of refreshment until she said, 'I won't tell anyone.'

'I can't offer you alcohol, Jess,' I said. I knew that I had already crossed a fairly hefty line – probably the one that mattered the most – by letting her into my house on a Saturday night, but as long as alcohol was kept out of the equation (ha ha), I was confident that I could persuade her to leave before very long, and no harm would be done.

'Okay,' she relented with a smile.

'What would you like?' I asked her, trying to recall what I had in my fridge. 'There's lemonade, I think. Or milk.'

Milk?

'Surprise me,' she said, which to her credit made the choice sound a lot more exciting than it was.

I headed into the kitchen and stuck my head in the fridge, eventually locating the lemonade can where it had been pushed behind an ancient jar of mustard. On emerging again, I realized that Jess was behind me, leaning against my kitchen worktop, watching.

I stepped into the space between us and passed her the can. 'Thank you,' she murmured, meeting my eye conspiratorially like we were outside the toilets at a nightclub and I'd just done her a deal on a handful of Es.

She cracked open the can and put her lips to the rim to catch the fizz, holding my gaze with steady grey eyes, her creamy blonde hair a waterfall framing her face and glancing off her cheekbones. I swallowed, not quite sure what to do with myself, and half turned away. But then – for what could only have been a couple of seconds – she closed her eyes, tipped the can up and drank. The movement made her neck extend, drawing her long hair down between her shoulder blades as her back gently arched. And without warning it suddenly reminded me of . . . oh God.

I'd known that she was pretty before, in an objective sort of way – anyone who claims that becoming a teacher has bestowed them with a mysterious ability to no longer notice these things is lying. But right now, against the unlikely backdrop of my Formica-heavy kitchen, Jess's good looks felt less like a realization than an assault: they'd crept up without warning and swiftly floored me, leaving me dazed and anxious, blood rushing hotly to my stomach.

She lowered the can then, drawing the back of her hand slightly clumsily across her mouth. 'Mr L,' she said, like she wanted to tell me something. There was a slight wobble to her voice that made me fear what might be coming next, but the disconcerting progression of thoughts inside my mind was scaring me more. So I took the only option available to me, which was a sharp exit left into my living room.

Sitting back down on the sofa, I wondered if perhaps I *was* drunk. But I'd had a mere can-and-a-half of beer, and unless the brewery had upped the percentage significantly since last Tuesday, I knew that the volume I'd consumed was unlikely to have distorted my mind to the point where I could find one of my own pupils attractive.

I briefly examined the can anyway before putting it down again, resolving not to touch it until Jess was safely on her way home. She'd already stayed longer than she should have done, which was (if you were interested in canvassing popular opinion, which unsurprisingly I wasn't) around ten seconds – the time it might normally have taken me to establish she was lost and lend her my *A-Z*.

84

You need to ask her to leave. Ask her now.

It wasn't long before she came out of the kitchen and perched next to me on the sofa. The scent of her was synthetically floral, girly – of that body spray they were always passing around the room while they were supposed to be thinking about fractions. I tried very hard to breathe out and not in.

'You want me to leave, don't you?' she said nervously.

I shifted uncomfortably then – a subconscious reflection, perhaps, of my reluctance to heartlessly boot her out of my cottage and on to the street – and as I moved, our dangling legs collided, the bare skin of my right foot coming to rest against the polka-dot cotton sock of her left one.

It should have been easy to deal with, not least because accidentally bumping body parts happened more regularly at Hadley Hall than you'd think – mostly between teachers during departmental meetings in Mackenzie's office, where there wasn't enough room for everybody's personal space to fit around the table. But, deep down, I suppose I was quietly relieved that Jess hadn't instantly recoiled in horror, or tutted, or offered me the mandatory muttered apology – any of those little social signals universally understood to mean you find touching a particular person to be at best inappropriate, at worst repellent.

I didn't know anyone who would have preferred to be confirmed as repellent. But I did know it was now up to me to move decisively away.

It's only a foot.

I experimented briefly with the thought. *Only a foot. Big deal.* If Jess was Sonia, I'd doubtless have come into contact with much more of her anatomy than that by now. But Jess wasn't Sonia, it wasn't only a foot and it was a big deal. So I removed myself from her as politely as I could.

She didn't really react, though I did think I could detect the faintest rising blush to the apples of her cheeks. Her head was resting against the back of the sofa, blonde hair splayed across the leather, bunched up around her shoulders. She was regarding me with an intensity I recognized from maths club, chronically misinterpreted to date as earnest concentration. It was slowly starting to dawn on me that she probably wasn't that fussed about what x equalled after all.

My heart was pumping faster now. I was aware of everything beginning to gradually collide in front of my eyes, like some world-of-nature calamity that suddenly becomes beautiful when you watch it in slow motion: the smell of her perfume, the twitch of her foot, the arresting effect of her gaze.

Stop it.

'Jess,' I said then, in an attempt to halt the thought-cascade. 'You really shouldn't be here. This is –' I released a breath of self-reproach – 'not right.'

She nodded, because we'd already established that, but still I got the feeling I needed to explain it to her again. 'What would your friends say if they knew you were here?'

She offered me a half-smile. 'Do you mean, how many people know I'm here?'

I hadn't meant that actually, but if she was offering to tell me, I wasn't going to turn her down. The rest of Jessica's year group was perpetually itching for gossip like this, always so desperate to spread salacious rumours that if there weren't enough of them to go round, they simply started making them up. Given this ever-present appetite for scandal (whether real or imagined), it would be helpful to know exactly what I was dealing with.

'Nobody knows I'm here, Mr L,' Jess assured me. Our

eyes met again then, and I realized that she was asking me to trust her.

But it wasn't only Jess's friends I had in mind. 'What about your mum? Your sister?' I probed, though I did make a conscious effort not to sound too alarmist. Nobody likes a walking panic attack.

I knew that Jess's dad wasn't around – or, to be more accurate, that he was dead. He'd been a solicitor until he keeled over, according to the rumours, of heart failure at his desk. Overwork: surely the worst way to go. I briefly pictured myself flat on my back in the staffroom at Hadley Hall – death by equation overdose – while Sonia made the most of the best opportunity she'd had yet to feel me up, scarlet fingernails running unchecked all over my dead body. I shuddered, then realized Jess was confiding in me.

'My mum's whacked out on diazepam and my sister just watches TV,' she was saying, looking down and fiddling with the ring pull on the lemonade can. 'Neither of them has any idea what I do on a Saturday night.' She thought about it. 'Or any night, actually.'

I was well aware that the pastoral carer in me was obliged to be concerned about this revelation. I knew I should make a note of it, ask her more, follow up on Monday – and I would. But for now I needed to park it in favour of labouring a point.

'Jess, listen. You can't tell anyone that you came here tonight, that you were in my house. You do understand that, don't you?'

To my relief, she nodded. 'Of course. I'm not stupid.'

'I should probably call you a taxi then.'

'Okay. Or there's a bus in fifteen minutes,' she said, turning her wrist to glance down at her watch. I caught sight of the scar on her hand again then, still bright pink though the stitches had been removed. For some reason – guilt, perhaps, because I'd been the one who'd failed to prevent it all from happening – I couldn't take my eyes off the ragged seam of it, the way it knitted shut the two halves of her palm with an unflinching, accusatory rawness.

Eventually I managed a nod of acknowledgement. Fifteen minutes: that was okay. Fifteen minutes to make sure she got home safely. Fifteen minutes to pull myself together, which should have been achievable, given that it was a time window far longer than the ones I normally offered my pupils in which to start behaving responsibly.

'Hey, Mr L,' she said then, a soft smile inching across her face. 'Before I go, will you settle a bet for me?'

I was starting to feel more relaxed now. Teacherly. Perhaps her question would be something related to school. *Finally – back on track. Nothing to see here.* 'Well, I can try.'

'Okay.' She bit down on her bottom lip. 'Do you have tattoos?'

I couldn't help smiling at my own misplaced optimism. 'Okay, Jess. You really shouldn't be asking me stuff like that.'

She laughed then, feigning surprise like I was teasing her. 'Mr L! Why not? We all reckon you have.'

Well, the answer to her question was no – but, in fact, I had been thinking of getting one. I'd seen a picture in a magazine of a guy with a crow tattoo on his back, but it wasn't filled in – it was more like a doodle, made out of hundreds of tiny coils. The overall image was huge, powerful. It looked pretty cool.

Recognizing this detail to be not entirely pivotal to the conversation, I rubbed my chin. 'Why, er . . . why did you think I'd have tattoos, Jess?'

She sent another smile my way, this one more coy. 'You're

the coolest teacher at Hadley. I mean, you've got long hair, and you wear cowboy boots.' She hesitated. 'You look like a rock star.'

Assuming this to be a compliment, I allowed it to imbue the air between us for a couple of seconds. Quite what she wanted me to do with it, I wasn't sure. Maybe I should have taken the opportunity to point out that being the coolest teacher at Hadley Hall really wasn't much of a challenge. To pick an example at random, Derek Sayers wore his grey beard long, rotated a selection of grimy-looking bow ties and sported a comb-over with misguided pride in the manner of someone who had once been told it took ten years off him. Meanwhile Bill Taylor's NHS-issue glasses came complete with a string, and he carried a pocket watch, which he'd slap emphatically on to the table at the beginning of staff meetings like the thing was a sodding hourglass. (I had once thought about leaning across and turning it upside down as a sort of joke; but I also knew that Bill drank alone at bars in his free time and occasionally liked to ram people with his front bumper in supermarket car parks, so I'd opted for keeping my shins intact at the last minute instead.)

But rather than say any of that, I said the only thing that sprang to mind – which seemed not only to be a bad habit I was developing, but one that got worse whenever I was with Jessica Hart. 'Yeah, and I'm a maths teacher. Lots of cool points for that one.' I gave her a slightly moronic thumbs-up, before instantly (and quite rightly) regretting it.

But Jess didn't seem to think I was a moron. 'I think you're cool,' she murmured. It slid out of her mouth like a confession. 'We all do. Haven't you noticed how we're always trying to get your attention?'

You're flirting with me, Jess. I almost said it out loud, just in case she didn't know, because she did emanate that type of natural charm which meant this wasn't entirely outside the realms of possibility. I thought perhaps I should call her on it, tell her to stop – but the crazy thing was, I pictured myself reaching out and grabbing her hand while I said it so she didn't feel too embarrassed. Given the context, this had the definite potential to make me either a glaring hypocrite or a rampant opportunist, so I opted to be neither and simply shook my head instead – an effort to dispatch a plasma blast or similar to break up the gradually snowballing thoughts in my mind.

Misreading my headshake as a wordless reply to her question, Jess tilted her head down slightly so that she was looking back at me through dipped eyelashes, and said, 'Well, we are. All of us. All the time.'

It was then that a flicker of suspicion brought me up short. Only a couple of months ago, she'd told me that everybody was messing about because they couldn't understand a word I was saying. Since then I'd been genuinely trying to slow my lessons down, with a noticeable uptick in good grades, I'd thought. Now she was telling me they played up because they thought I was hot. Which was it?

Is she fucking with me?

'So if you don't have tattoos,' Jess was saying now, 'do you have a six-pack?'

(I did, as it happened, along with biceps that popped nicely when I flexed them. I was proud of my physique, and grateful to my dad for the DNA, because I actually did precious little to warrant it aside from lifting a few weights now and then, and steering clear of crisps. But none of that mattered now, because I was starting to think my hospitality and – let's face it, my gullibility – were about to turn around and bite me on the arse.)

'Is that a bet as well?'

She went very still and blinked at me.

'Is that why you came round here, Jess? This is all a bet, a joke?'

It took only a couple of moments' silence for my sense of conviction to collapse dramatically. Jess's face – a perfect, compact heart that angled gently at her chin – began to crumple and flush; and straight away, I wished I could scoop up all my words and stuff them back into my mouth where they belonged.

'No,' she said eventually. Her voice shrivelled to the decibel level of a small creature attempting to avoid predators. 'I told you, nobody knows I'm here.'

I'd got it wrong. She'd been attempting to flirt and flatter me, not shaft me – though it was becoming increasingly difficult to decide which was worse. 'Sorry,' I said, shaking my head. 'It's just, sometimes, those girls you hang around with –'

'The Witches?'

I stared at her. 'What?'

To my relief, the dimples made a tentative comeback. 'I know that's what you call us.'

'Them,' I stuttered, 'not you. Them. What? How do you know that?'

'I saw it on your notepad, last week. You'd written: "Wednesday. Witches flicking rubber bands. Again."'

I inhaled deeply. There was something about this girl. It was like she was one step ahead of me the whole time.

'Them,' I repeated. 'Not you. I like you.'

'I like you too.'

I swallowed, wondering for a moment how best to correct her before deciding the mistake was mine, not hers. I needed to watch my words.

'I just meant,' I said, to clarify, 'that you're better than those girls. You shouldn't stoop to their level.'

'I don't,' she said simply. 'I just sit with them.'

It was a fair point. I liked a girl with a logical view of the world, and Jess definitely had that. It was just a pity that this gift for sound reason seemed mysteriously to evaporate when it came to basic arithmetic, but I was working on it.

In the brief pause that followed, Jess plucked several times at the ring pull on her lemonade can, a gentle, rhythmic *thunk*. Her fingernails were a shade of hot pink they hadn't been when I'd last seen her (I would have noticed – we'd been using protractors for what was fast becoming one of my all-time favourite lessons. The girls took a slightly different view, which was essentially that they detested geometry).

'I'll take it off before Monday,' she told me.

'Take what off?'

'The nail varnish,' she said, holding up the back of her hand and wiggling her fingers.

They weren't supposed to wear nail polish at school, but it didn't exactly bother me. I tended to let things like that slide, given that I occasionally wore leather to work.

I shook my head like, *Don't worry about it*. 'I never saw you, remember? You were never here.'

She smiled happily in response, like I'd confided something in her. 'Of course. I can keep a secret, Mr L.'

'You shouldn't be keeping secrets at your age,' I insisted, 'and you definitely shouldn't be here on a Saturday night. You should be out having fun.' I thought about it. 'Or, you know – in studying.'

'I could say the same for you. Why are you all by yourself on a Saturday night?' She took another sip from her drink. 'I didn't actually think you'd be here when I knocked.'

As a rule, I hated to let people down – and the fact that I'd failed to live up to Jess's baseline expectation that I would turn out to be a normal human with somewhere to be on a Saturday evening was a bit annoying. On the other hand, I quite liked the idea of myself as the pensive maths teacher, staying up late into the evening to drink beer, be alone with my thoughts and do great things with calculus. I thought that persona had definite enigmatic potential.

'Well, I had plans for tonight,' I informed her. 'But they fell through.'

She smiled. 'With Miss Laird?'

'Jess . . .' I said, and then shook my head and started laughing. 'Jesus Christ.'

'What?' She started laughing too. 'Miss Laird fancies the pants off you, it's so obvious. She's always staring at you in assembly.' And as she spoke she gently admonished me for being the object of Sonia's affection with the lightest of play-ful shoves to my right pectoral.

Even I was surprised by how hard I found it to resist reaching out and shoving her gently back.

Fortunately, Jess continued talking, which gave me a few seconds to gather myself. 'I watch Miss Laird all the time,' she was saying. 'She's always looking at you and trying to sit next to you and following you to the staffroom. She tripped up the other day, chasing you in her stilettos.'

Despite myself, I laughed again. 'Tell me that's not true.'

Jess grinned back at me, like she loved to make me smile. 'It's one hundred per cent true! She dropped all her books. Running after you,' she added, in case I'd not caught this bit the first time.

'Well,' I said, 'it's not reciprocated.'

'How come?'

Because I was enjoying myself, and because I suspected it would make her laugh, I was tempted to tell Jess all about my night with Sonia at the restaurant. But I realized how it might have looked: even Sonia, who'd been very much in attendance on the most bogus date in history, was utterly convinced that my forced participation was irrefutable proof of my lustful intent – despite the fact she'd virtually had to abduct me in order to secure it.

Plus, Sonia was a fellow teacher, and much as I would have loved to tell Jess about her retching into passing flower beds, I knew it wasn't fair. Mackenzie was a firm believer in sticking together, and would even occasionally go as far as to describe us as one big family – usually on Friday mornings during the rousing motivational speech he delivered off the back of his one and only coffee of the week. I wouldn't have taken it quite that far, but it was hard to come up with a meaningful argument against the general sentiment.

So instead I just said, 'Not my type,' as neutrally as I could.

'Oh. What's your type?'

'Complicated,' I said.

I knew as soon as I'd spoken that it was a poor choice of word. I must have been trying to articulate what I'd always suspected, which was that Sonia was pretty vacuous, with nothing going on underneath all that blusher and mascara and bright red lipstick. Yes, she was more than capable of making her presence felt – but I was pretty sure that beyond her maniacal tendencies, her head was just an empty space. On the few occasions I'd attempted to engage her in proper conversation at the pub, before everything had kicked off between us, her limited contribution had been to sling back oversized glassfuls of warm white wine and agree with every

94

word I said. I wanted something deeper. It didn't have to be an ocean, but it had to be more than something so shallow it barely counted as a puddle.

And why wouldn't I want complicated, for God's sake? I was living on my own in North Norfolk, teaching at an all-girls private school and hanging out with other teachers. I had never really travelled, or ridden a motorbike, or jumped out of a plane, or done anything that could be seen as remotely remarkable. My risk-averse parents – well-intentioned as they were – had always persuaded me to walk on the safer side of life. If I was honest, I'd actually been feeling for a while that my life was in a bit of a rut – so, right now, complicated was just up my street.

I did not mean her.

I swear. I did not mean Jess.

'How complicated?' she asked me then. And that was the moment when everything spun 360 degrees because suddenly her hand was on my thigh. The feeling of her touching me shot straight to my stomach like a lightning bolt, but this time, I didn't move away.

Conversely enough, the expression on her face was almost one of innocence. With berry-red lips parted ever so slightly, she was simply waiting patiently for my response to the pretty straightforward question being posed by her fingers on my leg. *Yes, or no?*

My heart began to pump so urgently it could have passed as the bassline to an acid-house anthem. I knew by then that I wanted to kiss her, but I also knew that I didn't want to go to prison. In an effort to mobilize my last remaining vestige of self-control, I moved my leg from beneath her hand and leaned forward, hanging my head like I was getting a quick prayer in before everything went sideways. My hair fell across my face, and I breathed hard for a few moments, my heart still hammering.

Teacher plus pupil equals pervert was whirling round and round my mind. There was nothing complicated about that little equation whatsoever.

'Jess,' I said eventually.

She didn't respond.

I turned back round to look at her. She was sitting very still, grey eyes wide, waiting. 'I'm sorry. I think you should leave. This is very wrong. You know how wrong this is, don't you?'

Her eyes glassed over then.

Please don't cry. Oh God, please don't cry.

'Don't you like me?' she breathed, just about holding it together.

It occurred to me then that I wanted to answer that question by grabbing her and kissing her, just to show her how much I *did* like her – a realization that struck me in the pit of my stomach like the fist of a heavyweight boxer with an anger problem.

Forget it, I told myself then, sternly. *Theoretically, all this is still under your control.* As the (supposedly) responsible adult here, I had to at least try and claw back some daylight. I'd created this problem by inviting her in and letting her flirt with me before waffling on to her about 'complicated' – so now it was up to me to shut it down, and fast. 'I like you, Jess,' I said softly, 'but I'm your teacher, and you really need to leave now.'

'Actually, I am leaving,' she said quickly. 'After Christmas, we're all moving to London to live with my aunt.' It was only after she had swept a swift yet shaky fingertip underneath each of her eyes, her mouth slightly ajar, that I realized she was slowly weeping.

'Oh,' I said. 'I'm really sorry to hear that.' And I was. 'How come?'

She slung her head back and stared at the ceiling for a couple of seconds, taking deep breaths, attempting to compose herself. I gently took the can of lemonade from her and set it down next to my half-drunk beer because she didn't seem to know what to do with her hands.

'My mum's basically an alcoholic, and she can't cope,' she said eventually. 'She needs to go to bed and stay there for about six months, she reckons.'

'Jesus,' I muttered.

'There's only three weeks left of term,' she said, looking at me again. 'And then I'm gone for ever.'

I realized then that I would miss her. I realized that I looked forward to having her in my lessons. I realized that I was chuffed she'd joined maths club. And at roughly the same time as I realized all that, I realized I must also be a class-A, top-grade scumbag, because she had started to very slowly trace her fingers up and down my thigh and I wasn't doing a thing to stop her.

Jess's hand began to inch upwards in the direction of my groin. 'You've got to go, Jess,' I whispered to her, surprised to realize that my eyes were brimming with tears. *Please stop. Don't stop. Please stop. Keep going.*

She promptly ignored me by leaning over and kissing me, hard.

Instantly I succumbed, grabbing the back of her head with my hand and pulling her against me. Her silken hair ran through my fingers like water, my cock already embarrassingly stiff. I groaned as her tongue found its way into my mouth – sweet and citrusy, sticky with lemonade – and grappled with my own.

She was a strong kisser. She felt experienced. It felt as if she knew exactly what she was doing. *Irrelevant, irrelevant*, I reminded myself, even as our legs began to tangle together, our kissing becoming more and more fierce.

'Jesus Christ,' I groaned into her mouth.

I couldn't stop my hands from moving all over her body, smothering her in great sweeping motions like I was rubbing her with oil. She had one hand buried in my hair and the other gripping the back of my neck, making me intermittently shudder and adding great shocks of voltage to this unbelievable kiss.

Then suddenly she moved a hand downwards, and I felt her fingers brush my flies. And that was it – the small, single movement that was pretty much equivalent to my mother karate-kicking my front door in, snapping on all the lights and barking at us both to go home. I had gone too far – *fuck*, way too far – and I withdrew myself from her quickly, blinking and panting like I'd just woken with a start from a really vivid dream. Or nightmare, depending on which way you looked at it.

'I'm so sorry,' I gabbled, shuffling backwards on the sofa, untangling my legs from hers, trying to arrange myself so my cock wasn't pointing skyward. 'I'm so sorry, I'm so sorry.'

She started crying then, properly. Her hair was all over her face. 'Don't say you're sorry. Please. You want it as much as I do.'

'Yeah, but that's the point, Jess, isn't it? I shouldn't do. I'm your teacher.' It felt like the right moment to stand up then and start striding purposefully around the room, but I didn't want her to see how desperate I was for her. 'This is wrong. This is very, very wrong.'

For Christ's sake. I sounded like sodding Mackenzie discussing vandalism to the school daffodil patch.

She'd pushed her hair back now. The inch of skin surrounding her lips had turned pink-sore from our kiss. 'It doesn't feel wrong to me.'

'You really need to leave, Jess.' It was the only thing I felt certain of at this point. Everything else was shifting like quicksand.

'I've missed my bus.'

'Then I'll drive you,' I said. 'I'll drop you off at the corner of your road.'

'You can't, Mr L, you've been drinking.'

Out of the mouths of babes. 'Believe me, Jess, drink-driving is nothing compared to what's just happened.' I was probably on the cusp of the limit, but even that felt irrelevant – I knew that unless we got in the car straight away, we would very quickly reach the point of no return. And I reasoned that I'd rather lose my licence for driving under the influence than be arrested for having sex with a schoolgirl.

I reached out and fumbled on the coffee table for my car keys, before getting to my feet and offering her my hand. As she took it, I pulled her against me one last time, and then – for no better reason than being unable to help myself – I started kissing her again. My hands were glued against either side of her head, and I was pumping my tongue desperately in and out of her mouth like I was a sodding teenager. She had one hand caught up in my hair and was moving the other steadily underneath my belt and on to my backside.

I took a great shuddering breath and pulled away from her. 'Come on. We have to do this now, before it's too late.'

What are you saying? It's already too late.

As we drove in silence back to Jess's house, Sonia Laird was for some reason looming reproachfully in my mind. I silently informed her that the whole thing had been a mistake, a one-off – that, somehow, I would fix it. I had no idea how, but I knew I had to fix it.

From her unauthorized little stakeout in my conscience, Sonia looked less than impressed.

8

A new-build development at the edge of the village, Carnation Close bordered an idyllic expanse of shimmering, green-gold hay meadow. At its far end, where the contour of the landscape dipped sharply beyond the field's hawthorn boundary, Jess could just about discern a tiny blue triangle of sea tucked in between the sycamore trees. Swifts swooped low above the grass as she paused to soak up the view, a bright decoration of poppies making tiny scattered beacons amid the weaving stems, backlit by evening sunshine.

The houses, in contrast, carried about as much natural appeal as a budget hotel on the Gatwick arterial. From six identical mock-Georgian villas, each with a front door in a primary colour and a thick carpet of shingle on the drive, Jess guessed number four to be Will and Natalie's place, as there was music emanating from inside. Simply Red, she noted. *Interesting.*

Jess felt her heart give way slightly when Natalie answered the door. She was simply dazzling, classic perfection in a black-lace cocktail dress, her mouth a slash of scarlet lipstick, hair a glassy curtain cut sharp against her face. She smiled tightly with a rigidity that seemed to be more about not cracking the lipstick than any predisposition to be hostile, though she did loosen up enough to bellow Will's name as they passed the foot of the stairs on their way to the kitchen.

Jess dutifully began unpacking the food while Natalie vanished back upstairs to finish her make-up. She had received flurries of barely decipherable texts from her hostess over the past few days, an unwelcome brain dump of nonsensical ideas for tonight's menu that mostly involved bizarre suggestions for themes and unworkable ingredients. However, a lifetime of dealing with her bossy older sister, Debbie, meant that Jess was unfazed by authoritarianism, preferring to rely upon her own expertise in the same way that a doctor might incline towards medical science as opposed to the half-cocked theories of hypochondriac patients when considering diagnoses.

It had also transpired that Charlotte suffered from a serious peanut allergy, though Natalie was resolute in her assurances that since she wouldn't be eating the party food, Jess had no reason to worry. But after several nights of waking up at two a.m. envisioning the disastrous consequences of a snatched canapé, Jess opted to preserve her sanity and create a menu that was nut-free. She spent longer than usual checking, then double-checking, all her ingredients – but she had to be sure.

The kitchen was a spotless combination of gloss white and faux granite, making Jess's look like a squat in comparison. Unable to discern a single stray breadcrumb, greasy olive oil bottle, filthy recipe book or leaking box of cereal, she now understood what Will had meant by living in a sanitized house.

Natalie eventually stalked back through to the kitchen from the living room, holding two gin and tonics and extending one to Jess.

'Oh, no thanks,' Jess said quickly. 'Not while I'm working.'

Natalie tilted her head, shooting Jess a smile that narrowed her eyes. She'd added lashings of liner and charcoal to her already smouldering look, Jess noticed.

'So, how's that leg of yours?' Natalie sipped from her drink, speaking in a manner that suggested Jess's right thigh was like a troublesome child with behavioural problems.

'Oh. Not too bad. Lots of ice and painkillers.' Jess attempted to mirror her hostess's perfunctory tone, then realized she was probably only succeeding in coming across as a little bit sarcastic.

'Such a nightmare.' Jess could feel Natalie watching her. 'Will was distraught.'

'He shouldn't feel bad,' Jess mumbled, struggling suddenly to meet Natalie's eye. 'It wasn't his fault.'

Natalie crunched down loudly on to an ice cube. 'No, thank God.'

Jess waited, unsure if she should perhaps acknowledge the money Will had offered her on Natalie's behalf. But then Natalie switched on a smile, saving Jess from that particular discomfort yet launching her headlong into one that was, in reality, far worse. 'He's just through here. Come and say hello.' She flicked her silken mane gently back in the direction of the living room.

Jess took a breath, having no choice but to follow her. As they reached the double doors, Natalie paused and whipped round, clamping her gaze on to Jess's feet. 'Sorry, no shoes,' she said. 'Do you mind?'

'Of course not.' Jess removed her pumps and padded through self-consciously behind Natalie in her socks, feeling dowdy and ridiculous in comparison to her elegant hostess.

For a short-term rental, the house was terrifyingly well presented, the level of spotlessness such that Jess began to panic that her socks might not actually be clean. The carpet, walls and requisite furniture were bland enough (Jess assumed the place had come furnished) but touches of

Natalie were still evident everywhere, as if she'd spun through all the rooms with her home improvement wand, whacking it against various fixtures and fittings so that people wouldn't think she took her style inspiration from online rental listings. The coffee table in the centre of the room bore an enormous arrangement of calla lilies, candles in hurricane vases adorned every surface, and from the hearth a scent diffuser hinted heavily at the presence of a nearby pomegranate plantation. Jess also noticed two bottles of antibacterial spray on the bottom shelf of a half-full bookcase – presumably tucked away ahead of the party, to be squirted liberally around the place tomorrow. The books themselves she assumed to be Will's – though he'd never been much of a reader before. She struggled somehow to imagine Natalie losing herself in the post-modernist ramblings of James Joyce, Philip Roth or Joseph Heller, or the scathing satire between the pages of all the *Private Eye* magazines.

But by far the most arresting item in the room was the enormous photo-on-canvas of Natalie, Will and Charlotte hanging above the gas-effect fireplace – the only evidence Jess had seen so far in the entire house to suggest that a small child lived here too.

They were posing for that studio photography classic – the three of them lying forward in a row, Natalie and Will flanking Charlotte, bare feet crossed playfully at the ankle. Charlotte had been styled to look like a catalogue model, beaming cheerfully through her teeth and hair with shiny camera-ready perfection. Natalie herself was a photographer's dream, her very glance a sultry suggestion, though it contained just the right amount of virtue for a family shot. Will had clearly been groomed as well (as much as a person with a shaved head and zero beard can be groomed – Jess suspected fake tan) and primed to smile as if he'd just had the best sex of his life. The contrast between this photo and his appearance back then – his rock star look, as he had jokingly liked to call it – was quite astounding.

Seeing him on display like that, one third of a happy trio, brought a sudden stiffness to Jess's stomach, so she turned her gaze away – only for it to land on the real-life Will instead. He was standing next to the sofa wearing jeans and a shirt in a shade of blue that somehow made him look even browner, even more handsome, than he had the other day. But the expression on his face was of someone who could quite happily have eaten his own fist.

'Will, you remember . . .' Natalie hesitated for a moment.

'Jessica,' she supplied quickly.

Will extended a hand to Jess, who wiped her own against her apron before shaking it. His grip was firm and he looked her right in the eyes. Even to touch him made her gently shiver.

'Hello again,' he said. 'How's your leg?'

Jess swallowed and shot him a hopeful smile. 'Still in shock, I think.'

To her immense relief, he smiled back. Then, tipping his head at the music, 'Simply Red. You a fan?'

'Simply Red.' She pretended to think about it. 'Is the lead singer that guy out of *Men Behaving Badly*?'

He laughed. 'Er, no! Good guess though.'

'Oh, you're so *young*,' Natalie exclaimed sharply, and she sounded so alarmed about it that Jess instantly felt guilty.

Will looked away and reached for the remote, cranking Mick down a few notches. 'I hope you've cooked us up a feast, Miss Hart.'

She nodded. Her mouth felt dry. 'I tried.'

'Is Charlotte ready, darling?' Natalie enquired, gently swaying away to 'Fairground'.

Will shook his head and avoided Jess's gaze. 'Not yet. Helen's still doing her hair.'

'Well, what on earth's she doing to it?' Natalie said impatiently, removing the cocktail stirrer from her glass and licking it.

Will shrugged. 'I don't know. Plaits?'

'You're going to think we're terribly lazy,' Natalie declared, addressing Jess, 'but we do have a part-time childminder, even though Will doesn't work per se. Everybody needs their own space, don't they, darling?' She looked across at him but gave him no time to answer. 'And it's not like we can't afford it, so . . .' She gave a little shrug.

'I don't think Jessica really needs to hear the finer details of our childcare arrangements,' Will remarked.

'Hiring help is nothing to be ashamed of, darling,' Natalie countered, as if this was a couples therapy session and Will was being resistant.

Jess thought she saw Will flick his eyes briefly in the direction of the ceiling. Sensing the acuteness of his embarrassment and feeling it too, all the way to her toes, she concentrated too hard on the blank television screen behind him.

It was then that she spotted it.

A little statue in copper, about six inches tall, of a long-haired guitarist, head thrown back, rocking out. It was positioned prominently on its very own shelf above the television.

Unbridled, her heart began to pound. Over to her left, Natalie was experiencing her own lack of control, lost in a little dance tribute to Mick.

Jess simply couldn't take her eyes off it, staring for so long that eventually she felt Will follow her gaze. The room swelled with a loaded silence to which only Natalie, apparently, was oblivious.

'So, do you have everything you need?' Will asked her then, briskly. His eyes were pleading with her to nod and retreat.

She swallowed and offered him a faint smile. 'Yes, I do.' She hesitated. 'Thank you.' And then she turned and disappeared into the kitchen, her heart still thumping.

Natalie came in after her only a couple of seconds later, pulling the living-room doors shut behind them.

'You'll have to excuse him,' she said in the abrasive manner of someone freshly bolstered by alcohol, 'he gets like that sometimes.'

'Like what?'

'Irritable.'

'Well, I'm probably the last person he wants to see again. You know, after the accident,' Jess mumbled, for something to say more than anything else.

'Between you and me,' Natalie said, leaning a little closer, 'that was actually part of the reason I asked you.'

Jess gaped at her. 'How . . . how do you mean?'

'He's just been utterly floored by the whole thing. Understandably of course,' Natalie added hastily. 'Anyway, I thought it might help if he could see for himself that you're recovering okay.' She winked inappropriately, in a way Jess suspected she might not have done sober, before slinging down the last of her drink and stalking off back to the living room.

Two hours later and Natalie was slowly getting drunker. Jess could see and hear her through the double doors of the living room, holding court on the sofa with a gaggle of women from the village. She was gushing loudly about the renovations on the holiday home, her audience cooing in chorus over photos of the damp course like she was showing them pictures of a newborn baby.

An earlier well-practised scan of the party guests had told Jess most of what she needed to know, which was firstly that they all seemed to be intent on getting wasted, possibly to the point of throwing up in Natalie's wheelie bin, but also that nobody appeared to be handing a dossier of Jess's past around the room like security intel at a cabinet meeting. She had become expert over the years at separating in one glance those who knew from those who didn't, and the ratio was continually calibrating in her favour anyway as old faces moved out and others moved in. Still, she always mentally readied herself for someone to make the connection at an event like this, because she deemed there to be a much better chance that way of snuffing out the spark before it became a flame.

Tonight, thankfully, nobody had particularly looked at her twice, other than when she'd done a quick round of the room to hand out her business cards or to top up the canapés. She felt as confident as she could do that Natalie's new circle, as it currently stood, was safe enough.

'Well, they're starting to knock down the interior walls,' Jess could hear Natalie informing them now, 'so in a couple of days' time we'll either be looking at something out of *Architectural Digest* or a very big pile of bricks.'

One of the women said something Jess couldn't quite catch.

'Oh no, we're going absolutely the whole hog,' Natalie responded brazenly. 'Adding two storeys to the back while we're at it. The garden's easily double the size it needs to be, so it makes sense to extend south as well as north. The neighbours despise us already.' She laughed throatily. 'They picked a fight with my builder the other day and I just told him: "Kevin, you know what to do."'

Another woman leaned over, presumably to ask her what it was that Kevin allegedly knew to do.

'Took his pneumatic to the boundary, of course,' Natalie declared, face flushed with self-satisfaction. 'Broke up some residual concrete just for the hell of it. By the end of the day they were ready to put their own place on the market.'

Cue raucous laughter from her audience. Jess winced and turned away, unable to prevent herself from wondering exactly how the Will she knew was able to handle co-existing day-to-day with a woman like Natalie.

Still, the night had gone well so far. She'd been right to follow her instincts on the menu: the sweet pork meatballs had vanished within minutes, her vodka gazpacho shots coming a close second. In a few minutes she'd start clearing dishes from the canapés to take out the lemon meringue tartlets and cream-stuffed profiteroles.

And then, once again, her mind made an unexpected detour towards the little copper statue in Will's living room.

He must look at it every day. Does that mean he still thinks about us?

Fortunately, Natalie's party hadn't so far been the sort of occasion where people stumbled into the kitchen with their eyes half shut and tried to go to the toilet in the sink (she'd catered plenty of those). As yet she'd had only a couple of interruptions – someone sticking their head round the door and asking for an orange juice, another guest complimenting her on the excellent canapés – and she hadn't seen Will all night. Twice, she'd felt as if perhaps he was watching her; but when she'd turned round, there had been no one there.

Now, though, she did have a visitor: a dark-haired child in

a fuchsia pink dress that looked as though it was probably something to do with a Disney film. She was a perfect little princess with deep green eyes, observing Jess with innocent curiosity.

'Hello. You must be Charlotte.'

The girl nodded shyly.

Jess smiled. 'Pleased to meet you.'

As she crouched down to Charlotte's height, Jess felt her damaged leg twinge, and hoped that the child didn't recognize her from the accident. She was fairly sure that it would have been traumatic for a seven-year-old to witness, especially as she'd been marooned in the back seat of the car the whole time with nothing by way of a coherent reassurance forthcoming from any of the adults.

Searching Charlotte's face for signs of her father, Jess could see him straight away in her eyes and her little chin. Her heart was in momentary danger of snapping in two.

The girl frowned. 'I'm seven,' she informed Jess. 'And Mummy wants some more meatballs.'

Jess laughed. 'Well, as luck would have it, I think I do have some more in here somewhere. Would you like to help me carry them through?'

The child furrowed her brow, stuck a thumb in her mouth and shook her head, which made her curls bounce gently.

'Okay,' Jess said. 'Do you know what else I have up there?' She gestured above their heads to the worktop, and Charlotte's gaze travelled upwards to where the desserts were ready and waiting.

Jess stood up. The profiteroles, drizzled in melted couverture chocolate, were stacked tall to make their grand entrance. She lifted the platter carefully from the work surface and squatted down with it to Charlotte's height. 'Do you think you can take this one from the top?'

Charlotte's eyes widened and she nodded eagerly as Jess held the platter out. With chubby fingers the little girl reached up and gingerly removed the top profiterole from the stack, not pausing as some children might have done to check if she was allowed to eat it, but stuffing the whole thing quickly into her mouth in one urgent motion. Her entire face bulged for a few moments as she worked her little jaw against the pastry and cream, the chocolate sauce making a thick dark smudge around her lips.

'Ooh, that made a nice mess,' Jess said with a grin, reaching up for a napkin. She squatted down again and paused as Charlotte finished chewing before drawing it gently across her face. As the child waited, her gaze lowered slightly, eventually fixing upon a dark slick of chocolate sauce that had landed squarely down the front of her dress. Instantly, she started to cry, a long, thin wail, like a cat at midnight.

'Oh Jesus,' Jess muttered.

'My dress,' she began to bawl hysterically, 'my dress.'

A door opened behind them.

'What's going on?'

It was Will. He rushed straight over to Charlotte and squatted down in front of her, the handsome white knight arriving to rescue his princess. In that moment, forming a little circle on the kitchen floor, the three of them could have been mistaken for a family.

'I'm sorry,' Jess breathed, 'I gave her a profiterole.'

Will snapped his head round to look at her. 'Didn't Natalie tell you about her allergy? She's only supposed to eat her own food.' His tone was thunderous, his face dark.

'It's okay,' she gabbled. 'I checked everything before –'

'Is there any peanut in there? ANY PEANUT?'

'No,' she stammered. 'No, no. None. I'm so sorry, I didn't think . . .'

He didn't look at her after that. His arms were round his daughter, who by now was wailing a continuous note at a very high pitch. 'Hey, darling, shush. Shush. It's okay. We'll fix your dress.'

His comfort felt like a reproach. 'I'm really sorry,' Jess said again.

He still didn't look at her. 'Shush, darling. Shush.'

Feeling increasingly like she was intruding on a private moment, Jess stood up. 'I think Natalie wanted more meatballs, so –'

'Charlotte needs changing,' Will said sharply, and for a brief, terrifying moment, Jess thought he was asking her to do it. 'And then we need some more ice.' Still, he wouldn't look at her. Charlotte's howl had now turned into dramatic, shuddering sobs.

'It's in the garage,' he added and, finally, he looked up and their eyes met. 'Take those meatballs out to Natalie, I'll sort Charlotte out. And then I'll come and give you a hand.'

9

Most of the daylight had by now been lost, and the air was damp and cooling. The handful of guests who'd been chatting and drinking outside on the back lawn had retreated indoors, leaving footprints imprinted in the gathering dew and a smattering of empty cups on the patio.

Jess waited while Will fiddled with the key in the lock. 'Fucking thing.'

Inside, the double garage was cool and dark, the sort of place someone might realistically need as a bolthole if they lived with a woman like Natalie. The space seemed cavernous, housing only a weights bench, Will's car, a chest freezer and a small stack of groceries along the far wall. Jess was pleased, though, that the strong, comforting scent of damp concrete and engine grease still hung in the air. It reminded her of perching on her father's work bench as a child, watching him painstakingly restoring his Triumph Spitfire, both of them listening to political programmes she didn't understand on his faithful Roberts radio.

Jess let her eyes rest briefly on the groceries: curries-in-a-can, baked beans, sliced pineapple, bottled water. She guessed it was the work of Natalie; for what purpose, she couldn't quite imagine.

As Will turned to face her at the car's front bumper, Jess thought about complimenting him on the size of his garage to break the ice. She thought about saying sorry for Charlotte's dress again. She thought about saying sorry for everything else.

'We should keep the lights off,' he said. 'I don't want anyone to see us.'

She nodded. 'Okay.'

There was a brief pause.

'Hello again,' he said. 'Sorry about that, with Charlotte. I panicked.'

'No, I'm sorry. I wasn't thinking. Is she okay?'

'Of course, she just . . . we bought that dress especially for the party. She's an occasion girl, like her mother.'

'She's beautiful,' Jess said softly.

'Thank you,' he said warmly, like he somehow knew what it took for her to be gracious about it.

'There's a lot of people in there.' She had the impression he was relieved to be getting some air.

'Yeah. Natalie's something of a fast mover – socially, I mean. I don't know how she does it. Catered house parties aren't really my thing. No offence,' he added quickly. 'Your food was the best bit. Nothing says a good party like an asparagus cigar.'

'I think you might be the only one still sober enough to appreciate it,' she said with a teasing smile.

'Ah. That's because they all got pissed on your tomato vodka. They're a discerning lot.'

'Vodka gazpacho shots,' she corrected him, trying and failing to keep a straight face.

'Well, they went down a storm, Jess. You'll have to come again.'

There was a pause.

'So,' Jess said, lowering her voice, 'what are we doing in your garage?'

'Ice?'

'Ice.'

Neither of them moved for a moment or two, during

which time Jess's gaze settled on Will's weights bench. She smiled.

'What's funny?' He was watching her, amused.

'No, nothing, it's just . . .' She let a tiny laugh escape.

Will laughed too, like it was catching, his eyes lighting up. 'What?'

She tucked a strand of hair behind her ear. 'I noticed before that you'd –' she puffed her cheeks out slightly and made a shrugging motion with her shoulders that was supposed to indicate upper body bulk – 'so I was going to ask if you'd been working out.'

He laughed again, loudly. 'Nice. The opener to beat all openers.'

'I resisted. I'm too classy.'

'That much I do know,' he said with feeling. He leaned back against the chest freezer then, regarding her with soft eyes. 'I actually had a dream about you last night.'

She said nothing, sensing from his expression that this would not be a story that came with a punchline.

'You were sitting in my living room with Natalie, and you'd told her everything.'

'That's really what you think? That I'm going to tell Natalie everything?'

'That's what my *subconscious* thinks,' he corrected her. 'Look, I'd understand, in a way. You've got every reason to hate me.'

'Does it seem to you like I hate you?'

He shrugged stiffly. 'Perspectives change a lot in seventeen years. You were fifteen back then. You're over thirty now.'

'That doesn't change what happened between us.'

There was a brief silence. Jess eased the weight from her right leg, feeling the blood rush and then subside to a gentle pulse.

'And how do you see it – what happened between us? Be honest.'

She could tell that he was half expecting her to talk about a gross abuse of trust, a disgusting act of power play. 'We fell in love,' she whispered, looking right at him.

He exhaled sharply, like she'd just shoved a fist into his stomach. 'Okay,' he said. 'You really still think that?'

'You don't?' she breathed, a ripple of sadness moving through her.

He kept his gaze fixed firmly on the concrete floor. 'Well, I did. I'm not so sure any more.'

'Why not?' Her voice was tiny, barely audible, even in the silence.

'Well, unfortunately that's what a prison sentence and enforced psychological assessment does for you. Oh, and let's not forget all the hate mail from members of the public I'd never even met.'

'I'm sorry. I thought our plan would work. I really did.'

'Well, of course you did,' he said, his voice slightly dazed, 'you were fifteen.'

'Don't keep saying that,' she said, 'like you've had it drilled into you. It's crap.'

He laughed then, a proper laugh. 'It's crap? Would you like some selected highlights from the assassination of my character to date?'

'No,' she whispered.

'I'm a monster,' he said. 'I'm evil. I deserve to die, to be chemically castrated. I should never be allowed near children again, never work again, never be happy again. I'm an animal, clinically insane, a danger to society. I should be locked away in prison for the rest of my life. I should never stop looking over my shoulder. I should be stabbed to death, have my throat slit, my genitals mutilated.' He looked at her. 'What do you think about that?'

She shook her head, wiping away a single, silent tear that had dribbled down her cheek.

'Or I could tell you all about what happened to me in prison, if you like? They were waiting for me, Jess. Do you want to know?'

She shook her head again, and he appeared to check himself. As a silence descended, the gloom seemed to intensify. From somewhere that sounded very far away, she could just about hear the music – 'This Love' by Maroon 5 – drifting towards them.

'Sorry,' he said, shaking his head. 'Sorry, Jess. It's not your fault. It's just that tonight is the first time in a while that I've been forced to shake hands and make small talk with strangers, and I'm terrified. I've literally spent the entire night hiding out in the playroom with Charlotte, telling everyone that she doesn't want to come out, that she's shy. No wonder my girlfriend thinks I've got mental health problems. I had to take a sedative just to make it downstairs tonight.'

She said nothing, waiting.

'I thought I was ready to come back to Norfolk, Jess, and start meeting people again, but . . . I'm not. I'm terrified that I might bump into an old face. Or that someone could see you and me in the same room together – that it might jog a memory and they might remember something, recognize me, tell the papers. And that's it, my life would be over. Natalie would leave, I'd lose Charlotte. Or they might . . . you know. Something might happen. I don't care if they hurt me, but I love my daughter, Jess.'

I care if they hurt you.

'I do the same thing myself all the time,' she told him. 'I

think about who's around. But there's no one in there who knows. I promise.'

He swallowed and nodded. 'Funny. That's exactly what my sedative said.'

She permitted herself a careful smile at his joke. 'Would it help . . . I mean, don't take this the wrong way, but maybe you'd be better off back in London.'

'We've already had that conversation,' he said. 'And by conversation I mean screaming row. Coming to Norfolk, doing up the house . . . it was Natalie's big plan for family time. If I go back, she and Charlotte are staying and I can find somewhere else to live.' He hesitated. 'She puts up with a lot, you know.'

'You really can't tell her? She might surprise you, Will, she might understand.' Jess swallowed. 'She clearly loves you.'

He smiled faintly. 'She loves who she thinks I am, and that's not her fault because she doesn't know that Will Greene isn't real. For God's sake, I chose her because she'd been in America while everything was happening. We met online, Jess: I picked her out of everybody else because I knew she'd be ignorant. I wanted to date her for the sole reason that I could lie to her more easily.' He shook his head, like he couldn't quite believe it himself. 'Added to which, she campaigns for women's rights, you know? She fundraises for Women's Aid. She helps to run a rape crisis helpline every other weekend.' He looked at Jess. 'Trust me, she wouldn't understand this.'

A moment passed.

Will frowned, working his jaw, lost in his thoughts. 'She saved my life, actually.'

'How . . . how do you mean?' Jess asked him, her voice small.

'She made me feel like I had a horizon again,' he said without hesitation, as if it was something he had thought about a lot. 'You know, like I had somewhere to look other than at my feet. I actually think . . . I've become a better person since I met her.'

From outside, they heard Maroon 5 get louder, and then a voice – not Natalie's – calling his name. A door slammed. They both froze, waiting for the sound of footsteps crunching on gravel. None came.

'Jess,' Will said then, into the gathering darkness. 'I know this is coming about seventeen years too late, but . . . thank you for your statement. I just wanted to say that.'

She shook her head, a rejection of his gratitude. 'Don't be crazy. I just told them the truth.'

'Well, it helped me. So thank you.'

'I'm so sorry I couldn't be there,' she said, her voice a rush of remorse. 'In court. Me and Debbie were at my aunt's in London, with my mum. She wouldn't let me go back, not even for the sentencing. And when you went to prison . . . social services banned me from seeing you.'

'Don't apologize, Jess. Seriously, the whole thing was a big fucking mess. It must have been hell for you too.'

She could only nod, disarmed for a moment as the secret she had yet to confess to him rose rapidly in her mind once again, silent but ominous like the lick of a flame.

'Jess.' An expectant stillness briefly settled. 'What happened with your mum? I mean, I read about what happened, but not . . . what *happened*. If that makes sense.'

'Well, there's not much to say, really,' she replied, meaning only that the story wasn't at all complex.

'Please tell me. I need to know.'

Jess kept her eyes on the floor. 'Okay. Well, it was . . . it was a Tuesday night. She'd cooked shepherd's pie for me and

Debbie. We were all sitting round the kitchen table, listening to Jeff Buckley.' She released a breath, slow and steady. 'And then she just . . . got up and walked out of the front door.' Swallowing, she looked up at him. 'Me and Debbie were still eating.'

He was just watching her, saying nothing.

'I had this strange feeling about it. It was late, dark. She hadn't taken the car, or her wallet, or a coat.'

Silently, he reached out and took her hand, giving it a tiny squeeze and bringing tears to her eyes.

'She'd planned the whole thing. It was a huge tide. She'd borrowed a shotgun from her friend Ray, and she just . . . shoved it into her mouth and pulled the trigger. We heard it from the house. So I went out to the salt marsh and found her on her back, floating in a creek.' She shook her head, remembering the sight of it, the smell, the deathly sound of the bitter silence. 'I mean, it didn't really look like her, though. Her head was . . . well, it was obliterated, obviously. From the force of the blast. I just couldn't grasp the fact that I'd only seen her walking around our kitchen ten minutes earlier. Still can't, actually.'

'What did you do?'

'Um, I just stood there. And then I threw up all over my shoes. And then I waded in there and pulled her out.'

'Fucking hell,' he muttered.

She was quiet for a long time before she spoke again. 'I think that was the beginning of the end, for me and Debbie. Life went downhill for her after that and she never really recovered from it. She blames me. Although –' Jess paused, and looked down at where their hands were welded together – 'I'm actually glad that it was me who found my mum, and not Debbie. I don't think she could have handled that.'

120

'Well, in fairness,' Will said, 'no one should have had to handle that.'

She made to nod, but she wasn't sure if she entirely agreed. She had always partly felt that being the one to find her mum was a form of just punishment for what she had done.

'Did she leave a note?'

Jess shook her head. 'No. Nothing.'

'You don't know why . . . ?'

'Well, we'd had a fight the night before. About . . .' She trailed off. 'It doesn't matter.'

'God, Jess. I blame myself. Everything that happened with us – it must have been devastating for your mum.' His voice wavered slightly as if he was battling some deep internal pain. 'I didn't really realize what I'd done to you until I had a daughter of my own. I had a hard time coming to terms with that, after Charlotte was born.'

'Don't ever feel guilty about my mum, Will.' Her voice grew quieter. 'You know what she was like.'

'Jess,' he said, all at once abrupt like there was something he'd been trying to tell her. 'I want you to know. I came back to find you, before –'

But then Natalie's voice came sharply at them, a drunken bark across the lawn.

'I should go,' Will said, into the dark, though his fingers firmed around her hand.

'Okay,' she said. 'I like your garage, by the way.'

'Oh, thanks. I'd give you a tour, but it'd be a bit bumpy.'

'So who's been stockpiling the non-perishables?' she asked, nodding somewhere in the direction of the groceries. 'Is there some impending doom I should be worrying about?'

'Erm, I get this stupid phobia sometimes, about running

121

out of food. It's ever since . . . well. Being in prison.' He sounded slightly embarrassed. 'I had a bit too much time to come up with conspiracy theories while I was in there too. You know – apocalypse, solar flares, Doomsday . . . that kind of thing.'

'Oh.'

'Yep, I'm that guy,' he said, his voice like a wince. 'Just a scare story away from keeping emergency gas masks in my garage.'

She smiled sadly. 'But you're only here for a few months.'

'Well, you know, global cataclysm applies to all postcodes. It's very non-discriminatory in that way. Wherever you are, Jess, you need canned goods.'

'Thanks for the tip,' she said.

And as she spoke he squeezed her hand again, the cluster of their fingers a small misshapen orb suspended in the darkness between them. 'Sorry again. I feel like I'm just going to keep apologizing to you for the rest of my life.'

'You really don't have to.'

'Don't be too nice to me, Jess. I'm not sure I'm mature enough to handle it.'

And then, without meaning to at all, she stepped forward and placed a hand on his chest, finding his lips with her own and kissing him as definitely as she dared, putting her other hand against his face to steady herself. She waited a moment for him to respond, and he did for just a second more before pulling away from her, breathing hard with shock or something else.

'If you wanted to know how I really feel about everything that happened,' she said, her voice quivering with emotion, 'that's how.'

And then she let herself out of the garage and headed back towards the house, limping fiercely like a defective clockwork toy. She would dish up dessert, she told herself firmly, then leave quietly, without a trace.

10

Matthew

Monday, 29 November 1993

My heart was pounding like a copper on the door of a drugs bust as I made my way across the school car park. A whole Sunday had passed with no reproach – no phone calls, no vigilantes chucking bricks through my living-room window, no friends-of-Jess walking threateningly past the cottage. I knew this because I had spent most of the day eyeing up the road outside my house like I was putting in a stint for the Neighbourhood Watch, replaying what had happened the previous night over and over in my mind, desperate to convince myself that perhaps a stupid drunken kiss could be forgotten – that it could even be laughed about, in time. (I wasn't quite sure who I thought would be laughing about it: distinctly unamused thus far, were they to learn the truth, would be Mr Mackenzie, Sonia Laird, Jess's mother and the PTA. And I had the uncomfortable suspicion that, after them, my next available sphere of influence was typically to be found sitting inside a Vauxhall Astra with a blue flashing light on the roof.)

Striding as purposefully as possible into school, I was half braced for a cacophony of cat-calling and verbal abuse. I had already prepped my defence: if challenged, I would say she had a crush on me, that it was all in her imagination.

I knew that this strategy was cowardly in the extreme – but I reasoned that I could always apologize and make it up to her after the event. Like, *way* after. During university or something. Right now, I had to focus on damage limitation.

But my little plan – the same one that had seemed so watertight at home on a Sunday afternoon over a packet of nuts and a bottle of warm ale – seemed ridiculous now, almost laughable. What if she could describe my living room? What if someone had seen her go inside? What if she had swiped something from my kitchen – a little memento that would later serve as indisputable evidence, placing me beyond doubt at the scene of the crime?

I had made, as my mother would say, some highly unwise decisions on Saturday night. There was evidence enough of *that* anyway.

'Morning, Mr Land-*lay*!' Steve Robbins clapped me hard on the back as I entered the staffroom, an annoying habit I had not yet got round to confronting him about. As the school's IT technician, Steve was inexplicably permitted to turn up at work every day wearing a *Red Dwarf* T-shirt, jeans and a pair of bright white Hi-Tecs trainers. He positioned himself in front of me, blocking my path and bending his knees slightly as if we were about to wrestle, which we definitely were not.

'Two words for you,' he said, arms stretched out, palms inward, like he was preparing to karate chop a chunk of wood with his bare hands. 'Stallone. Awesome.'

Inhaling the bitter smell of substandard coffee, I scanned the room. Nobody seemed to be paying me the slightest bit of special attention. Even Sonia Laird was deep in conversation with Lorraine Wecks, which told me everything I needed to know. I was sure that Sonia would have been crouching behind the door with a meat cleaver if she'd caught wind of me kissing a fifteen-year-old.

In that moment, I couldn't have felt more relieved if I'd been a cardiac patient hearing the doctor say they'd had a fuck-up with the notes and I didn't need open-heart surgery after all. 'Oh yeah?' I said jauntily to Steve, patting his shoulder a couple of times as I moved past him and headed for the kettle. A couple of strong coffees – however chemical the aftertaste – and I might just be able to make it through the morning.

'Yeah.' Steve made a machine gun from each of his index fingers and sprayed several rounds into the staff noticeboard. 'Why didn't you come, dude? You'd have loved it.'

I frowned. Steve wasn't fully up to speed on the whole Sonia Laird drama and he wasn't known for his subtlety either. I decided to gloss over it. 'Headache.'

'Jesus. You sound like my girlfriend.'

We both knew that Steve didn't have a girlfriend, but details like that weren't important first thing on a Monday morning. I made us both a coffee (foul, just foul), claimed my usual chair near the window and, still wearing my favourite denim jacket with the sheepskin collar, stretched my legs out across the carpet tiles to wait for the start of the Monday-morning staff meeting. I'd put on my cowboy boots today – for luck or something. Somewhere over to my left, I could see Bill Taylor swinging his pocket watch backwards and forwards like a menacing little pendulum.

As the chatter around me continued, I finally felt my little fog of fear begin to lift. All the signs were positive so far – if I could just make it to the end of the day without incident, I could go back home, lock all the doors and spend another few hours refining my defence (as if the situation were no more serious than being busted by my parish council warden for nicking flowerpots from the gardens of kindly dithering pensioners).

When the staff meeting eventually kicked off, it became clear beyond all doubt that nobody had a clue about Jessica and me. I knew this because top of today's agenda was a decisive show-of-hands on whether the ladies' staff loos were to be made temporarily unisex until the end of term (the ladies, understandably, were not keen) while maintenance works were being carried out on the gents' (which all the men knew to be code for industrial-level cleaning) – not the fact that I had been entertaining a pupil in my cottage on Saturday night. I felt fairly safe in assuming that, had it been public knowledge, the latter would have trumped the former on this particular agenda. Then again, Miss Gooch was in charge of setting it, and everybody knew she had an almost pathological hand-washing problem.

Fucking hell, it felt amazing.
Stop thinking about it.
Stop thinking about it.

Now all I had to do was figure out if any of the kids knew, but this would only entail the very lightest of detective work, if any. Sniggers, sly looks and missiles fashioned from an interesting variety of sanitary items would more than give the game away.

I made it through double maths with the lower fourth and morning playground duty without incident. I made it through a lunchtime rehearsal of the sixth-form play, *The Caucasian Chalk Circle*, without incident (unless you counted all the props that kept going missing – so far we'd mislaid two Cossack hats, a fake baby and an entire tin bath). I made it through an early-afternoon session of marking test papers (oh God, hopeless) without incident.

One thing I did not do, however, was make it through the day without thinking an inappropriate thought about Jessica Hart.

It seemed that the more likely I was to escape death by lynching for what had happened, the happier I was to allow my thoughts to wander off-piste, back to my living room and the way I had taken her face and hair in my hands while I kissed her.

I kissed her.

It felt good. Oh, shit. Why did it feel so good?

Now what?

'Matthew?'

I jumped so suddenly that I flung almost an entire mug of tea over my own lap. It soaked straight through my trousers and stung like shit. I leapt up and virtually into the arms of Sonia Laird, who I now realized had been standing in front of me in the staffroom for the past thirty seconds or so, trying to get my attention by repeatedly whimpering my name.

'*Fuck*,' I growled, much to the disapproval of the grey-haired couple – yes, they were actually a couple – who ran the library. If you happened to be looking for the last word in classification, the Pattersons were it. They could literally stun you with their expertise in cataloguing and index cards. Stun, as in, bolt gun.

Sonia pouted and fluttered about with a grotty-looking tea towel. 'Sorry, Matthew. I didn't mean to scare you.'

Reluctantly I took the microbe-infested tea towel from her, mumbling something barely comprehensible about corduroy not being as hard-wearing as you'd think.

'Sorry,' she said again, and I wondered then what she was really apologizing for. 'I just came over to say . . .' She lowered her voice. 'I don't want things to be "awkward" between us.' She spoke delicately, as if we were discussing a case of genital warts (hers, not mine). 'I know you had plans to come to the cinema on Saturday, and I hope you didn't drop them on my account?'

I swallowed. I'd convinced myself up to this point that I didn't really care if Sonia cottoned on to the fact that I was avoiding her, but now that she was virtually asking me outright, it seemed a bit harsh to confirm that I thought she was slightly deranged.

'Headache,' I muttered, recycling the excuse I'd given Steve for continuity.

I had been trying to dab at my crotch with the tea towel in a way that wasn't too obvious, but now I stopped. It felt strange to have my hand anywhere near that region of my body at the same time as being in touching proximity to Sonia. Unfortunately, Sonia seemed to interpret this as an open invitation for her to pluck the tea towel from my grasp and offer to take over, so I sat swiftly back down without saying anything else and hoped that she wouldn't join me.

My hope was short-lived. 'We could go together, if you like?' she suggested in a voice that was becoming worryingly guttural as she settled into the chair next to me. 'I wouldn't mind seeing it again.'

I cleared my throat, which was probably a subconscious effort to encourage Sonia to clear hers. She had evidently arrived at the conclusion that the first time I'd declined to kiss her had simply been an error of judgement on my part. I needed to help her arrive at a different conclusion, namely that it hadn't been.

'Don't you think your boyfriend might have something to say about that, Sonia?' I asked her as tactfully as I could.

She simpered, offered up a light shrug and put one hand on my knee. 'Not if I don't tell him.'

My heart was beating faster now, and not for any reason

remotely complimentary to Sonia. Attempting to skin my own legs with boiling water hadn't helped, and to make things worse, Lorraine Wecks had walked back into the room and seemed to think that the occasion of me and Sonia sitting next to each other warranted a series of un-subtle winks from over by the kettle. Some people can pull off a wink, and Lorraine wasn't one of them. They were so clumsily executed I couldn't even tell if they were aimed at me or Sonia.

The whole thing was starting to get out of hand. 'Should go,' I muttered.

'But you've got a free period,' Sonia protested.

I scooped up my book bag and got to my feet. 'I really need to dry these out,' I told her, meaning my trousers, which unfortunately only gave her the green light to once again start eyeballing my groin.

I turned the collar up on my jacket, taking care to avoid Lorraine's convulsing eye, and strode quickly from the room.

Steaming across the playground like an oil tycoon fleeing a leaking wellhead, I was stopped in my tracks by the sound of a voice calling my name. This time, for a change, it wasn't the vacant mewl of Sonia Laird. This time, it sounded upbeat and excitable.

'Mr L!'

My heart pounded. It was Jess. She was walking swiftly towards me, wrapped up in a woollen coat and grey knitted scarf, bag slung over one shoulder like she was ready to go home.

I observed straight away that she didn't look as if she was about to give me a slap or the heads-up on my arrest war-rant. She actually seemed ridiculously happy to see me. I felt awash with relief.

'You're supposed to be in PE, Jess,' I told her, surprising myself with a knowledge of the lower fifth timetable I didn't know I had.

'I know, but –' she held up a bright blue tub of decongestant ointment – 'having problems with my sinuses.'

Her eyes were shining, her gleaming curtain of blonde hair flipped over itself. She was smiling at me like I was someone who mattered. I was pretty sure that if I had been staring a few years into the future, I would have been looking at the girl of my dreams.

Seriously. Get it together.

I swallowed. 'You didn't have any sinus issues the last time I checked.'

I didn't mean it to come out as dirty as it sounded. Honestly.

She gave a simple shrug and an even simpler smile. 'Well, you *are* my teacher . . . so I can neither confirm nor deny.'

I smiled back. It was becoming clear that I hadn't needed to dread this moment after all. She was making it stupidly easy on me. 'I haven't seen you then.'

'Thanks, Mr L,' she said, and that was her cue to depart, except she didn't. She lingered, shifting her bag on to her other shoulder and gently tossing the tub between her left hand and her right.

It was my turn.

'Jess, can I have a word?' I said formally, rubbing my hands together against the cold.

She nodded.

'In private would probably be best,' I said, starting to walk in the direction of the drama studio, away from the playground, which for all the three-storey buildings that surrounded it might as well have had a permanent follow-spot

131

trained on to anyone daring to cross it. I kept walking until we reached the side of the studio, where I knew that a well-concealed footpath led into a patch of stiff shrubbery. Against my better judgement, I took it.

After a couple of turns, the path petered out at a wooden bench dedicated to an ancient tap teacher. *For Peggy, teacher of tap and modern dance 1977–1989, from her friends. She loved this place.*

I looked around the laurel bushes. *This* place?

Our hideout was concealed from view, and it looked dry. An excellent place to sit down and sort this all out.

'Have a seat,' I told her, already mentally defending myself to the person who might happen to stumble across us with, *We're just sorting out her sinus problems.*

We both sat down and Jess folded her hands patiently in her lap, generously opting not to question why I deemed all the foliage to be necessary.

I fumbled around with the words in my head for a few moments before saying – in a deep voice that was supposed to convey my regained sense of responsibility but ended up sounding more Leonard-Cohen-with-laryngitis – 'Saturday night was a mistake, Jess.'

Oh, fantastic. Very original, Landley. A-star for effort.

To her credit, Jess smiled. 'Have you been practising this?' Her breath was freezing in tiny little clouds between us.

'No,' I said quickly, frowning, 'why?'

She looked relieved. 'Thank God. It's *rubbish*.'

I went for solemn but ended up laughing. 'Sorry.'

She settled back against the bench and crossed her legs, probably to help her keep warm. 'No, don't be,' she said, biting her lip like she was really trying hard to take me seriously. 'I'm sorry, I shouldn't have laughed.'

How can she be so cool about this? When did girls this cool ever exist?

'Well,' I said, clearing my throat as she offered me another stab at saying anything that meant something, 'I shouldn't have kissed you.' And then I stuffed my hands into my pockets because I was really starting to feel cold.

She smiled into the folds of her scarf. 'Wasn't it me who kissed you?'

True.

No – irrelevant. Get a grip.

I shook my head. 'Jess, I kissed you back and I shouldn't have done that. I don't know what I was thinking. I'm your teacher. You shouldn't have even been in my house.'

She looked more serious now. The smile had melted off her face. I wanted to quickly reconstruct it, put it straight back where it belonged.

'I was the one who knocked on your door, Mr L. It wasn't like you came looking for me.'

Another tick to confirm my good character. If Jess didn't think I was a pervert, then maybe – *maybe* – I wasn't. 'The point is,' I said softly, 'we made a mistake and we have to pretend like it never happened, okay? There's a lot of people who'd be really angry about this if they found out.'

Even though she was the person whose opinion should have mattered least to me, Sonia Laird was for some reason in my mind as I said this. *Bloody Sonia Laird.*

Jess frowned, looked down and picked at a tiny hole in the leg of her black tights. She was starting to shiver with the cold. I wanted to grab her hands and blow some warmth into them. 'Well, *I'm* not going to tell anyone,' she said. 'But I want you to know that Saturday night was the best thing that's happened to me all year.'

We both froze as a clatter of footsteps rounded the other side of the shrubbery. Girls were laughing, gossiping about boys.

'Jess,' I said as soon as their voices had receded, 'you shouldn't say that. You're young; you've got plenty of great experiences ahead of you.'

'I told you we're moving to London after Christmas,' she said, with a slight shake of her head. 'I'm really going to miss you.' She looked across at me then, her grey eyes small and sad.

I remembered what she'd said to me about her mother needing to take off to bed for six months. 'Is your mum going to be okay?'

'Define okay,' she said softly, the shadow of a smile across her face.

I didn't need to attempt it to know that amateur mental health analysis was unlikely to be one of my strengths – but I also didn't want Jess to think I'd just been asking out of courtesy. She got that all the time: teachers checking up on her with one eye on the clock before they dashed off to supervise hockey practice or back-slap each other for being the world's biggest egghead.

'Is it . . .' I hesitated. 'Because of your dad?' Even as I said it, I knew I should have at least tried to pretend I didn't actually think things were that simple.

'No,' she said, shaking her head. 'Actually, my mum was sort of relieved when my dad died. She'd always wanted to travel the world, but he wanted her to have us, so . . .' She offered me a little such-is-life shrug. 'She was finally free.'

Jesus Christ. 'Who told you that?'

She blinked at me, shivering a little more intensely now. 'She did.'

'Jess . . .' I struggled to find the words, probably because I'd never before been challenged to find the upside of someone telling her kids she was glad their dad had carked it. So I decided to position it as some sort of good-natured misunderstanding. 'She didn't mean it. You know that, don't you?'

'She did,' Jess replied simply, shooting down my ignorance. 'She tells us all the time.'

'It's probably the alcohol talking.'

She smiled. 'What you're really thinking comes out when you're drunk, Mr L.'

Well, if that was true, then I was definitely some sort of child molester.

'How long has she been like this?' I asked her, slotting my hands under my thighs and jiggling my legs gently, an attempt to generate some warmth.

'Forever,' she said. 'She fell off a horse when I was five and got addicted to the painkillers. Then she got depression and started drinking. My dad hated it. They were hardly speaking – you know – at the time he died. She only cried at the funeral because she was hung-over.'

For a mother to afford her own comedown more pity than her dead husband or grieving children was not really defensible in my book, so I didn't even bother trying.

Fortunately, Jess didn't seem to be waiting for me to put a positive spin on the behaviour of egotistical lunatics at major life events. 'I miss my dad,' she was saying, 'but it's made me more determined to follow my dreams. I'm going to be a chef when I leave school.'

Admittedly, I was slightly relieved that her goals didn't in any way rely on her being good at maths. 'That's great,' I said with feeling. 'You should do it.'

She smiled and then paused. 'So what's your dream, Mr L?'

Caught off guard, I wavered, wondering if her question somehow meant I habitually appeared jaded or pissed off around my pupils. I hoped not, since that would have put me in the same personality category as the unsmiling Derek Sayers and his unwashed comb-over.

'Er . . .' I scratched my chin. 'Well, I like teaching.'

'No!' She brushed my thigh with a fingertip, probably reflexively. 'I mean . . . what's your *dream*?'

I smiled. It was sort of nice to indulge the thought for a moment that my life's desire might not actually be to hang around with Sonia Laird and play pretend karate with Steve Robbins all day.

'Well. To travel, I guess. I always wanted to, but . . .' I trailed off then and glanced at her, aware that the last thing she probably needed right now was another adult whining on at her about unfulfilled ambition.

But her eyes were wide. She seemed to be hanging on to my half-sentences like they were the most fascinating thing she'd ever heard.

I couldn't really come up with a meaningful conclusion that wasn't something predictable about the Hadley job having been a real opportunity, and not wanting to let Mackenzie down. 'Life takes over sometimes, Jess. That's why you need to do this stuff while you're still young. Which you are,' I added cheerfully, because I was conscious I'd started to sound a bit like my dad, who spent most of his time complaining about his knees and writing to *Points of View*.

'So, go somewhere next summer,' she said. Her teeth were chattering now, though she hadn't seemed to notice. 'You get long holidays. There's nothing stopping you.'

I looked across at her, trying to recall at what point the focus of our conversation had shifted from her alcoholic mother to my motivational shortcomings.

'Where would you go?' she pressed me.

'Italy,' I said, without hesitation. 'It's not exactly exotic, but . . . my grandmother's Italian. We've got family out there.'

'You've never been?'

'Well, for holidays and stuff when we were kids. But I always sort of promised myself I'd go out there one day, maybe do some teaching. Learn the language. I mean, I know a few words and phrases, but it'd be great to learn properly.' I rubbed my hands together and blew into them, briefly envisaging Italian sunshine.

She brushed her hair from her face and looked into my eyes then, like she was about to make a confession. 'I've always dreamed of having my own Italian restaurant. You know — a little trattoria.'

That was a good dream. 'Yeah?' I said, leaning forward.

'Yeah. Mr Michaels was telling us about this amazing little place in Puglia.' She became animated, her eyes widening. 'They built it into a cave, but there's no signs, and they don't have a menu, and it's all lit up with candles inside. And they serve you wine straight from the barrel. I mean, they actually have the barrels *in* there.'

(I had to smile. On the one hand, it was encouraging to hear that Brett Michaels, Hadley's head of languages and long-time advocate of Kentucky Fried Chicken, had updated his definition of a good dinner spot to include whether or not it sold wine by the vat. On the other, it was mildly concerning. I liked the guy a lot, but if there was ever the embodiment of a functioning alcoholic, he was it.)

'Have you ever been?' I asked her. 'To Italy?'

She shook her head. Her teeth were chattering more sharply now.

'Well, what about the Venice trip in February? Mr Michaels is running it. There's still spaces.' (Hadley Hall pupils didn't go to Stonehenge or Hadrian's Wall for their field trips. Oh no – they went to the Dolomites, Barcelona, Stockholm, New York. And now, it seemed, Venice.)

'I'll be living in London by February, Mr L,' she reminded me with a sad smile.

I must have sighed then, because my breath became a fleeting patch of fog in front of my face. 'Oh, yeah.' I frowned. 'Sorry.'

'It's okay,' she said mildly. 'My mum would never pay for me to do something like that anyway.'

I'd overheard talk in the staffroom before about Mrs Hart's substantial inheritance, a portion of which had apparently been ring-fenced for the children's school fees. Much of the (admittedly rather presumptuous) conversation had then proceeded to centre on why the woman was still so bloody tight with money. I could only assume that having a full-time drinking habit left one with very few available hours in which to generate a stable income – as well as an accumulation of ruptured facial capillaries that no amount of charm or foundation could make up for at interview.

'Are you going?' Jess asked me now.

I shook my head. 'There's enough teachers already signed up.'

'Well, you should go to Italy by yourself. Next summer. Find your family.'

I glanced over at her, feeling strangely grateful that she was so willing to share her optimistic outlook. In truth, I was mystified as to where she found the strength for it. Most girls in her situation would have been arrested by now for shoplifting and dabbling in recreational drugs. 'Yeah,' I told her, feeling suddenly inspired. 'Maybe I will.'

She smiled. Her lips were beginning to tinge blue from the cold. 'Well, don't forget to send me a postcard.'

I almost said it. Ridiculously, in that moment, I almost said, *You should come with me.*

Fortunately, a small but crucial cluster of my brain cells kicked in just as the words were leaving my mouth. 'You should get home, Jess,' I ended up mumbling without conviction. 'It's freezing out here.'

But instead of nodding and leaving, she reached out and placed a hand on my leg. It was the softest and lightest of touches, but – *whoosh!* – I felt exactly the same as I had on Saturday night.

You've not been drinking, Landley. There was no excuse then and there's even less of an excuse now.

It shocked me to realize I could do this sober.

'Jess,' I said, but my voice caught clumsily in my throat. I moved my hand down to gently brush her fingers from my leg but I ended up just taking her hand and holding it. Our fingers were squeezed tightly together: hers felt marginally warmer than mine, which were ice cold. I closed my eyes.

'This stops now,' I whispered.

'I like you so much,' she breathed, reaching up with her other hand and placing it against the back of my neck, her fingers through my hair, sending unbelievable little waves of something electric down my spine. I thought about gabbling some further protest, but I knew by then that it was pointless. I shut my eyes.

If she kisses me, I'll kiss her back, just to let her know I like her too, but after that, it stops. I don't know how, but I'll make sure it stops.

Just as I was coming up with this remarkably shoddy action plan, I felt her mouth against mine. Her lips were shaking with the cold. Straight away I dropped her hand and took each side of her face between my palms, just as I had done on Saturday night, and kissed her, hard. Our tongues began to do battle, a fierce friction that got more intense by the second. Her hands slid inside my jacket, ran over the ridges of my ribcage, worked down to the small of my back. I pulled her in tight, mouth still locked on to hers, and then even tighter, until finally she hooked a leg over my thigh and eased herself quickly on top of me. She was so light I barely realized she had done it until I felt the rub of her crotch against my own.

The sensation was incredible and alarming all at once.

I pulled back urgently from her then, ashamed to discover that I was on the verge of tears. 'No! This is wrong – this can't happen.'

I shifted sharply underneath her and she slid off me. With some effort and an amount of inelegant reorganization, I managed to get to my feet.

'Okay,' she nodded. 'Okay.' And now she was actually crying, whereas I was just scuffing round the edges of it, almost numb with shock that I'd just been kissing one of my own pupils behind the drama studio while all her classmates were doing shuttle runs around plastic cones. *How did I let this happen? What sort of guy have I become?*

I ran a hand through my hair. 'Jess, I like you a lot but this has already gone way too far.'

She nodded, doing her best to stem her tears with her fingertips. 'Okay. I'm sorry.'

I shut my eyes briefly, tried to gather myself. 'Please don't say that,' I told her. 'This isn't in any way your fault.'

Jess picked up one edge of her scarf and quickly wiped her mouth. That small, self-conscious movement finally did it. I started to cry. 'I'm so sorry, Jess,' I said, crouching down and kneeling in the mud, taking her hands between my own. She was shaking, and trying not to; sobbing, but attempting to stop. Even now, she was being braver than I was.

'Forget about me, do you understand?' I told her. 'I'm the worst kind of bastard.'

She shook her head. The trails from her tears were snaking all over the smooth, plump skin of her cheeks. 'I don't think you are.'

'One day you will. Believe me. One day, you'll get what I'm talking about.'

There was a long pause as she stared into her lap. 'That's really patronizing, Mr L,' she said eventually with a sniff, and then raised her head slightly to look at me again. 'I know how I feel.'

Her expression was so earnest that my heart could have ripped in two. 'You think you do,' I told her, with some determination, 'but trust me. You really don't.'

After that, we didn't speak again. I just watched as she stood up, adjusted her scarf and bag, and slid me one final, tearful sideways glance before picking her way back through the shrubbery and padding off down the path towards the school gates.

I remained where I was in the mud, literally unable to move. I stayed there until it was dark, knees in the dirt, shivering my bollocks off.

II

Monday morning, and Jess awoke to an interesting soundtrack of vigorous whisking and the Stereophonics. Upon further inspection it turned out to be Zak downstairs at the Aga wearing tracksuit bottoms and her ancient Blur T-shirt, scrambling eggs and humming along to the music.

They'd rowed bitterly the previous night. Jess's christening had overrun, thanks to a frustrating little domino of disasters that had kicked off with a long delay in getting everyone to sit down for dinner, whereupon some of the guests then forgot they were not at a wedding and kept standing up to make speeches during the main course. Fortunately, the final (interminable) discourse had been brought abruptly to a halt by a lengthy scuffle between two opposing branches of the father's family, most of whom were apparently not even supposed to be there. But by the time everybody had calmed down and was seated for dessert, it was gone seven, at which point she'd already missed four calls from Zak, who was sitting in the Brancaster White Horse with his parents, waiting to order.

When she finally arrived back at the cottage, it was late, and Jess was half asleep with exhaustion. Zak, however, was wide awake, having spent the past few hours at a steady but furious simmer. His parents, apparently, were not the sort of people who indulged weak excuses like running late at work, a trait which was obviously genetic, because neither did Zak. His main line of argument seemed to be that Jess was inherently disorganized. Hers was that she wasn't, plus he was being an unreasonable dickhead. Zak had responded to this by swiping his arm along the length of the mantelpiece, which turned out to be an efficient way of dispatching some of the junk he despised so much.

Eventually they had made it up in the early hours of the morning in the same way they always did, and now Jess was battling waves of deep confliction over her kiss with Will on Saturday night. Despite it having been only the briefest of moments, it had left her feeling something that was obviously incompatible with Zak being in the room next door, arranging rashers of bacon in a frying pan on her behalf.

When the knock on the front door came, she only just registered it over the music and sizzling pan. Smudge scampered through from the kitchen to alternately bark at the intruder and wedge his nose against the bottom of the door, inhaling for clues. Jess set down her coffee and fiddled with the latch before swinging the door wide and locking eyes with Will.

In dark jeans and a fitted shirt, sunglasses perched on top of his head, he looked like something out of *Esquire* or an advert for an urbane brand of denim. He was jangling his keys in his hand and, stupidly, Jess glanced past him to scan the road for Matthew's car, before remembering with a jolt that it was crushed years ago.

'Morning,' he said with a smile, and then hesitated. The kitchen could be seen from the front door and, straight away, he clocked Zak at the Aga. 'Sorry,' he said. 'I thought you'd be . . .'

It was at this point that Zak seemed to sense the air change, and looked over his shoulder.

Please stay where you are, Jess begged him silently. *Just stay in the kitchen.*

But Zak cherished all opportunities to assert himself,

especially when it came to strange men turning up at his girlfriend's front door. He set down his wooden spoon and wandered through to take up position directly behind Jess, slinging one arm up against the door frame and extending the other, palm open. 'Zak Foster.'

He shook it. 'Will Greene.'

Jess felt a flash of anger towards Zak for behaving as if both she and the house belonged to him. 'Will's a client.'

'I'm sorry,' Will said. 'I've caught you at a bad time.'

'No, no,' Zak said firmly. 'You're fine, mate, absolutely fine.' The way he said 'mate' was passive-aggressive in the same way that warring females called each other 'sweetheart' in city-centre bars. 'Come in, come in.' Zak put an arm round Jess's waist and pulled her close to him, giving Will space to pass.

Jess caught Will's eye as he hesitated. 'Actually,' he said, 'it's not important. I'll catch you another time.' And then he turned and began to head off.

She couldn't just let him walk away. 'Won't be long,' she said quickly to Zak, wriggling free from his grasp. She pulled the door firmly shut behind her and headed across the front lawn after Will, Smudge at her heels, though he quickly became distracted by the scent of bonemeal at the base of her hybrid tea rose.

It couldn't have been much past ten a.m., and the sun was already warm and high, forcing her to squint into it. Will had pulled his sunglasses back down on to his face. Through the open window of the living room the music drifted out to them, sentimental and melodic.

'Hello. That was awkward,' Will said as they faced one another at the foot of the lawn.

Jess recalled their split-second kiss in the garage on Saturday night, and how great it had felt. As she batted the thought away, she felt a wave of guilt over Natalie and Charlotte. Because he was no longer hers to kiss.

She looked over her shoulder to see if Zak was watching them. He was, steadily, through the living-room window.

'Sorry,' she said. 'Now's probably not the best time.'

'No, you're right.' He hesitated. 'Are you okay, though?' It seemed for a moment as if he might have wanted to take her hand, before deciding on the safer (wiser) option of maintaining his distance.

She nodded. 'I'm okay. You?'

Taking a breath to speak, he let it go again. 'Christ, this is –' He gave a barely perceptible head tilt towards the cottage. 'I feel like I'm on stage.'

'Sorry,' she said, shaking her head in mild frustration. There was so much she wanted to say, so much she wanted to hear.

He smiled faintly at her. 'I was sort of hoping we could talk, but I'm not sure it's an *ideal* three-way conversation.'

'Later?'

'Natalie's out tomorrow night. I could call you.'

'You could come over if you like.'

'Ah.' He rubbed his chin. 'Not sure it's quite the conversation for a seven-year-old, either, actually.'

'I keep forgetting,' she said, embarrassed. 'Sorry.'

He shook his head with a hazy, forgiving smile like, *Don't.* 'What's your number?' he asked her. 'Natalie tends to deal with all the road-traffic accident admin in our household.'

She gave it to him and he tapped it into his phone.

'Out of interest,' Will said, his face tightening slightly as he slid the phone back into his pocket, 'does he always watch you this closely?'

'Zak's just like that,' she said lamely, resisting the urge to look. 'He doesn't really mean anything by it.'

'Sorry. Don't want to cause you problems.'

'You haven't,' she said quickly. 'I can handle Zak.'

Will cleared his throat pointedly then and nodded towards the cottage. Jess turned to see Zak striding across the lawn to join them. Clearly, he'd got bored of waiting.

Slinging a possessive arm round Jess's shoulders and delivering a patronizing peck to the top of her head, Zak started talking loudly at Will. 'You know, I can't quite place you, but you look very familiar.'

Jess was stunned. It would have taken nothing short of a forensic mind to match Will Greene with Matthew Landley purely from sight. She was sure – almost beyond doubt – that he couldn't possibly know.

Unless someone's told him.

Above their heads, a trio of wood pigeons cooed softly from their perching place atop the pantiles as if expressing their fascination for the dangerous little drama playing out beneath them on Jess's front lawn.

'I don't think so,' Will said brusquely, matching Zak's tone.

'No, you do,' Zak needled. 'You definitely do.'

'Zak, Will needs to go,' Jess said quickly. 'I'm sure it'll come to you.'

'Okay, baby,' Zak said with a shrug, and Jess could almost see Will mouthing *Baby?* at her in disbelief. 'I'm sure Will and I will have the pleasure of meeting again soon. You know – this village being the size that it is.'

Jess rolled her eyes. Will smiled tightly, and with dignity said, 'I look forward to it,' before turning his back on them both and heading for his car. Zak's arm remained firmly clamped round Jess's shoulders as the car roared off.

'For fuck's sake, Zak,' Jess couldn't help but mutter at him, swatting away a kamikaze fly.

'Don't tell me *you're* annoyed. Who the fuck is he, standing out here like he owns the place?'

'I could say the same about you.'

'Come on, Jess, I'm serious!' He looked down at her. 'Who the fuck is that guy?' His eyes were simmering with something that definitely wasn't love.

'Well, why don't you tell me?' she said, her voice trembling with anger as she shrugged his arm from her shoulders. 'You were the one going on and on about him seeming familiar.'

Zak let out a puff of frustrated half-laughter. 'Come on, Jess. I saw him whip his phone out. What is he, your secret shag?'

The sunlight was hot, and she was starting to melt standing still in it. 'I think you should go home, Zak.' And then she steamed past him back into the cool gloom of the cottage, where for want of anything obvious to vent her frustration on she grabbed the abandoned egg pan from the hotplate of the Aga, discarding its contents like vomit into the bin before slinging it in the sink. She wanted to insist that he leave, but she couldn't handle a screaming match right now. She rested both hands against the worktop and attempted to steady her thoughts.

'You're welcome for breakfast, by the way,' Zak said behind her from the doorway. 'Oh, and while we're on the subject of withholding the truth, I think you should tell me what the fuck you've done to your leg.'

Jess stayed where she was. 'We've been through this. It's nothing.' She had initially intended to tell him, but after much agonizing had been unable to think of a way of explaining it all that wouldn't have resulted in Zak hot-footing it to the nearest police station – or, even worse, Will's front door. So she'd opted instead to meticulously keep the bruising covered up, even insisting on having sex with all the lights off, much to Zak's displeasure.

'Oh, really? Then why does your thigh remind me of roadkill?'

'It looks worse than it is.'

'That wasn't the question.'

'I knocked it.'

'Against what, traffic on the M25?'

'I fell into a creek, out on the marsh.'

He gave a contemptuous little laugh. 'Sorry – which is it? Did you knock it or did you fall into a creek?'

She turned round to face him then. 'Both, okay, Zak? I knocked it as I was falling into the sodding creek!'

He let her defence hang weakly in the air for a couple of moments before turning the screw a little tighter. 'Oh, that's strange,' he said, all sarcasm and upper hand, 'because that type of bruising is actually more consistent with a road traffic accident than it is with a fall.'

She swallowed, all out of ideas.

'If there's one thing I hate,' Zak said then, 'it's lying.'

There followed a pause that lasted long enough to make Jess feel really uncomfortable.

'Just go home, Zak,' she said softly, eventually.

'Oh, really? Just go home?'

'Yes, go home! I can't talk to you when you're like this.'

'I think as your boyfriend I'm within my rights to ask why you look as if you've been hit by a fucking freight train!'

Like a firework, Zak's temper had a definitive trajectory: in the wake of the initial explosion, it was generally best to regard him from a safe distance until he burnt out. Asking him to stay calm was about as effective as pleading with a Catherine wheel to slow the fuck down.

'IF YOU WON'T TALK TO ME, JESSICA,' he

shouted, 'THEN WHAT THE FUCK AM I DOING HERE? ¡*Joder!*'

Smudge padded quietly up to Jess and positioned himself at her feet in a silent show of solidarity.

'Please just go,' she said again. 'You're scaring the dog.'

He was evidently angry enough by now not to care about her leg any more. 'Jesus. Fuck the fucking dog.' He left the kitchen and steamed back into the living room and up the stairs, cursing heavily in Spanish as he went.

Jess sank down on to the sofa and put her head in her hands, waiting for him to come back down and deliver his final shot.

He reappeared quicker than she'd expected. 'By the way, if I find out that prick on your doorstep had anything to do with that mess on your leg, I will fucking kill him.'

The following evening, as daylight faded, Jess used one hand to dig fervently into a bowl of milk chocolate mousse left over from the christening and the other to clamp a bumper bag of peas to her elevated leg. She was sitting with Smudge, watching a gaggle of grocery-wielding suits rampaging up and down the streets of central London in the opening episode of *The Apprentice*, seemingly to do little more than ambush unsuspecting City workers with inedible makeshift lunches that they didn't actually want.

Her phone buzzed.

'Are you watching this? It's like the world's weirdest lunch break.'

She laughed. 'I know! It's compulsive though. What exactly is it they're supposed to be doing again?'

'Haven't got a clue. I don't think they do either.'

There was a pause.

'So, any thoughts on the other night?' Will said carefully, like he thought it was a topic that might need easing into.

'Well, I should apologize. For kissing you. I'm not normally like that. You've got a girlfriend and . . .'

'Come on, Jess,' he said softly. 'Hello? It's me.'

Relieved, Jess attempted a silent spoon-lick.

'So how did it pan out with your boyfriend yesterday?' he asked her. 'I sensed an imminent threat to my kneecaps.'

She frowned. 'Sorry about that. Zak's . . . you know. Very passionate. He says what he thinks. He's half Spanish.'

There was a short pause. 'Not that Spain's not one of my favourite ever countries, Jess,' Will said eventually, 'but I find that to be a bit of an odd logic.'

Jess agreed, actually. She was never quite sure why she used Zak's Hispanic roots to excuse the worst of their fights.

'He's convinced he knows me,' Will said.

'I'm pretty sure he doesn't. If he did, he'd have said so by now.' This much she knew to be true. 'Zak's not really one for delaying gratification.'

'Right.' A pause. 'He sounds great, by the way.'

'Well, he has his moments,' she said, feeling a sudden rush of guilt about Zak, because it wasn't exactly his fault that Will had driven back into her life. And if it had been obvious yesterday morning from her slack jaw and halting speech how she felt towards Will – there was definitely a danger of that, after all the years she'd spent swamped by pit-of-the-stomach regret – then who could blame Zak, really, for feeling defensive? She recalled Octavia, and Zak's brother, and was instantly overcome with shame.

'Did Natalie say anything after I left yours?' she asked Will now. 'Did she wonder what you were doing in the garage?'

'Actually, she was so pissed she virtually passed out. Spent most of Sunday in bed,' he said, and Jess could tell he was making an effort to talk neutrally about her. 'She honestly wouldn't have known if I'd treated all her guests to fifteen rounds of naked charades.'

'She definitely doesn't know we know each other?' Jess probed softly, swallowing another slim spoonful of mousse.

'Believe me, Natalie's sole priority on Saturday night was making a good impression on our new neighbours,' Will said. 'Ironically enough. We had to wrestle the karaoke mic out of her hand at about three a.m.'

There was a long pause.

'I'm so sorry I kissed you,' Jess said again. 'That was . . . really unfair.'

'Oh, I'm not a big believer in what's fair and what's not these days, Jess.'

'So . . .' She wavered slightly. 'What now?'

'I think this is the bit where we say it's best we don't see each other again, isn't it?'

She nodded into the phone, bracing herself to hear the words.

But to her relief, he hesitated. 'Do *you* think it's for the best?'

She shut her eyes. 'Oh God, don't ask me. Evidently I'm completely the wrong person to ask.'

'Well,' he said eventually, 'that makes two of us, Jess.'

In the silence that followed, she felt the bag of slowly defrosting peas discharging little rivulets of water along the contour of her right thigh. 'So what do you think we should do?' she asked him, her voice drawn-in and low.

Will let out a sigh that sounded almost painful. 'Well, put it this way, Jess – Natalie's due back any minute and it's nothing I can articulate against the clock.'

12

'I started my period,' was the first thing Anna said when Jess and Smudge arrived for supper.

No doubt freshly ejected from a yoga session, Anna was dressed in harem pants and a T-shirt that said, *Go with the flow*. Most of her hair was hidden beneath a large woven headband and she was looking super-toned, as if someone had taken a suction pump to each of her limbs.

'Oh, shit.' Jess gathered Anna into a hug, holding her tightly as she began to convulse. She felt weak and delicate in Jess's arms as she sobbed, exhausted like someone who had just been winched off a cliff face or rescued by a SWAT team from a hostage situation.

'I'm not sure how much longer I can do this for, Jess,' Anna gasped through a mess of snot and heartbreak.

Jess wasn't sure either, but she knew that for now she had to brazen it out with complete and unwavering faith. She squeezed her tighter. 'Anna, you're the strongest person I know.' This much was definitely true.

'Yet completely incapable of managing the easiest thing in the world?'

'It's not the easiest thing, and it's not your fault,' Jess whispered into Anna's hair, just in case she was in any doubt.

Anna shook her head and murmured something incoherent about Rasleen.

'What?' Jess drew back so she could see Anna's face, which by now had reached a level of blotchy that would normally warrant antihistamines.

Anna hesitated, then wiped her eyes with the hem of her T-shirt. 'Rasleen says I'm stressed. She thinks I need to iron out the wrinkles in my life and be stricter about sticking to the rules.' With a shuddering sigh, she attempted a smile. 'Which means no more takeaways, so . . . I cooked. Now's your last chance to leg it, Jess.'

Smiling back, but privately frustrated on Anna's behalf, Jess shook her head and followed her inside, Smudge bounding ahead of them to sniff out stray crumbs – of which Jess knew there would be precisely none – in the kitchen. She observed with sadness that the Lava Lamp and submarine mammal song had been switched firmly off, and that even the gentle tang of patchouli from the incense had now been replaced by the unusual aroma of a split-pea vegan lasagne charring slowly in the oven.

'Rasleen's talking rubbish, Anna,' Jess said as they sat down together on the sofa. 'Your life's not . . . wrinkly. Unless you count being guilt-tripped by third parties.' She dug around in her bag for Anna's all-time favourite pick-me-up and slapped it into her palm. 'Now have a fucking Crunchie.'

Breaking into a weak smile, Anna shook her head and handed it back, helping herself instead to a kiwi from the small harvest in her fruit bowl. 'Better not. Thanks anyway, Jess. You have it.

'Oh God, though,' she groaned as she peeled off the kiwi sticker, transferring it absent-mindedly to the coffee table for Simon to swear about later. 'I thought it was being pregnant that turned you into a complete emotional wreck, not the bit before you even get there. I am *so* pathetic now.' She bit fiercely into the kiwi fruit, hairy skin and all, making Jess blanch slightly. 'I mean, look at me. Pregnancy is all I talk about, and I've even started reading sex memoirs.'

'You've started reading what?'

Anna withdrew a hard-backed copy of a memoir penned by a self-declared sex expert and slung it on to Jess's knee. 'You know why I'm reading this? To remind myself what it's like to have sex for fun. I'm one of *those* women now, Jess. Reading about proper sex because I no longer actually have it.'

Grateful that Simon was well out of earshot downstairs somewhere in the bowels of the hotel, Jess smiled.

'Never mind,' Anna said through another hairy mouthful of kiwi fruit. She nodded down at the cream and gold embossed card marking her page in the book. 'Are you coming to George's head wetting?'

The card, Jess now recalled, was an invitation sent by Anna's youngest sister, Cara, and her husband, David, for the head wetting of their third child. She had an identical one propped up on her mantelpiece back at the cottage.

'Sorry. I completely forgot. When is it?'

'Friday, but we'll probably head down Thursday night. Mum's desperate for you to be there. I think she's getting withdrawal symptoms from not having seen you for a couple of months.'

Jess faltered. Last Wednesday she'd received a text from Will suggesting they get together on Friday. He'd not mentioned Natalie, or Charlotte, so she could only assume he was free for the day. And although the prospect of spending time together filled her with a guilt that occasionally more closely resembled dread, her overriding emotion was that of irrepressible excitement.

'Please,' Anna was imploring her, oblivious to the reason for her hesitation. 'I'm going to be surrounded by people with babies talking about babies, asking me when I'm going to have babies.' She shook her head. 'Urgh. *Please* come, Jess.'

Jess continued to hesitate.

Anna started reeling off the names of mutual friends in an effort to persuade her. 'Sarah and Louise are going to be there. And Dee, and Jo.' She gave her a cajoling smile. 'Come on, Jess. We can take the piss out of Cara's fascinator.'

Without looking Anna in the eye, Jess muttered something about her leg not being fit for public consumption as she picked the kiwi sticker off the coffee table and folded it up into a very, very compact half-moon.

There was only a short silence before Anna made a noise like she was dying from something horrible. 'Oh God. You've got plans with Matthew, haven't you?'

Jess braced herself. 'I'm seeing him on Friday.'

'Seeing as in seeing?'

'No,' Jess said quickly. 'Seeing as in . . . spending a finite amount of time with.'

'That's dangerous.'

'It's not like that. We're just catching up,' Jess insisted, though she wondered if she was trying to convince herself more than Anna.

Anna expressed her scepticism nasally and got up to make a pot of raspberry-leaf tea, mumbling something about it being Rasleen's prescription for fertility-friendly hydration and supposedly a substitute for alcohol (which Jess thought frankly to be an insult to alcohol). And as she clattered about, flinging teabags into the teapot and almost breaking the pottery mugs, Jess tentatively filled her in on Zak, and Will, and Will's oblivious girlfriend. She told her about the party, and the kiss, and the ugly argument with Zak a week ago that had started on her front lawn and concluded with Zak storming out, slamming the front door behind him with such force that it had knocked two picture frames off Jess's wall.

Jess picked at a thread on her shirt sleeve. 'I'm nervous that Zak's heard gossip. About Matthew – Will – being back. You've not said anything, have you?'

'To Zak?' Anna said, which wasn't exactly the confirmation Jess had been hoping for.

'To anyone. Simon?'

Crossing back over to the sofa with a tray, Anna made a face that could equally have been antipathy or offence. 'Don't take this the wrong way,' she said, 'but I don't consider Matthew Landley to be particularly newsworthy.'

'But if Zak knows, someone must have told him,' Jess insisted. 'What if the papers get hold of it?'

Anna frowned and passed Jess a mug. 'If Matthew's really that worried, he should just go back to London,' she said, and Jess could tell she was trying very hard not to make any references to crawling or rocks. 'Remind me why he's here in the first place?'

Jess took a measured sip from her tea. It tasted like very weak, hot blackcurrant squash, minus the satisfying sugar kick. 'He can't go back yet,' she said. 'They're doing up that house. It's not that simple.'

'Nothing ever seems simple where Mr Landley's concerned.' Anna shook her head, apparently baffled. 'I can't believe you're having an affair with him all over again.'

'I'm not. He loves Natalie. He loves his daughter.' Even just to mention the other women in Will's life brought a little thump of guilt to Jess's chest.

'I don't think he loves them if he's kissing you, Jess,' Anna pointed out gently, though with a note of surprise that this should need saying at all.

'I kissed *him*,' Jess clarified quickly, 'and it was just a stupid kiss, for a second. It didn't mean anything.'

It was a limp excuse that Anna decided to underline by staring pointedly into her fruit tea, just as Jess was wishing silently that she had a glass of wine in her hand.

'So, does this mean you're not coming to the head wetting?' Anna asked her eventually.

Jess took a breath. 'I just –'

'Never mind,' Anna said, though her face betrayed her disappointment. 'God, this all feels a bit déjà vu, Jess.'

'Just please don't say anything to anyone,' Jess said in exactly the same tone of voice that she'd probably used the last time she was asking Anna to keep a secret for her.

'Do you want my advice?'

'Yes,' Jess said with hesitancy, because Anna tended to express her views on Matthew about as sensitively as an environmental campaigner with a megaphone.

'Stay away from him. He's got a girlfriend now, and a daughter. Even if you didn't have all that history, it would be completely inappropriate for you to keep seeing him. There's no way this can end well.'

'History's a nice way of putting it,' Jess mumbled, her face growing hot with shame.

But Anna didn't smile back. 'Okay – damning previous. It all boils down to the same thing: Matthew Landley is bad news.'

'It's Will,' Jess said, to remind herself more than anything else. 'His name's Will now.'

Anna made a face that said, *Oh, he'll always be Matthew Landley to me.* 'So does your sister know he's back?'

Jess shook her head. 'I'm not giving Debbie any more sticks to beat me with. We're still fighting about the cottage.'

Jess's cottage in fact belonged to her older sister, who

since inheriting it from their mother and getting married had permitted Jess to live there at a knock-down rate a month (maths never having been her strong point, a trait that clearly ran in the family). But now Ian, her husband, had apparently found himself to be in something of a financial black hole, and Debbie was becoming increasingly adamant that selling the cottage was her only viable option for digging him out of it.

'She's really going to sell it?'

Jess nodded. 'She and Ian are having financial problems. He's been spending too much money on the girl he was seeing. He bought her a convertible.'

Anna's eyes widened. 'Christ, he's having *another* affair? How many is that now?'

'Three,' Jess said, trying to ignore the voice in her head that was curtly reminding her she'd not been so different to Ian herself on Saturday night. 'Anyway, they need a lump sum. They're defaulting on everything.'

In fact, Jess believed that deep down, living in Wanstead with Ian and two young girls while all her friends achieved their various career goals (the highlight of Debbie's professional life to date being a brief period organizing the diary of her now husband at a stationery supply company) was the real reason her sister wanted to sell the cottage. Booting Jess and Smudge out of their sweet little seaside home and into a bedsit in King's Lynn was probably the only way for Debbie to feel temporarily better about her own life.

Anna shook her head. 'Why the hell would she sell her own cottage to pay off the debts from her husband's affair? That woman is such a doormat.'

Jess thought it was more that Debbie had a really bad aim when it came to directing her anger at the right people. She was angry with Ian, so she screamed at the children and blamed Jess; she was angry with their mother, so she screamed at Ian and blamed Jess. In the end, it always boiled back down to Jess, which was nothing new. She'd been living with that for the past seventeen years.

'You could always move in with Zak,' Anna suggested tentatively. 'You know he wants you to.'

As far as Jess was concerned, cohabiting with Zak was not likely to happen – but they'd been wrangling over it for months. Unable to understand why she refused to be turned on by fashionable London postcodes, Zak was doggedly persistent in selling the idea to Jess with all the creative fervour of an estate agent presenting top-floor bedsits as penthouses. He was particularly fond of informing her that Octavia had moved in with him after only six weeks, which Jess thought to be a slightly odd choice of sales tactic given all the irreconcilable differences that had followed.

Jess frowned and shook her head. 'I'm still trying to build up the business. I don't want to have to start all over again in London.'

'What about buying the cottage from Debbie?'

From down on the rug, Smudge positioned himself so that his belly was angled skyward, his legs akimbo. Obligingly, Jess rubbed him with her foot. 'No, I'd never get a mortgage. I can't even go into my overdraft without the bank shining a light in my eyes. God, maybe I'll have to move in with you.'

Anna looked uncomfortable and cleared her throat. 'Actually, I don't think you could, Jess. Not with Smudge.'

Smudge lazily flicked one ear at the mention of his name and flexed his paws, but his eyes remained firmly shut.

'Anna, I was joking.'

'Well, no. It's more that . . .' Anna released a short, tense breath. 'Rasleen asked me last night if I spend much time around domestic animals.'

Jess felt a small stone begin to form in her stomach.

'I mean, she's advised me to cut them right out.' Anna aimed wide eyes at Jess, pleading with her not to be angry.

'Cut them out . . . like cigarettes?' Jess said, feeling punctured as she wondered exactly when Rasleen had managed to turn yoga into a byword for bollocks.

'Sorry,' Anna said, and Jess realized that Anna was actually asking her not to bring Smudge over any more.

From his spot on the floor, Smudge registered Jess's unauthorized break in stroking his belly and opened one almond-shaped eye as if to try and ascertain what could possibly be stopping her.

'Anna,' she protested, 'I feel like Rasleen's trying to lay all the blame at your door. Or mine. Or Smudge's. Or possibly anyone's except her own.'

'It's not that. It's more just . . . a process of elimination.'

Thinking it a little odd that Rasleen referred to the various components of Anna's life as if they were toxic by-products, Jess exhaled. 'God, I really need a drink.' But as soon as she'd said it, she felt a twinge of self-reproach, recalling the wine and champagne she'd accidentally made Anna drink at Carafe a fortnight ago.

'Rasleen hasn't had a drink for *nine years*,' Anna remarked solemnly, as if this were a fact to be admired.

'But she's her,' Jess pointed out gently. 'And you're you.'

'But Rasleen's got six kids,' Anna whispered.

Jess's voice cracked as she tried to protest, the tears springing quickly to her eyes. She swallowed and grabbed Anna's hand, wanting to squeeze it full of reassurance. 'That's nothing to do with it,' she managed to say eventually.

'I think you should stop seeing this woman. What a horrible thing for her to say to you.'

'Jess, I'd do anything to get pregnant,' Anna said, beginning to cry. 'I'd literally do *anything*. What's a fucking glass of wine when you don't have a family of your own? When you're surrounded by kids and none of them are yours? Do you know how sick I am of people telling me how great I am with kids? They tell me I'd make a fantastic mum, Jess. And I have to smile and thank them like I'm *fucking flattered*.' She spat out the words as if they were poisonous.

They stared at one another then for a couple of moments, helpless and heartbroken, before Anna began to gabble, 'I'm sorry, Jess, I'm so sorry.' And Jess knew exactly what she was saying sorry for, and the two girls wrapped their arms round one another as they sobbed over a horrible past and uncertain future.

Smudge, who had always been sensitive to sadness, sat up at this point and slid his chin on to Anna's knee, causing Anna to break down completely. He sat there quite patiently as she bent over and buried her face against his neck, allowing her tears to soak into his fur. Occasionally he would swivel his eyes towards Jess as if to seek reassurance that everything was going to be okay; but really, she didn't know if it was.

'I'll walk you down,' Anna said as Jess prepared to leave later that evening. 'Simon's still on shift. I might be able to talk him into a quick swim.' Swathing her slender frame in a creamy cashmere cardigan, she grabbed her keys and phone, following Jess and Smudge out of the flat and down the fire-escape staircase leading to the car park. The air was warm and still, the scent of peonies lingering from the perfectly manicured flower beds.

It was too late by the time Jess spotted the car parked up next to hers. They'd already begun to cross the gravel, and Anna clocked him straight away, sitting outside on the low wall in front of Jess's bumper, his back to them.

'Well, look at that,' Anna declared loudly. 'He's turned up four days early.'

Smudge began to strain at the lead, tail batting furiously from side to side. Clearly, like Jess, he was a big Will Greene fan.

'So, thanks for having us,' Jess mumbled, attempting rather awkwardly to pull off their goodbye while they were still only halfway across the gravel. 'Thank you for supper.'

Anna shot her a look and kept walking, flip-flops snapping sharply against the soles of her feet. 'Nice try.'

Turning his head as they approached, Will stood to greet them, dressed for the heat in scuffed jeans and a T-shirt with sleeves that capped his biceps. Jess could see him hesitating, trying to gauge Anna's body language, before eventually opting to slip both hands into the back pockets of his jeans and brace himself against whatever onslaught was doubtless coming his way.

'I saw your car,' he explained swiftly to Jess as the two girls drew to a halt in front of him. He glanced at Anna. 'Hello, Anna.'

'Mr Landley,' Anna clipped, her voice abrupt and unwelcoming. 'Fancy seeing you here.'

Jess saw Will swallow, though his expression revealed nothing. She bent down and let Smudge off the lead, whereupon he instantly scampered over to Will and began making frenzied circles around his legs.

Will glanced down at Smudge but chose to remain standing. 'How are you?' he enquired of Anna, his tone polite but warm.

Anna simply nodded, after which there followed a long, excruciating pause. 'Well, you two obviously have plans. Don't let me hold you up.'

'I was just driving past,' Will said quickly, meeting Jess's eye. 'I sent you a text.'

Her phone was buried deep inside her handbag. 'Sorry, I –'

'Well, take care, Mr Landley, won't you?' Anna cut in sharply, turning her back on him to envelop Jess in a hug. 'Call me,' she whispered, before stalking off in the direction of the hotel lobby without looking back.

'Sorry,' Will said with a grimace as soon as Anna was gone. 'I was only going to hang on for ten minutes. Should have stayed in the car.'

'It's okay. She was just surprised to see you, I think,' Jess improvised.

'I assumed you'd be alone. I thought you might be using the gym or something. Sorry.' He squatted down then to stroke Smudge, who by now had rolled on to his back and stuck his paws in the air, eyes squeezed shut.

'I'm glad you stopped,' Jess said, looking down at him with a hesitant smile.

He glanced up to meet her eye. 'I've been out for the afternoon. Charlotte's at home with the childminder.' A pause. 'Natalie's away at the moment.'

Jess swallowed. 'Oh.'

He rubbed Smudge's belly for a couple of moments more before straightening up. 'I was only going to say . . . do you fancy popping over for a nightcap? Charlotte'll be asleep by now. I just need to relieve the childminder, and then . . .'

'If you're sure it's okay?'

'Yes, it's fine.' He paused, then added, 'Just a catch-up.'

She nodded. 'Well, I'll go and drop Smudge off first.'

'I'll text you.' Their gazes briefly locked before Will

turned and got back into his car, much to Smudge's displeasure.

As Will's car made a wide sweeping circle of the gravel before heading out on to the main road, Jess remained where she was, caught once again in a bitter and reluctant wrestle with her conscience. But it was Anna's voice in particular that was shouting far more loudly and insistently than any of the others in her mind.

Stay away from him.

Stay away from him.

13

The house was dark except for one lamp in the corner of the living room and the soft glow of Will's sound system playing Buddy Guy blues on low. The room smelt of a fragrance designed to imitate freshly laundered linen.

Will had thrown all the windows open but the evening heat still clung, and Jess was glad she'd taken the opportunity at home to change, swapping her shirt for a sleeveless tunic. Perched at the end of Natalie's pristine sofa, she made a mental note not to spill anything or leave any sort of trail to say she'd been here. She was struck once again by the complete lack of evidence to indicate that Charlotte lived in this house – no Disney DVDs on the side, felt-tips on the coffee table or tiny fingerprints on the screen of the iPad. Nothing. She felt sure the neurotic addiction to order was Natalie's, and was starting to wonder how she coped with the reality of having a small child, with all the associated tomato ketchup, poster paint and chocolate cake on birthdays this normally entailed.

Jess allowed her gaze to rest on the little copper statue above the television. She thought back to the night she'd given it to him and permitted herself a smile at the memory.

'So, Anna Baxter. There was a distinctly uncomfortable blast from my past.' Will was facing away from her, fiddling with the volume on the sound system. Jess couldn't help noticing that every exposed inch of his flesh was tanned, from the back of his neck right down to his feet.

'I know, I'm sorry,' she said. 'Anna's just . . . she's trying to look out for me.'

'No, don't apologize. It was stupid of me to pitch up like that. I saw your car from the road and thought . . .' He shook his head and straightened up, turning towards her again. 'Never mind. So you're still friends?'

She nodded. 'We have been since school. Anna and her husband actually own that hotel.'

He laughed, once, and ran a hand over his head. 'Oh, fuck. Even stupider.'

'You weren't to know.'

'So should I be worried?' he asked her, though the flicker of a frown across his face told her he already was. 'Anna used to put me on edge, a bit. I always felt like she was . . . I don't know. Watching me. Can't really explain it.'

'She knows we've seen each other,' Jess said quickly, 'but I trust her. She won't tell anyone.'

'Okay.' He nodded, seeming to accept this. 'Right. Drinks. What would you like? I have anything and everything.'

Jess smiled. 'Surprise me.'

'Okay.' Smiling back, he tipped his chin down to meet her eye. 'You're sure, though? I have a bit of a thing for flaming sambucas.'

'Positive.'

Surveying the room while he was gone, Jess noticed a giant bouquet of blooms in creams and peaches bursting like a floral firework from a vase on the edge of the hearth. Wondering with a spark of envy if he bought flowers for Natalie every week, she quickly averted her gaze, only for it to land back on the family canvas above the mantelpiece instead.

It did something strange to her insides, to look at that photo of a little girl and see Will written across her face,

166

her smile, her eyes. To see his existence etched on to hers was oddly bewitching and, at the same time, completely heartbreaking.

She'd managed to compose herself by the time Will returned a few moments later with two glasses of white wine. 'Thought I'd play safe,' he said, handing her one. 'We can work up to the pyrotechnics later.'

'Thank you,' she said.

They regarded each other briefly.

'It's okay,' he said after a few moments, so expert still at reading her thoughts. 'I invited you. This is all . . . above board. Just two friends catching up.'

She swallowed. 'I know.'

He looked then as if he wanted to say something else to her, before appearing to change his mind. 'I tell you what's weird – being able to pour you a drink without feeling like I'm grooming you.' He raised his glass and took a seat on the armchair near the sofa. 'We should toast to that.'

Jess smiled and raised her glass back. 'Although I do seem to remember helping myself on more than one occasion. To be fair, I think you did try to stay above the letter of the law.' She took a sip of her wine. It was crisp, dry and deliciously cold, as if it had been in the freezer.

'Yeah, and failed miserably. As evidenced by my prison term.' He took a lengthy swig from his glass, and she wondered if he wasn't quite ready to joke about it yet after all.

'You brought it with you,' she said then after a light pause, tipping her head at the little copper statue above the television. She wondered what back story he had assigned to it for Natalie's benefit.

He cleared his throat. 'Didn't want to leave it gathering dust for six months.'

'I'm so glad you kept it.'

167

'What would I have done – thrown it away?'

'Things get lost sometimes.'

'Not things like that.' Resting his head back against the armchair, he watched her for a couple of moments. 'It's nice to see you again, Jess. Not in my garage.'

'And you. Although it wasn't bad, you know. As garages go.'

His smile was drily appreciative. 'I actually can't quite believe you're here.' He tilted his head then, like he needed to get a better angle on the reality of her. 'And the bizarre thing is, I don't even have to hide my past with you. Because – guess what? You *are* my past. Do you have any idea how fucking incredible that feels? *Hey, it doesn't matter if she finds out you went to jail because SHE ALREADY KNOWS*. You're the only person in my life acquainted with the full facts of my shady history.' He made a wry toast with his glass towards her. 'You should feel extremely privileged, Miss Hart.'

She smiled sadly. 'Well actually, it always felt like sort of a privilege to know you.' She took another sip of wine and sank further down into the sofa, tucking her legs up underneath her so she was curled up like a ball in the corner of it. 'There you go – an incredibly-corny-but-true sound bite, just for you.'

'Thank you,' he said, like he meant it. 'Do you mind if I replay that in the middle of the night when I'm feeling like a complete scumbag?'

She nodded. 'Feel free. Although in my opinion you're not. A scumbag.'

'Ah, well, the last thing I do before I go to bed is kiss my daughter goodnight while she's sleeping. That's a killer for making me feel like the world's *biggest* scumbag.'

She didn't say anything, just waited while he frowned into

168

his wine glass like he'd spotted a foreign object floating there and was trying to work out what it was. 'I've sort of got into this habit of looking at her fast asleep, and her face is all glowing from her nightlight, and I start imagining the day she finds out that her father's a liar and a convicted sex offender.'

'That's not a very good habit,' she said softly, trying to ignore the regret she felt bunching up inside her chest.

'I know. I'm a full-on insomniac these days, so I do it every night, and I can't stop. That's the thing about having children that the parenting manuals don't tell you. You love them compulsively, and it's not always healthy.'

'Is it since prison?' she asked him quietly. 'The not sleeping?'

He shrugged lightly, as if to reassure her. 'Yep. I'm used to it now though.'

Jess looked away from him and down at Natalie's carpet, which was unnervingly speck-free in the manner of a show home. *Loving compulsively*, she thought. *I can relate to that.*

'It's one of those bastard rock-and-hard-place situations,' Will carried on. 'You know – Natalie and Charlotte are in the dark, and I'm lying to them every day of my life; or I'm honest, and I never see them again.' He puffed out his cheeks and released a tense breath. 'But that's the way it's got to be. I accepted that a long time ago.'

As they both took a contemplative sip of wine, Jess rested her head back against the sofa, memories crowding into her mind. 'Do you remember that first ever night, at your cottage, when you insisted on driving me home even though you'd been drinking?' She smiled faintly at him.

He looked over at her. 'Ah, yes. My finest hour – kiss a schoolgirl, drink-drive her home. What a gentleman.' He shook his head. 'Still not quite sure what you saw in me.'

'You *were* a gentleman!' she laughed. 'You were trying really hard to stop kissing me. It was me seducing *you*.'

'That's one thing I still don't get with you,' he said, looking at her like she was something particularly challenging to do with Pythagoras's theorem.

'What?'

'That you seem to think I'm a nice guy, not a predatory monster.' He scratched his chin. 'Weird.'

'Well, maybe that's because I know the real you.'

Buddy Guy moved on to 'Slippin' In', and Jess briefly shut her eyes. In later years, it had been one of her mother's favourite songs for drinking to. 'My mum loved this,' she mumbled. It wasn't exactly a fond memory, since her mother's drinking sessions had mostly entailed her slumped helplessly somewhere while dribbling, muttering and occasionally wetting herself.

Jess took another long, cold slug of wine. It had flooded her bloodstream by now, lulling her into relaxation, and she allowed her eyes to explore the room again. Once more they were drawn to Will's bookcase, and the collection of paperbacks in haphazard stacks on the lower shelves.

'I never had you down as a bookworm.'

Will glanced over at the bookcase. 'Well, I wasn't before I went to prison. But the library sort of kept me sane.' He grimaced gently. 'Think they might be the wrong kind of books though. I'm probably more in need of a self-help manual than I am *American Psycho* or *Top Ten Conspiracy Theories*.'

Jess shook her head. 'You seem okay to me.'

He met her eye and smiled. 'You always were too generous, Jess.'

They fell quiet for a moment.

'So, how are things with Zak?' he asked her. The question

seemed tentative and carefully phrased, a bit like asking someone with arthritis how the manual dexterity was going.

'I'm not sure.'

He nodded, just waited.

'We fought after you left last week.' She looked down. 'He's a bit . . . protective.'

'I noticed.'

'It's not his fault,' she said quickly, her brows knitting together. 'He had a bad experience with his ex-wife.'

'I'm sorry,' Will said then. 'I'm fucking everything up for you.'

'No, you're not – it's the opposite. I'm so happy you're back.' A small pause. 'I just –'

'Don't,' he said quickly, smiling at her with his eyes. 'Don't caveat it. I liked the first bit. Don't say anything else.'

'I'm worried,' she confessed, thinking of Zak, Natalie, Charlotte.

'I know,' he said softly. 'It's written all over your face.'

Her frown deepened slightly. 'Zak . . . wants me to move to London with him.'

After a moment's hesitation, he nodded. 'And do you want to?'

She shook her head. 'Not really. I love it here. I mean, don't get me wrong, there've been times over the years when I've thought maybe it would be easier to move away, start again. But Norfolk's my home. And, anyway, my business is here, all my clients . . .' She sighed. 'Zak won't leave London though.'

'How come?' he asked, but slightly begrudgingly, as if he'd fully expected Zak to be pig-headed like that.

'His work. He doesn't think A & E in Norfolk would be quite the same as in London. He gets more stabbings and bullet wounds there.'

'Oh, I don't know,' Will said. 'I'm sure there's an untapped supply of perverse thrills to be had from mutilation-by-farm-machinery.'

She permitted herself a smile. 'I suppose we're at a sort of stalemate.'

He shot her a sympathetic look but said nothing.

'So where's Natalie this week?' she asked him cautiously.

'Oh, she's in Birmingham. Something to do with financial services. She's not supposed to be working at the moment, but she got offered stupid money to do it, so . . .' He glanced at her. 'Anyway. That's where she is.'

As he trailed off, Jess felt as if they could have been sitting across the room from one another in his little flint cottage near Holt all over again, waiting to see how long they could hold out before the first kiss that would see the rest of the evening descend into sex and carpet burns on the living-room floor, sharing fags and a bottle of gin, laughing about Miss Laird or Laura Marks, naively making soppy little plans for their future.

She looked down into her glass and spoke almost without thinking. 'I wonder what Miss Laird's doing now.'

He paused for the briefest of moments before saying, 'Not much, by all accounts.'

She waited for him to elaborate.

'She's dead.'

Jess blinked. 'What?'

'Four years ago, London. Car mounted a pavement on the Essex Road.' Having imparted the facts, he lifted his glass back up to his lips, his face emotionless, and took another healthy gulp of wine as if he was quietly toasting Miss Laird's demise.

'Oh my God. Who told you?'

'Google,' he said. 'I set alerts up on my phone.

'Twenty-four-seven rolling Sonia updates.' He shook his head, like even to recall it still made him uncomfortable. 'I found out she'd moved to London, so I guess I wanted to be the first to know if she started teaching at a nearby school or did anything notable within a fifteen-mile radius of Chiswick. I always felt as if we had unfinished business, me and her. That was partly why I changed my name.'

Jess tried to think of something positive to say. 'At least . . .' she began, then trailed off.

'At least what?'

She hesitated. 'No, I was about to say something awful.'

'Jess, the woman was a complete cow while she was alive.' Will knocked back another mouthful of wine. 'She completely shafted us. I don't see how death could have imbued her with any particular qualities of charm. Go on, I couldn't care less what you say about her.'

She hesitated again, but only for a moment. 'I was just going to say, at least now you don't have to worry about her turning up. You know – unannounced.'

A long silence followed.

'Yeah,' he murmured eventually, fixing her with those green eyes of his. 'Unscheduled reunions can be such a bitch.' He stood up then and gestured to her glass, even though it wasn't quite empty. 'Top-up?'

'Please.' She downed the last inch of the wine in one and handed it to him. He disappeared into the kitchen.

Resting her head back against the sofa, Jess tried to steady her breathing. Perhaps she should leave now. It was starting to feel impossible to sit across the room from Will and not feel the old emotions come flooding back, not recall the times they'd shared all those years ago. Yet he was now a father and Natalie's long-term partner, she reminded herself. He had steadied his life – and here she was, threatening to derail it.

Just as she was wondering if she had the strength of mind to tell him she was leaving, to get up and walk out of the front door, he returned with her topped-up wine glass and she knew straight away that she didn't.

'You're not having another?' she asked him as he passed her the glass.

'Better not,' he said, tipping his head gently up towards the ceiling. 'With Charlotte.'

He joined her on the sofa then instead of returning to the armchair. Jess swallowed, said nothing.

'Sonia used to write me letters when I was in prison. Well, it was more like hate mail, actually. She'd say there were people waiting for me to get out so they could finish me off.' A flicker of bitterness ignited in his eyes as he spoke. 'It wasn't enough for her to have done what she did – she wasn't going to be happy until someone had physically lynched me.' He thought about it. 'Or – you know – brought back the death penalty.'

He was so close now she could grasp the scent of him. He smelt of something delicious, familiar (was it by Hugo Boss?), but she took a couple of quick breaths and attempted to focus. 'And were there? People waiting for you?' she asked, almost afraid of what he would say.

'Actually, I don't know. My cottage was long gone, so I went straight to my sister-in-law's family's farm when I got out. Stayed there for a year. Anybody who wanted to get to me would have had to wade through three fields' worth of cow shit first, so I don't think anyone bothered in the end.'

She laughed, and then caught herself. 'Sorry. It's not funny.'

He smiled. 'No, please – *please* laugh. I never thought I'd get the chance to find any of this amusing.'

She smiled back at him. 'Do you still see them?'

'Katy and Richard?' He shook his head. 'Nope. And I have two nephews I've never even met.' He shrugged, almost as if this was to be expected. 'I think Katy and her parents started to look at me slightly differently after the boys were born. Because obviously I'm a dangerous sexual predator who will naturally be looking to abuse her sons at some point. So they'd rather have me out of their lives for good. It's neater that way.' He swallowed. 'And I don't just mean for them. I can't take the risk of Natalie finding out, so . . . it's better if we don't see them. Or my parents. It's not better for Charlotte, obviously, but –' His voice cracked slightly.

Jess felt her heart swell with sorrow. 'You don't speak to your parents?'

He shook his head. 'We stopped speaking before I even went to prison. Mum especially. She went through the whole thing – blaming herself, fighting with my dad, becoming a social pariah. They actually threw her out of crochet club. Turned all the lights off and shut the curtains until she went away.'

'That's awful,' Jess said. 'I'm sorry.'

He shook his head but said nothing further.

'Why does Natalie think you don't speak?'

'Oh, you know – ancient family rift. I told her I caused it, which she can fully believe. She's never met any of them.' He let out a breath of contemplation. 'So Natalie and Charlotte – they're really all I've got now. If you don't count Natalie's friends, who I keep at arm's length. I'm pretty sure they all think I'm a bit odd, as boyfriends go.'

Jess looked down into her lap. 'That's horrible What a mess.'

He reached out then and grabbed her hand. 'Don't, okay? It's not your fault.'

She stared at him, feeling his fingers grip hers and touch the edge of the scar across her palm, sending her stomach into free fall.

He turned her hand over gently, laying it flat to expose the scar. She looked up, meeting his eye, and he shook his head. 'I remember that day so clearly. You just opened your fist and all this blood came pissing out and I was trying to play it cool but I fucking hate blood, Jess . . .' He smiled. 'God, I was trying so hard not to let you see me panic.'

She laughed briefly. 'Well, you did a good job. I'd never have guessed.'

'That was mostly down to you, actually. You kept really calm.'

She swallowed. 'I have something to confess.'

He was still holding her hand. 'Go on.'

'I did it myself.'

His smile faded and his fingers slackened slightly. Her gaze rested on his tattoo, the one on his left arm. *It can't be night for ever.* She couldn't meet his eye.

'I cut myself, with my own scissors. I wasn't trying to get the scissors from Beth. I did it to get your attention.'

'Fuck,' he breathed. 'Why?'

'I have no idea.' She shook her head, incredulous as she was every day that she'd done it in the first place. 'It was stupid. I guess I liked you and I wanted you to notice me. I remember having this thing about Laura Marks, thinking that you were going to fall in love with her.' She shook her head again. 'Stupid, obviously.'

'But now you have this,' he said sadly. He traced a finger across the jagged shape of bunched-up tissue.

She nodded. 'It should probably be a reminder to myself not to do any more stupid stuff.'

They were now well beyond the moment when he should

have dropped her hand, but they stayed sitting like that for a couple more minutes, feeling each other's pulses thudding gently as he continued to explore her palm.

'Jess,' he said, pushing his index finger gently across the length of her scar, 'if we're doing confessions, I have one too.'

She felt her heartbeat quicken slightly. *Is that what we're doing? Then there's something else you should know, Will. Something I never told you.*

'I came back to find you, after I got out,' he said. 'More than once.'

'When?' she asked him, feeling a strange churn of panic at having missed him, which was slightly irrational given that he was sitting next to her, holding her hand.

'Not long after I was off licence. On your nineteenth birthday, actually. I'd read about what happened with your mum, so . . . I knew where to find you.' He continued to trace her scar with his finger. 'Anyway, I asked around, but someone said you'd gone to France.'

She stared at him. 'Only for five weeks. I was doing a course. Pâtisserie,' she blurted out, unable to bear the thought that while she'd been practising her piping, Will had been in Norfolk looking for her.

'Well, I was happy for you, Jess. I took it as a sign that you were making something of your life, so I just went back to London. And soon after that I met Natalie. I wanted to try again – just to say sorry, to apologize for everything – but all this time had passed and I kept losing my nerve. Anyway, I finally mustered up the courage to come back on your birthday a few years later, but I bottled it on your doorstep. Same thing happened when I saw you in the pub on New Year's Day three years ago.' He let out a measured breath, his forehead creasing slightly. 'And then on Christmas Eve the year

177

before last, I finally did it – I knocked. Tried again the next morning too. But you weren't there.'

'I spent that Christmas at Debbie's,' she said, thinking out loud and experiencing a stronger-than-usual surge of resentment towards her sister. At the same time as Will had been standing on her doorstep, Jess had been curled up on Debbie's sofa with Tabby and Cecilia, resolutely attempting to watch *How the Grinch Stole Christmas* while Debbie screamed at Ian in the kitchen for failing to pick up the turkey or some other seasonal crime.

'Then Natalie suggested moving here while we did up the house,' Will continued. 'But the idea of being in Norfolk full time with her and Charlotte – that was different to the occasional trip on my own. I was terrified. All I could think about when we got here was whether you'd call the police if you so much as caught a glimpse of me, and if I'd be arrested in front of Natalie and Charlotte for harassing you or God-knows-what-else.'

She shook her head. 'I wanted to find you too. But I had no idea where you were. I actually wrote to your parents a few times, to see if they'd tell me.'

His fingers squeezed hers. 'Seriously?'

'I thought you might be staying with them. They never wrote back.'

'They moved to Hampshire after my arrest. Couldn't cope with all the scrutiny. I think finding a pack of photographers hiding out in Dad's hydrangeas was the final straw. My mum's sister lives in Winchester, so that's where they ended up. They're still there.' He sighed stiffly and offered her a grim smile. 'So you reached a dead end?' he guessed.

'Well, searching your name was the first thing I ever used the internet for. But I didn't know you'd changed it. I just assumed you didn't want to be found.'

He gripped her hand so hard then that she was overcome with the urge to kiss him out of sheer relief that he was finally by her side.

But with great effort she fought it, gently withdrawing herself from him and clearing her throat. 'Can I use your toilet?'

He nodded. 'Of course. There's a cloakroom at the bottom of the stairs.'

She headed out of the room and into the hallway. Hesitating at the foot of the staircase, she glanced upwards.

She had only meant to be a minute. She had only meant to look. But, of course, as soon as she pushed open the door to Will and Natalie's bedroom, the temptation to trespass became irresistible. She had been denied so many details of his life for so long that she was curious just to see how he spent the first and final minutes of every day (though admittedly the overwhelming scent from a bowl of bright purple potpourri on the windowsill made her think that staggering to and from the en suite with a damp flannel clamped across his face was a very definite possibility).

Lined with fitted wardrobes, drawers and a vanity unit in oak-effect MDF, the room was plain and functional, almost entirely lacking the efforts at personalization that had been made downstairs. In fact, the space felt so clinically sparse, it could easily have passed for the budget tariff option at a mid-end B & B, the sort that served only dusty cereal for breakfast and still went in for shower curtains. There was a plastic alarm clock and a copy of *Generation X* on one bedside table; on the other, a lipstick-stained glass and a bottle of hand sanitizer. The only other evidence of life, aside from the potpourri, Natalie's straightening irons and a make-up bag, was propped up on a chair beneath the window – a single cushion screen-printed with Charlotte's beaming face (thrown in, Jess supposed, if you'd purchased a big enough canvas).

She thought sadly back to Matthew's old bedroom at his cottage – to the plump, dark bed linen that had always seemed so seductive, the dimmed lighting, the stereo rotating Morrissey, the Stone Roses, Nirvana. To their discarded clothes, the giant plastic replica whisky bottle that collected his spare coppers, the wobbly pile of travel guides to all the places he dreamed of visiting one day – Italy, Spain, Panama, Amsterdam.

But other than the single dog-eared paperback, there were no hints at all in this room as to who Will was when he was with Natalie. Jess began to feel a strange compulsion to open drawers and rifle through their things for clues like a contestant hunting cardboard points on a low-budget game show, so in an effort to resist, she sat down heavily on the edge of the bed instead.

The room was too hot now, humid. For a moment she considered throwing a window open, but she was too afraid of making a noise – not to mention the fact that she was struggling to recall what had even possessed her to come up here in the first place.

Shaking her head, she got up to leave, just as Will appeared in the doorway.

'Fuck,' she breathed. 'I'm sorry.'

He leaned against the door frame and regarded her quietly for a few moments.

'I'm sorry,' she said again, hot and embarrassed.

To her relief he smiled, and offered her an easy shrug. 'It's all right. It's not exactly a sacred space.'

They stood there silently for a couple of seconds. Jess felt uncomfortably conscious of the flush on her neck.

Will took a step towards her then that seemed instinctive, his eyes bright, and for a moment they just looked at one another, on the brink – she knew this – of touching.

It seemed that one of them would need to diffuse the charge in the room, so Jess exhaled slowly, a controlled breath, and momentarily averted her gaze to break the spell of his. 'So, what's your place in Chiswick like?'

His smile slipped slightly. 'It's . . . very well put-together.' *Just like Natalie.*

'Well, that's good,' she said, though she sensed Will's feelings towards Chiswick might actually be lukewarm. 'I always really hoped everything would work out for you.'

'Yeah,' he said, putting a hand to the back of his neck in what seemed to Jess to be a small gesture of frustration. 'I mean, it's a nice house.'

'Chiswick's lovely,' she said, strangely unable to let go of the idea of it, speaking with firm positivity like a mother persuading her child that moving up to high school was going to be fun.

'Lovely, yes,' he said simply, because that was a given. 'But it's not Norfolk.'

Jess knew that someone like Zak would guffaw sarcastically at such a remark. But she understood exactly what it meant to Will, and all at once she felt indescribably sad.

He spoke abruptly then, his words spilling into the space between them. 'Do you ever think about us, Jess? I mean, if they hadn't found out and we could have just carried on?'

Staring at him, she saw that his eyes were swimming with regret. She felt it too, right down to her toes.

'Yes,' she confessed, only just stopping short of adding, *I do, I think about that all the time.*

He nodded, seemingly relieved he wasn't alone. 'It's just a

bit bloody ironic, isn't it? Standing here like this today . . . a ten-year age gap means nothing.'

Yet back then it meant everything.

'But you have Natalie now, and Charlotte,' she felt obliged to point out, though the words physically stuck in her throat, coming out only half formed.

He held her gaze for just a second more before looking down at the carpet. 'Yep,' he said, his tone now artificially bright as he appeared to collect himself. 'You're right. All things considered . . . I'm actually pretty lucky.'

'That's not what I meant,' she said quickly, her voice rushing out to meet his in alarm. 'I just wanted to say – you have a family, which . . .' But then she wavered, unable to finish.

'. . . is an amazing thing,' he supplied firmly, though his voice was quiet.

She felt a strong compulsion then to bolt over to him and wrap her arms round his waist, bury her face against his chest. But she forced herself to resist, to remain marooned there where she was.

'I owe her everything I have,' Will mumbled, like the hasty recollection of a mantra he repeated dutifully into the bathroom mirror each morning.

'I didn't mean that you owe her anything,' Jess said softly.

'No,' he said, looking over at her again. 'But the fact is, I do.' A couple of moments passed before he shook his head. 'Hey, let's talk about something else. Oh – you might like this, actually.' He moved to his left and opened a wardrobe door. Rummaging briefly, he turned to face her. 'Ready?'

She smiled, grateful for the distraction. 'Oh God. Am I? I don't know.'

He grinned, and slowly withdrew a pair of tan cowboy boots from the back of the wardrobe.

Jess clapped a hand over her mouth. 'Wow.'

'I know. Weird.'

'Do you ever wear them?'

He shook his head. 'Kind of past my cowboy phase now. But . . . I always knew I'd keep them. They're my memento of being carefree.'

She smiled, thinking back to all the times she'd seen him wearing them at Hadley Hall and thought how cool he was. If she was honest, she still thought he was pretty cool now.

'I won't model them for you. They don't look quite as good with middle age.'

'Well, I can remember what you looked like in them as if it was yesterday.'

She noticed him swallow. 'Anyway,' he said, looking down at the boots, 'I stashed them in the car when we moved. I like to keep an eye on them. Natalie's been trying to smuggle them to a charity shop since the day I met her.'

'Thanks for showing me.'

'Any time,' he said, setting them gently back down on the carpet.

There was a pause so light it was barely there. Will exhaled. 'We should probably go downstairs.'

She nodded. 'Okay.'

But neither of them moved.

'Only because,' he added, 'if Charlotte wandered in here now, I'm not sure how I'd explain entertaining you in my bedroom to her mother.'

She nodded, and made to move past him, but as she did he reached out and grabbed her hand. Instantly, her chest cramped with longing, and she wrapped her fingers back round his. His hand felt hot and firm. Her heart began to pound.

Will shook his head as he studied her, like he thought she

might in fact be a ghost, like the very idea of her didn't make logical sense. 'I'm sorry. It's just . . . weird getting used to being around you, Jess. All the rules are different this time.' But he didn't let go of her hand.

They stared at one another for a couple of seconds, a wordless asking of impossible questions.

'I think about you a lot more than I should,' Will confessed then, his words catching against the stillness of the room. But before she could tell him, *I think about you too*, he was stepping forward, taking her face in his hands and kissing her, hard.

She felt as if her heart might explode with the familiar, urgent passion she had once known so well. There was no feeling their way here, no waiting for permission, no gentle exploration. In an instant his tongue was in her mouth and his body against hers. The taste of him was hot, intoxicating.

They took a few stumbled steps together until Jess's back was touching the wardrobe. Now he had her, one hand on either side of her shoulders, kissing her harder, pressing himself against her. 'It's you, Jess,' he mumbled, the words falling from his mouth into hers. 'It's always been you.'

And then, from the stillness beyond the bedroom, the sound of thick, urgent shuddering. Instantly, instinctively, Will pulled back to listen. It was the unmistakable sound of a child's sleep-ridden sobbing.

'Dad-dy,' came a thin, confused cry. 'Dad-deeee.'

'*Fuck*,' he groaned.

They stood there, still holding one another, breathing hard but not moving, hoping perhaps that Charlotte might lull herself back to sleep. But the sobbing grew gradually louder.

Will rubbed his face vigorously before pacing a couple of

times across the room as he called out, 'Coming, sweet-heart.' And then, as soon as he could, he made his exit, footsteps heavy on the landing as he jogged next door.

Jess rested her head back against the wardrobe and shut her eyes, her blood pumping, her underwear damp, her skin flushed. She tried to steady herself. *Oh my God. I cannot be doing this. This cannot be happening.* They were in Natalie's bed-room, in Natalie's house, with Natalie's daughter clearly having some sort of traumatic sleep experience next door. The whole situation was completely reprehensible, yet she wanted him so badly she thought she might expire if he didn't come back into the bedroom and kiss her again within the next few seconds. She waited and waited, her heartbeat slowly returning to normal. Eventually she moved to the bed and sat down on the edge of the mattress, knowing she should feel relieved that the whole thing had been stopped in its tracks before it had got out of hand.

It's for the best.

It's for the best.

After a few minutes, he reappeared in the doorway, look-ing strained. He put a finger to his lips and came towards her as she got to her feet. Her legs felt as if they might give way at any second.

'Charlotte's wet the bed,' he whispered, so quietly she could barely hear him. 'I'm sorry.'

She knew what he was saying. Of course, she had to go.

They stared at one another for a few more moments. 'I'm so sorry, Jess,' he said, and she didn't dare to ask him what he was apologizing for because she wasn't really sure she was ready to hear the answer.

For the faintest of seconds she thought again about mak-ing her confession, giving oxygen to the little flame of guilt that flickered constantly inside her. But she had no idea how to begin; and then she realized he was waiting, in the politest of ways, for her to leave. She forced her face into a smile and made to move past him.

'Wait,' he whispered, and for a moment her heart leapt. Then he tilted his head towards Charlotte's bedroom. 'I'll just run some water in the bathroom. I'm . . . nervous she'll hear you.' He left the room and, a couple of seconds later, a tap began to roar.

She cleared her throat, pushed the hair back from her face and straightened her top. Her strapless bra had slipped down partly on one side. She hitched it back up, and in that moment, she felt as cheap as she knew it was possible to feel.

In the whole time she'd known him, he had never once made her feel like that.

14

Matthew

Saturday, 4 December 1993

Less than a week after I found myself kissing Jessica Hart in the middle of a laurel bush, the snow began to fall.

I was freezing alone at home in the cottage, the thick skirmish of a blizzard outside. My ancient central heating system just wasn't cutting it, so I'd ended up in a sort of staring contest with my gas fire as I tried to work out how long it would take for the carbon monoxide poisoning to kick in if I lit it. The thing had recently been condemned by my landlord's handy man, whom I suspected to be less than qualified and under orders to ingeniously lower the gas bill by way of a fat yellow sticker slapped over the 'on' dial.

It turned out to be a winning tactic because, when it comes down to it, nobody laughs in the face of a condemned sticker. So I decided to drink some brandy instead, on the basis that it had warming properties not dissimilar to naked flames, and (if I stuck to my units) came with the added bonus of not being life-threatening.

Some weeks earlier, I'd found an ancient bottle of the stuff hidden away under the stairs, along with some blunt screwdrivers and a length of nylon rope – all of which must have belonged to my landlord. My first thought had been that I didn't want my fingerprints getting mixed up with any of *that*; but the combined effect of the snowstorm and my piss-weak radiators was finally forcing my hand. So I wrapped myself up in my grandmother's old tartan blanket, turned my back on the fraudulently redundant gas fire and cracked open the brandy.

Before I drank it, I had envisioned the taste of a tenant's sweet revenge. After I drank it, what I actually tasted was the closest I'd ever come to sampling paint stripper. Still, it had the desired effect.

I was halfway through removing my own oesophagus – and feeling considerably the warmer for it – when I registered the sound of tapping on wood. The number-one suspect, as always, was Mrs Parker. We'd recently been having one of those subtly hostile neighbour debates about encroaching tree roots (mine under her lawn), which she liked to kick off a couple of times a week by striding purposefully into my garden and rapping on the back door.

I decided this time to invite her in and show her the gas fire, which I thought would be an easy way of demonstrating that if she expected my landlord to be putting his wallet behind any form of horticulture this side of the millennium, then she was going as senile as the old man five doors down who quite regularly took a turn down the local B-roads stark naked.

I pulled the rug tight round my shoulders and padded through to the kitchen, thinking that perhaps if she saw me wrapped up and swigging from a brandy bottle I might also be able to convince her that I was unwell, and perhaps postpone our little tree-root war until I'd made my (protracted) recovery.

But it wasn't Mrs Parker who was standing on my back doorstep.

My only contact with Jessica Hart since our tearful kiss on Monday had been yesterday, during double maths. I had tried and failed to avoid her eye, pushing away any thoughts relating to Venice or Puglia, and sidestepping the topic of homework when it became pretty obvious from her nervous fidgeting that she'd failed to do any.

'Jess,' I said, and then – because she already looked as if she was trying really hard not to laugh at me – broke into a bemused smile. 'What?'

'You look like a homeless person!'

I glanced down at myself wrapped up in my grand-mother's blanket, brandy bottle swinging from my hand. 'This isn't all I do, you know,' I felt obliged to clarify as I attempted to straighten my face.

'Okay,' she said, eyes sparkling, smile still wide. 'I believe you, Mr L.'

'It's snowing,' I said, as a kind of explanation. Normality went on hold when it snowed, wasn't that how it worked? The everyday became the extraordinary.

We stood facing one another. Her hair was littered with thick white flakes, and she was quivering against the cold. She wasn't even wearing a coat, just an Aran-look sweater and some skinny brown cords that had darkened to halfway up her calves with the wet. On her feet was a pair of grey Converse pumps, and they looked soaked through. I had a strong urge to take off my blanket and wrap her up in it but, ungallantly, I stalled.

I couldn't let her in.

'I know,' she said, meeting my eye as I dithered.

'You know what?'

'That I'm not supposed to be here. I know I shouldn't keep turning up, but I just . . .' She trailed off, sounding exasperated. With whom, I wasn't quite sure.

'It's okay,' I said, even though we both knew it wasn't. I wanted to help her – as her teacher aside from anything else – but this was one of those scenarios that fell into the surprisingly sizeable grey area surrounding my educational remit like the gloomy chasm of a moat.

I could feel my resolve gradually weakening as I stood there staring down at her, trying to remind myself why Jessica being snowed on in my garden was more sensible than her being two steps further forward in the (relative) warmth of my kitchen.

Her teeth were starting to chatter. 'My mum and my sister are fighting. I just needed to . . .'

And then – because she looked sad and snowflakey, and I was full of brandy – I thought, *Sod it*. So I stepped forward and unwound the rug from my shoulders before leaning across to slip it over hers. As I pulled the edges together in front of her she reached up to take them from me, and our eyes met. I swallowed hard, then put a hand to her back and guided her inside.

She knelt down on the doormat to remove her shoes and socks, the blanket covering her back like a cape, and I couldn't help noticing that she'd painted her toenails. Midnight blue, flecked with glitter. I swallowed again, maybe audibly this time, because something about her bare feet in my house suddenly made everything feel shockingly intimate.

'So what were they fighting about?' I asked her as I shut the door. The draught brought with it a final little flurry of snowflakes that wafted delicately to rest on my socks like tiny pirouetting ballerinas.

Standing up again, she shrugged from somewhere beneath the blanket like she was trying not to care. 'My mum ran out of vodka. And our TV never works when it's raining.' She sighed. 'Or snowing.'

Realizing that it would be inappropriate to continue

casually ingesting biohazards while Jess confided in me, I silently set the brandy bottle down on the countertop.

'It's okay, Mr L,' Jess said quickly, watching me. 'I'm . . . unexpected.'

'Yeah. You are,' I frowned. 'You're completely fucking unexpected.'

She didn't say anything for a couple of moments, just let her gaze rest against mine while she carried on quivering under the blanket. The silence called for one of us to make a constructive suggestion, and I sensed it should be me.

'Let me do something,' I said. 'About your mum.'

'It's not up to you,' she replied, but in a tone that was matter of fact rather than ungrateful.

'It is,' I protested softly. 'I'm your teacher. I should help.' I felt this to be true, even if I didn't know it for a fact.

'You already do.'

'How?' I couldn't think of anything I did in particular except let her into my cottage after dark on Saturday nights and try very hard not to think of her as anything other than a pupil.

'You're always so calm,' she said simply, like that was the only quality she would ever seek out in someone. As she spoke, she was still wobbling away like an injured animal under the rug.

'Sit here with me,' I told her then, remembering a tip from the previous tenant. 'There's a hot-water pipe running under this patch of floor. Keeps you warm.'

So we slid down together on to the pitted linoleum, our backs against the kitchen cabinets. It seemed quite natural for me to put my arm round her then, and as she tucked herself comfortably into the crook of my shoulder, I found myself wondering how something so wrong could feel so fucking right. It made me angry, almost. Like someone else was making up all the rules and the people who really mattered didn't get a say.

'I was thinking about Italy last night,' she murmured then. 'Tell me what it's like.'

Her breath made a wistful sigh against my neck as she spoke, and I felt my skin become studded with goose pimples, though not from the cold. I realized then that Jess had become like a tiny shooting star across my black imagination, destined after Christmas to vanish into darkness, leaving only the glimmer of a light stream to mark her path.

I looked down at the top of her head. All the snowflakes had melted into her hair, leaving it flecked with little spots of damp. I thought about telling her what I knew of Italy, which was that my grandmother's family lived in Tuscany. They were in the alabaster trade, and owned a rolling estate in the countryside stuffed with olive trees and sunshine. Alabaster, apparently, could afford you quite a nice lifestyle if you played it right, and from what I'd heard, my dad's uncles and cousins had done just that, and now spent most of their time dining al fresco, eating gelato and drinking Chianti. (Quite why my father had opted to stay in England after university rather than head out to Italy was anyone's guess. For my part, I was convinced that I'd be a lot more suave and a lot less idiotic if I lived in Tuscany and had made it big in alabaster.)

But there was something about describing all this that felt a little too much like telling her a bedtime story. So, instead, I ended up mumbling, 'It's just . . . it's really hot out there. You're so pale, you'd burn. You'd need sun cream.'

Jess seemed to think this was hilarious. 'I thought you were going to tell me all about the wine and the architecture and the language and the history! I can see why you became a maths teacher!'

I smiled. She was right. And then I felt relieved, because it was obvious now that she definitely didn't think I was trying to be smooth, or charm her. Somewhere along the path of my paternal bloodline, my Italian DNA had clearly gone MIA.

She nudged into me then with what could have been an elbow – though given that all her various body parts had now been welded into one by the blanket, it was hard to tell. 'So why *did* you become a maths teacher?' she asked me.

'As opposed to an English teacher?'

'As opposed to anything.'

I wanted to say it was because I'd hoped to do some good in the world, but then again, the question was coming from a fifteen-year-old girl who was somewhere in the region of my left pectoral, and with whom I already had two illegal kisses to my name. 'Well,' I ventured, deciding to opt for a response slightly lower down the hypocrisy scale, 'I guess I thought I might be good at it.'

'You are.'

I looked down at her against my shoulder and smiled. 'Ha. No offence, Jess, but your grades are fairly consistent in suggesting otherwise.'

She smiled back up at me with her eyes. 'Well, if I'm going to be a chef, that won't matter, will it? I only need to be able to cook.'

'You'll need maths if you open your own restaurant. Who's going to do your books?'

'Well, maybe I'll just call you,' she said teasingly, with a grin.

We were quiet for a few moments then, and I tried to concentrate on the sight of the snowstorm beyond the windowpane as opposed to the feeling of Jess beneath my arm, the closeness of her form against me. From somewhere under the lino, the water pipe was starting to slowly heat the seat of my jeans, and I was about to ask her if she was feeling any warmer when she turned her face up to mine and murmured, 'What are your parents like, Mr L?'

'My parents?' I repeated.

She nodded against my chest. 'Do you get on?'

I hesitated, but I couldn't pretend. 'Really well,' I told her, feeling almost guilty about it. 'I mean, they like what they like, but we're really close.'

'I'd love to meet them,' Jess said, but it seemed like less of a request than a modest ambition to one day encounter a real-life family who weren't all certifiably insane. 'Have you got any brothers or sisters?'

'One brother. Richard.'

'What's he like?'

Ah, Richard. *Where ambition goes for a quick lie-down*, I thought. By his own admission, all Richard needed to be happy in life was a sofa, a TV, the complete James Bond video library and a small circle of like-minded nerdy friends to share it all with. And of these, he already had the lot – so in theory, at least, he was perfectly content.

I probably used to be a bit condescending about the way Richard chose to live his life, until he pointed out to me that I wasn't doing such a great job of striking out and doing anything particularly awe-inspiring myself. In a way, I realized, it was me who was the loser, because I wanted to be so much more than I was, whereas Richard was perfectly at peace with his own mediocrity (his words, not mine).

'Actually,' I said with a smile, 'Richard's great. You'd really like him.'

'Is he younger or older?' Jess asked me.

'Two years younger.'

'Lucky you. Anna's got younger sisters too. I hate being

the youngest. Debbie's so bossy. Plus she never got on with my dad. She always said I was his favourite.'

Something about that made me think that discerning an affinity or otherwise with her father had been, until he died, Jess's quick-fire measure of a person's character. So far we had her alcoholic mother and slightly strange sister who didn't get on with him. I was sensing a pattern.

'What was he like?' I asked her carefully.

'Oh, the best,' she said simply. 'He was funny. We used to laugh all the time about really stupid stuff. He was so much fun. Wound my mum up something rotten.'

She was speaking into the hem of the blanket, the lower half of her face obscured. Only her nose was sticking out, her grey eyes blinking, like she was hiding from something or someone. But that someone couldn't have been me, because she wriggled an arm free then and reached out for my hand, pulling it on to hers beneath the tent of the wool.

I turned my head and looked down at her. Her fingers felt icy in my palm. She'd started to quiver with the cold again, shuddering softly against me.

'You're still freezing, Jess,' I said with a frown.

'Warm me up?'

Her words struck me somewhere between my stomach and my groin, and for a few moments, neither of us spoke or moved. But we were both breathing pretty damn hard.

Then Jess lifted her head and put her lips against mine. They felt damp and plump, warm compared to the rest of her. For a couple of perilous seconds I hesitated, balancing on the brink again of fighting what I felt for her – but it wasn't long before I surrendered, wrapping both arms round her back and drawing her into me, my eyes squeezed shut like I was dropping down the face of a rollercoaster ride. I felt her break free of the blanket and her hands slide up my back to my shoulder blades as she pushed her tongue between my lips. I let her in, breathing fiercely through my nose like an animal. After that, it took me approximately twenty seconds to muster the good grace to pull away.

We're talking grace in relative terms.

I was so desperate to say what needed to be said that I started speaking even before her tongue had fully left my mouth. 'Jess . . . if we . . . if this goes any further, we won't be able to take it back. You know that, don't you?'

'I won't want to take it back,' she murmured, moving her lips to my neck. 'Ever. You?'

I swallowed and attempted to focus. My cock was so stiff I was almost tempted to reach down and touch it myself. 'I've been trying really hard, Jess . . . not to think of you like that.'

'But you do?' she asked me, breath hot against my skin. 'Think of me like that?'

Admitting it was more difficult than I thought.

'Sometimes,' I confessed eventually, my eyes shutting against the sound of my verbalized guilt. 'But I don't want to.'

The worst part is, deep down I knew exactly what was going to happen. If it's possible to really and truly lie to yourself, I was doing it right then – because afterwards, I tried to reason that I had only intended to kiss her, that I had never meant for it to go so far.

But if that was true, I would have pushed her hand away when she started to unbutton my flies. I wouldn't have unzipped her cords and slipped my fingers inside her underwear. I would have decided against clambering on top of her, jeans around my knees. And I definitely would have been a bit more shocked when she'd whipped out a condom from her back pocket.

I think deep down I knew that I was her first. And yes, as her maths teacher with a decade on her in years, I was well aware that this made it far, far worse.

And so it began. I was captivated, enraptured, unable (but also unwilling) to stop what we had started – and the fact that Jess was forcibly being relocated to London after Christmas made everything seem more urgent somehow. Her imminent departure meant that justifying my recklessness was marginally easier – but the prospect of losing her, now that I had found her, was also what kept me awake at night. I would find myself wide-eyed at three a.m., blinking into the blackness as I tried to conjure up ways to keep our relationship going after she moved (my masterplan, in the end, turned out to be a fairly unimaginative combination of forward planning, late-night trains and cut-price motel rooms). The idea of her being taken so far away from me already felt wrong, like an abduction in broad daylight I was powerless to prevent.

Our last night together in Norfolk was to be 22 December. School had broken up a week earlier, I hadn't seen her for several days, and now we had merely a few hours of alone time left before Jess headed off to east London the following evening. I was trying not to think about that part too much, because whenever I did it brought a curdle of dread to my stomach.

I was freezing my nuts off (again), shivering outside Jess's mother's house like a stalker with a drink problem, waiting for Jess to come out. We'd said seven. *Where is she?* With the amount of dubious skulking I'd been doing of late, I was surprised nobody had yet become suspicious and reported me – at which point I'd probably have been forced to whip out my Hadley Hall credentials and claim I'd heard this was a really good street for researching right angles or something.

Then the sound of a door banging and light footsteps against gravel. She was almost upon me before I could make her out in the darkness.

'Hi,' she whispered, standing on tiptoe to plant a kiss against my numb lips. 'Sorry. My mum's not well.'

I was familiar enough by now with Jess's home situation to understand that she didn't mean a common cold. 'Is she going to be okay?' I took her hand in mine and gave it a reassuring squeeze (well, that's probably what it felt like to Jess. In reality, it was more of an adrenaline-charged excitement spasm brought on by seeing her out of school hours again. Yep, I was the teenager, not Jess, as evidenced by my involuntary bodily functions and propensity to scuff about on street corners after dark like I was trying to make a bit of extra pocket money dealing Class-B drugs. I was aware that all this was less than ideal, given that I was a maths teacher at a private school and not a delinquent from the local comprehensive, but the fact remained that I didn't have a clue how to change the way I felt about her. Literally – I had nothing).

She took in a sharp breath. 'You're freezing!'

'No, I'm fine.' Hand-in-hand, we started walking briskly towards the car, and I gave silent thanks yet again to the local residents' committee for campaigning so vehemently against the proposal for street lighting put forward by the council last spring. The darkness meant we had a chance at least of slipping away unseen, like thieves.

'It took ages to get her off to sleep,' Jess was saying. 'And quite a bit of diazepam.'

I attempted to ignore the sharp flash of anger in my

stomach at the thought of Jess being forced to soothe her own mother to sleep each night. 'Jess,' I said then, though already I was praying her reply would be no, 'do you want to stay with her?'

Jess stopped and stared at me in dismay, like I'd just suggested slipping dog waste through local letter boxes for kicks. 'No,' she said emphatically. 'My sister's with her. She'll be okay.'

I firmed my grip on Jess's hand, and this time the motion was smooth and voluntary. She looked up at me and grinned, something she did a lot when we were together, which incidentally was already a major factor in my moral quandry. She didn't ever appear troubled, concerned or abused when she was with me – just stupidly happy. It never once struck me that she was reluctant or fearful. And that made it hard for me to feel that what we were doing was wrong: because it didn't *feel* wrong. If I thought about it logically, of course, I knew how wrong it was – there were laws against people like me for a reason – but it never *felt* anything other than completely and utterly right.

We reached the Golf and climbed in, pausing to share a kiss across the handbrake in the frigid air. Jess moved a hand to my leg. 'Not here,' I breathed, pulling away from her. 'Not here.'

She smiled and turned to fasten her seatbelt. I was really anal about obeying the law whenever we were together in the car; and the run-up to Christmas, when the police liked to people-bait by pulling them over just for the hell of it, was making me super-nervous. I stuck religiously to the speed limit, and was getting increasingly obsessive about checking my headlights and tyre tread before picking her up. Sometimes I would even walk round the car two or three times before driving it, to ensure everything was in order. I wore driving glasses, maintained the correct braking distance and slowed down well ahead of red lights. I could only hope that Jess appreciated my reasons for behaving so neurotically and didn't just think the Highway Code really turned me on or something.

I reached into the back seat and pulled out the bunch of carnations I had waiting for her. White and hot pink – the same combination I had picked out for her twice previously, which both times had made her beam with pleasure. I would happily have paid double the price just to see the smile they brought to her face.

I drove out to the edge of town, past the long driveway that led to Hadley Hall and towards the beach. Between us, we had the tide times pretty much down pat by now. This was out of necessity rather than a casual interest in oceanography: we had been forced to reassess the suitability of the cottage as a meeting place after Mrs Parker had enquired about Jess one night as I was returning from work. I had muttered something about private tutoring before scuttling indoors like a cockroach and spending the rest of the night in a sweat-infused panic, rehearsing my little speech for the police over and over in my mind. To my shame, I even had a tenner and a stack of maths text books permanently arranged on my coffee table, so if the knock ever came, I would be ready.

Worse, I'd practised my defence in front of the bedroom mirror, crinkling up my forehead again and again until I felt I had conveyed the appropriate combination of shock and innocence. To my eternal shame, I had briefed Jess too.

Yes, private tutoring, she had repeated, blinking. *I'm sorry – should I have told my mum?*

But, as yet, not even my worst fears had been terrifying enough to make me end it with her. Occasionally, overcome with guilt, I would promise myself that the next time we were alone together, I'd finish it: no negotiation. But then I'd see her in the flesh, and she'd take my hand and start chattering lightly about her day and cracking her stupid little jokes that I loved, and all my best intentions would melt away. I was, as it turned out, the very epitome of weakness. Newborn babies had more gut resolve than me.

As I took the road that led to the car park, 'Nightswimming' by R.E.M came on over the radio. And at exactly the point I was turning to Jess, to tell her how much I loved this song, she looked across at me and smiled. 'I love this song,' she murmured dreamily.

Fuck what everybody else thinks, I told myself then. *This is real.*

I smiled back at her. 'I love it too.'

We reached the beach car park, and I parked up at the end of it, switching off the headlights. 'It's really cold,' I said, which was actually a good thing, as it meant we were more likely to be alone. The doggers would be taking a night off. 'Are you sure you want to walk?'

Jess always wanted to walk. She appreciated any opportunity to get out and see the world – even if it was only the same little corner of North Norfolk, over and over again. She smiled and waggled mittened hands at me. 'I'm all wrapped up. Let's go.'

So we made our way to the edge of the footpath, then took our usual sharp left. It was high tide, and from somewhere beyond the dunes I could hear the sea gently working the shoreline. Everything was cold and calm.

Our favoured spot was a bird hide nestled in the shadow of a thick clump of trees, with a view that took in the grazing marshes and, beyond them, the road. It was a place to which birdwatchers flocked during daylight hours – but after dark, we always had it to ourselves. Admittedly, heading to a bird hide wasn't quite as exciting as disappearing into the dunes to frolic about in the sand, but it was probably a few degrees warmer and had the added benefit of enabling me to watch for headlights.

Despite it being the more considered choice, I knew that, in reality, the pair of us sneaking off to a bird hide was still up there with checking into a motel that rented rooms by the hour or steaming up a car in a lay-by off a B-road. Jess didn't agree, though. She always said she thought it was romantic.

I hated to hear her say that, because it only reminded me that she was still too young to know what real romance was if she thought I was spoiling her by bringing her to a frigid wooden hut in the middle of nowhere. I imagined again how she'd view me in ten years' time, certain that between now and then she would wake up to what a pervert I was and quite rightly begin to hate me – but that only made me more determined to savour the tiny sliver of time we had left together now.

Reaching the hide, I pushed open the door. It was pitch dark inside and utterly silent, just the way we liked it. I lifted one of the wooden shutters and fastened it at the top; it let in a rush of icy air but at least I could hear road noise now, spot lights moving. We straddled our usual bench, facing one another, and I reached out, taking her face between my hands as I always did, and started to kiss her. She shuddered deeply, either with cold or excitement, I couldn't tell.

'Wait, wait,' she mumbled into my mouth, pulling away from me. 'Get the torch.'

I hesitated for a moment, then obeyed, clambering to my feet and fishing around in the rafters for the torch we had hidden there a couple of weeks previously. I fumbled with the switch as I sat back down on the bench, my fingers half frozen, and eventually snapped it on. An anaemic beam illuminated our knees and threw a piss-weak glow across our faces.

'I've got something to tell you,' she said then.

I licked my lips. The taste of her was all over me. 'Okay. What's up?'

She took a breath, her eyes glistening. 'I'm not going to London any more.'

I stared at her. 'What?' I breathed, my heart breaking into a spontaneous little tap dance of hope.

'I sorted it.'

Rather worryingly, it transpired that my natural reaction to this was to come out with the same sort of low and reverent whistle as made by my dad whenever someone told him a British coarse fishing record had been broken again. 'How?'

Jess's smile was like a quiet plea for my praise, but I knew I had to withhold it until she'd confirmed at least that her mother wasn't drugged up to the eyeballs and chained to a radiator on an indefinite basis. (Well, maybe not the part with the drugs – we could take it as a given that this was happening as we spoke – but I did need to find out exactly how Jess had managed to pull this off.)

'Debbie's always reading my diary,' she began softly, in the sort of voice I might have used to start reading a children's story. 'And then she goes to my mum and tells her what I've written.' Jess rolled her eyes. 'She thinks I don't know.'

I nodded, hoping the frozen smile on my face would somehow negate the small swell of fear I could feel in my stomach. Surely she wasn't about to tell me she'd written something down about us? Teenage diaries – naively, I'd never even considered it.

'Er, like what, Jess?' I asked her, casually scratching the back of my neck as if my heart wasn't at that very moment attempting to abscond from my ribcage.

She shrugged. 'School stuff. Friend stuff.'

I couldn't bear it any longer. 'Me stuff?'

Her expression faltered slightly. 'No, of course not.'

Oh, thank fuck.

'I knew there had to be a way to make my mum change her mind about London.'

'Okay,' I said, reaching out and taking her hand, feeling instantly guilty that I hadn't given her a bit more credit.

Fortunately, Jess didn't seem to be too hung up on my apparent lack of faith in her. 'So, I wrote in my diary that Anna's mum was worried about me and Debbie. I said she was planning to ring social services and report my mum if we moved away – that she was going to tell them all about the drinking, and the tablets.'

I wasn't too familiar with Anna Baxter myself. Hadley's strange little system of staff hierarchies meant that top-set pupils very rarely mingled with bottom-set teachers, as if by doing so they might somehow contract stupidity. But I knew that Anna was Jess's best friend, and that her mother was something of a substitute parent to her. It was for this reason that even the idea of the Baxter clan (there were sisters too, I'd heard) made me incredibly nervous. I guessed that as a surrogate mother Mrs Baxter would defend Jess like one of her own if ever she needed to.

Jess was leaning forward, her eyebrows lifted with hope. 'It worked, Mr L. My mum panicked and called it off.'

I exhaled, steadily, unsure how to decide whether Jess's

little ploy had been reckless or genius. 'You're really not going?'

'Well, we are – but just for Christmas. My mum had a bit of a meltdown on the phone the other night, so my aunt said she'd talk to this guy she knows who runs an alcohol support group, see if he can come over while we're down there.' She slid me a tentative smile. 'Which means you're still going to be my teacher. I get to stay here, with you.'

'Wow,' I said. 'I mean, I'm happy for you, Jess, but . . .' I hesitated. I was overjoyed for myself, of course – but even so, I could appreciate there was a bigger picture to all of this. I had to play devil's advocate – it was my duty as a semi-responsible adult, never mind a teacher. 'I just hope it's the right thing, staying here. For your mum, I mean. If your aunt can help her . . .'

Jess shook her head. 'My aunt doesn't actually want us. My mum's just got nowhere else to go, that's all.'

'Are you sure?'

She shrugged gently, like she was all out of ways to convince me. 'Yes. That's what my aunt said to Debbie.'

I suddenly had the strange idea that maybe I could be the one to look after Jess, if nobody else was going to bother. I certainly felt confident I could do a better job of it than the various questionable role models who'd been making a complete hash of things to date.

'So it's good news,' she confirmed, leaning forward like she thought we should celebrate with a kiss.

'It's definite?' I asked her, holding her off for just a second more in order to clarify. 'How do you know your mum won't bring it up with Mrs Baxter?'

Jess shook her head, and for a moment I thought that

would be the extent of her answer. Then, possibly sensing my need for detail, she said, 'They don't speak. Plus my mum told my aunt she'd try and lie low for a bit.'

If lying low was addict-speak for pressing pause on the substance abuse, then I might have felt a bit more optimistic on Jess's behalf – but instead I suspected it to have the far less cryptic meaning of being steadfastly horizontal while off one's tits on prescription painkillers. Attempting to evade the attention of social services didn't sound like a great long-term solution to me either, but if Jess was happy, then – for now – I resolved to be too. Maybe we could revisit it after Christmas, I told myself. Who knew – perhaps her mother would turn out to have an undiscovered talent for sticking doggedly to New Year's resolutions, and we could boot her towards sobriety that way.

'As long as you're sure it's the right thing,' I told Jess firmly, 'then that's really great.'

She kissed me again then, her lips feeling colder than they had before. But just as I began to try and work some warmth back into them, she pulled away from me and reached inside her shoulder bag, the one she took with her everywhere she went. If there was one thing I had learned about this girl over the past few weeks, it was that she was super-organized. She always had a street map and a packet of condoms in there, a lighter and some tissues. It really wouldn't have surprised me if she'd whipped out a kettle and a couple of teabags to mix us up a nice hot drink.

Hers was a calm sort of practicality, a quality I knew would come in handy when she eventually became a chef. I could easily imagine her working in Brett's little Puglian trattoria, serving up pasta with one hand, tossing pizza dough with the other and flinging Parmesan over everything while her boss secreted profanities in Italian – all with a graceful smile on her face.

My mum would love this girl, I thought to myself. And not for the first time, that realization made me really sad. It's rare you find yourself doing something so illegal that you know your own mother wouldn't hesitate to shop you if she found out.

'I bought you a Christmas present,' Jess said, handing me a wrapped packet that had the rough dimensions of a brick but about a tenth of the weight.

I felt a pang of regret. The previous Saturday, I had bought her a silver necklace from the first high-street jeweller I had stumbled across (the class of retailer least likely, I'd reasoned, to make me sweat with awkward questions about the lucky recipient so they could convince me their prices were at least partly based upon personal service). But afterwards, of course, I'd promptly lost my nerve, stashing the box away in its crappy plastic bag inside my kitchen drawer underneath the takeaway menu for the China Garden and the council reminder about Christmas and New Year bin collections. *What use is she going to have for jewellery? What's she going to say when her mum or her nosy sister ask her where she got it? What if she doesn't like it? She's way too polite to say so, etc., etc.*

I took the gift from her now, wishing I'd had the courage of my convictions and brought the necklace along. 'Thank you,' I told her. 'You didn't have to get me anything.'

'I wanted to,' she said, and I believed her. Then she laughed softly. 'Don't get too excited, Mr L,' she said. 'You might hate it.'

I knew straight away that I could never hate anything Jess gave me. I pulled off the wrapping paper – two of Santa's little helpers sharing a kiss under a bunch of mistletoe – and opened the cardboard box inside, removing the bubble wrap from the object within.

It was a little copper sculpture of a long-haired figure, head thrown back, rocking out on an electric guitar. Roughly the size of an outstretched palm, it was cold, heavy and beautiful.

'Jess . . .' I said, turning the figure over in my hand, like I'd just been presented with some sort of award (for being the world's biggest pervert, maybe) and was working out how best to thank those closest to me.

'Do you like it?' she whispered, squeezing my leg in anticipation. 'He reminds me of you.'

I recalled what she had said to me about looking like a rock star. 'I love it,' I told her truthfully. 'I've never loved anything more.'

'Anna helped me choose it,' she whispered.

My heart slithered into my shoes, lay down and refused to get up.

'What?' I breathed. Jess had sworn to me that she hadn't told anyone about us. Perhaps naively, I'd believed her. 'What do you mean, Jess? When did you tell Anna?'

Jess blinked at me. 'I haven't told Anna. I haven't told anyone. I said it was for my uncle.'

I didn't know whether Jess had an uncle or not, but I quickly discovered that I didn't really care either way. Relief slapped me in the face as firmly as Mrs Baxter herself might have done, had she happened to pop her head round the door of the bird hide.

'Shit, I'm sorry,' I told her, wrapping my arms round her. 'Panicked. Sorry.'

I knew this was probably the first time she'd ever bought a present for a boy (or man, if we were really splitting hairs about it), and it was making my heart wilt slightly. I had bought her nothing – or, at least, nothing she knew about – yet she was still smiling excitedly, so pleased I'd liked my gift. She wasn't the same as other girls, always expecting. I got the impression that in return I probably could have presented her with the slightly dubious copy of *Teaching Today* that had, for some reason, been lingering in the gents' loos since the start of term, and she would have been ecstatic.

'I, er . . . forgot yours,' I told her – the half-hearted excuse of tossers everywhere. It was Christmas, for God's sake. 'I left it at home. I'm sorry.'

She frowned away my apology. 'Don't. I don't care. I don't want anything. I just want you. I'm not going to see you now for nearly two weeks.' She leaned forward and started to kiss me.

I promised myself right there and then that, since she was staying in Norfolk, my actual present to Jess would be getting her on to that Venice trip in February. Much more meaningful than a crappy old necklace. If I had to pay for it myself on the sly, I would do it. I wanted her to see for real the world she probably dreamed of before she went to sleep each night.

Whenever she kissed me, it was like tipping kerosene over a naked flame: we were suddenly hands everywhere, pulling at clothing and ripping down zips, like vandals breaking into one another. I lost myself in her straight away, and let my little statue clatter to the floor.

We were at it so hard and for so long that night in the bird hide that by the time we finally emerged, warm enough to be virtually giving off steam in the night air, the battery in the torch had completely died. We left it there, up in the rafters – there would be a next time now, after all – and made our way back along the beach path in the dark, both laughing, both relieved, both naive.

Even at that point, her move to London already a distant memory, I think we both thought it would be for ever.

15

Jess stretched out in the back garden with Smudge, her feet partly hidden in a luscious carpet of grass. Together they were soaking up the blooming, delicate heat of Norfolk in early summer. It was somewhere approaching nine a.m., Radio 4 was playing on her father's battered old Roberts and she had a strong black coffee in hand with a plate of home-made churros by her side. Smudge, it turned out, was a big fan of churros – though his personal definition of appreciation was allowing them to briefly graze his oesophagus as he wolfed them down whole.

She was always pleased, especially at this time of year, that she allowed her garden to grow wild. Bees buzzed busily through the clover that was dappled confetti-like across the unshorn grass. The borders were resplendent with foxgloves, geraniums and catmint, glorious shocks of pinks and purples against a rich jungle of green. Climbing roses with bursting, creamy blooms snaked carelessly across the flint and brickwork of the garden walls. The pigeons were cooing sweetly in the crab-apple tree, politicians were receiving their daily dose of provocation on Radio 4 and, for a few brief moments, Jess felt truly content. Then she remembered Will, and her happiness sagged slightly.

She'd received a text from him on Tuesday that simply said, *Really sorry will call asap*; and another yesterday – *Crazy week really sorry Jess* – but other than that they had not communicated. Now she was in limbo once again, not knowing if he'd forgotten their plans for today, wondering whether to pop over there or call him, unsure exactly when Natalie was due back from Birmingham.

Natalie. Charlotte. In the glare of bright Friday-morning sunshine, it was much harder to unravel that little knot of guilt from her mind, especially without Will to distract her.

Not to mention Zak. He had driven up from London on Tuesday afternoon to surprise her, but she'd been in Norwich until late, catering an event for a digital design agency. The theme of the evening had been Mexican – something to do with expanding into emerging markets – so Jess had provided the bite-sized burritos and twice-baked quesadillas while the hosts supplied the mariachi music and tequila slammers.

On arriving back at the cottage, she had discovered Zak on her sofa with Smudge at his feet. Waiting for her on the coffee table was an elaborate bouquet of flowers and a box of luxury chocolates, but the bigger gesture – the shining symbol of his atonement – came in the form of a small turquoise box in the palm of his hand.

He was contrite, sorry he'd broken her things, begging her once again to move into his mews house in Belsize Park, as convinced as she was not that sharing square footage was the answer to all their problems. And then he urged her to open the little Tiffany box, which she found to contain a classic heart pendant in sterling silver, the same one she'd commented on several months ago when he'd paused outside the window on Sloane Street and pressed her to tell him what kind of jewellery she liked.

In the end she let him stay for two nights, and on the second they had hot, drunken sex after spending the evening at Carafe, because she finally failed miserably to resist that way he had of charming her.

As soon as he set off back to London the following

morning, Jess took Smudge out with her across the salt marsh. Timing their passage against the tide, together they crossed the two deep channels that marked the access point to the fringe of pinewoods overlooking Wells. It was an isolated spot, risky to reach and, as such, somewhere that virtually guaranteed solitude, their only company perhaps the occasional intrepid birder on the lookout for rarities blown off-course from far out at sea.

Having climbed to the highest point of the woods, Jess located a patch of shade and Smudge proceeded to skip about chasing insects. She could see the coloured beach huts of Wells from where she sat, bright splashes of paint against the canvas of pine trees, day-trippers peppering the strip of hot yellow sand that sloped into the sea. She'd been hoping the view would prove calming, a way to help clear her head – but in the end she was unable to get past one recurring, repetitive thought that kept spinning through her mind like vertigo: *I don't know what to do. I don't know what to do.*

She reached down now and absent-mindedly fondled Smudge's ears, tilting her face up to the sky and half-heartedly trying to follow a segment on the radio about fiscal stability in the eurozone, which given how frequently the presenter was interrupting all three studio guests was proving to be an intellectual challenge in itself. So much so that she didn't even register the sound of a car door slamming from somewhere near the front of the cottage.

It was only when Smudge jumped to his feet and sent her coffee cup flying that Jess sat up and turned round, squinting into the sun. Will was standing by her back door, sunglasses on.

'Hey,' he said, and then squatted down to greet Smudge, who was whimpering with excitement. 'Hello, you.'

She swivelled round to face him properly, her heart

213

thudding, awash with relief that he had not forgotten her. She was suddenly very conscious that she was still in her nightwear of a flimsy vest top and tiny shorts, and that most of her right thigh was covered by a creeping bruise in a shade of yellow that looked almost radioactive. 'Hi,' she said.

She watched his Adam's apple bob gently as he swallowed and took her in.

This was no good. Her nipples were hardening.

'Wait there,' she said. 'I'll be two minutes.'

Inside the house she pulled on a dressing gown, applied deodorant and ran a comb through her hair, before grabbing an extra coffee cup and heading back outside.

Will was sitting on the edge of the back step with an upturned Smudge, obligingly rubbing his belly as he basked in a pool of sunshine. 'How's your leg?' he asked her as she came towards him, his eyebrows knitted together in concern.

She smiled. 'It's okay. The bruising's actually fading, if you can believe it.'

Her cafetière was still half full on the patio. She filled both cups and handed one to him. 'Is this . . . ?' he said, looking up at her.

Though the pattern was now faded by seventeen years of dishwashing to an unattractive outline of shadows in pastel, the word *Venezia* was still clear around its circumference. She nodded. 'It's my favourite, actually. Has a very comfortable grip.'

He laughed. 'Well, that's good to know, Jess. I'm glad it's come in useful.'

They shared a smile and she sat down next to him. Two electric-blue dragonflies zipped past their noses, in search of water and somewhere to bake in the sun.

'God, this is great,' he said, inhaling the sight and scent of her ramshackle little garden. 'You're actually growing things. Bucking the national trend for widespread stunting.'

She smiled. 'Well, I like bees too much.' She reached for the plate of churros and was about to offer him one when she realized firstly that it was empty and secondly that Smudge was licking sugar crystals from his nose. She started laughing. 'I would offer you breakfast, but I think Smudge has just eaten it.'

'That's okay,' he said with a smile, 'I have plans for breakfast.'

She felt a twinge of disappointment.

'Sorry that I'm such a cliché, by the way,' he said then, taking a sip of coffee and nudging her shoulder gently with his.

'How do you mean?'

'Not calling you. This week's been a bit crazy.'

'Oh.' She nudged him back. 'It's no problem, honestly. Is Charlotte okay?'

'She's fine, but the bed-wetting's been a bit of a thing recently. I think it's to do with being in a new house.' He looked across at her. 'Sorry about all that the other night.'

'God, don't be,' she said, shaking her head, though she wasn't quite sure which bit of the night he was apologizing for.

From somewhere down the road, a lawnmower purred into action.

'So . . . do you have any plans for breakfast?' he asked her.

She smiled into her coffee.

'If you still fancy doing something, Charlotte goes to Helen every Friday,' he said. 'The childminder. I have the day free.'

From the Roberts, the heated discussion was fast becoming both a blazing row and radio gold. The studio guests were out of control, bellowing en masse into each other's microphones. From the crab-apple tree the pigeons began to coo more excitedly too, as if they also had deep-rooted concerns about the macroeconomics at the heart of this debate.

Will was watching her, amused. 'Do I get the feeling you're not loving the idea?'

'No! I absolutely do love it. Sorry – hang on.' She leaned over, snapped off the radio and beamed at him. 'I'm all yours.'

He met her eye with a wry smile at exactly the same time as she very nearly blushed. 'Do I skip the obvious joke?'

She laughed and plucked the head from a nearby daisy. 'Yes please.'

The sound of dogs barking drifted over the wall from the direction of the salt marsh. Smudge flicked an ear disdainfully, but it wasn't enough to make him move from his hot little patch of grass.

'So, Jessica. I have a one-time offer for you.'

She smiled. 'Wow.'

'Well, hang on. You don't know what it is yet.'

'Too late. You've talked it up. Go.'

Feigning apprehension, he blew out his cheeks. 'Okay. Fancy a day trip to Norwich?' He waggled his eyebrows. 'My car has air con.'

'Stop it, Will. I don't think I can cope.'

They faced one another over brunch in a cafe at the foot of Elm Hill, which offered good views of the snaking cobble-stoned street beyond the window. The sun was angling through the glass, gently baking their bare arms; and from the radio behind the counter floated the melodious strains of acoustic guitar. The scent of Italian coffee billowed.

'So when did you shave your head?' she asked him, scooping up a forkful of pillow-soft, pan-fried root vegetable hash.

The cafe was packed – mothers and toddlers, couples taking the day off work, writers on laptops enjoying an early lunch. Jess was grateful that the gentle burble of chatter was enough to drown out their own private conversation.

Finishing his scrambled eggs, Will wiped his mouth with a napkin before picking up his coffee. 'The day I left the farm. Needed a disguise. I told you, false noses are so 1992.'

She smiled. 'How did it feel?'

'Not that great at the time, actually. Katy did it for me.' He winced at the memory. 'Managed to make me feel like a convict all over again.' He nodded at her. 'You kept your hair short. Not quite as short as mine, thankfully.'

'Do you like it?' she asked, putting a hand up self-consciously to touch it.

'Yeah, I do,' he said, like that much should have been obvious, and then set down his cup. 'It's funny, I spent a lot of time looking in the mirror after I moved to London, trying to decide whether anybody would recognize me if I stepped outside.'

'And did they?'

'Nope. Or if they did, they didn't care. London's a pretty good place to be anonymous.' He smiled faintly. 'I did actually think about going to Italy, after I got out. But I was still on licence, and the farm was the best place for me to hide. Then I moved to London, and I was broke, so going abroad wasn't really an option. And after that . . . I met Natalie, who had no idea who I was, and for the first time in five years I could pretend to be a normal fucking person. I loved it. I felt like a kid at Christmas.'

Jess speared a cube of sweet potato with her fork as she

worked up the nerve to broach the most delicate subject of all. 'Don't take this the wrong way,' she said carefully, 'but I'm kind of surprised that you had a baby.'

He raised one eyebrow but said nothing, waiting.

'I just mean that babies are . . . complicated.' She swallowed, struggling for a moment to get the words out. 'I wouldn't have expected you to opt for extra complication at that point in your life. Or maybe ever. You know – after everything that happened.'

'Well,' he said, equally carefully, 'I didn't exactly opt for it.' And then he pushed his knife and fork together on his empty plate, sat back in his seat and waited for his words to make an impression.

They did.

'Oh,' was all she could manage at first. She set down her fork and took a long slug of coffee while she attempted to process what he'd just said. 'So, it wasn't planned?'

'Well, Natalie was on the pill when we met. Or so she told me. Anyway, I was a bit of a mug about it – I knew she got all gooey around children but I never really paid much attention to what that meant in the context of me *not* wanting them – and the next thing I knew . . .'

'Ouch.'

'Yeah, it was a bit.' He frowned at the memory. 'So then I had to decide, am I going to be a complete wanker and leave her or am I going to be a nice guy and stay?'

'So you opted for nice guy.'

'Well, of sorts. Natalie made it easy on me, really. I was living in her flat, she was climbing the ladder at work, determined to be the breadwinner . . .' He took a sip of coffee. 'But, yeah. If you can call it that, I suppose I opted to be a nice guy. Or nice-ish. We argued a lot.'

'What about?' she asked quietly.

'Um, lots of things. She couldn't understand why I felt so weird about us having kids, for one.'

Jess waited, sensing he wanted to elaborate.

'I don't know, Jess,' he said eventually. 'I guess I always just imagined . . . having children with you. It seemed to me like that was the natural order of things.' He glanced at her. 'Natalie was three months' pregnant when I came back to find you that second time. That's why I bottled it on your doorstep. I just – I couldn't bring myself to tell you I'd got a girl pregnant. Stupid, I know.'

His words struck Jess right in the gut, a series of little punches, and it took her a couple of moments to regain her composure. 'You did the right thing,' she managed eventually, feeling him watching her. 'With Natalie.'

There was a short pause. 'Well, I did the proper thing. Pulled myself together. Learned to cook. Cut back on booze. Decorated a room for Charlotte. Carried on doing my odd jobs for old dears.' A short pause. 'Tried to become responsible, I suppose.'

'Odd jobs?'

'That was how I paid my rent before I met Natalie. You know – painting, putting up shelves, trying my hand at plastering. Which is harder than it looks, by the way.' He smiled. 'Some people are definitely born to be teachers, Jess. Turns out I'm one of them.'

Jess looked down at her coffee, suddenly overcome with memories of Matthew scrawling frantic formulas across the blackboard at Hadley Hall, shouting them out as he wrote, jabbing his stick of chalk to emphasize each point, so passionate that his class should grasp what he was telling them. It made her want to weep with regret.

'Where were you living?' she asked him. 'When you met her?'

'Converted cupboard in Bethnal Green. I had to go with the first landlord who didn't want to check if I had a criminal record. So when Natalie asked me to move in with her, it felt like . . .'

A relief, Jess thought.

'. . . everything was going to be all right.'

There was a pause.

'So she fell pregnant –' Jess prompted him.

'Oh, yeah. Well, we were living in Camden back then and . . . you know, ever since leaving prison I'd had this craving for outside space. It was a bit of a compulsion. I did it all the time when I was single – just took myself off to the nearest park to look at the sky, feel the air on my face. So whenever me and Natalie had a fight I'd head out on to Primrose Hill and sit there on the grass, thinking about . . . everything.'

'Everything like what?'

He sipped from his coffee. 'You. Us. Prison. Whether I should stay with Natalie.'

'You really think she did it on purpose? Stopped taking the pill?'

He nodded. 'Well, that was part of the reason we were fighting. You know, I'd make accusations, she'd deny it and start crying – and then I'd look at her standing there in front of me all hysterical with her little baby bump sticking out over the top of her trousers, and I'd feel like the world's biggest bastard. And then I'd remember how she'd rescued me from that cupboard in the East End and . . . you know. There was give and take on both sides, Jess.'

Jess swallowed away a surge of some very acidic thoughts about Natalie.

'Anyway, a few years ago, she got really pissed on her

birthday and admitted it. Said she'd done it to keep me, because she thought I seemed a bit twitchy.'

'Shit.' Jess shook her head. She looked down at the contents of her bowl, a little autumn rainbow topped off with the yolky yellow remains of a perfectly fried duck egg. Her hunger had suddenly evaporated. She felt almost nauseous.

'She tried to make me feel as if the whole thing was my fault for not wanting a family with her in the first place,' Will continued. 'Anyway, the next morning I got up and looked at Charlotte across the breakfast table and . . . well. Let's just say it's impossible to have any sort of valid regret when your three-year-old takes your hand in hers, squeezes it really tight and tells you not to be sad.'

From somewhere in the corner, a baby began to wail. Jess felt entirely sympathetic.

'Fucking hell,' she mumbled. 'She really did trap you.'

'Yeah, but if she knew the truth about me . . .' He trailed off, his face folding into a frown. 'She would say that my dishonesty is worse than hers ever was.'

Jess shook her head. 'You're just too afraid to tell her. That's different to –' she hesitated – 'deliberate deception.' She leaned back in her chair again as the mother with the wailing baby passed their table and headed out of the door in an attempt to placate him with some fresh air.

'Anyway, I've got Charlotte now,' Will said eventually. 'She makes up for most things. To be honest, Jess, I live for her now. I don't have a job, I have no means of really supporting myself . . . All these years, without Natalie and Charlotte, I would have had nothing. And I don't just mean financially. They put purpose back into my life when every last shred of it was gone.'

Jess finished her coffee and tried to pretend she wasn't experiencing fierce stirrings of resentment towards Natalie.

He observed her for a couple of moments. 'You know, I don't think I've ever seen you angry before.'

'It has been known.' But then she found herself unable to meet his eye, so she glanced over at the counter instead. 'Let's get the bill.'

They wound their way back up Elm Hill and along the end of Princes Street towards the city centre, meandering slowly, not wanting to rush. Though Will had his sunglasses on again, she sensed somehow that his eyes were scanning the street as they walked, like he was half expecting a paparazzo to hop out from an innocuous doorway and have them plastered all over the front page of the *Sun* by tomorrow morning.

'But you've managed to avoid marriage, so far,' she said as they crossed at the lights opposite the church. From somewhere behind them, the cathedral bells began to chime, a heavy, comforting clunking of timeless song.

'Well, that's not difficult. Natalie's been married before – she was young, only eighteen – and I made it clear from the start that I wasn't keen. I mean, she can engineer a pregnancy, but she can't exactly frogmarch me down the aisle.'

Jess became momentarily distracted by a horrifying vision of Natalie crushing narcotics into Will's cornflakes so she could drag him unimpeded to a registry office and elicit his dribbled consent to a lifetime of sham marriage. By the time she had reached the top of Bridewell Alley and Will had haplessly slurred his way through the wedding vows, Jess realized he was no longer at her side. Turning to look for him, she saw that he had been chatting to a *Big Issue* seller and was now jogging to catch up with her, magazine in hand.

'I feel bad,' she said. 'I never stop.'

'Force of habit. We do the soup kitchen thing each Christmas.'

She looked across at him. 'Seriously?'

He laughed as they began to walk again, deep in the channel of winding, medieval streets where ancient buildings bowed towards one another above their heads. 'Well, it's like a White family tradition. Natalie used to do it with her mum every year. I always get goats for my birthday too – you know, like for a village somewhere in the depths of Burkina Faso.'

Jess wrinkled her nose and said nothing. Right now, she wanted to despise Natalie, not hear Will eulogizing about her philanthropic charms. Arriving at the top of the hill, they headed straight on to Back of the Inns, past all the clothing retailers, before turning right through the Royal Arcade.

'This is going to sound really lame,' Will said, 'but spending time inside really does make you appreciate the little things. It brings you a bit closer to people who have nothing.'

She looked across at him. 'But Natalie doesn't know that.'

'God, no. She just thinks I'm really into swapping goats for birthdays.'

She laughed. 'And what does Charlotte get?'

'Oh, all the same old plastic tat as the other kids. Especially at Christmas, to bribe her into the soup kitchen with us. Seven's a bit too young to force selflessness on her.'

They emerged together on to the bustle of Gentleman's Walk. The street was noisy and hot, packed with tourists and insurance workers on lunch breaks and shoppers stamping sweatily from one store to the next. There were dogs on strings, girls in hot pants handing out money-off vouchers, boys crouched down low on BMX bikes, weaving their way through the crowds. It was a good day for basking at a pavement table outside a coffee shop, for sitting in the square under the shade of the lime trees, for heading up to the castle to dangle bare feet into the cold water of the fountain.

'So what do you want to do now?' Will asked, turning to face her.

'Let's go back to the car,' she said.

He hesitated, and winced. 'Can I be stubborn and say I really don't want to go home yet?'

'Me neither. I've got this crazy idea.'

He smiled. 'Excellent. It's been a long time since I had one of those.'

They drove to a budget hotel in the south of the city.

Will checked them in, paying with cash and mumbling something unnecessary to the receptionist about coming back down for their bags. Then he grabbed Jess's hand and gripped it tightly as they moved wordlessly through carpet-freshened corridors, their eyes flicking from door to door to identify the right number.

Eventually, reaching their room on the second floor, they faced one another. 'You okay?' he asked her, because it was obvious that once they were the other side of that door, there would be no going back.

She nodded, and he turned the key to let them both in. The space inside was gloomy and stale, the watered-down sunlight filtered by net curtains and dust motes thrown around by some poorly executed vacuuming.

They sat down together on the edge of the bed. The sheets on the thin mattress were stiff and off-white, a row of mismatched coat hangers was dangling half-broken from an open rail and a yellowing notice slapped wonkily on the mirror above the television reminded them bossily to neither smoke nor expect breakfast. The whole place felt devoid of soul; perfect, then, for an act of ill-judgement.

Jess edged a nervous smile at him. 'Did we really just do that?'

'Check into a dodgy hotel mid-afternoon?'

She winced and nodded.

Will looked down at his hands, resting chastely in his lap. 'We've done worse before now.'

She thought about it. 'No, that was good,' she said. 'This . . . this is bad.'

He laughed softly and looked across at her. 'I love that you think it was good. You know we're the only ones in the world who think it was anything other than completely despicable?'

'We were also the only ones there.'

'Truth,' he said thoughtfully.

Jess hesitated. 'Look, just so you know, I don't normally behave like this,' she said, at exactly the same time as Will said, 'So on a scale of one to ten, how obvious do you think we were back there?'

'Ten being obvious?'

'You're right. Probably about eleven. Oh, and by the way, I'm hardly sitting in judgement over how you behave. Hello? It's me.'

'For the record though,' she said, 'this is probably the worst thing I've ever done.'

He rubbed his jaw. 'Budget hotel with wipe-clean curtains? You're right, this is all a bit crime-against-culture.'

She rocked into him with her elbow. 'No. I didn't mean that.'

'What did you mean then?' he asked, reaching out to brush the hair from her face.

Briefly, she let her gaze travel the room. The brown bloom of a water stain decorated the ceiling, and a cobweb laced its way from the bedside lamp to the MDF headboard. The place was grubby and suggestive all at once, and it struck her that maybe they had rooms reserved especially for a certain category of guest. 'I mean,' she said, 'checking into a hotel with someone else's boyfriend.' She failed to mention Zak, though he was as heavy in her mind as Natalie.

By now Will's hand was resting gently against the back of her neck. 'Seriously, Jess – we don't have to do this.' As he paused, his fingertips felt like little electrodes against her skin. 'Honestly – we can go right now, if this isn't what you want.'

Even as he was speaking, Jess's heart was pounding, and she already knew that she didn't possess the willpower to leave. 'Wouldn't that count as the shortest-lived clandestine affair in history?'

Will frowned. 'Oh, yeah. Well, in that case, we'd better stay for a bit. You're right, I don't think my ego could quite handle walking back into reception after only –' he glanced at his watch – 'four-and-a-half minutes.' He exhaled, steadily. 'Maybe we should find something to do. You know, to fill the time.'

'Um, like what?'

'Um, like this.' He leaned across, taking her face between his hands, and in the next moment they were kissing urgently, their mouths all over one another, starting where they had left off the other day – or was that the other decade?

Will saw fit to skip the introductory chapters they already knew so well, and Jess wasn't about to protest. He unzipped her dress at the back with one hand and she lifted his T-shirt up over his head. She was surprised to see that his torso too was now covered with tattoos, but had zero inclination to stop and remark on the fact. He was tanned and muscular, but not overly so – just perfect.

He pulled the straps of her dress roughly down over her shoulders, before unsnapping her bra as she unbuttoned his flies. Groaning as she took his cock in her hand, he responded by reaching down and slipping his fingers between her legs. She let out a cry of pleasure, coloured by all the years that had gone before. They kissed and touched one another like that for what seemed like hours, hands and legs and mouths everywhere, their bodies starting to gleam with sweat, before Will finally pushed her on to her back, straddling her with jeans around his knees. Moments later he was finally inside her once again, moving quickly and vigorously, the muscles in his arms and torso pumped. She shut her eyes and abandoned herself completely, feeling only delirium. 'Look at me,' he growled, lowering his face so his breath brushed her neck. 'Don't shut your eyes. Look at me.' So she did, and even as they both began to lose control, their gazes remained locked tight until eventually came the sweetest relief of all.

They spent the rest of the day in that strange little room, the semi-plastic curtains shutting out the sunshine as they alternated between talking, laughing and fucking each other sore.

It was different to how it had been before. It had always been passionate – their own private thrill – but this time there was an edge to it, something raw and rough and seemingly uncontrollable. She had always remembered Will as sexually confident, but this time he almost overpowered

227

her. It excited her: she felt a hunger for him that made sex with Zak feel like taking afternoon tea at Beelings.

They opened the curtains again, flung open a window and basked like cats in the sun as the breeze rushed in and tickled their bare skin. Rush-hour traffic began to build – always gridlock on a Friday in Norwich – and they listened to the sound of the everyday, gears crunching and engines revving as office workers inched their way homewards, the occasional blast of music drifting out of car windows.

'So I hate to bring this up,' Will mumbled to her as she lay with her head on his chest, tracing an index finger lazily across his warm skin, 'but what would Zak do if he knew you were here?'

Jess swallowed. What Zak would actually do didn't bear thinking about. 'He'd be devastated.' It was an understatement really, given everything that had happened with Octavia.

Will nodded in acknowledgement, the movement rough against the stiff, over-starched pillows.

'His ex-wife, Octavia . . .' Jess exhaled steadily, all too aware of her own hypocrisy. 'She cheated on him with his brother.'

A pause settled between them. Jess could feel the guilt pressing down on her like a thumb grinding into her sternum.

'You think he knows something's going on with us?' Will looked down, brushing the hair from Jess's face so he could see her properly.

Lifting her chin to look at him, she shook her head. 'If he did,' she said, 'we'd definitely know about it.'

He seemed to accept this. 'Is he in London at the moment?'

She nodded, drawing comfort from the strong, steady

thump of Will's heart against her cheekbone. 'I'm supposed to go and see him tomorrow.' She shut her eyes. 'I'm going to cancel. I can't do this and then . . . do that.' Her face crumpled up with self-reproach. 'He doesn't deserve this.'

'No,' he agreed. 'Nobody does.'

'What . . . what about Natalie?'

'What about her?' he replied, but only because Jess's question could have had a million meanings.

'Do you think she suspects?'

He shook his head. 'Honestly? I think she's been too busy to think about it. Her mind's been on the renovation and not a lot else. If she didn't have that to distract her . . .' He paused. 'Yeah, there's a risk she'd figure us out. She's sharp, Jess. She doesn't miss much.'

Jess felt her insides turn clumsily at the thought of it. 'God, Will – I know what it feels like to grow up without a dad. What if she . . . ?'

'She doesn't know anything, Jess,' he said, and she realized that, for now, this was all the reassurance he could offer her. She suspected that he couldn't bring himself to think about life beyond this afternoon any more than she could. The thought of the devastation they could cause was too horrible to contemplate.

As the sunshine turned to dusk, she rolled on to her front to examine his tattoos. The one across the firm curve of his left pectoral resembled a crow, but it was inked on with hundreds of tiny coils, like doodles with a fine-liner, to form the overall picture. It was beautiful. A large tribal design stretched down the right side of his body, from the front of his shoulder to the bottom of his ribcage.

'They're amazing. I love them.' She smiled. 'And pleased, obviously, that you've kept your six-pack.'

Will slung one hand back behind his head and glanced

down at his chest before throwing her an uncharacteristically bashful smile. 'Thank you. Natalie hates my tattoos. She won't let Charlotte see them.'

'Charlotte's never seen them?' Jess was incredulous.

'Well, she's had the occasional glimpse. But Natalie's always bitching at me to put a T-shirt on.'

'Why? They're stunning.' *And why the hell would you want this man to ever put a T-shirt on?*

'Oh, she thinks body art is psychologically damaging to young female minds.'

Though Jess tried to push it back, she couldn't stop the thought from coming. *She doesn't love you like I would have loved you.*

Through the open window came the impatient peppered stamping of car horns, someone swearing.

'Okay,' Jess said, propping herself up on one elbow. 'I have a big philosophical question for you.'

He shifted slightly. 'I'm abstaining.'

'Abstention denied. And you don't know what I'm going to ask you yet.'

'Yes, I do,' he said. 'You're going to ask me what I'd do if my fifteen-year-old daughter started shagging her maths teacher.'

She smiled. 'How did you know that?'

'Let's call it a hunch.'

She bit down on her bottom lip. 'Okay. So?'

'Well, first of all, my daughter's only seven, so we're still a little way off that stage.'

'Fine. Fast-forward eight years.'

He examined her face, almost like he was seeing her for the first time. 'Why do you want to know this?'

'I'm interested,' she murmured. Her mouth felt dry, salty with dehydration.

He looked thoughtful. 'On what basis? Sociologically?'

'Idle curiosity. Humour me.'

'Okay. Do you really want to know?'

She nodded, tracing tiny shapes with her finger across his torso.

There was a brief pause. 'Well,' he said carefully, 'I'd render his legs unusable for one.' He registered her expression with some amusement and then shrugged gently. 'What? You asked.'

'You know that's completely illogical, don't you? If everything that happened between us was right, what you just said makes no sense.'

'I never said it was right. And I also never said I didn't deserve a pounding for what I did.'

She frowned, continuing to doodle absent-mindedly across his skin. 'Well, my dad might have had something to say about it, I suppose. But I still don't think you deserved to go to prison.'

He cleared his throat and stared towards the ceiling. 'Yeah,' he said eventually, his voice sounding slightly roughed-up around the edges.

'Will. What was it like?' she whispered into the gloom of the room. From the pavement outside she could hear the click-clack of heels, giggling, the jostling of male voices. Doors slamming somewhere along the corridor. The soundtrack of the city getting ready to let its hair down.

'Desperate. Mundane. Noisy,' he said, his voice low. A pause. 'Not safe.'

'You said before that they were waiting for you. Tell me what happened.'

There was a long silence. 'You don't want to know, Jess,' he said. 'Trust me on that one.'

Letting it go, she settled down against his chest and they

lay there like that in the dusk for a few minutes, not speaking, just feeling one another breathe.

'I thought about you a lot while I was in there though,' he said after a while. 'I had insomnia pretty badly, so I'd spend every night running over and over this stupid little fantasy where you'd be waiting for me on my release date. I just imagined us heading straight back round to my cottage and starting everything up again, exactly where we left off.' He let out a short laugh. 'I thought about it every night. I was really pathetic about it.'

'And then what?' she asked him, her voice small.

He shifted his weight against the mattress. 'Well, when I first came back to find you after I got out, that was what I was thinking, I guess. That we'd . . . you know. Start over. But you were in France, so it was obvious you were rebuilding your life, and you didn't need me coming back to fuck it all up for you. And after that . . . I don't know. Things began to change for me. Any chance of a career was pretty much dead in the water, and I was living in that bloody cupboard scraping by on any odd job that didn't need a reference, panicking about how I was going to live, long term. I knew you'd be okay, that you'd go on to do amazing stuff, so . . . I guess I had to let the fantasy die. Accept the fact that my life was never going to be the same again. And then I met Natalie.' He looked down at her. 'But I never stopped thinking about you, Jess. You were always there, in my mind. That's why I kept coming back. Not . . . to start things up again,' he clarified – though she would never have questioned his intentions anyway. 'Just to say sorry, for everything that happened. Although I did start to wonder as time went on if you'd even want to see me again. I managed to convince myself that your feelings towards me would have changed, that you probably hated me. Which would have been completely justified, by the way.'

She shook her head, so relieved she'd had the opportunity to disprove his fears. 'So how long are you here for this time?' she asked him, terrified he would tell her they were all due back in London a week on Tuesday.

'We're supposed to be heading back in September,' he said quietly.

'Well, I'm secretly crossing my fingers for a delay,' she told him with a smile. 'I keep thinking your builder might go AWOL. Or maybe that you'll discover the house is sited on some sort of prehistoric settlement and you'll all have to down tools immediately.'

'Ah yes, a high-profile archaeological discovery,' he said, smiling at her. 'Nothing I love better than a media storm.'

She appreciated the joke by way of a nudge against his ribcage. 'But you'll be back after September?' she guessed. 'For holidays?'

'Well, that was the plan,' he said uncertainly. 'I mean, when Natalie first suggested buying it, I thought maybe a holiday home would be a safe way of enabling me to come back from time to time. You know, like I could always take off again if I needed to. But being here . . . it's not been as easy as I thought, Jess. I'm constantly looking over my shoulder. And, of course,' he added, pushing his fingers through her hair again with a sigh, 'there's you. It's not like I'm expecting to just keep popping in and out of your life. I don't want to do that.'

She was desperate to ask him what it was that he wanted to do instead, but she knew it was an almost impossible question. So she simply shut her eyes, allowing herself to be transported seventeen years into her past – to pretend that it was Matthew Landley's chest she was resting on, that he belonged to her. That she had double maths first thing tomorrow. That nobody knew a thing.

'I would love to say I have this all bottomed out,' Will mumbled gruffly then, like he was ashamed to be telling her otherwise, 'but not a single plan I've made in my entire adult life to date has come off. Even having Charlotte was a bolt out of the blue.'

During the long pause that followed, Jess felt for Will's hand, pulling his fingers into a little knot with hers. The weight of her secret was clumping up inside her once more like something cancerous, and she began to wonder again if she might finally have the courage to confess.

She tried to imagine how the words would sound, once she'd breathed them out, contaminating the perfect air between them; but just as her heart began to pump a little faster at the thought, Will suddenly jolted. 'Oh, *fuck*.' He reached over to grab his watch from where he'd discarded it on the MDF bedside unit. 'Fuck! Charlotte . . . Helen was only supposed to have her until seven.'

She sat up. 'What's the time?'

'It's nearly nine. *Shit*.' He leaned over and grappled in the pocket of his jeans, lying crumpled on the floor, for his phone. 'Fuck. I'm out of battery. Can I use yours?'

Remaining where she was, she nodded numbly. 'Of course. It's in my bag.'

He got up and retrieved it before sitting back down heavily on the edge of the mattress and tapping a number on to the screen. She watched his tattoos flex as he put the phone to his ear.

'Helen? It's Will. I'm so sorry. Have you been . . . ? Yep. Yep. Sorry. Yeah, my phone ran out of battery. Is she okay? Has she eaten? Oh, okay. Yep, that's fine. I'll be back shortly. I got delayed. Really sorry about that.'

Jess shut her eyes.

'Yeah, I know, I'm really sorry, Helen. Yep. Can you hang

on for another half an hour or so? Yep. Thanks very much. Thanks. Okay. Okay. Bye.'

He turned round and looked at her, and in that moment she felt cheapened once again, sitting there naked on a damp mattress in a budget hotel room.

Cheap is what happens when you do things like this.

'I've really got to go,' he said, like it physically pained him. 'I can't believe I forgot her. What a prick.'

Jess wrapped the bed sheets around herself in a self-conscious attempt to preserve her dignity as he pulled on his T-shirt, jeans and flip-flops, fished around for his sunglasses and car keys, and stuffed the dead phone back into his pocket.

'Jess,' he prompted gently.

'Oh! Sorry.' She reached down next to the bed and groped about for her underwear, painfully aware that she needed a shower, to wash her hair, to change her clothes.

But as she bent down, something caught her eye on the floor.

It was Will's leather bracelet, snapped cleanly off. She'd only just noticed it, dark as it was against the grey-purple carpet – an odd choice of colour scheme that reminded her a bit of feral pigeons. She couldn't believe she hadn't realized it was missing from his wrist until now.

'Will,' she said, picking it up and holding it out to him.

He paused for just a moment, then took it from her. 'Bollocks.'

'Anna would say this is a bad omen.'

Smiling faintly, he closed his fingers round the bracelet, then slipped it into the pocket of his jeans. 'It's just old, Jess. I'll fix it. Don't worry.' He shot her a reassuring smile. 'Good spot, though. They might have posted it back to me in a branded envelope.'

Jess's eyes widened. 'Oh, Jesus.'

He laughed. 'Maybe someone's watching over us.'

'Or warning us.'

There was a brief pause. 'Well, that's one way of looking at it.' He held her gaze for just a moment. 'Sorry, Jess, but . . .'

'Right. God, sorry.' She pulled her things on quickly, grabbed her bag, looked back to check the room and then took his outstretched hand.

'Sorry to rush you,' he murmured as they left the room and made their way back down the corridor. 'I feel like I've spent my entire life telling you where to be and when.'

'It's the teacher in you,' she said with a smile, squeezing his hand to let him know it was okay.

He looked down at her then and for a moment she thought he was welling up, but he turned away before she could be sure.

They paused at Reception to return their key, Will gruffly muttering something about a change of plans while Jess feigned a sudden and unlikely fascination with the tourist information display.

16

There was something about trying to make a baby that seemed conversely akin to having an affair, Jess was realizing, in that it appeared to entail a similar amount of sneaking off to bed at strange times of the day and snatching one-off opportunities to shag each other stupid. Unfortunately, Jess had been slow to equate this curious new phase of her best friend's marriage with remembering to call her before popping over – because to do so would have felt weirdly formal and bizarre, given that she and Anna had been wandering in and out of each other's houses quite freely since childhood.

So, unannounced as usual, she stopped by on Sunday evening with some leftover party bites from a client tasting. Of course, she was half expecting Anna to reject the food in favour of some sort of fertility smoothie made from royal jelly or similar, but what she hadn't been predicting was a sweaty and breathless Anna to wrench open the front door wearing nothing but a gingham apron and a strange expression on her face that could equally have been profound impatience or the early stages of an orgasm.

'*Fuck!* Sorry,' Jess gasped in surprise, suddenly engulfed by disturbing images of Simon prowling naked around the kitchen in a chef's hat, brandishing a spatula.

Anna sort of gaped at her for a couple of seconds before pushing her hair back over her bare shoulder and resting one elbow on the door frame, which was possibly the worst impression of composure that Jess had ever seen. 'Oh, hi, Jess. You okay?'

Jess smiled. 'Baking?'

Anna dropped the pretence straight away and started laughing. 'Oh, bloody hell. I only grabbed it to answer the door. It was the nearest thing! Lucky it was you, Jess.'

'Sorry,' Jess said, covering her mouth to try and stifle a chuckle as Anna succeeded in projecting fluster and amusement all at once. 'I just brought round some . . .' She passed over the cool bag, packed with Anna's usual favourites (miniature salmon puffs, pizzette, Parmesan crackers). 'They're just nibbles . . . Save them for later.'

Anna looked pleased. 'Thanks, Jess. Hey, we'll only be a minute. Can you hang on?'

Jess's jaw slackened slightly. 'You can't be serious.'

'Wait downstairs in the sports bar for me? Please?' Anna begged. 'I really want to catch up with you.'

'Christ. Only if you promise not to wear that apron.'

So Jess reluctantly but obediently headed downstairs to the sports bar, where she ordered a glass of overpriced Argentinian Malbec and sat down at a table overlooking the swimming area. It was only a token pool – the variety favoured by health clubs and hotels that was designed for bobbing about in rather than racking up any sort of mileage – but tonight it was mesmerizing, spot-lit and still with the water sparkling emerald over the green mosaic tiles.

Also mesmerizing – though admittedly in a slightly less hypnotic sense – was the group of middle-aged women from the next table who looked as if they were at the tail end of the most depressing hen weekend in history. The atmosphere was so sombre that the occasion could easily have been mistaken for a funeral wake, were it not for the requisite reluctant smattering of pink sashes and feather-trimmed cowboy hats, and predictable rotation of pop music loosely related to having a good time playing over the sports bar sound system. At one point the group made a half-hearted attempt at some dance moves vaguely reminiscent of the conga, which culminated in one of the women knocking over a champagne bottle and being issued with a sharp slap from the flame-haired bride-to-be. Chaos threatened to descend, with the barman forced to step in and mediate before the hen party started to resemble an early-hours brawl on the pavement outside a provincial nightclub.

A couple of friends whom Jess knew from catering college stopped by to chat then, a good opportunity to catch up over a glass of wine, until Anna eventually appeared and Jess's friends headed back over to the bar. Embarrassingly, Anna had brought Simon with her, reminding Jess of the time she'd arrived at Anna's London university digs to discover her wrestling half naked on the sofa with a boy from her course, after which Anna had insisted on them all sitting round the kitchen table together and sharing a can of tomato soup.

'Sorry, sorry,' Anna fluttered, tottering over with a tray bearing a bottle of mineral water and two glasses. Jess wondered guiltily if she should quickly lean over and tip her red wine into an adjacent pot plant.

'Tomorrow's the start of my fertility window, so we had to . . . well, you know.' Thankfully, Anna had swapped the apron and bare skin for skinny jeans and a polka-dot blouse. Her hair now carried a post-shag tousle, her lips and cheeks a satisfied warmth.

Simon's cheeks looked warm too, but his were the shade of red most commonly induced by choking fits or particularly vicious chilli masalas. He'd thrown on a chequered shirt and a pair of cords from what Anna witheringly referred to as his 'food stain' collection (corduroy in shades of plum, mustard and raspberry – tonight was raspberry).

He had, however, failed to attend to his hair, which was sticking up at various conflicting angles like it had just done a couple of rounds in the kitchen's industrial salad spinner.

Greeting Jess with a nod, Simon pulled up a stool next to his wife. 'Ah, fertility windows. More fun than you'd think.' He said it like a slogan, smooth and sarcastic with a faux-American accent. Then he took up his glass of water and looked instantly depressed.

Jess smiled, privately thinking it quite fortunate that Simon's acerbic sense of humour was one of the reasons Anna had fallen in love with him in the first place.

As Anna beamed at Simon in a way that suggested they would revisit his sarcasm later, Jess noticed she'd almost lost the apples to her cheeks. She was thinner than when Jess had last seen her, but oddly so – she looked strangely angular, as if she'd lost too much weight too quickly. (Then again, Jess thought, maybe it was just the sports bar down-lighting. With its polished brass bar rails and stripped pine surfaces, the bar catered for the – mostly male – golfing crowd and the sort of guys who liked their pint to come with Sky Sports on a plasma screen. It wasn't exactly a romantic dinner destination, so flattering lighting had never really been required.)

'Is this a bit awkward?' Jess enquired casually, taking a sip from the second glass of wine she'd ordered as she waited. It was delicious – round and smooth, with flavours of damson and warming spice. 'We could have done this another time.'

'Christ, no,' Simon said, a gentle dig at his wife. 'Nothing awkward about this whatsoever.' Jess noticed that even as he spoke he was staring intently at her Malbec as if she'd conjured it out of a hat and he was trying to work out whether or not it was real.

'Oh, come on, you two,' Anna chided briskly. 'We're all adults.'

Just as Jess was thinking she might offer Simon some wine, since he was clearly weighed down by abstention-related misery, it occurred to her that – lighting aside – Anna really was looking alarmingly thin.

'Have you lost weight?' Jess asked her, concerned that in the single week since they'd seen one another, it could possibly be this obvious.

Anna glanced down at herself as if to check, realizing as she did so that her shirt was misbuttoned. She tutted and started again. 'I think I'm just toning up from the yoga. It's quite intensive.' Now that Jess thought about it, Simon looked as though he'd lost weight from around his jaw-line too.

'So how good are your yoga moves, Simon?' Jess asked him, partly to see if she could break him out of the little staring contest he seemed to be having with her wine glass.

'Well, Jess, you'll be pleased to know I'm now two centi-metres closer to touching my toes.' He held his hands up. 'I know, I know. I'm a bendy genius. Although it has taken an inordinate amount of dedicated stretching.' He fired a wry wink in Jess's direction. 'I'm knackered.'

'You're knackered because you've been working too hard,' Anna said, missing the subtle sarcasm. 'I keep telling you to take it easy.'

'Well, someone's got to stump up the cash for Rasleen's extortionate hourly rate.' By now Simon's gaze had returned firmly to the Malbec.

Anna tipped her head until it reached an angle that said pissed off. 'Define extortionate.'

Clearly lacking the energy to come up with an answer that would satisfy an already prickly Anna, Simon chose not to reply. Instead, he leaned across the table and grabbed Jess's wine glass, as if the klaxon had just sounded on some sort of speed-drinking contest. 'You don't mind, do you, Jess?' Without giving her a chance to respond, he began to glug – and it soon became clear that he wasn't going to stop. So he just kept drinking, and drinking, while Jess and Anna simply watched in astonished silence. In the space of about ten seconds, the entire contents of the glass were gone, at which point Simon set it back down on the table as casually as possible and breathlessly wiped his mouth with the back of his hand.

'Sorry, Jess,' was the first thing he gasped after coming up for air. 'But I really fucking needed that.'

'Simon,' Anna said, her voice pure acid. 'What the fuck do you think you're doing?'

'I haven't had a drink for two weeks, Anna.'

'That's Jess's wine!'

'I'll get you another,' he said to Jess, though she observed to her amusement that he didn't sound in the least bit sorry. 'Fuck me, that was good.'

'Jesus, listen to yourself,' Anna berated him furiously. 'If I was pregnant I'd have to stop drinking for a whole nine months. I wouldn't be able to just go around downing other people's wine whenever I felt like it. If that was even socially acceptable in the first place. Which, in case you were wondering, it's not.'

'If you were pregnant there'd be a light at the end of this sodding tunnel,' Simon snapped back at her, his capacity for self-preservation clearly now perilously reduced by the alcohol.

'This. Sodding. Tunnel,' Anna repeated slowly and deliberately, so they could all have a chance to reflect on her husband's choice turn of phrase. 'What an eloquent description of our future son or daughter.' She blinked at him, which was her way of requesting an apology.

Instinctively compelled to referee, and in the interests of fair-mindedness, Jess considered pointing out that, in fact, Anna had also been known to equate the conception process with tunnels, black holes and, occasionally, hell pits – usually between mouthfuls of Crunchie after getting her period.

But Simon and Anna were obviously having so much sex that post-coital unity no longer really needed to come into things. 'Fuck it,' Simon said, standing up. 'I'm getting a fillet steak and fat chips. Sorry, Jess,' he said as he moved past her, squeezing her shoulder. 'I'll ask them to bring you another glass.'

'I shouldn't have ordered wine,' Jess said guiltily as soon as Simon had steamed off down the length of the bar and banged through the double doors in the direction of the kitchen.

'Oh, please. He's lying about not drinking. He drained a bottle out of the wine rack two days ago then filled it back up with flat cola. I check,' Anna added sadly, clearly aware that these were not exactly ideal behaviour patterns.

'We should have done this another day. Probably the last thing he wanted was to come down here and sit with me.'

Anna shook her head in disagreement. 'Rasleen's been reminding me of the importance of keeping my life in balance. Seeing my friends, that sort of thing.' Her face lifted into a smile. 'I really wanted to catch up.'

Jess felt slightly concerned that Anna seemed to think a reminder necessary, as if their friendship was no different to a car due for servicing or bikini line regrowth in need of a warm wax strip or two.

'Rasleen really wants to meet you,' Anna was suggesting

now, as from somewhere over her shoulder the hen party let up a half-hearted cheer to the opening beats of 'Love Shack'.

'Me? Why?' Jess asked, still reeling from Anna's comment and now instantly suspicious.

Anna looked surprised. 'Because you're my best friend. Like I said, Rasleen's approach is very holistic. It's not just about the yoga.'

Jess wrinkled her nose. 'I don't think so. What if we don't get on?'

Anna laughed. 'Of course you'll get on. Rasleen gets on with everybody.'

Jess personally thought this could only be true if the accepted definition of getting on with everybody had recently been expanded to include not getting on with anybody.

'Do you think . . .' She rubbed at the over-polished table with her thumb, attempting to find a tactful way to phrase what she wanted to say, wary of being perceived as a negative energy or whatever label it was that Rasleen-slash-Linda assigned to anyone daring to express independence of thought. 'Do you think Rasleen's getting a little bit dogmatic? I mean, all this pressure she's putting on you . . .'

'I'm putting the pressure on myself, Jess. Look, there's eight months to go until we're eligible for IVF. And who knows how long the wait will be after that? Or if it'll even work. And by then I'll probably be too fucking old to be a mum anyway.'

A waiter appeared at Jess's shoulder then and set down a fresh glass of Malbec to replace the one Simon had necked. 'With the compliments of Mr Beeling,' he declared smoothly and serenely, like he was brokering an international peace deal.

Clearly unimpressed by her husband's attempt at making

244

amends, Anna switched on the kind of forced smile she normally reserved for difficult guests, like last week's group of birdwatchers who had angled their telescopes at the hot tub then tried to claim they were looking past it to the treeline. 'Thanks, Sam.'

'Mr Beeling only ordered one glass.' He frowned, seemingly thrown by Simon's lack of foresight. 'Can I bring you anything else?'

Anna shook her head. 'Fine with the water, thanks, Sam.'

'So, how was your nephew's head wetting?' Jess asked Anna as Sam scurried back to the bar. She took a sip from the wine, savouring the comforting warmth of it inside her belly.

'Great, how was Matthew Landley? I take it he's not downstairs in the car park waiting for you tonight?'

Jess tilted her head. 'I'm serious, Anna. Tell me all about it. I'm sorry I couldn't be there. How's your mum?'

'Missing you,' Anna relented. 'The whole thing was a bit OTT. There were speeches. And people kept passing me their babies to hold. I think they were hoping I might catch the right hormones or something. Oh, and my mum's organizing a family get-together in Spain, in August. She wants you there, Jess. She told me to tell you – you don't have a choice.'

Jess smiled. She missed Christine too. 'At the villa?' she asked, trying not to be distracted by the sight of the hen party moving off, a big gaggle of pink feathers, VPLs and moulting glitter. She couldn't help wondering where they were heading to next and if she should perhaps text Philippe at Carafe to warn him.

Anna nodded. 'Yep, it'll be at the villa. You can think about it if you like. Let me know.'

Jess had fond memories of childhood holidays with

Anna's family, happy times when even Anna's infuriating younger sisters had seemed bearable. 'Okay.'

'You could bring Zak.'

'Ha.'

'I'm actually serious. Bring him.'

'I don't think we're quite in the market for family holidays just yet,' Jess said with a frown as she traced an absent-minded circle of the brass number thirteen screwed on to their table.

Anna frowned. 'Why not? Has something happened?'

Jess chewed on the inside of her lip.

Anna took a deep breath, as if she was preparing to jump off a very high diving board. 'Are you about to say something that's going to really upset me?'

'Like what?'

'Like, you slept with Matthew.'

Jess remained silent. Anna emitted a long, low groan of frustration, provoking a display of minor alarm from the two golfers at the next table.

'Please don't give me a hard time, Anna,' Jess mumbled, trying to simultaneously take a fortifying swig of wine and smile reassurance at the golfers.

'I'm your best friend, Jess. If you're doing something stupid, it's my *job* to give you a hard time.'

'It only happened once. It's not . . . ongoing.'

Clutching at her mineral water like she thought it might be able to offer some form of psychological support (Jess doubted it), Anna spoke with incredulity, like the only possible explanation could be that this would all turn out to be an honest mistake – that Jess had somehow, in the wrong light perhaps, managed to confuse Matthew with Zak. 'But he has a wife and *child*.'

'She's not his wife,' Jess said, before she could help herself.

246

'This isn't like you,' Anna said, setting down her glass and grabbing Jess's hand, forehead all corrugated with concern. 'You don't do stuff like this. You're not this person.'

Jess remained silent, wondering for a moment if she should perhaps explain to Anna that Natalie had tricked Will into having Charlotte, that it hadn't even been his choice to become a father. This detail of his biography felt important to Jess – insofar as it showed, perhaps, that he and Natalie were together for reasons other than love. But every sentence she tried to form in her head made it sound as if Will had been arrested for drink-driving and Jess was attempting to plead peer pressure in his defence.

'So have you finished things with Zak?' Anna asked her.

Jess frowned. 'No, I mean . . . I'm not *with* Will, Anna. It was a one-off. I told you that.'

Still, she had cancelled on Zak yesterday. She'd been supposed to travel down to London in the afternoon, but had called him in the morning to tell him she had the flu.

'In the height of summer?' Anna ventured, with a level of disbelief that was verging on amusement.

Fortunately, Zak hadn't seemed to be suspicious, which in a way had made it all seem worse. 'I know. I'm not proud of myself. I know I'm no better than bloody Octavia.'

Anna's face dropped. 'Exactly. If he finds out you're lying, he'll completely lose his shit.' She enunciated the last three words very deliberately. 'You know what he's like about stuff like that.'

Jess frowned. 'I know.'

'Shall I tell you what I thought the other night, when I saw Matthew?'

Jess shrugged, because she wasn't anticipating a compliment.

'I thought . . . he doesn't *suit* you.'

247

Jess made a face. 'What does that mean?'

'I don't know, Jess. He looks . . . old.'

He still looks twenty-five to me. 'Er, Will's only a year older than Simon,' Jess pointed out. 'There's nine years between you two – or did you forget that?'

Anna rolled her eyes against the discrepancy. 'Me and Simon met as adults.'

'The age gap's still the same.'

'Oh, no moral difference?'

Jess paused. 'Well, yes – if you happen to be the CPS.'

Anna almost spoke over her. 'Look, the long and short of it is, you need to choose between them, Jess. Will, or Zak.'

'It's not about choosing, Anna. I'm not *with* Will. If he left his family for me . . . there's a massive risk he'd never see his daughter again. And I don't want that for him.'

'So, what – you're just going to see each other on the side?' Anna let the question hang, but Jess got the feeling she would probably have liked to add, *Nice – and who are you turning into, by the way?*

She drew a steadying breath. 'No, I'm not. I know I need to stop it.' She'd not felt able to admit it to herself before now.

'Yes, you do,' Anna agreed. 'And never mind him leaving his family for you – there's a good chance Natalie could beat you both to it. She's probably not as stupid as you think, you know.'

'I never said she was stupid.'

'You just need to sort things out with Zak and never see Will again,' Anna pressed, a quick refresh on society's moral codes. 'He ruined your life the first time round, Jess. Please don't let him do the same thing again.'

He didn't ruin my life. Matthew was the best thing that ever happened to me.

But Anna wasn't letting up. 'You need to think about how much you're prepared to throw away for the sake of Matthew Landley. You do this –' she paused – 'all the time.'

'Do what?'

'Every boyfriend you've ever had – including Zak – you compare to him.'

'No, I don't.'

'Yes, you do. You always say, *Matthew would never have said . . . Matthew would never have done . . . Matthew used to say . . .*' She shook her head. 'The thing is, you were never really together.'

'Yes, we were,' Jess said fiercely. 'You're a little bit in denial about that, Anna.'

'Jess,' Anna said then, and suddenly all the features on her face seemed to tighten slightly. 'Have you told him . . . ?'

'No,' Jess said quickly, more sharply than she had intended. 'No. I haven't.'

There was a long, horrible pause.

'So when's he supposed to be going back to London?' Anna asked her eventually.

'September. That's the plan, anyway.'

On the television above the pool table, Sky Sports was showing Formula 1 from Monaco. A car had come off the track against a run of advertising hoarding and, watching it in slow motion, Jess was suddenly reminded of what Will had told her on Monday night.

She turned to Anna. 'Will told me Miss Laird died in a car crash. I mean, she was walking. The car mounted the pavement.'

Anna swallowed and looked down at her glass of water. 'That's awful.'

There was a strange pause then, as if Jess had said something really tactless.

'I'm not really sure how I feel about it,' she confessed, thinking perhaps she'd come across as slightly blasé.

'I'm assuming Mr Landley feels abundant glee.'

'No, of course not. Why would you assume that?'

Anna shot her a look that said, *Be serious*. 'What did he say then?'

'Not much, really. What could he say?'

She shrugged. 'I don't know. Something nice?'

Jess took another sip of wine, resisting the urge to do a Simon and sling back the whole lot in one. 'Because she died?'

Anna fixed her with a patient smile. 'I think that's traditional.'

'Yes, maybe if you're in earshot of her family at the funeral,' Jess conceded. 'Otherwise, why should he? She completely screwed him over. She's responsible for everything. *Everything*.'

Anna shut her eyes like she was waiting for Jess's ill will to leave the room, and when she opened them again, she looked grave. 'Please come and do some yoga with Rasleen. Come tomorrow. I think your solar plexus may be blocked. Do you feel it here?' She placed a hand on her upper abdomen.

'Er . . .' Jess looked down at her top. 'Not really.'

Anna appeared unfazed. 'So you'll come? One session. You'll get to meet Rasleen and, you never know, you might even start to see Matthew Landley in a completely different light.'

'I'll think about it,' Jess said, but what she was thinking was that this all sounded more like low-grade hypnotism than it did yoga, so she definitely wasn't going.

'That means no,' Anna surmised.

'Probably,' she admitted after a moment's pause.

250

Anna made a huffing sound and downed the last of her water like she once would have downed a tumbler-full of late-night whisky.

An hour later, as Jess headed back home, having wished Anna luck with her next fertility window and before she really had time to think about what she was doing, she dialled Will's number. But it went straight to voicemail.

It was late when he returned her call.

'Sorry,' he said. 'I keep forgetting that everyone else has normal sleep patterns.'

Jess smiled. 'Where are you?' She was curled up on the sofa, rubbing Smudge's belly with her foot and cradling a mug of warm beef broth, a rainy-night throwback from early childhood, at a time when her mother still had the capacity to be nurturing. It was one of those comfortable old habits she'd never quite felt the urge to shake off.

'Erm, it's raining outside and I'm sitting in my garden shed. My arse is wet and I'm also wearing an undersized cagoule and red wellies, in case that picture wasn't quite attractive enough for you. I look like a sodding garden gnome.'

She started laughing. 'Oh *God*.'

'Yes, I'm sitting in the pitch dark with my hood up like a weirdo, and to cap it all off, my dick has gone hard just hearing your voice, which is most un-gnome-like of me.' He sighed heavily. 'So what are you doing? Come on, you must be less tragic than me right now. It wouldn't be difficult.'

'Um – right now?'

'Excellent.' She could hear his smile. 'Go on.'

Jess grinned, hesitating for just a moment. 'Pyjamas and beef broth.'

There was a disbelieving pause. 'You're not seriously drinking gravy?'

'Broth is not gravy! And it is raining,' she reminded him.

'Yes, but it's not the 1970s. Or January. And I'm assuming you're not at a football match.'

She smiled faintly into the phone. 'Want to come over and try a cup? You never know, you might like it.'

There was a long pause.

'Sorry, Jess. Much as I am a big fan of hot stock . . .' He trailed off, and they were quiet for a moment.

'Is Natalie back from Birmingham?'

'Yeah, she is.'

'Was Charlotte okay the other night?'

'Oh, fine. I told Natalie I got stuck in traffic. Apparently Helen did microwave pizza for Charlotte while they were waiting, and that's literally all I've heard about since.'

Jess swallowed. For some reason, to hear this made her eyes prick with tears. 'I really . . . I had a really good time on Friday.'

'Me too, Jess.'

She swallowed, wanting to ask him what they should do now, but knowing that he wouldn't have the answer to that. How could she possibly expect him to?

'Look, Jess . . . I'm not a big fan of under-the-radar.'

'We can hardly be over it,' she said sadly.

He sighed heavily. The impossibility of it all felt suddenly overwhelming.

'I'm sorry I called you,' she concluded eventually. 'I know I shouldn't.'

'You don't ever need to apologize,' he told her. 'For anything. You can skip that bit with me, Jess.'

She fought back a sharp and sudden urge to disagree. *Actually, there is something I need to apologize for. Something I never told you.* 'Okay. Well, maybe I can see you soon.'

'Yeah, I'll . . .' He trailed off again.

'You'll what?'

'No, I was going to say "I'll be in touch" and then I realized that sounded like just about the crappiest thing I've said to anyone, ever.'

She managed a soft smile. 'Let's not say anything then.'

'Okay.' He exhaled with some force. 'Right. Need to try and get out of this sodding shed now.'

She hesitated. 'Are you stuck?'

'Erm, sort of. The door's jammed shut. I think the wood's swelled up.'

Despite herself, she started laughing. 'Would you like me to call 999?'

'No, you can spare me that indignity, thanks very much. I'd rather succumb to hypothermia.'

'You know, on second thoughts, I think you might actually be more tragic than me tonight.'

'Well, actually, that's where you're wrong, because just as soon as I get out of this –' there followed the sound of thumping against wood – 'fucking shed . . .'

'I'll leave you to it,' she said through her laughter. 'That sounds like it might need both hands.'

'Oh, no need to be so smug,' he said, and she could tell he was struggling to suppress a smile. 'Enjoy your beef broth. Never knew that about you.'

Her laughter took over then, and she couldn't say anything else.

17

Matthew

Wednesday, 5 January 1994

I hadn't slept. Like, at all. So by three a.m. I had given up and started making vats of strong black coffee in the I-heart-maths mug that Steve had bought me for my birthday (he'd assumed this to be a masterstroke in irony, which was ironic in itself given how much I did, in fact, heart maths). The mug was roughly the same size as your average household bleach bucket, and for its part the coffee was so strong, made as it was from pure exhaustion, that by the time I arrived at Hadley Hall I was literally shaking. The overdose of caffeine had worked its way inelegantly to my bowels, and as soon as I reached the school gates I was forced to make a hasty detour to use the toilets in the drama studio.

Yes, I hadn't seen Jessica for the sum total of twelve short days, and I was, quite literally, crapping my pants.

If it had been up to me, I would quite happily have pitched up in Jess's garden shed the previous night, when she'd finally returned home from her festive family trip to east London; but I had resisted on the basis of the reindeer notecard she had sent me shortly after arriving at her aunt's flat. It had informed me, in her familiar stop-start handwriting, that they would be getting back really late on the Tuesday night because they were going to see *Swan*

Lake at the . . . well, it could have been anywhere. It could have been the MGM Grand for all I knew, because I hadn't read any further. The first four sentences had been enough to send me crashing into the sort of doom spiral that always seems so much worse during the festive season (and would doubtless be exacerbated this year by my over-consumption of sherry and cheese straws, and enthusiastic masturbation several times a day because Jessica was more than a hundred miles away, leaving me alone in my cottage-slash-igloo with very little but the onset of frost-bite to occupy my mind). The rest of the note, I learned afterwards, had gone on to explain that she wouldn't be able to call me either, as her aunt's phone was in the family kitchen where everybody had to sit all day because her aunt was too much of a tight-wad to heat the rest of the flat. And she definitely wouldn't be able to leave the flat to find a payphone because apparently her aunt's estate in Dalston was full of predatory men looking to jump young teenage girls.

The irony of this was not lost on me. Ha bloody ha.

So I decided, at the very last minute, to spend Christmas with my own family. Richard had brought his new girl-friend, Katy, home (new being code for first ever), so I wasn't allowed to make my usual jokes about his hair or expanding waistline, and neither could we sit up together late into the night – as was by now tradition – swigging from our mother's festive bottle of Baileys while working our way through Richard's entire library of James Bond videos and talking, mostly theoretically, about girls.

Over the past couple of months, I had thought a lot about discussing Jess with Richard, but each time I thought I might broach the subject, I bottled out at the last moment. I sensed, somehow, that my brother might disapprove – and this was Richard, who didn't have much of an opinion about anything, except maybe the declining quality of the Christmas television scheduling, and whether the internet really had any potential as a money-spinner (he thought that, on balance, it probably did).

So Richard's disapproval would really have meant something to me. In fact, I knew it had the potential to drive an irreversible wedge between us, so for that reason, I didn't see the point. I decided to wait, perhaps until Jess turned twenty-one, before breaking the news to all my various friends and relatives.

I also got the feeling that Katy might not be the sort of woman who'd approve of sexual activity with a minor, and as she appeared to make Richard happy, it hardly seemed the ideal time to regale her with the story either.

With Katy in tow, Richard had conveniently ditched the James Bond obsession, and was even wearing a shirt with sleeves and a button-down collar, which thrilled our mother virtually beyond speech or movement. Given that the signs were now all pointing to a new unspoken Katy-regulation warning me off any mention of 007, I figured it would have been rude of me to suggest cracking open the video library, so I simply sat silently in the corner throwing nuts down the back of my throat and trying very hard not to fantasize about Jessica's tits.

Our mother was irritatingly on-edge for the entire festive period because apparently Katy's family was something to do with landed gentry and had maids to clean their various houses, which my mother didn't. So everyone had to keep removing their shoes and doing bizarre stealth runs with the Hoover whenever Katy was in the toilet. On Boxing Day I found a copy of the Yellow Pages with the page turned down on Molly Maid.

Katy herself spent most of the time perched on the edge of the sofa wearing an expression of faint repulsion as if my father had just exposed himself from behind the piano, while my mother waved bowls of cheese and onion crisps under her nose and waffled on about how pretty her hair looked.

I got the impression that Katy didn't exactly take to me, mostly because whenever I tried to talk to her, she'd ignore me, squeeze Richard's hand and look in the opposite direction. So I'd end up trailing off like an idiot while Richard picked up the baton and started talking about what holidays they had planned for next year or how well Katy's dad's sheep were doing on his farm. This annoyed me, because I knew for a fact that Richard didn't and wouldn't ever give a shit about anything to do with the countryside, or to be more specific, the importance of his girlfriend's family flock to the UK wool industry.

Maybe Katy disapproved of my long-haired look, given that she was dating a man with a buzz cut, and not a very good one at that. I'd realized that some women were inexplicably distrustful of men with hair that had grown anywhere beyond an inch from the scalp. If that was the problem, she would fit in well at Hadley Hall. Interestingly, I could imagine her getting on with Sonia Laird like a house on fire.

Richard-and-Katy's (*seriously? Joint gifts already?*) present to me that year was a box of Cuban cigars, picked up cut-price as part of a bulk purchase made by Katy at José Martí International Airport during a trip to Havana that July, before she'd even started dating Richard. Given that not once in our lives had Richard and I ever shared a cigar, I thought it was a bit of a weird, cop-out present, and hoped this wasn't the shape of things to come. As I saw it, having a girlfriend was not a good enough excuse for becoming thoughtless, boring or both.

I'd been hoping too to use my little festive interlude to have a chat with my dad about getting in touch with our Italian relatives, perhaps even mooting the idea of making a trip out to Tuscany in the summer. But with a guest in the house my dad was under strict orders not to deviate from his list of pre-approved conversation topics, for fear of causing the only girlfriend Richard had ever had to scarper in the direction of the ring road without looking back. Whenever an opportunity presented itself for us to chat, my mum, who had an in-built radar for this kind of thing, swatted my dad with her oven glove and ordered him back into the living room with a top-up for Katy's bitter lemon – so I was forced to compromise by spending my downtime with my head in a travel guide to Italy, which seemed a bit of a waste when you had real-life Italian flesh and blood to talk to.

I'd planned to stay for New Year's Eve, having imagined Katy (before I'd had the non-pleasure of meeting her) to be the sort of girl who might want to head to the pub for a few drinks and a drunken attempt at 'Auld Lang Syne' on the stroke of midnight. But apparently Katy's family was in the tradition of making health-related New Year's resolutions, none of which involved finding yourself awake and pissed at one a.m. on New Year's Day, since that was likely to interfere with running five miles before breakfast or drinking unpasteurized milk or whatever it was they did to make themselves thinner.

So I headed home to my little cottage before the main event, pausing only at a petrol station to purchase eight cans of lager for myself and a carton of eggnog for Mrs Parker. I had never bought eggnog before, but after presenting it to her, I planned straight away to do it again – she received it with such awe and gratitude, you'd have thought I was Jesus Christ himself standing there on her doorstep. Mind you, with my hair and beard as they were then, in silhouette I was probably doing a passable impression of him – and to be fair she had once mistaken the milkman for Ian McShane.

My doorbell chimed just before midnight. I was watching Jools Holland's Hootenanny and sinking my fourth lager, miserably contemplating the idea that Jess was probably partying somewhere in the West End with her cousins, meeting rich young boys from Chelsea and getting drunk on champagne. Watching the Hootenanny she most certainly was not.

On hearing the doorbell, I had a surge of hope that it might be her; that they'd been forced to flee Dalston because her mother had drunk too much coffee liqueur and caused a fire in the high-rise by knocking over the Christmas tree or something – which probably accounted for why I flung the door open with such gusto.

I stared, dumbfounded, at the vision that greeted me.

It was Sonia Laird in high heels, raincoat held wide open to reveal a stupidly tiny Sexy Santa costume in some cheap fabric that half resembled plastic.

I was just about drunk enough to let my mouth fall open while it still contained lager; and Sonia took advantage of the ensuing confusion to slip past me into the living room while I swore and wiped my chin furiously with the sleeve of my freshly soaked jumper.

It was freezing, so I shut the door behind us, even though I really wasn't keen on sharing an enclosed space with Sonia for any length of time.

'Sonia . . . what the fuck are you doing?' I asked her from the doorway. If I hadn't been thinking by now that she definitely had something missing, cerebrally speaking, I might have found her little outfit funny.

Sonia's unique way of answering my question was to purr, 'Merry Christmas, Mr Landley,' before removing her raincoat entirely and letting it fall to the floor. The vision of her standing there with her red shock of over-styled hair, limbs so white they were almost transparent and yellow teeth adorned with a smudge of crimson lipstick was in turn-on terms about as kinky as watching my own grandmother attempt a striptease.

'Sonia,' I said, and then wasn't sure how to continue. What I really wanted to do was eject her from my house, but even I could appreciate the guts it must have taken for her to stand there half naked in front of someone who had visibly recoiled when the coat came off.

But Sonia clearly wasn't planning to back down with her dignity intact. 'Come on, Matthew,' she crooned doggedly. (You had to hand it to her, she was nothing if not tenacious.) 'You're single. I'm single. Let's have some fun. Or did you want to sit here on your own and watch –' she glanced at the television – 'the Hootenanny?' She pronounced it in a stupid Scottish accent, like a school bully ridiculing the class nerd. I felt oddly protective of Jools in that moment.

'Sonia, you're not single,' I reminded her. It felt like I had been reminding her of that since the first day I'd met her.

'Actually,' Sonia replied perkily, as if she was about to impart some nugget of information that would make me fall spontaneously and passionately in love with her, 'Darren and I have split up.'

My immediate thought was, *Lucky Darren.* And then I took a long swig of lager.

'So . . .' Sonia said, obviously convinced that my next

260

move would be to vault the sofa and attempt to remove her Sexy Santa costume with my teeth.

'I have a girlfriend, Sonia,' I said, before I'd even had a chance to think it through.

She gave a tight little scoff of disbelief. 'No, you don't.'

That annoyed me. On the one hand, Sonia was always seemingly trying to get off with me; on the other, she appeared consistently determined to make me feel like the biggest loser who'd ever walked the planet. 'And how the fuck would you know?' I said.

Sonia didn't move. She stayed where she was, swaying slightly on those stupid high heels of hers. She looked so unstable on them that I was tempted to extend an arm and give her a shove. 'Well, Steve Robbins would know, which means Josh would know, which means the entire bloody staffroom would know,' she retorted eventually.

'Well, actually, none of you know,' I said, which was pushing it slightly, given the particular circumstances of my current relationship.

'Well, where is she then?' Sonia said, looking around the room, presumably to illustrate just how much of a fantasist I was. 'It's New Year's Eve, and your *new girlfriend* is nowhere to be seen!'

She even had the nerve to use air quotes too.

Just then, the clock struck midnight and fireworks began to explode outside. My cottage backed on to the village playing field, where swathes of functional-though-slightly-pissed middle-class parents clutching polystyrene cups of microwaved mulled wine had gathered with their well-adjusted children to cheer in another successful and prosperous twelve months. Meanwhile, I was being held hostage once again – this time in my own home – by a woman I had once stuck my head in a coat stand to avoid, who was wearing nothing more than plastic underwear and having the audacity to claim it was all for my benefit.

I was drunk, and I was confused. All I really wanted was to be holding Jess in my arms – and right now, I didn't even know if I would ever get to hold her again.

I wanted to scream with frustration, which probably explained what happened next.

'WHAT DO YOU WANT FROM ME?' I shouted at Sonia. 'I HAVE NO IDEA WHAT YOU WANT! ONE MINUTE YOU HATE ME, THE NEXT YOU WANT TO FUCK ME! WHICH IS IT? WHICH IS IT?'

Outside, the fireworks boomed and screamed.

'I love you,' she said then. 'I love you, Matthew.'

I stared at her. At no point in time had I ever expected her to come out with anything as stupid as that.

I put my head in my hands, knowing that I had to kill this, now. 'Well, I don't love you,' I told her. 'I never will. I love my girlfriend. I love her more than you will ever know.' And in that moment, I knew that was it: I loved her. I loved Jess Hart. I wanted to jump on the next train to London and tell her, right now, how much I fucking loved her. Screw that Chelsea crowd. Screw her spaced-out mother and weird sister. I probably loved Jess more than the lot of them put together.

In front of me, Sonia was still standing in the middle of the room, working her jaw with humiliation, blushing scarlet.

Because that makes sense, I wanted to say. *You can stand in front of me in polythene pants but you blush when I tell you I love another girl.*

'I'm sorry, Sonia,' I said, though it was probably pretty clear that I wasn't sorry at all.

'Shut up,' Sonia barked. She began to make her way to the door, tottering in her heels. She was in such a hurry that she left her raincoat lying there on the floor.

'So now I'm the bad guy?' I exclaimed, incredulous. 'Jesus, Sonia, I didn't ask you to come here . . .'

'Just stay away from me,' she snapped. 'Don't come anywhere near me again.'

'Fine,' I said. I was exhausted by the whole thing. 'That's absolutely fine.'

And then she turned to me and spat, 'You know something, Matthew? You're a real cunt.'

It was the last thing she said before yanking open the door, forgetting that I had a front step and snapping her ankle bone clean in two as she wobbled straight off the top of it.

A few days later was the start of spring term, and the story, of course, had spread around the whole school before lunchtime. A group of pupils from Hadley just so happened to have been trooping back with their parents from the firework display while Sonia was still writhing around on the pavement outside my cottage, screaming in agony – so our entire little drama was played out in front of a sniggering, tittering audience containing far more people with whom I was on first-name terms than ideally I'd have liked (zero really being my upper limit).

Once the paramedics had arrived, I'd gone inside to fetch Sonia's coat in an effort to preserve what was left of her dignity (which to be fair wasn't much), so I couldn't even claim she'd just been tottering drunkenly past my house. Then I had to endure a lengthy interview with the police, who were trying to get me to say I'd pushed her off the step, just so they'd have something more exciting to process than another festive drinker with an ankle injury. By this point I was half wondering if I could call Jess in to back me up on how useless Miss Laird was at doing anything in heels.

I spent almost an hour in with Mackenzie as soon as I arrived back at work on the first day of term. In expectation of getting a hard time for bringing the school into disrepute, I had ironed a shirt, pulled my hair into a ponytail and for-gone the cowboy boots. Fortunately, none of it was necessary: Mackenzie seemed to agree that Sonia appeared to have unravelled somewhat over the Christmas break, so I was duly excused from much of the start-of-term rigmarole that I would usually have had to endure – including an abnormally lengthy staff meeting and the launch of some weird educational tombola to raise funds for a school in Dji-bouti. I was more than happy to escape both events, if only for the reason that they would have involved extended exposure to the icy, will-stab-you glare emanating towards me from Lorraine Wecks, which was almost as bad as hav-ing her wink at me.

But the whole day passed before I could speak with Jess – an entire seven hours of vacant teaching and nervous fidgeting. Eventually I spotted her crossing the atrium near the main hall, head down, and I stepped into her path, not caring if I was being obvious, barely concerned that we could be seen. I had to talk to her.

'Hello, Jess,' I said, in my best could-I-please-have-a-quick-word-about-your-homework voice. 'Could I please have a quick word about your homework?'

I had no idea where to take her that would be private enough to say what I wanted to say; but I started walking anyway and, to my relief, she followed.

Finding an empty classroom – ironically enough, Miss Laird's home ec lab – I pulled the door shut behind us.

Grabbing a load of textbooks from a shelf, I spread them all out on the bench in front of us to feign legitimacy in case anyone should happen to walk past; although quite how, as a maths teacher, I planned on explaining this impromptu lesson in home economics I had not, admittedly, fully thought through.

'I know what happened,' Jess said, her voice shaking, at around the same time as I came out with, 'I've really missed you, Jess.'

I spoke again quickly before she could say anything else. 'No, you don't,' I said. 'You think you know what happened, but you don't.'

'Well, I already knew that Miss Laird had a thing for you.' She stared at me with a strange expression, like she'd forgotten who I was. It was making me panic slightly. 'I said that to you before.' Her grey eyes were full of tears. I wanted to kiss them away. 'Everyone's laughing about it.'

'Yeah – *she* has a thing for *me*,' I said desperately. 'She turned up on my fucking doorstep, Jess, wearing that stupid fucking costume, and I told her I had a girlfriend I was in love with.'

It was a cheap time to play that particular card, I knew that; but I also knew that I wasn't lying. I loved this girl – *loved* her – and I wanted her to know.

'What?' she breathed. 'What did you say?'

'I said, I love you,' I repeated, my voice quiet but firm. 'I mean it. I would never touch Sonia – Miss Laird. It's you I want. I've missed you so much.'

'Oh my God,' she said, and then she began to cry. 'Oh my God. I've missed you too.'

'Hey,' I whispered. And then, because I knew to step forward and hug her was too risky, I just stood there limply, one hand pointlessly half extended into the space between us as I mumbled, 'Don't cry. Don't cry.'

Despite this winning effort at being ineffectual, Jess shone me a smile through her tears before wiping her eyes and cheeks with the cuff of her white blouse. 'I'm crying because I'm happy, Mr L,' she said, offering me a relieved giggle to confirm it.

For possibly the first time in twelve days, my whole body relaxed. I leaned back against Sonia's workbench, my hands resting next to my hips, feeling suddenly warm with reassurance. Still, I felt compelled to glance up every now and then at the classroom door, just to check we didn't have an audience. We should have been safe, given that Sonia hadn't made it from her sickbed into school; even so, it wouldn't have exactly shocked me to look up and see her face mashed against the glass window in the door, eyes aflame with a mixture of outrage and triumph. Bitter experience was starting to teach me that Sonia liked nothing better than to catch me off guard. She was in that same vein of sly as someone with press accreditation and a red-hot deadline.

'So how was your Christmas?'

'Oh, you know – okay,' Jess replied delicately, as if her Christmas had been the familial equivalent of gastroenteritis and she was only just entering the recovery period. I'd almost have preferred her to be saying she'd been partying non-stop with the same rich boys from Chelsea who'd been gallivanting boorishly and illogically around my head since the day she'd left.

She sighed. 'My mum thinks Christmas is just a really good excuse to get wasted.'

Well, we all thought Christmas was just a really good excuse to get wasted – but I sensed Jess's mother probably took it to a whole new level. I envisaged less carol singing and Quality Street, more wrestling the sherry bottle from someone else's grasp while hurling strings of profanities at the Queen's speech. I didn't picture her happily tipsy on the sofa getting all the answers wrong to Trivial Pursuit (*Is Washington a city or a state, for fuck's sake? Who in God's name is Imelda Marcos?*) but bawling bitterly to herself in her bedroom, party hat on the piss, cheeks a similar colour to the cranberry sauce and last-night's mascara all over her face like she'd given Santa's elves free run of her make-up bag.

'I'm sorry,' I said. I really was. I would have loved to have taken Jess home, introduced her to my family and *Elvis' Christmas Album*, allowed my mum to darn her socks and my dad to force-feed her mince pies and Ferrero Rocher. Wasn't that how Christmases were supposed to be?

'It's okay,' Jess said, accepting and pragmatic as ever. 'That guy from the support group came round and gave her a book.'

'Oh,' I said, nodding as if this was a positive step forward and not just a way for ex-alcoholics to occupy their time in the hope of preventing themselves from falling off the wagon. Never mind it being the sort of thing that nobody did at Christmas ever. 'Well, maybe that will help.'

'I really hope she uses it,' Jess said with a frown. Then her face brightened. 'But the good news is, I spoke to my aunt. She's going to pay for me to go to Venice. I asked Mr Michaels today.'

'Wow. That's brilliant, Jess.' I'd been planning to offer her the money myself, but I hadn't yet worked out the logistics of how she would explain popping off to Italy for a week cost-free to her mother. Now, I didn't have to.

'She'd already got me a present, but she said I could have the school trip instead.'

'What did she get you?' I asked, thinking somewhat smugly that it would have to have been pretty awesome to top Venice.

'Cookbooks,' she said. 'They were really nice, actually. But it's fine. She's taking them back for a refund.'

I thought that was pretty shitty. Even my own family – set in their ways and routines as they were – would never have done something like that. If her aunt could afford to drop several hundred pounds on Jess's school trip fee, I was sure she could have written off the cost of a few cookbooks. I made a mental note to find out what the books were next time I had a pencil on me, promising myself I'd go straight out and replace them.

'So what about your sister? Is she going to Venice too?'

Jess made a face. 'No. She hates holidays. She got home-sick after twenty-four hours in Dalston.'

I smiled, trying to think of a polite way to suggest that a week in her aunt's east London flat was not in quite the same league as the Hadley Hall trip to Venice. 'I have a feeling Venice will be a bit different to Dalston, Jess.'

She fixed me then with her gaze in a way I was beginning to find addictive. 'You should see if you can come.'

I hesitated, not because the idea of being in Italy with Jess didn't sound like the most exciting thing I'd heard this year (unless you were counting this lunchtime's forty-five-minute update on the school gym refurbishment, which I wasn't), but because I already knew there was no room for any more teachers on the Venice trip. Almost instantly, I began to experience a surge of indignation towards the lucky few who'd clearly been paying attention, rather than taking it upon themselves to descale the staff kettle, when the trip was first being announced.

'Venice,' Jess was whispering, her eyes like pale grey magnets drawing me towards her. 'Come to Venice. It would be amazing. It would be perfect.'

And then she leaned forward, stood on tiptoe and kissed me. But only a second after I'd responded she pulled away, glancing over at the classroom door before grabbing my hand.

'Come on,' she breathed.

As she tugged at me to follow her, a choir of startled voices began to bellow at me in my head, a chorus of alarm to inform me that this was one step too far – that yes, I was clearly stupid, but surely not *that* stupid?

Actually, I was that stupid.

The extent of my protest was to urgently say her name several times as she led me by the hand in the direction of the home ec store cupboard – because even the prospect of what she wanted me to do was enough of a turn-on to make this more of an argument with myself than with her. 'Jess, seriously – we can't.'

But as it turned out, we could.

The cupboard was narrow and windowless, and smelt faintly of bread and cinnamon. It was also fucking freezing. We left the light off and shut the door, and I let Jess push me up against the shelves at its far end. She felt for my outstretched hand, lifting her other hand to my face before delivering an urgent kiss to my mouth. Everything I had been worrying about over the past couple of weeks evaporated as I kissed her back. 'I love you too, Mr L,' Jess groaned, the words sliding off her tongue on to mine. 'I love you too.'

I don't know how long we were kissing for. It could have been seconds or it could have been minutes. It felt more like days, and I hoped it would never end. There was something just so incredible about being there with her like that in the dark, about knowing that – given our surroundings – this

269

couldn't go any further than a kiss. It was tantalizing to the extreme; beautifully excruciating. The sweetest form of torture possible.

Until, that is, she reached down and gently unzipped my flies.

I knew I should resist and for a few moments made a weak attempt to do so by mumbling incoherently, 'Jess, we can't. We can't. Not here,' as she undid my belt and let my trousers slip to the floor. But then she was easing down my boxer shorts, dropping to her knees, taking my cock in her mouth. And that was it. I was gone, catapulted into a state of frenzied euphoria.

In a way, I thought later, I was glad the cupboard was dark that day. I didn't particularly want to look down and see the picture of myself, trousers round my ankles and boxers at my knees, while one of my pupils – a girl in school uniform – engaged me in the oral sex session of my life. Oh, I was painfully aware that the skirt she had on was a little too short; that she was wearing those pull-up black stockings (all the rage at the time among the top four year groups); that her tie was knotted up high over her thin, white blouse (which I was technically supposed to tell her off for – all ties were supposed to reach down to below the ribcage). Oh yes, every ingredient of the stereotypical male fantasy was right there in front of me. But that wasn't what I got off on. I got off on *her* – her sweet laugh, her charming, uncomplicated personality, how easily she seemed to love me back. I fancied her as much when she was slobbing about in her ripped jeans and T-shirt as when she was in her uniform – more probably, because it didn't make me feel like quite so much of a pervert.

Because that was what was going round my head after Jessica left the store cupboard that afternoon. I stayed in there alone for a little while longer, attempting to revisit planet earth so I could psyche myself up to act normally on my walk back through the school to the car park – but all I could hear was an unidentifiable voice barrelling around inside my mind chanting: *Pervert. Pervert. Pervert.*

18

Jess probably hadn't spent the whole of Friday night sleeping
at altitude, but that's what her dry mouth and headache were
telling her when she woke up on Saturday morning. Smudge
was downstairs barking hysterically, the alarm clock said
eight a.m., and somebody was under the misguided impression that now would be a good time to repeat-dial her
mobile. She had been exhausted last night after spending
the afternoon pitching for a slot on the catering roster with
three different events venues, which she'd followed up by
staying out late in Carafe, gabbling on to Philippe about
God-knows-what. She'd finished off the night by climbing
into bed still wearing all her clothes.

Jess finally located her phone on the floor and, speech
failing her, opted simply to listen.

'You're where?' she croaked eventually.

'On your front doorstep,' came the reply.

The two sisters faced one another at Jess's kitchen table. Jess
had run out of Philippe's Colombian coffee, so they were
having to make do with the slightly solidified contents of an
ancient jar of instant she'd located at the back of a cupboard.
Debbie, who had her arms folded (as far as she could) across
her ample chest, was wearing a sour expression.

'So you forgot.'

'Not exactly,' Jess mumbled guiltily, even though of
course she had. The entire arrangement had completely
slipped her mind. She'd even let both Debbie's calls go to

voicemail yesterday evening in the bar, unwilling to assign any part of her Friday night to what she'd assumed would simply be another pointless bout of bickering with her sister.

'Well, I was at King's Lynn station at the time we agreed, and you weren't. Flat tyre, was it?'

Jess raised her coffee cup to her lips and sipped. It tasted as good as she expected it to, which wasn't very. 'I'm surprised you didn't bring your key.'

'I didn't think I'd have to!' Debbie's chin fat quivered with outrage. 'Shall I send you the bill for the taxi and the Travelodge?'

'If you like,' Jess replied, 'but I'm not really in a position to pay it.' She'd shoved all her final-warning bills – which normally sat unopened on the kitchen worktop – into a drawer while she was making the coffee. She didn't need the humiliation of Debbie knowing just how much financial trouble she was in.

'I'll subsidize your disorganization then,' Debbie snapped back. 'And just so you know, I had a really lovely evening with my McDonald's Extra Value Meal watching back-to-back episodes of *Ice Road Truckers*.'

Thinking privately that Debbie probably wouldn't have got much closer to her dream night in if she'd planned it in advance, Jess placed a plate of home-baked coconut macaroons in the middle of the table as a form of truce. But to make her point, Debbie – a woman who had recently admitted to eating fourteen cake pops in as many minutes at a children's birthday party with the dubious justification of 'not wanting to appear rude' – was resolutely refusing to touch them.

'I don't like coconut, actually she sniffed, shrugging huffily.

'What's wrong with coconut?' Jess asked, at a loss.

'Huh. What's right with it?' Debbie muttered.

Jess glanced down at Smudge, who was gingerly sniffing the sole of Debbie's left foot as if he didn't quite trust her. Admiring his perception, she wondered if perhaps her sister gave off warning fumes in the manner of a skunk or similar.

'What the hell were you doing last night anyway? You look a state, if you don't mind me saying.' Debbie, as always, was impeccably blow-dried and painted-on, as people did tend to be when they had too much time on their hands.

'Adding "if you don't mind me saying" to the end of a sentence is not a catch-all caveat to insult someone, Debbie,' Jess grumbled.

'Out on the town with that man of yours?' Debbie ploughed on loudly, like a gossip columnist ambushing a z-list celebrity. 'What's his name . . . Walt? Victor?'

'Zak,' Jess replied, to save them both the tedium of exhausting every letter at that end of the alphabet. 'And no. He's in London at the moment,' she added, wishing that the same could be said for Debbie – or at the very least that she was back in the King's Lynn Travelodge, marooned there indefinitely by gridlock on the A17.

And then, with impeccable timing, came another knock at the door.

While Zak captivated Debbie with heart-warming stories from accident and emergency, Jess tore into a butter-soaked croissant and sipped from a takeaway coffee, both courtesy of Zak. The coffee was at least fulfilling its basic obligations by being fresh, roasted and strong – but Jess still couldn't help wondering idly at what point of the morning it might be acceptable to sink a quick gin without being classed an alcoholic.

'So remind me, Debbie,' Zak was saying, in an apparent effort to charm Jess's sister, 'what do you do?'

She'd left them alone together while she was in the shower, trying and failing to wash away her hangover and dark mood.

Debbie pulled her usual martyr's grimace. 'Look after two little girls, I'm afraid. Full-time job.'

'Wow,' Zak said, as if this were fascinating and nobody in the world apart from Debbie had ever given birth before, 'and how old are they?'

'Eight and six. They're going through a bit of a phase at the moment though. Ooh, these croissants are *amazing*, Zak,' she added, tearing another chunk from hers while glaring pointedly at Jess's offending macaroons in the middle of the table.

'They decorative?' Zak asked Jess through a mouthful of croissant, nodding at the macaroons.

In Ralph Lauren piqué cotton and slim-fitting beige chinos, Zak was looking particularly like one-eighth of a polo match today, Jess thought. Shaking her head, she resisted the urge to ask him why he thought someone would display platefuls of home baking around the house like ornaments, in the manner of collectible snow domes or crystal figurines.

'So, what's this phase your little girls are going through?' Zak asked Debbie with a smile, clearly expecting her to reel off harmless tales of reading after lights-out or refusing to eat carrots.

'Biting,' Debbie intoned gravely. 'It's becoming a real problem.'

Zak looked across to Jess for some assistance. She shrugged.

'Oh,' was all he could come up with.

Debbie adjusted the waistband of her jeans, which on closer inspection looked to bear a suspicious resemblance to elastic. 'We were hauled in to talk to the head teacher a couple of weeks ago,' she said. 'Me *and* Ian. Like they didn't trust me to deal with it.'

They probably didn't, thought Jess, taking another mouthful of croissant.

'Anyway, they asked us if we'd considered psychological intervention.'

'Good idea,' Zak said quickly. 'Nip it in the bud.'

Debbie made a face that looked a lot like a simper. 'I keep forgetting you're a doctor.'

Jess rolled her eyes.

'Have you been to your GP about it?'

'God, no,' Debbie said quickly. 'What if he calls social services?'

'He won't do that,' Zak chortled, as if bringing in social services was equivalent to conducting an unauthorized rectal exam. 'He'll probably just refer you to a specialist. What does your husband think?'

'My husband?' Debbie repeated, like this was the first she'd heard of him.

'Yeah, Ian?' Jess prompted her.

There was a short pause. 'Well, unfortunately Ian has been a bit distracted by his PA recently. *Saskia.*' Debbie spat the name out witheringly while staring very hard at the Aga, like she was hoping Ian and Saskia might turn out to be slow-cooking inside it. 'The girl I used to call a million times a day. The girl who is so *stupid* she doesn't even know what "penultimate" means.'

Jess tried to envisage a phone message from Debbie for Ian that would have necessitated use of the word 'penultimate'.

When the news of Ian's third affair had first broken, Jess had responded with genuine sadness, especially on behalf of her two beautiful nieces – but this was now giving way to a renewed sense of guilt over Natalie and Charlotte. How was she any different to Ian's slow-witted secretary?

'He's sacked her now, of course,' Debbie said briskly. 'I made him do it.'

'Er, is that legal?' Jess said, not altogether supportive of her sister's Napoleonic tendencies.

'Of course it's not. She's threatening to sue, *of course*,' Debbie said, with a roll of the eyes like this sort of thing happened to her every day of the week. 'But I told him. It's me or her.' She polished off the last of her croissant, brushing the flakes from her fingers.

Jess pushed away an ungenerous thought that involved Debbie and Saskia standing side by side and the choice being fairly obvious. 'So what now?'

'The long and short of it is, I've got to sell the cottage, Jess. Affairs cost money. There's been a lot of wining and dining and hotels and expensive jewellery. And I told you about the sodding convertible.' Debbie sat back and shot Jess a bizarrely smug expression, like nobody would have believed that Ian had been cheating on her unless he'd given himself away by sticking a soft-top on his credit card. 'Someone's got to pay for it all.'

'Can't it be Ian?' Jess asked, wondering why it had to be her.

'God no, not with the size of our mortgage.'

'Think yourself lucky you've even got one,' Jess muttered, remembering all her unpaid bills.

Debbie was starting to get snotty. 'Look, we don't sell, we go under. All four of us. The girls too: your *nieces*. Is that what you want?'

Jess stared into her cup like a fortune teller into tea leaves, trying to foresee a day when she wouldn't be trying really hard not to hate her sibling. The croissant had left an oily film on her tongue that reminded her of bacon fat. She attempted to break it up with the last of her cooling coffee, which was a bit like trying to wash up a grill pan with tap water and no soap.

Somehow, despite the words that were coming out of her sister's mouth, Jess knew that any decision to sell the cottage would always be less to do with Ian's debts than Debbie's long-standing resentment towards her.

Zak cleared his throat. 'I might just take Smudge for a quick stroll.' He got up and emitted a short whistle, the aural equivalent of waving a steak under Smudge's nose. 'Lead?' he asked Jess.

She came with him to the front door and passed over Smudge's lead. He clipped it on before turning to face her.

'Nice surprise?' He bent down to kiss her.

She nodded limply.

'Fully recovered?'

'Yes thanks,' she breathed, hating herself for the lie.

'You know,' he said, 'when you say you've got flu, you probably just mean you've got a common cold.' He smiled apologetically, like he was delivering bad news. 'It's not actually the same thing.'

Despite herself, she smiled weakly. 'My mistake.'

He paused for a moment, hand on the door, seemingly searching her face for something he'd lost. 'Unusual in summer, though.' And then he held her gaze for just a moment more before turning his back and exiting with Smudge.

She let her head hang for a couple of seconds, staring down at the floorboards until Debbie's voice came at her from the kitchen, shrill like a marauding peacock. 'I could murder another coffee, Jessica.'

Turning and heading back into the kitchen, she passed Debbie wordlessly and snapped the kettle on.

'You've really done well there,' Debbie said to her sister as she sat back down. 'I think we've just solved our housing problem.'

Jess felt her stomach lurch. 'What are you talking about?' she whispered.

'Oh, come on,' Debbie hissed across the top of the croissant bag. 'You're dating a man with *two houses*.'

Jess stared at her. 'Are you serious?'

'Yes! He told me that while you were in the shower.'

'I don't mean about having two sodding houses, Debbie! I mean are you seriously telling me you think it's okay to make me homeless because Zak happens to have a bit of spare cash in the bank?'

'Oh, Jess, for God's sake. Stop being so dramatic. I sell this house, he'll look after you – simple. You *know* you're not going to end up on the street – but I might, if I don't sell.'

'Debbie, look at me.' Jess leaned forward and made a mouth with her hand. 'Watch my lips, okay? I am not moving in with Zak. It's not that simple.'

'Why-ever-the-fuck-not? Belsize Park, isn't it?' She cast a disdainful glance around Jess's ramshackle kitchen. 'I know which I'd prefer.'

Forced to assume it was moments like this that Anna practised yoga to rise above, Jess struggled to contain her outrage. 'The point is, Deb, I don't want to be coerced into moving in with someone because I have nowhere else to live! Do you know how ridiculous that is?'

Debbie shook her head and shrugged at the same time. 'No it's not. People do it all the time.'

What people? she wondered.

'I'm sorry, Jess,' Debbie said, and the way she said it made Jess think she wasn't sorry at all. 'I have to put the cottage on the market. In fact . . .' She took a breath.

'Oh God. What?'

'. . . that's why I'm here so early. I've got an appointment at the estate agent's at ten. To arrange a valuation.'

Jess put her head in her hands.

'I'm sorry,' Debbie repeated, and the words were starting to sound more hollow every time she said them.

Jess looked up at her. 'Debbie, I know Mum left the house to you, but . . . please. Just think about this.'

'Don't tell me you've got happy memories of this house,' Debbie said, her ability to become very quickly affronted never far from her fingertips. 'The only thing I remember when I sit in this kitchen is horror, pure and simple. I shall be glad to be rid of the place, frankly.'

They sat in silence for a few moments, Jess pushing croissant flakes into little piles with her thumb. 'Can you at least give me time to find somewhere first?' she asked, humiliated by having to beg Debbie to take pity on her.

'We can ask Zak when he gets back if you like,' Debbie suggested, clearly not quite finished with goading her yet.

'That's not funny,' Jess snapped.

Debbie sighed, and finally the truth came out. 'We're about twelve weeks away from repossession. Ian's been in arrears on the mortgage for months. If I don't sell the cottage now, the bank's going to take it anyway.'

Jess stared at her sister. 'Fuck,' she said eventually.

'As you can see, for once, Jess, it's not all about you,' Debbie said, firing her final shot.

'Why don't you leave him, Debbie? How much more of his bullshit can you take?'

'If I could find someone rich enough, I'd be gone in a heartbeat,' she retorted. Not for the first time, she eyed the remaining chunk of Jess's croissant. 'Aren't you going to eat that?'

19

The following lunchtime they all decamped to the beer garden of the Three Mariners, where Debbie began to work her way through a bottle of overpriced Petit Chablis on the basis that hair-of-the-dog had at some point been medically proven, while Jess (who suspected it hadn't) stuck judiciously to cola. Smudge settled into a contented doze beneath the table and Zak went inside to order the food, an early lunch since they'd all skipped breakfast. Jess had offered to cook a traditional Sunday roast, but Debbie – in much the same way as she'd suddenly developed an irrational fear of coconut – was now claiming an aversion to meat on the bone, so they'd decided to come out to eat instead.

The morning's already humid air had thickened in the space of a few hours, and Debbie was using the menu to alternately fan herself and bat away flies.

'You're quiet today,' she remarked. 'Stay up late last night, did you?'

Actually, Jess had stayed up late – it had been almost two a.m. by the time Zak had finally fallen into a wine-infused slumber on the sofa, mouth slack and legs splayed, the tickle of a snore vibrating in his cheeks. Jess had left him there and padded barefoot with Smudge to the bottom of the garden, where she'd fashioned a hole in the hedge two summers ago to give her a better view of the salt marsh. And although they were shrouded entirely in darkness – too cloudy for stars – she pulled up a garden chair and turned to face the sea, tucking her knees under her chin and staring out into the blackness. The only sound to be heard was the faint rumble of the pushing tide in the distance, overlaid with Smudge breathing heavily, nose against the grass. Occasionally she caught the edges of a ghostly shadow, the dark wings of a barn owl passing over as it silently swooped for prey.

And then it began to come at her, the echo of Anna's voice, a relentless reverberation. *You need to choose between them, Jess. Will, or Zak.*

Will, or Zak.

Jess looked over at Debbie and shook her head. 'Not for the reason you're thinking,' was all she said.

'We had a nice day yesterday. What's so wrong with him?'

It was true – they *had* had a nice day yesterday. After Debbie had finished barking orders at her new estate agent, Zak had suggested taking a boat out of Burnham Overy Staithe to Scolt Head Island for an impromptu picnic. Jess had packed them up a feast (roasted potato salad, shredded crab and lemon-lime chicken, left over from Friday's client pitches) and had thrown in a bottle of Prosecco at the last minute too, a kind of insurance policy against wanting to smother herself to death under Debbie's Union Jack beach towel by lunchtime.

But, in the end, the day had been okay. The three of them had lazed about together on the sand dunes between clumps of whispering marram grass, devouring the picnic while Debbie read out extracts from Saturday's *Guardian*, most of which were from the Family supplement and involved her sneering at somebody else's parenting techniques. Later, back at the cottage, Jess cooked a posh chilli made with slivers of steak and bitter chocolate, and because Debbie had sunk at least a whole bottle of Pinot Noir to herself by that point, she even forgot to object and claim she'd developed an allergy to chopped tomatoes or steak in slices or something.

Jess had trodden carefully around Zak all day, unable to shake the effect of his knowing glance and flu remark by the front door that morning. She was wary of upsetting him, conscious of having deceived him, and half expecting Debbie to announce to him her grand plan for them both to move in together at any moment.

'There's nothing *wrong* with him exactly,' Jess said now. 'Things are just a bit complicated between us at the moment.' She took a sip from her cola. It had evidently been mixed with the wrong quantity of syrup, coming out so sweet it made her tongue flex. She winced and set the glass back down.

'So, what's new?' Debbie said with a shrug, wiping graffiti into the condensation on the wine chiller with her thumb. 'It's not like you've always gone for straightforward. You've always plumped for complicated.'

Jess refused to take the bait. 'Well, maybe it's time for a change then.'

'Or maybe you should stop trying to find the perfect man. Maybe he doesn't exist.'

Actually, he does.

'Zak can be . . . I mean, he has his faults,' Jess mumbled, unsure even as she was speaking why she would ever confide in Debbie.

'So do you,' Debbie sniped smugly, with enough of a smile to be able to pretend she was joking.

'You only want me to be with Zak so you can feel less guilty about making me homeless,' Jess said, leaning back in her chair and squinting against the sun, wishing she'd remembered to bring her sunglasses.

'I don't feel guilty about it,' Debbie replied simply, picking her glass up and taking a supercilious sip.

Jess looked beyond her sister's bloated face to the children's playground, which was positioned conveniently in front of the main dining-room windows so that all the full-time working parents could have five minutes to themselves to sink a weekend vodka and tonic relatively guilt-free. The children were shouting with delight and intermittently standing on each other's heads as they battled for supremacy, swarming like brightly coloured ants over the monkey bars and climbing frame. But then a streak of dark brown curls and a high-pitched squeal stirred something in her mind. She frowned and narrowed her eyes. *Is that . . . ?*

'Fuck,' she breathed out loud.

Debbie turned to look. 'What?'

Jess swallowed. 'Oh, nothing. I thought that boy was about to fall, but . . .' She smiled brightly. 'He's fine.'

Turning in her seat, she made a quick scan of the tables out on the lawn. There was no sight of Will and Natalie – they had to be inside, she concluded with relief, in the main dining room. Not that she wasn't desperate to see Will, but she didn't really fancy a five-way showdown with her sister and Zak taking centre stage.

Debbie frowned. 'What boy?'

'Never mind. He's fine.'

Debbie shrugged and turned back round. 'I never let Tabby or Cecilia play on climbing frames. Too much potential for falling the wrong way and ending up paralysed. And that would be *all* I need right now,' she added, as if paralysis was on a par with turning her whites wash pink or succumbing to a bout of hay fever.

Jess resisted the urge to suggest to her sister that this embargo on fun was probably the exact reason her daughters found biting to be so entertaining. She attempted to offer some constructive advice. 'A little bit of danger isn't necessarily such a bad thing, Deb.'

Debbie laughed bitchily. 'You know, funnily enough, it's only ever childless women who come out with claptrap like that.'

Childless. It was not only the word, but the way she pronounced it with utter contempt that made Jess want to issue her sibling with an impromptu but very thorough Petit Chablis shower.

Zak unwittingly reappeared just in time to save a smug-faced Debbie. 'Here you go.' He set down a block bearing a numbered wooden spoon and stuffed his over-stocked wallet back into his pocket. He was playing it suave today, in a fitted denim shirt and aviators.

'Wine, Zak?' Debbie schmoozed sweetly, retrieving the bottle from the chiller.

'Better not, thanks,' he said, nodding at his own glass of cola. 'Driving back to London later.'

'Ooh, going anywhere near Wanstead?' Debbie crooned as she topped herself up, knowing that he was.

'Well, I'm in Belsize Park, so I can happily drop you off,' Zak said charmingly, and Jess got the idea he was trying to prove to her what an Awfully Nice Chap he could be when he wasn't in the mood for belligerence. She massaged her temples with her thumb and index finger while Debbie started twittering on about how to get to Wanstead, like Zak didn't already live in London and have a hard-disk navigation system built into his brand-new four-by-four.

Zak took a sip from his glass. 'Mmm,' he declared. 'Delicious.'

Jess rolled her eyes.

Ten minutes later, their food arrived. 'So, go on,' Debbie

said to Zak, plucking a couple of chips from the mountain on her plate and stuffing them into her mouth. 'Say something in Spanish.' She chortled. 'Bet you get that all the time, don't you?'

Jess cringed inwardly while Zak smiled serenely. 'Not really.' Speaking Spanish on demand was one of his greatest pet hates, rivalled only by Mormons on the recruitment trail and dawdlers in the outside lane of the M25.

As for Jess, she was well aware that her general indifference towards Zak's linguistic abilities set her apart from the rest of the female population. It was one of the (admittedly more minor) reasons she suspected that Zak might not be the man for her. He deserved to be with someone who would go weak at the knees whenever he declared *Estoy enamorado de ti*, surely?

'Go on then,' Debbie goaded.

Zak cleared his throat. 'Er, okay.' He took a breath. '*Lamento tener que decirte que estás clínicamente obeso.*'

Even Jess could make out what the last couple of words meant. Despite herself, she smiled and looked down at her food.

'Oooh,' Debbie fluttered, gooey-eyed. 'Swoon alert.' She pretended to fan herself with her hand in the manner of a middle-aged woman being shown a photo of Gary Barlow.

Already resigned to the fact that she was completely and utterly at odds with her own sister, Jess shook her head and took a mouthful from her lunch, lukewarm chargrilled vegetables shoved carelessly into a slightly burnt baguette. It was bland, and the burnt bits weren't helping. She got up. 'Anyone else want salt? Ketchup?'

Debbie simply put up a hand and shook her head, as she was by now busy gabbing to Zak through mouthfuls of cheeseburger about hooking him up with Ian for a game of golf in Essex (Jess knew this to be pointless because Zak played golf in Hertfordshire, and only on a particular type of grass). Zak looked as if he might want to ask Jess for something but was suddenly doing a good impression of being the sort of person who was far too polite to interrupt people when they were talking – never mind the fact that he had just called Debbie obese to her face without so much as blinking. Jess wondered momentarily how much covert abuse he dished out in Spanish while attempting to jump-start people's hearts in A & E.

She headed back towards the pub, sticking close to the flint wall along the boundary of the garden to minimize any chance of being spotted from the window. It was pretty, this idyllic country pub, with its facade of brick and flint, and crimson roses bejewelling the arch of the doorway.

Fortunately, the condiments table was positioned just inside the main door, next to a slightly grubby stack of menus and a Visit England information rack. Jess picked up a salt cellar and some sauces, and was just about to head outside again when the dining-room doors swung open behind her.

Somehow, she knew it was him, and turned round. The sound of clinking cutlery and Sunday-lunch chatter was bubbling gently away behind them like an orchestra tuning up.

'I'm not stalking you,' she said. 'I promise.'

'That's okay. I've been known to do a bit of casual stalking myself from time to time.'

He looked lovely. Brown, handsome, lovely. His arms were slightly pumped, like he'd spent the morning in his garage doing bench press. She swallowed away a vivid flashback to the last time she'd seen him, when he'd been naked on top of her in a budget hotel room.

'Something very weird has just happened to me,' he said then.

His face was set straight, almost strained, and she knew at once that he didn't mean good weird. 'What?' she asked him, though she suddenly felt afraid.

'I bumped into Steve Robbins.' He spoke quickly, like the name would be familiar to her.

She stared at him. 'Who? Steve who?'

'Steve Robbins. Mr Robbins. He did IT at Hadley.'

Jess flipped urgently through a mental index of faces but she couldn't recall who he meant. 'Steve Robbins . . . I don't . . .'

'You do, you do – white trainers. Hair like he glued it on. *Red Dwarf* T-shirt.'

The image fell unexpectedly into place. 'Oh my God,' she breathed. 'I do. I do remember him. Mr Robbins. He used to . . . set up projectors and things.'

Will nodded. 'I just bumped into him. We were good friends.'

'Oh, fuck.'

'Really good friends,' he said, like he was still struggling to take in what had happened.

'Did you speak to him?'

'Um, barely. We walked past each other outside. He must have been going back to his car. He didn't recognize me at first, then we both looked back at the same time, and he just put his hand up, like . . .' He swallowed and shook his head. 'Wow. Sorry.'

'Are you okay?'

'Yeah, I just . . . Steve's the first person I've seen here who's definitely recognized me.'

'But if he's a friend . . .'

'Well, he was. I haven't spoken to him since, obviously. And he was never exactly the most subtle of people.'

The flicker in his eyes was betraying his urge to panic. 'Don't worry,' Jess said quickly. 'He doesn't know your name. No one can find you. Has he gone?'

Will nodded. 'I saw him drive off. I'm a bit worried he might come back though. Steve's the kind of person who would really need to know if prison's what it looks like in the films. Nice guy, but about as tactful as a tabloid journalist.' He caught her eye. 'Sorry, Jess. Sorry. Let's . . . talk about something else. It's fine,' he said, exhaling. 'Nothing happened.'

Shaking her head to dismiss his apology, she glanced down, noticing as she did that his bracelet was safely fastened back round his wrist. 'You fixed it.'

'Well, *fix* is overstating it,' he said, following her gaze. 'It's a patch job. And by patch I mean superglue.' He smiled grimly. 'Natalie thinks I should bin it. She not-so-secretly hates it.'

'Where does she think you got it?' Jess couldn't resist asking him.

'I told her Richard gave it to me.' He paused. 'Emotional attachment is the sole reason it's not yet met an untimely death-by-Hoover-nozzle. Good thing she doesn't very often bump into Richard.'

Something about the way he said this made Jess suspect the breakage might not have been a one-off. 'Has it broken before?'

He laughed softly and scratched his chin. 'Um, yeah. Fourteen times.'

She stared at him, incredulous. 'You've mended it fourteen times?'

'Well, I've glued it,' he said. 'Which basically involves being a bit too heavy-handed, fucking it up and sticking bits of myself to the table.' He hesitated. 'Not on purpose, obviously.'

Fourteen times. It means that much to you.

'It was just bad luck that it broke the other night then,' Jess said. 'If it wasn't the first time, I mean. Not a bad omen after all.'

He smiled in agreement, and there followed a light pause. 'So . . . Sunday lunch,' she said, an attempt at a change of subject, though she could tell he was still half thinking about Mr Robbins.

'Natalie's idea of heaven, mine of hell,' he said, rubbing his chin. 'Usually prefer to sweat my heatwaves out in the privacy of the back garden. Without the aid of a carvery roast and a climbing frame crawling with ADHD.'

She knew what he meant. Coming here on a sunny Sunday lunchtime seemed only one step removed from spending the morning in a soft-play centre with a raging tequila hangover.

She smiled at him. 'You're secretly annoyed you can't swing from the monkey bars, aren't you?'

He shrugged and slid her a sideways glance. 'Well, I can always sneak back and do it later. You can join me if you like.'

A waitress rushed past them then from outside, making them both jump. She was staggering beneath a tower of empty plates so tall they almost reached her chin.

Will held Jess in his gaze for a moment before nodding in the direction of the beer garden. 'So how's it going out there? With your Spaniard,' he added with a loose smile for clarity, though she knew he'd meant Zak.

For a moment Jess had no idea how to respond. Irrationally enough, spending time with Zak had already started to feel a bit too much like betraying Will.

'I mean, he's not technically Spanish. Only on paper, fifty per cent. It doesn't really count,' she ended up mumbling lamely.

291

He paused, as if trying to decipher the strange language she'd just been speaking. Abandoning the effort, he moved on. 'And your sister – Christ, I haven't seen Debbie since I had to give her detention for being menacing in charge of a lacrosse stick.'

Jess smiled weakly and a silence settled between them.

'Sorry to labour a point,' Will said then, 'but how exactly is it going with you and Zak?' His eyes were wide. 'I mean, don't get me wrong, I am fully aware that I'm not in a position to even ask you that. Just . . . humour me.'

She stared at him, inviting an explanation.

'Sorry,' he said. 'After Steve – and with Charlotte playing outside – I've been glued to the window for the past twenty minutes. Watching you was compulsive viewing, I'm afraid. Didn't want to look but couldn't quite help myself.'

'Creep,' she offered, smiling to let him know she was joking.

There was a pause like a held breath.

'I think about you all the fucking time.'

For a moment, Jess just stared at him, unable to speak.

'I have no idea what you want me to do with that,' she said eventually, trying to prevent herself from welling up.

He swallowed and nodded. 'Well, that makes two of us, Jess.'

'Are you asking me to leave him? Do you want me to tell you to leave Natalie?'

'*Fuck*.' He turned his back to her then, putting both hands to the top of his head in an expression of pure frustration. He stayed like that for a few seconds, breathing hard, while Jess attempted not to be distracted by an oversized gilt-framed watercolour to her right that depicted a pack of beagles tearing a terrified-looking fox into pieces.

Eventually he turned round. 'Look, this is none of my

business. You can go out with whoever you want, of course you can. I'm just going to go back to my table and finish my lunch, and you should do the same. Ignore me, I'm sorry, I'm acting like a twat.'

He wasn't angry with her, she realized. He was angry with himself.

'It doesn't have to be this way,' she said, her voice soft. 'Zak's going back to London tonight. Maybe we can . . .'

'Don't, Jess,' he said, cutting her off sharply. 'Go back to your lunch. Eat your baguette, talk to your sister, spend time with your boyfriend. That's what summers are for. You deserve it.'

Do I? she wondered. *Would you still say that if you knew what I'd done?*

But just as that familiar little shiver of sadness and shame began to rise once more inside her chest, Zak wandered through the front door and came to an abrupt halt in front of them both.

'Hello again,' he said, tilting his head at Will and speaking in the manner of a Crown Court barrister warming up to decimate the witness box. 'Will Greene, isn't it?'

'Now heading off, I'm afraid,' Will muttered, at the same time as Jess grabbed Zak's elbow to try and steer him back outside.

'Don't be daft, mate,' Zak said, shaking Jess off. 'Come out and join us. No good hiding in here on a nice day like this.'

Will regarded him steadily. 'Thanks anyway, but I was just leaving.'

'You know,' Zak said, taking a step forward, hands in his pockets, oh-so-casual and wearing a self-satisfied little smile, like he knew something they didn't, 'I still can't think where I know you from.'

Will swallowed. 'Then you probably don't. Excuse me.'

Zak put out a hand. 'Oh, hold on! Sorry – you look like you can't wait to get out of here – but I've been thinking perhaps you could help me with something.'

Jess's heart began to pound. She didn't dare to imagine what Zak was about to say next.

'Did Jess ever show you that bastard leg injury of hers?'

'Zak,' Jess said, her voice rigid with fear, 'shut up. Come on.'

'We really don't know each other that well,' Will said. 'Sorry. I can't help you.'

'Oh, that's funny,' Zak said. 'Because you two seem to have your heads together every time I see you.'

There was a dangerous pause.

Will took a single step towards Zak. 'Maybe, if you've got something to say, you should just come out and say it. I'm here with my family having lunch, so I really don't have time to piss about.'

'But you have time to chat up my girlfriend?'

His accusation hung in the air for about five seconds and then, from out of nowhere, Zak followed it up by throwing his fist against Will's jaw. Jess registered a collective gasp from four generations of the same family frozen in shock just outside the front doorway, no doubt arriving for a nice civilized Sunday lunch without anticipating the forced digestion of actual bodily harm before they'd even seen the menu.

Will's reply to Zak's provocation was swift. Muttering, 'This won't take long,' in the direction of their aghast audience, he delivered a hefty punch to the centre of Zak's face, the force of which sent Zak staggering backwards through the open doorway on to the gravel drive. As he struggled to regain his balance, Will advanced. Jess tried to grab his arm and pull him away, but he shrugged her off.

Zak put one hand to his face and raised the other in a quick, reluctant surrender. 'Fucking hell,' he spluttered at Will through the torrent of blood streaming from his nose, 'okay, okay.'

'Okay?' Will hovered for just a couple of seconds more before turning away and heading wordlessly past Jess, back inside.

Jess stared at Zak. Blood was dripping through his fingers and landing in fat crimson splats on the gravel. 'Fucking animal,' he heaved.

'You started it, mate,' someone called out. Their little audience had expanded now, and with it came a line of raised smartphones, held steadily up in the air like lighters at a Coldplay concert.

'Yeah, all right,' Zak spat out in the direction of the voice, still holding his face together with one hand. 'Thanks for that. Fucking dickhead. Go back to your fucking lunch.'

Despite her own anger, Jess leaned over him. 'Are you okay?'

'Call the police.'

'We can't,' she said, beginning to panic that Zak might not be the only one to have had that particular brainwave. 'You started it. They were all filming you.'

She managed to convince Zak to stay put while she went to fetch Debbie, who thankfully had been oblivious to the whole drama, concentrating instead (her jaw set in disgust) on the sight of a nearby mother who was allowing her children to run laps of the beer garden wearing only their pants.

By the time Jess had persuaded her sister to part with the

remainder of her lunch – though Debbie did insist on necking the last of the wine before they left – there was no sign of Charlotte anywhere, and Will's car had disappeared. For once, she felt grateful that she'd missed him.

Zak headed back to London with Debbie just after seven. Jess had spent the rest of the day trying to get her sister to shut up about Zak's nasal injury, while Zak occupied himself by sulking in front of the mirror, rearranging his hair to divert attention from his bright pink punch mark and pretending he was going to call the police. When that didn't make him feel any better, he attempted to repair his battered ego by ardently making a play for Jess whenever her sister left the room.

While Debbie waddled to and from the car with her multiple bags, gabbing on about the estate agent who was coming round on Tuesday to value the cottage, Zak – who though slightly more charming than Debbie was no less exasperating – wrapped his arms round Jess and whispered into her hair, 'Move to London with me, Jessica. Please. It'll be perfect, I promise.'

'I need some time to think,' she replied, pulling back from him, wondering if it was normal to view a fist fight as the prerequisite for a fresh start.

He looked at her like she'd just turned down the offer of a trolley dash around Louis Vuitton. '*Cariño*,' he said. 'Tell me you're not still pissed off about that dickhead at the pub?'

She had to admire his attempt to brazen it out, pretending that Will's right hook to his face had been nothing more than a heated exchange of words over a spilt pint of lager.

'No,' she said, shaking her head. 'London . . . it's a big decision, Zak. We've talked about this. You'd better go.' She shifted uncomfortably from his grasp, not wanting to get drawn into any more discussion about it.

'All right,' he said, feigning deference by delivering a chaste kiss to her cheek. 'But I'm not going to give up, Jess. You do know that, don't you?' And though there was a twinkle to his eye, the veneer of a jocular grin on his face, there was something about his expression that was almost daring her to underestimate him.

It made her strangely nervous.

He squeezed her hand then, slightly more firmly than he needed to, and headed outside to wait for Debbie.

Despite the fact that he'd seemed to be hovering pretty close to the truth, Jess was still convinced that no one had actually told Zak about Will mowing her down with his car last month. Self-restraint in the face of damning evidence was simply not Zak's style – had he known the facts, he'd have speed-dialled the police within minutes, hungry for blood in the manner of Ian last summer when some teenagers tried to ride their bikes near his special edition Mondeo.

Debbie pulled Jess in for a hug on her way out. Jess noticed she'd combed her hair, changed her smock top and reapplied her Dior Poison for the ride home.

'Listen,' Jess said as Debbie deposited a couple of half-hearted air kisses somewhere near her face, 'Zak doesn't know anything.'

'Hmm?' Debbie pulled back. 'What do you mean?'

'About the past. Our past. My past. He doesn't know anything and I'd like to keep it that way.' She simply couldn't risk him putting two and two together about Will.

Debbie pushed a stubborn clump of fringe out of her eyes. 'Well, *I'm* not going to be the one to tell him. I find the whole thing embarrassing, frankly.'

Jess swallowed and looked down at Smudge, who was making anxious herding circuits of their legs.

'Come on,' Debbie said. 'Tell me now while he's outside, quickly. Who-the-fuck is Will Greene, and why were they fighting?'

Clearly Zak – probably for reasons relating to personal pride – had not yet succumbed to Debbie's repeated requests for information, and Jess wasn't about to either. 'He's no one,' Jess said. 'I don't know. Who knows?' Her words came out scattered, like she'd plucked them from her mind and thrown them haphazardly into the air.

Debbie exhaled. 'Ok-ay!' she sing-songed, like she was personally of the opinion that Jess was nuts, a view that Jess thought to be slightly ironic. 'Don't forget the estate agent on Tuesday. Don't go out or anything. This is really important.'

'Thanks for reminding me.'

'It's nothing personal,' Debbie threw back at her smugly, which Jess concluded was exactly the same sort of bullshit platitude as used by bankers when they were running around firing each other for cocking up the Libor.

'Look, Debbie,' Jess said then, thinking that she might as well throw her pitiful hand of cards down on the table, 'I'm not planning on moving in with Zak, okay? So don't spend the whole journey back to London going on at him about it. Just leave it alone. Things between us are . . . they're complicated at the moment.'

'So make them simpler,' Debbie clipped. 'Stop trying to do everything from opposite ends of the motorway.'

As her sister turned to go, Jess picked up a wodge of business cards from the sideboard and handed them to her, desperate to salvage if she could at least one positive thing from the weekend. 'Look, if you come across anyone who needs catering . . . I'm willing to travel.'

Debbie looked doubtful. 'You know, no offence, but I normally recommend my woman from Chigwell. She's a bit more of what I'd call a . . . classic cook.'

'Oh, really?' Jess mumbled, trying not to feel humiliated. 'What sort of thing?'

'Well, you know. All the favourites. She does a really great sausage roll.'

The call came at midnight.

At first, all she could hear was the gusting sound of a stiff breeze.

Then came his voice. 'Jess. Fancy a swim? The water is warm as fuck.'

She sat up quickly, her heart pounding.

'Night swimming,' he continued. 'Reminds me of . . . what's that song, again?'

'"Nightswimming",' she supplied weakly.

'Yes! That's the one. Couldn't remember what it was called.' Behind his voice she could just about make out the sound of lapping water. 'UB40.'

'R.E.M,' she corrected him softly.

'Yes! R.E.M.' He paused. 'What did I say?'

'Will,' she whispered, 'where are you?'

'Well, I started off near you, as it happens. Not there any more though. Bastard longshore drift.'

'I'm coming to get you,' was all she said, hanging up.

She took Smudge with her – she had never headed out across the marsh after dark without him. Thankfully, the moon was almost daylight-bright, so there was no need for a torch. She didn't want to be out there waving one about anyway, inviting some kindly old soul to spot the beam from their conservatory and call the police.

The tide was on the push, so they didn't have long. An hour at most, she calculated. And tonight, it would be huge – the whole salt marsh would flood, as well as the creeks.

As soon as she was far enough away from the little line of houses that backed on to the sea lavender, she began to shout his name, suddenly terrified that he might have come out here to do something stupid. She dialled his mobile, over and over, but each time it just rang out.

The creeks were already filling up. She used the footbridge to cross the deepest of them, but she had to walk thigh-high through the rest, holding her phone aloft to keep it dry and forcing her mind to reject any memories of the last time she'd waded into a creek to drag someone out of it.

Despite the warm night air and tranquil sky, the early summer seawater was still the approximate temperature of the plunge pool at Beelings, and she gasped for breath, inhaling the scent of salt and mud as her chest constricted against the cold, her heart pounding with fear and adrenaline. Smudge kept close to her the whole way, delighted to be bounding over familiar territory by moonlight with the opportunity for a quick dip into the bargain.

To guard against getting stuck Jess tried to move quickly, but her shoes were drenched and heavy now; and though the final remnants of pain from her thigh injury had all but disappeared, the effort of moving forward at even the most slug-like of paces was starting to make her legs ache.

By the time she heard him shout out her name in reply, she was soaked in saltwater and covered with sticky black creek clay, her wet clothes clinging unforgivingly to every contour of her body. Still, she felt grateful that she'd had the foresight to slip on a pair of shorts and a T-shirt, rather than try to wade out here in jeans and a fleece.

Teeth chattering now, she rehearsed her speech. *This is how people die out here, Will. They get stuck in the mud in the bottom of the creeks, and then the tide comes in, and they can't escape. And then they drown. Especially if they get pissed first.*

For the last few hundred feet she allowed Smudge to lead her to him. She could see his black outline, an eerie silhouette: he'd made it over the dunes and was wading about in the water's edge, the silver light of the moon glancing sharply off the water as it rippled. The sea where they were was only calf-deep but the tide was rising, and the wind had picked up.

'Will!'

He turned to face her as she waded out towards him, Smudge cantering ahead of her and kicking up inordinate amounts of spray, like a horse on a wind-whipped Irish beach.

She was so relieved to finally reach him that she forgot her anger and extended her hand, willing him to grab it and follow her back to dry land. 'Will, the tide's coming in. The creeks are already full. Come on, we have to go.'

He didn't move, and for a few moments they just stood there in the water, staring at one another. Smudge had come to a patient halt between them, as if his being chest-high in the sea at one a.m. was perfectly normal. He was even trying to wag his tail but the water was weighing it down.

'Not quite as warm as I thought it would be,' Will said eventually, his voice jerking slightly with the cold as he spoke. Jess noticed that a deep purple bruise the colour and size of a small aubergine had spread across the left side of his face from where Zak's fist had met his jaw.

'What the fuck are you doing?' she whispered.

He appeared to think about this for a moment. 'Does

301

wanting to feel alive rather than dead-behind-the-eyes make any sense to you?'

It did, but she wasn't about to indulge him now. 'Well, if that's what you're looking for then you should sign up for a bungee jump, or rob a bank, or mow down some more people in your car or something, not come all the way out here on a high tide.'

He smiled, fished in the back pocket of his jeans and extracted a hip flask, holding it out to her. 'Jess. You look like you could use some spiced rum.'

The wind was arriving now in punchy, biting gusts, like it had blown straight in from Scandinavia and wasn't about to give either of them a break. Shivering, she ignored the flask. 'Will, it's dangerous out here. The tide's massive tonight. Please come back with me.' She held out her hand again.

'I thought you and I could have a bit of a flirt with danger,' he said, like he hadn't even heard her, flipping the top from the flask and taking a slug. 'You know – how we used to in the old days.'

'If we get caught out here together,' she said, 'Natalie will find out, Will. Is that what you want?' The water was now at her knees. Somewhere over to their right, Smudge had wisely retreated back towards the sand dunes.

A couple of moments passed, during which he regarded her with scepticism, like he was really pissed on a night out and she was trying to talk him down from solo karaoke.

'I'm not sure it's going to end well between me and your boyfriend, by the way,' he said then. 'In terms of me not having to punch him in the face again, I mean.'

If there was one thing Jess was certain of, it was that Zak no longer felt very much like her boyfriend.

'Where is he now?' Will asked her.

'He's gone home.'

'Home where?'

'Belsize Park.'

Will gave this some thought. 'Well, that's close enough to Chiswick to really piss me off,' he concluded eventually.

'You've got several boroughs of London between you. I doubt you'll run into one another.'

'Lucky for him,' he muttered darkly.

'Is your face okay?'

'My what?'

She motioned to her chin. 'Your face. Where he hit you.'

'Oh.' He waggled his jaw a couple of times. 'Well, that's the thing about spiced rum, Jess – it tends to knock out most of your vital pain receptors. If you drink enough of it.'

'What did Natalie say?'

'Oh, I told her I collided with a hanging basket. You know, one of those wrought-iron ones that don't really yield when you walk into them with your face.' He shook his head.

'Did she believe you?'

'Well, yeah, but it backfired. Had to smuggle her out past the bins before she slapped the barman with a lawsuit.' He grimaced and took another swig from the hip flask. 'Can I tell you a secret?'

'That depends. Can you tell me while we're walking?'

He paused for a moment. 'Yeah, okay.'

They began to wade back towards the sand dunes, Jess's legs now numb from the cold, though she could still feel the drag of the tide, pushing, pushing against her calves. She kept one eye fixed on the twinkling cottage lights peppering the horizon and the other on the white flash of Smudge's tail as he bounded along ahead of them, guiding them home.

'So?' she prompted, sensing Will's train of thought had drifted. He was walking a few paces behind her. She turned and waited, to let him catch up. 'What's your secret?'

'Natalie wants to start trying again.' Pause. 'For a baby,' he clarified as he arrived at her shoulder, in case Jess wasn't familiar with the universal code for fucking-to-order.

She stared across at him, feeling her stomach shrivel in the manner of a slug being doused liberally with rock salt. 'Oh,' she managed eventually. 'Well, congratulations.'

'No, Jess – don't . . . don't *congratulate* me. That's not what I meant.'

She turned away, unable to bear the image of Will and Natalie in Chiswick cradling a pink-faced little newborn, surrounded by flowers and gift-shop balloons and stupid oversized cards. The tide swelled dangerously against her calves once again and she started to wade off.

He began to shout after her then. 'It should have been us, Jess!' His voice was tight, catching against the cold. 'It should have been us, with the marriage and the baby and the perfect fucking life!'

She felt her grief rise forcefully in her throat like vomit – a regret so intense it made her feel dizzy – and it took all her effort to contain it, to prevent it erupting messily from her mouth.

'Is that what you and Natalie have?' She turned round and began to shout back at him, her voice a fierce gust to join the storm of coastal wind. 'The perfect life?'

'Of course not! Why the fuck do you think I'm out here off my face in the middle of the night? I'm not drunk on

304

domestic bliss, Jess!' He sounded almost angry. 'I miss you every single day for the sake of a few fucking months back then!'

She felt the tears come instantly, devastated afresh by the idea that just another birthday might have made all the difference. She forced herself to turn away from him and start walking again, or at least attempting to. It was only down to chance that they hadn't both snapped an ankle by now on the uneven underwater terrain.

'Jess!' Within seconds she felt him catch her up, his arm finding her waist as he spun her gently back round to face him. He dipped his head to hers, his voice becoming an apology. 'I'm sorry. I'm saying all the wrong things, I know that. The last thing I want to do is chase you away.' His gaze fell momentarily to the hip flask in his hand, and he stared at it with exasperation, like he'd somehow been expecting the rum to make everything better, not worse.

'I feel the same as you do,' she confessed, her voice thick with tears as her flash of frustration began to subside. 'It's how I've felt for the last seventeen years.' She swallowed, struggling for a second to speak. 'I wish you hadn't told me about the baby.'

His mouth flipped open slightly, like he was lost for a way to explain it. 'I'm sorry. It's just . . . Natalie's not very discreet, you know? She talks to people, all the time – in the deli, the post office . . . Our builder's only just had his third, and she's been grilling the poor guy all week on age-gap siblings.' He shook his head. 'I've just been feeling paranoid, Jess, that you might bump into her or overhear something, and get completely the wrong impression. But look – don't say "the baby", like it's already in existence. It's not like that. It's not going to happen like that.'

She met his eye, attempting to swallow away the lump in her throat as she did so, but said nothing more.

They waded a few steps further until, finally, their feet found the edge of the sand dunes. Jess was surprised to notice as they emerged from the water that Will was wearing his cowboy boots. 'You've trashed them,' she observed sadly, looking down at his feet.

'Nah,' he said, though as he followed her gaze, he looked equally sad. 'They'll buff up.'

'So, what do you want?' she asked him, shivering as they ascended the bank that marked the edge of the salt marsh. Damp marram grass brushed their calves. 'Do you want another baby?'

'Not since I ran you over,' he said softly, and then paused. 'Is possibly the weirdest sentence ever spoken in history.'

She shook her head. 'No, the weirdest sentence ever spoken in history is, *I can't remember the difference between R.E.M and UB40.*'

He laughed. 'I think you could be right.'

They were silent for a few moments, though Jess's teeth kept threatening to break into a metronomic chatter.

She sensed the need for a change of subject. 'Have you made any plans for your birthday?' It was just over a week away, the ninth of June.

'Personally? No plans. Hate birthdays. But Natalie ...' He glanced at her and hesitated.

'It's okay,' she said gently. 'You can say it.'

'Sorry,' he said resignedly. 'I was only going to say ... birthdays tend to be more about Charlotte now. I let her get excited on my behalf.'

Jess smiled faintly, remembering what he'd told her

about villages in Burkina Faso. 'Well, maybe you'll get a nice goat.'

He took her hand again then before pulling her gently to a halt so they were facing one another. 'That reminds me, Jess.'

'Of what?'

He looked hesitant. 'At the risk of making an ever bigger twat of myself . . . I got you something.'

A goat?

'I figure the risk's quite small,' he qualified. 'I've already gone quite far.'

She nodded. 'Yep, tonight you've really excelled yourself.'

He ventured a smile. 'Well . . . this might help. Are you ready?'

Despite herself, she smiled back faintly and shrugged. Her teeth had started to chatter again. 'As I'll ever be.'

Suddenly brighter, he stuck his hand into the back pocket of his jeans. 'Close your eyes,' he whispered. 'Open your hand. All that jazz.'

'What?' she laughed, but she did it anyway. She felt him plant something light in the centre of her palm, and when she opened her eyes, she saw it was a small grey jewellery box. It looked a little battered, and was soaked through. 'What's this?'

'You'll find out if you open it.'

So she did. Resting on the gathered silk inside was a silver necklace with a single tiny pearl at its centre. Slightly tarnished, it looked old, like it belonged to somebody else.

'It's beautiful,' she whispered, and then looked up at him, waiting for an explanation. 'I mean, is there some sort of back story, or . . . ?'

He exhaled stiffly, like he was building up to make a revelation, taking a few squelching paces in the opposite direction before turning back round to face her. 'Okay, I'll say it quickly. I bought you that necklace for Christmas, Jess, 1993. I was going to give it to you that night in the bird hide, but I bottled it. Thought you might think I was being a cheesy twat.'

She stared at him. Her teeth had stopped chattering now.

'So I kept it. I kept it all this time because I had this stupid idea that one day . . . I might have the chance to give it to you properly.' Shaking slightly as he spoke, he reached out and removed the necklace clumsily from its little box before leaning across to fasten it at the nape of her neck. She lifted her fingers to where she felt it against her breastbone, and he moved his hands to her shoulders.

'How does it look?' she whispered.

He smiled and shrugged happily. 'Exactly as I thought it would.' Then he pulled her into a hug, and mumbled into her hair, 'Incidentally, I'm really sorry the quality's not up to much. That was my first stab at buying jewellery. You deserve classier than that after a seventeen-year wait, Jess.'

She admonished him with a squeeze to his ribcage. 'It's *so* worth the wait. Honestly. That's the sweetest thing anyone's ever done for me.'

'Jess, be serious,' he said, pulling back from her and dropping his chin slightly to meet her eye. '*That's* the sweetest thing anyone's ever done for you? Presented you with a crappy old necklace in the middle of a salt marsh at one in the morning?'

She knew he was teasing her really. 'Yes.'

'Then I think it's probably time to get yourself a new boy-friend,' was all he said.

She smiled and thought to herself that, on balance, she would have to agree.

20

Matthew

Wednesday, 16 February 1994

So my beautiful girlfriend was going to be in Venice with the lower fifth on Valentine's Day, and I desperately wanted to be there with her. But it had been looking like the only way that was going to happen was if I purchased my own plane ticket and stalked them all by water taxi.

As it turned out, however, Sexy Santa's broken ankle could not have been more perfectly timed.

Sonia was one of the teachers with her name on the list for the trip – but several weeks after I had somehow fractured her fibula by watching her fall off my front step, Mackenzie asked me to go in her place.

We'd not said a word to one another since New Year's Eve. Sonia was highly aggrieved and convinced that her ankle injury was a direct result of my failure to fancy her, so she'd spent the last few weeks getting most of the staffroom on side. This meant the vast majority of my (mostly female) colleagues now believed I'd tricked her into stripping off at my house before ejecting her on a whim that was no doubt related to lager, football or something I'd read in *Arena*. (I'd been naive enough to think we might both want to keep quiet about the whole thing in an effort to preserve her dignity, so to realize she'd been spreading pre-emptive lies about me in the staffroom really pissed me off.)

Mackenzie's reasoning for banning Sonia from the Venice trip was three-fold. One, she'd been behaving like she'd lost all four limbs in a motorbike accident and it was becoming increasingly apparent that supervising on a school trip was a risky choice of assignment for someone so feeble. Two, I had rudimentary Italian. Three, I got on well with Brett Michaels, who as head of the language department was running the trip. We had bonded previously over our mutual suspicion of the cheap instant coffee in the staffroom and of Lorraine Wecks (also Venice-bound as Sonia's partner-in-crime), as well as our shared disdain for Hadley's most pointless unwritten codes of conduct, like the one to do with keeping facial hair in check. (Brett had once thought it would be funny to ask Lorraine if she needed bringing up to speed on that, to which Lorraine had responded by carefully angling her cup of soup all over Brett's freshly shorn jawline. He had to stop shaving for a while to let the scorch heal up, which marked the start of a minor competition between us to see who could cultivate the hairiest face before someone lost patience and complained to Mackenzie. Our record so far was two working weeks, and I had won. Brett bought me a four-pack of Red Stripe lager as my prize.)

So I'd been all set to go, until Sonia turned up at school three days before the trip with a letter from her GP, claiming she was fighting fit. Brett chose to interpret this literally by going spare and nearly head-butting her. It culminated in the three of us battling it out in Mackenzie's office, with Sonia fake-crying and Brett arguing loudly and angrily over the top of her head.

The upshot, eventually, was that both Sonia and I would be going to Venice – because we all knew that, in reality, Sonia was an emotional wreck who barely had any place teaching at all, let alone limping along at the back and holding everybody up on an awesome holiday disguised as a field trip.

Brett and I exchanged a high five as we left Mackenzie's study. We also failed to hold the door open for Sonia, which wasn't deliberate but Brett thought in hindsight to be quite a nice touch. The battle lines were drawn. It was Landley–Michaels versus Laird–Wecks.

Oh, it was most definitely on.

The illusion of a free holiday faded almost as soon as the plane touched down at Treviso airport, when it dawned on Brett and me at roughly the same time that we were in charge of twenty teenage girls on a week off from private school with well-constructed game plans to fall in love with Italian men. For my part, I was in a state of such nervous distraction for the first twenty-four hours that I barely even noticed Jess, let alone remembered our shaky strategy for getting some alone time on Valentine's night. (She would wander out of her bedroom at eleven p.m. as if sleep-walking, at which point I would Just So Happen to be coming back from checking bedrooms. We'd then dart off down a corridor for a sneaky kiss. Perfect.)

Our second full day of sightseeing was St Mark's Square and a climb up the Campanile. Jess declared that she was scared of heights and wanted to stay down in the square. Like an idiot, I nearly busted us both by turning to her in surprise and saying, 'Are you? You never said.'

I tried quickly to cover it up by muttering something to Brett about checking phobias for insurance purposes before we flew out, and just about got away with it. Just.

Jess was mostly hanging out with her friend Anna Baxter in Venice. The Witches, thankfully, were all at home, no doubt spending their respective half-terms dispersed between shopping centres, bowling alleys and various fast food outlets. I'd recently noticed that Jess had begun to distance herself from them of her own accord anyway; in fact, she really seemed to be thriving at school. The difference was not so much evident in my maths classes – she'd unwittingly signed herself up for compulsory arithmetic progress the minute she became my girlfriend – but in the improvements she appeared to be making all-round. I'd overheard complimentary comments in the staffroom lately from several other subject teachers, and it had actually started to look as if she might be a realistic A-star prospect by the time it came for her to take her GCSEs next year. She was coming across as more studious on this trip somehow too, more engaged – even when Lorraine was monotonously lecturing everybody about Marco Polo with about as much dynamism as a brick at the bottom of the Grand Canal, and it was beginning to seem likely that one of us was going to have to push her in it.

All of this could not have made me happier. But there was something about Anna Baxter that slightly unnerved me, which was that she always seemed to be watching – Jess, me, gondoliers on the make . . . she wasn't so different to Sonia in that way. Wherever I turned, I got the feeling she'd turned there herself thirty seconds earlier and was waiting for me to catch up so she could catch me out.

Having publicly expressed my ignorance of my secret girlfriend's secret acrophobia (*not vertigo*, I informed the assembled group like a typical sodding teacher, *it's not the same thing*), I still only cottoned on to what Jess had been trying to do when the time came for everyone to head up the tower and she shot me a look. But, by then, it was too late.

'I'll stay with you, Jess,' Sonia said loudly. 'I can't get up there with these crutches. You go up, Anna. Jess will be fine down here with me.' And then she turned and smiled at me – only it wasn't a real smile, it was a hollow impression of one: the sort of smile a woman might give her husband if she'd invited the neighbours round for dinner, knowing all along that he was fucking one of them stupid every time her back was turned. It was the sort of look that said: *I know. I know about you two, and I'm going to get to her first.*

I started to panic, probably visibly. 'I could stay too,' I gabbled to Brett. 'Recce the cafes.'

'Nah,' Brett said, looking affronted. 'You're climbing the tower with me, Landley.'

As it turned out, there was a lift, meaning there had been no need at all for Sonia to bow out in the first place, which only served to heighten my suspicion and alarm. So the whole time I was at the top of the tower looking out over Venice, when I was supposed to be counting heads and pointing out the island of Giudecca and the Chiesa di Santa Maria della Salute, or whatever the hell it was, all I could think about was what Jess might be saying to Sonia down in the square. It was absolutely bloody freezing up there, but I was sweating like it was the middle of summer. I kept obsessively craning my neck to try and spot them over 300 feet below us on the ground – but, of course, they were nowhere to be seen.

Brett had one p.m. lunch reservations by the Rialto Bridge at some crappy tourist restaurant he'd picked out of the guidebook. We were all seated outside on the cobblestones, which thankfully came complete with patio heaters, the girls at three pods of tables closest to the bridge, and me with Sonia, Lorraine and Brett nearer to the restaurant itself.

Everyone was wearing their coats and trying to appreciate Venice's beauty on one of the bitterest days of the year.

Hunched up in my favourite denim jacket with the sheepskin collar, I personally would have killed for some rum in my cola. I was finding it challenging to be in the same room as Sonia, let alone share breadsticks and soft drinks across the same table, all the while wondering if she was about to bust me wide open for being a grade-A pervert.

I was desperate to get the chance to talk to Jess so I could find out what Sonia's little game was, and I didn't have long to wait. We'd only been seated about five minutes when I caught sight of Jess pushing back her chair across the cobblestones. I'd become somewhat adept in the art of peripheral vision over the past few months, and I managed to watch her glance at me, make her way to the restaurant and vanish inside it all without looking up once from my laminated photographic menu.

I knew I shouldn't get up and follow her until at least sixty seconds had elapsed, but my impulse control petered out at thirty. I got to my feet, muttering something about needing the toilet to Brett, who was arguing with Sonia about the correct pronunciation of *chiesa* (predictably, it was Sonia who was convinced it should be pronounced *chee-ay-sa*, and with a heavy English accent to boot). I shot a quick glance at Lorraine too, but she had her eyes on the bridge and a breadstick in her mouth. I couldn't be sure that any of them had even noticed me stand up.

Heading across the cobblestones with purpose, like a wino spotting an off-licence, I stepped inside the frigid gloom of the restaurant lobby where I saw off an overly eager waiter keen to seat me all over again. Jess was waiting for me at the foot of a spiral staircase that was cordoned off with a sign that threatened *Divieto di accesso!* along with a yellow hazard warning cartoon of a stick man tripping into an open flame. You had to wonder what the hell was up there.

Jess put a gloved hand out to touch me, but I shook my head. I really did look like a wino now, only one who'd located the off-licence and discovered it to be shut: I had started jigging edgily from foot to foot, partly to keep warm, but mostly because I was feeling really agitated.

'Is this about Miss Laird?' I asked her.

Jess looked nervous too, but it was hard to know if that was because of something Sonia had said or because my consternation was catching. Eventually she nodded. 'Yes.'

A little bud of fear bloomed inside me. I knew we didn't have much time – as soon as Sonia noticed that both Jess and I were missing, she'd be through here like a shot, broken ankle miraculously healed like a cripple on the Sabbath.

'Does she know?' I asked Jess.

'I think she might do.'

'Fuck.' I ran a hand through my hair. It felt damp from the cold. 'What did she say?'

Jess exhaled steadily. 'I made that stuff up about being afraid of heights.'

I admit I was privately relieved to hear that, because it hadn't really made sense to me before. 'Right.'

'Miss Laird's been trying to get me on my own ever since we left Norfolk. So I thought . . . might as well see what she wants.'

An open mind to engaging with Sonia – red flag number one. I bit my lip. 'Okay.'

Before now, I'd always thought it was a good thing that Sonia was about as subtle as a cockerel at dawn, because this generally meant it wasn't too hard to keep one step ahead of her. But I had a horrible feeling that I was about to watch that particular theory crash and burn, in a manner not dissimilar to the stick man who'd had the misfortune to venture up the staircase to my left.

'Um, so I sat with her in the square, and I just started telling her about my mum, and Debbie. You know – all the personal stuff I could think of. I wanted her to think I was cool with talking about . . . well, anything.'

This was a tactic that made sense, because Sonia was a stickler for boundaries, and everybody knew it. Even Lorraine teased her about it from time to time. She carried a 'Teacher Not Friend' key ring and referred girls to the school nurse if she found them crying. Sonia would never have started making conversation with Jess about her personal life unless she thought it was going to give her something she really wanted. Such as priceless leverage over me.

'And then . . . she just asked me.'

I felt in that moment as if I'd been shoved very firmly off the top of the Campanile, which probably explained why I shut my eyes.

'She asked . . . about you and me?' It was beginning to feel as challenging to form words as if I was, in fact, hurtling through the air at terminal velocity – but I had to know.

Jess let out a little gasp, which only served to exacerbate the sensation that I was about to hit the floor face-down at speed. 'No! Not that. Just – whether I had a boyfriend.'

I opened my eyes and, to my relief, everything looked calm and still. 'That's it? Just . . . a boyfriend? Not me?'

She nodded, her face still pink from the cold. 'Yes, that's it. She didn't mention you at all.'

I leaned back against the wall and tried to think, which wasn't as easy as it should have been, thanks to the repetitive strain of piped-in chamber music being spat sporadically through a pair of cheap defective speakers above our heads.

'And what did you tell her? When she asked you that?'

'I said I wasn't interested in boys. I told her I wanted to focus on school.'

Sensible.

'And she said . . . ?'

'She said that was good. But then we couldn't talk any more because Mr Michaels tripped over her crutches coming down from the tower and they started arguing.'

Normally this would have made me smile, but today I couldn't bring myself to feel anything other than deep unease. From out of the cheap imitation frescoes framed with gold plastic on the opposite wall, Sonia's face began to loom, and she was the one with the smile on her face. But it was a sickly triumphant smile – the sort that made my heart pump faster, and not in a good way.

'I think she knows something's up, Mr L,' Jess said then, in case I was thinking we were out of the woods, which I wasn't. (In fact I was wishing that Brett had been looking where he was sodding well going, because it sounded as if Sonia might have had more questions up her sleeve had they not been interrupted by his clown feet.)

Jess reached out to touch my arm, but I shook my head. 'Better not,' I murmured, shrugging her off as gently as I could. 'Someone might be watching.'

Obediently she withdrew and took a step back, glancing around the lobby as if she was worried there might be clones of Sonia hiding behind the polystyrene popes.

I took a couple of breaths that did nothing at all to calm me down. 'Listen, Jess . . . we'd better not be seen together for the rest of the trip.'

I saw her swallow back disappointment, and it truly broke my heart. She'd been so excited when I first told her I was coming to Venice and, like an idiot, I'd made it worse by feeding her all sorts of soppy Valentine's-inspired stories about how romantic Italy was.

'If Miss Laird asks you any more questions, I just need

you to tell her you think she's being inappropriate. Okay?' I didn't wait for her to answer. 'Jess – okay?'

She nodded twice in quick succession. 'She's being inappropriate.'

'And the same goes for Lorraine. Miss Wecks. Inappropriate. *You're being inappropriate.*'

She nodded again. 'Why Miss Wecks?'

'Because Miss Wecks is no better than Sonia. They're both sly as fuck.'

'Are you okay?' she breathed then, by which she probably meant I was coming across like I needed mental health intervention.

'Just don't talk to either of them. Don't say anything else.' It came out much more harshly than I'd intended, but there was no time for me to backtrack because our over-enthusiastic waiter had returned, this time to move us on by waving his menus at our legs like we were lethargic cattle as he gabbled furiously in Italian and gesticulated wildly at the stick man sign. It was time to go.

I exited the restaurant while Jess disappeared into the toilets. As I made my way across the cobblestones, shading my eyes against the bright winter sunshine with one hand and casually pretending to admire the beautiful stonework of the Rialto Bridge, I thought with escalating anger about what Sonia was turning me into. I had become, over the course of a lunchtime in February, the sort of man who whispers, *Don't breathe a word, it's our little secret* into the ears of young schoolgirls. The thought of what a twitching, edgy pervert I was now made me feel physically sick.

Sonia's hawk eyes followed me all the way back to my chair. I could feel the strength of her stare through the dark armour of her sunglasses.

'Point me in the direction of the toilets, Matthew,' she

said loudly enough for everyone to hear, as soon as I'd sat down. 'I'm bursting.'

I was bursting too, I wanted to bellow at her, but with rage. How dare she try to interrogate Jess? I looked after Jess, made her happy. Who was Sonia to start whipping out the intimidation tactics? I suddenly felt almost immeasurably protective of Jess, like I might just be forced to pluck the shitty little bottle of olive oil from the middle of our false-marble table and break it over Sonia's miniature beehive out of pure fury.

But instead, with all the self-restraint I could muster, I simply shrugged and said, 'Sorry, no idea. I went in there to chat up a waitress.'

'Ha!' Brett exclaimed, slamming the table with his palm, making our sad little selection of soft drinks jump. 'I fucking knew it!'

Did you? I thought, not altogether disappointed that Brett saw me as capable of such brazen audacity. From somewhere within my peripheral vision, I could make out Jess rejoining Anna a couple of tables away.

'Brett,' Lorraine hissed at him, her voice pure ice, 'would you mind keeping the expletives to a minimum please? This is a *school trip*.' (Like any of us could forget it. There was no other scenario on earth that would see me sharing a table at a pavement cafe with Sonia Laird and Lorraine Wecks next to one of the world's most romantic landmarks.)

'Oh, pipe down,' Brett snarled at Lorraine.

'I thought,' Sonia said, speaking over them but talking to me, her voice almost quivering with triumph like she was about to play her ace card, 'you said you had a girlfriend, who you loved.'

Brett let out a snort that should have projected cola all over the front of Sonia's cream coat, had he had the foresight to fill his mouth first. 'What? Landley doesn't have a girlfriend. He's more tragic than I am.'

I tipped my head quizzically at Sonia. 'I don't remember saying that. When did I say that, Sonia?'

Sonia went slightly pink as we both recalled her standing in my living room dressed as Sexy Santa with her slightly saggy, milk-white belly, wearing her stupid skyscraper heels, telling me she loved me. I gave her my best *Don't-mess-with-me* eyebrow-raise.

Brett turned to me. 'So? Did you get her number?'

I thought about it for a couple of seconds; thought about what I could say that would piss Sonia Laird off the most. In the end I accidentally-on-purpose picked up her drink, slung the last of it down the back of my throat, snapped a breadstick in half and said, 'Nope. Changed my mind. Her tits were too small.' Then I looked pointedly at Sonia's chest while Brett fell about in hysterics next to me, laughing so hard it was a wonder he didn't give himself a heart attack.

Even Lorraine Wecks allowed herself the very faintest of wry smiles. Sonia, however, simply sat there quite still, her face frozen and dark, like a lake iced over in winter. Even while I was laughing I had a horrible sinking sensation that on this occasion I might have taken it, as my mother would say, a step too far.

For the rest of the trip Sonia refused to speak to me, which suited me fine. I created my own reliable routine of dutifully allowing Lorraine to boss us all around with her clipboard and raised umbrella during the day, before thinking about Jess while masturbating furiously in the shower early evenings, then trying very hard not to stare at her over dinner every night (which thankfully was made easier by

321

the presence of Brett, whose entertaining approach to inhaling his spaghetti al pomodoro was a bit like watching a six-month-old with a bowlful of puréed carrot).

Eventually, on our fifth night in Venice, perhaps mistaking Sonia's post-Rialto wall of silence for sheepishness, I became foolishly willing to run risks again. I caught Jess's eye as she was leaving the hotel restaurant, and she hung back, pretending to peer into the darkened windows of the gift shop while I grabbed a print-out of Lorraine's itinerary for the following day and strode towards her with it. 'Did you get this?' I asked her loudly, waggling it in the air, pleased she'd tucked her own version out of sight in the back pocket of her jeans.

She could clearly sense my desperation. 'I'll be out the front at midnight,' she whispered, whipping the itinerary out of my hand and coolly stalking away from me to catch up with Anna Baxter.

We walked briskly in silence for five minutes or so, hands stuffed safely in our coat pockets, staring straight ahead like we were MI5 agents on our way to a hit. Venice at midnight in February was eerily quiet and dark, the only sounds an occasional clicking of footsteps and the gentle slapping of cold canal water against stone.

'Here,' I whispered roughly, desperately, as we reached a deserted square. The place was overlooked by an amphitheatre of tiny windows, so I grabbed her hand and pulled her out of sight with me into the arch of a building, hoping that its occupant wasn't planning to leave or arrive via the front door within the next ten minutes or so.

'We can't be long,' I whispered. 'If they find us both missing, we'll be in the shit.'

Seeming to take this as her cue to hurry things along, Jess

started to kiss me, hungrily. 'Don't worry,' she breathed. 'I crushed diazepam into Anna's vodka before we left.'

With some effort, I pulled away from her. Though happy to ignore the teacher in me shouting, *Vodka? What the hell were you doing with vodka?*, I did think it was probably wise to follow up on the prescription-drugs-cocktail revelation.

'What the fuck are you talking about?' Despite myself, I couldn't keep my eyes off her mouth. *Stop, Landley. We have to make sure Anna Baxter isn't dead in her hotel room.*

'It sends you to sleep,' she blinked, like that explained everything, which it didn't. 'I stole some from my mum before we came. I thought it might come in handy.'

Jesus. I knew Jess was organized, but I hadn't quite anticipated plotting to the degree of knocking her friends out by force-feeding them muscle relaxants.

'I haven't had any,' she assured me then, eyes wide.

'But Anna has? Jess, that stuff is really dangerous.'

Jess frowned. 'No, it's not. My mum does it practically every night. Has done for as long as I can remember.'

Oh, fucking hell. She thinks it's normal. 'Jess, that's kind of the point,' I said gently. 'Your mum's system is used to that stuff. Anna's definitely won't be.'

She shook her head, like there was something I wasn't getting. 'Me and Debbie have both done it before.' She shrugged. 'We were fine.'

I paused then because it suddenly felt as if I was scratching against the surface of a world that until now had only really existed in the shadow-dimmed edges of my consciousness. And, to my shame, that was exactly where I wanted it to stay.

'How did Anna look when you left, Jess?'

She slid me a grin. 'She was snoring. What about Mr Michaels?'

323

Brett had spent most of the evening sinking illicit Italian beers, and by the time I had tiptoed out of the room, he too was snoring, flat on his back with his mouth hanging open. My only risk had been walking past the peephole of the room next door – given that Sonia probably had one eye permanently clamped to the inside – but it didn't fly open as I passed. I had paused at the end of the corridor for a good three or four minutes too, in case her plan was to follow me out, which she didn't. For now, it seemed, we had got away with it.

'Snap,' I said.

She giggled. 'So we're fine then.' And then she kissed me again.

'I'm sorry it couldn't be just us, Jess, on Valentine's Day.'

'It's just us now,' she breathed. 'Tell me how much you love Italy.'

'I fucking love it,' I told her.

'We should move here,' she whispered against my neck. 'You and me, together. We should move here, together.'

Afterwards, I thought a lot about why I did what I did next. Maybe it was because she'd just hinted at the two of us having a future together and I was getting overexcited. Maybe it was the high of having slipped out of the hotel without being caught. Maybe it was for that exact reason that I wanted to raise the stakes. Whatever it was, I was apparently determined to push things further than they needed to go, because something about doing that seemed to represent the thrill I'd been missing all my life.

'Take off your clothes,' I told her.

She blinked at me, giving an involuntary and understandable shiver against the idea of stripping naked outside in February. 'What?' she breathed.

'No one can see you. Do it. Strip off.'

She trusted me, that was the fucked-up thing about it. I was painfully aware that she probably would have done anything I'd asked of her. And I never would have consciously exploited that – yet the words were leaving my mouth like they were entirely unconnected to my brain.

'Go on,' I urged, almost impatient, and she must have read in my face that I was deadly serious because she bit down on her bottom lip and started to unbutton her coat.

'Fuck,' I breathed, slamming my head back against the brickwork of the archway a little too hard.

She dropped her coat in a thick heap on the floor, kicked off her shoes and discarded her socks, gasping as her bare feet made contact with the cold stone.

'Hurry up,' I growled impatiently, my cock so hard I knew the minute she touched me it would all be over before it had even begun. The anticipation was fucking incredible.

She smiled obligingly and lowered the zip on her jeans, bending over to pull them roughly down and step out of them. I watched the shape of her move in her black underwear as she yanked her pale blue jumper off over her head and finally stood there, striptease nearing its climax, her skin white and shivering, her golden hair splayed across her shoulders like she was starring in some sort of shampoo advert, begging me with her eyes to touch her.

I stayed where I was, like someone had pinned me to the wall, and drank in the sight of her.

She took a pleading step towards me.

'Take off your bra,' I ordered, my voice now virtually gravel.

So with shaking hands she unclipped it and let it fall teasingly to join the rest of her winter clothing on the floor. And she stood like that in front of me for a good ten seconds or so, nipples swollen and stiff against the open air, while I looked at her until she shook, and I thought it was with cold but when I finally touched her I realized it was with desire.

Jess reached down and unzipped my flies at the same time as I pressed her right back against the wall. She drew a sharp breath of shock as its coldness touched her bare skin, but that didn't stop her grappling urgently with my belt, letting my trousers fall to the floor. I had a condom in my back pocket; it was a clumsy moment as I pulled down my boxer shorts, ripped off the foil and fumbled to slide it over my cock, all the while kissing her frenziedly. Finally with both hands free I lifted her up and she wrapped her smooth, long legs round my waist. Then, at last, we were fucking.

Looking back, I think it was then that I first got the feeling we were being watched – but I managed, somehow, to convince myself I was being paranoid. I knew that if I thought too much about that instead of this, the moment would be lost.

I came after only a couple of urgent minutes pressed against the icy stonework, and as I did I found myself whispering, 'I'm sorry, I'm sorry, I'm sorry,' over and over into her hair.

I tried to make it up to her before we went home, with a sappy belated Valentine's present of a *Venezia* mug from the hotel gift shop.

It almost broke my heart when she opened it because she reacted like it was the best present she'd ever received.

Like, ever.

21

Following a night of getting hammered alone on gin and tonics in her living room, alternating *The Best of R.E.M* with *The Best of UB40*, Jess woke up with a strong craving for caffeine, cake and Anna. For various reasons, mostly related to work, their only communication over the past two weeks had been some hastily composed texts and a couple of snatched phone conversations. So she called her.

They met at Cley in the cafe overlooking the nature reserve and sat side by side together at the window. Their seat afforded them an elevated view of the marshes, a vast green patchwork laid out like a thick rug beyond the road, hemmed at its far end by a high brown bank of flood wall and threaded along the horizon with a delicate blue ribbon of sea.

Anna was wearing a turquoise tunic yanked in at the waist with a cord belt, which only served to emphasize the fact that she really didn't have any waist left now to speak of. She looked tired, Jess thought, like someone who'd spent the past month working nights, failing to shower and existing on a diet of microwaveable cheeseburgers and white-label energy drinks.

Jess set down two plates of red velvet cake and pushed one meaningfully in front of Anna. 'Is everything okay?'

Stoically ignoring the cake in favour of a herbal tea and an apple juice, Anna shook her head. 'I've been getting teary. I'm due on in five days. I'm not pregnant, I can just feel it.'

A familiar clench of despondency took hold in Jess's gut, but she shook her head firmly in an attempt at reassurance. 'You don't know that.'

'I do. I can recognize the signs a mile off. So much for visualization.'

'Visualization?' Jess sank a fork into her wedge of cake, the scent of strong coffee ballooning deliciously from the cappuccino in front of her.

Anna nodded sadly. 'Rasleen recommends practising visualization during *viparita karani*. It's a yoga pose,' she clarified, demonstrating with her fingers on the side of her glass. 'You put your legs up the wall like this, then you think about your egg attaching itself to your uterus.'

Jess held the chunk of cake in her mouth, momentarily unwilling to swallow and at a loss to comprehend how Anna maintained such faith in a woman whose increasingly inventive recommendations for conception had yet to be confirmed as either successful or scientifically sound.

Seeming to sense she should address this peculiarity, Anna began to gabble endorsements. 'Simon and I met another client after our session yesterday who said visualization worked for her. Proud mum of two. And you know the woman who presents the local news – oh, what's her name? Looks half asleep?'

Jess shook her head and finally swallowed the cake, allowing herself to be distracted by the combination of sweet, salty frosting and chocolate-laced sponge. The shot of sugar to her bloodstream felt almost narcotic.

'Anyway,' Anna was saying, brushing away the small issue of her temporarily bogus advocate with one hand, 'she was actually visualizing *during* the six o'clock news. You know – while she was reading it.'

Jess wondered if perhaps that was why she looked half asleep. 'And then what?' she asked her.

Anna looked blank and shrugged. 'Weather?'

Jess let out a laugh. 'No! I mean, did she fall pregnant?'

'Within six weeks,' Anna confirmed sagely, with the all-knowing air of a pharmaceutical sales rep on commission for peddling the merits of amphetamines disguised as weight-loss tablets. Seeming suddenly brighter for her own propaganda, it looked for a moment as if she might even take a bite of her cake; but then she appeared to decide against it, slinging back some more of her apple juice instead.

'The cake's for you, by the way,' Jess said, in case Anna needed some encouragement. 'You look like you're still losing weight.'

'I've got five pounds to go before I'm at the optimum weight for conception.'

'You don't have five pounds to lose, Anna!' Jess exclaimed in shock. 'So what – now you're too fat?' She pushed Anna's plate a little closer. 'Please. Eat.'

'Wait,' Anna said, apparently unreceptive to calorific coercion by either subtle or overt means. 'I have to tell you something. I bought Abbie a yoga session with Rasleen, for her birthday . . .'

Jess considered this to have been quite a brave move, given that Anna's middle sister was extremely intolerant of anything she deemed to be New Age, bullshit or both. Her definition of these terms was fairly broad, in that she had huffed at the Glastonbury tickets Anna gave her for her birthday last year before sticking them straight on to eBay, and was innately suspicious of anything organic. She was about as likely to take a yoga guru seriously, Jess thought, as she would an old man with a hosepipe offering cut-price colonics to passers-by.

'Anyway, we went yesterday,' Anna continued. 'Essentially, Rasleen thinks Abbie's a control freak, and she said as much. So Abbie stormed out.'

'Anna,' Jess said, which was the mildest rebuke she could come up with. It was generally an accepted fact that Abbie overreacted to most things, but even Jess could see why she wouldn't want to stick around to be insulted at random by a woman she'd only just met.

'What?' Anna protested. 'She is one.'

'Yes, but you've had your entire life to come to that conclusion. Rasleen's met her once.'

'Well, I think that only goes to show how perceptive she is,' Anna said sniffily.

'Or judgemental,' Jess suggested, taking another stab at her cake. 'What can she possibly stand to gain from causing a rift in your family?' A thought occurred to her. 'Unless she's running a cult.'

Anna steadfastly refused to take the bait. 'She still wants to meet you, by the way.'

'Ha.'

'I'm serious, Jess.'

'I dread to think what she'd say about me,' Jess mumbled through a mouthful of cream-cheese frosting.

'Rasleen would love you,' Anna insisted.

Having heard nothing so far to indicate that Rasleen had ever loved anyone, Jess brushed a few stray crumbs from her chin. 'Well, I'm eating cake, and she wouldn't love that.'

'Once in a while's okay,' Anna said, demonstrating a sudden and uncharacteristic flair for missing the point of things entirely.

'Remind me again – why is she so keen to meet me?'

'I told you, it's part of the holistic approach. It's very

important she gets to know each of her clients as intimately as possible.'

Jess stared down at the walkers and birdwatchers dotted across the fabric of the marsh below them like brightly headed pins in a cushion, wondering exactly when Rasleen's definition of holistic had evolved to include slagging off her clients' friends and family. However, aware that she didn't currently possess the neuron speed to handle all the verbal jousting that would inevitably ensue if she said as much, she opted to remain quiet.

'Good?' Anna enquired, nodding at Jess's now-empty plate.

'I'm hungover,' she confessed, momentarily eyeing up Anna's untouched cake wedge before deciding to resist on principle.

'Carafe?'

Jess shook her head. 'Living room,' she said. 'Gin and nineties music.'

Anna looked wistful. 'Ah, gin. Was this a party-for-one?'

'Yes,' Jess replied firmly. 'And as an added bonus I didn't even need to turf myself out at two a.m.'

'Speaking of being turfed out,' Anna said with a frown, 'what's the latest on Debbie?'

Jess had been keeping Anna appraised of developments in her sister's grand plans for making her homeless, but it had still been a shock to them both when the 'For Sale' sign had finally been erected in Jess's front garden. Last night's little gin fug had inspired her to think she might run out there and take a flying high-kick at it – but she suspected that was the sort of thing estate agents probably charged for, so she'd resisted in favour of cranking up the volume on 'Losing My Religion' instead.

'They've lined up three viewings for this week already.

Debbie's still working from her completely baseless theory that it's okay to sell the roof over my head because Zak happens to be rich,' Jess told Anna now, sipping from her cappuccino.

Beyond the window, edging away from them towards the horizon, a flock of seagulls was swooping and dancing on the light summer breeze, little white balloons against a cornflower-blue sky.

Anna set down her cup. 'So exactly how in-the-shit are you? Financially, I mean.'

'It's bad,' Jess confessed. 'Then again . . . I do like to think bills are only real if you open them.'

Anna managed to frown and smile at the same time. 'Why didn't you tell me? We'll give you some money.'

'I've had a few other things on my mind,' Jess mumbled, by which she meant Will. 'And thanks, but I have so many creditors right now I think my head would explode if I had to add you to the list as well.'

'Not a loan. A gift. You don't have to pay us back, silly.' She took a sip of her juice. 'Is it just that you've not got enough work?'

Jess hesitated. 'Jobs are coming in, but not enough to justify paying myself a decent wage yet. And having to move house and fork out for rent at market rates isn't exactly going to help.' She thought back sadly to a conversation she'd once had with Matthew, sitting on his kitchen floor in the middle of a snowstorm, when she'd joked about asking him to do her books one day. Maybe, on reflection, that wouldn't have been such a bad idea.

'Well, Zak's desperate for you to move in with him. It could be the answer to all your problems.'

'Please don't,' Jess grumbled. 'You sound like Debbie.'

Anna paused for just long enough to let that little

quip slide by. 'Well, you *know* you can always move in with us if you need somewhere to stay. We just might need to find Smudge a temporary home for a little while. Would that really be the worst thing in the world?' she asked gently.

'Yes, it would,' Jess said, blinking away an image of Smudge being led off on a string to be spiritually healed or have his coat dyed purple by someone who would no doubt transpire to be a client of Rasleen's. She looked down at her coffee cup. 'I don't suppose you need any external caterers at Beelings?'

Anna shook her head apologetically. 'Sorry. Simon's still adamant we do everything in-house. I'll work on him. But look – I'll tout your card around in the meantime, punt it to as many guests as I can.'

'Thank you,' Jess said, grateful.

Anna shuffled a bit closer to Jess as two elderly bird-watchers squeezed in next to them on the bench. 'So what's going on with Matthew? Or Will. Or whatever his name is now,' she asked Jess, making a discernible effort to pronounce his aliases rather than spit them out.

Jess had exchanged only a couple of texts with Will since the incident on the marsh last weekend, of which she wasn't about to regale Anna with the details. She'd told her briefly about the fight at the pub, to which Anna had responded by coming down firmly on the side of Zak, despite him having instigated the entire thing.

'When I saw Will at the pub last week,' Jess said, 'he told me he'd bumped into Mr Robbins.'

Anna's recollection was instant. 'Mr Robbins,' she said straight away. 'As in *Red Dwarf*?'

Jess nodded.

'How did that go down?'

'I don't think they spoke. They were just passing. It scared Will a bit, though.'

Anna raised an eyebrow. 'Did it? I'm surprised it hasn't happened before, to be honest.'

'Will looks completely different now,' Jess said with a frown.

'Yet behaves just the same.'

Jess sipped from her cappuccino and said nothing.

'And how's Zak?'

'I haven't seen him. We've both been working.'

Anna appeared briefly to consider this before deciding not to buy it. 'Jess, this whole Zak–Matthew thing is on a collision course. Seriously – it can't possibly end well. You know that. I *know* you know that.'

Jess swallowed and looked down at her plate.

'You said you were going to put a stop to it,' Anna pressed.

'I know. I will. I know.'

'Jess . . . no matter what happens, I could never forgive Matthew for everything he put you through. So if you *did* ever get it together with him, where would that leave us? And what about Natalie, and his daughter? Not to mention Zak. The whole thing's such a *mess*.' She shook her head and said nothing further, presumably so Jess could take a moment to contemplate the inevitable carnage for herself.

If this wasn't emotional blackmail, it felt like its closest relative, and Jess couldn't remember when they had said it was okay to start slinging threats disguised as solidarity at one another.

'You know, he's really not as bad as you think.'

'Try me,' Anna replied, though it sounded like more of a challenge than a reassurance.

Jess made a taut exhale of breath. 'Well, he stayed with

Natalie when she fell pregnant, for one. She told him she was on the pill when she wasn't – but he did the right thing. He could have left, but he didn't.'

'That's what he said?'

'Yes, that's what he said. And now she's planning to do it all over again.'

'Do what?'

'Get pregnant. Force the whole thing on him whether he wants it or not.'

'Sorry,' Anna said, 'but it *is* his sperm.' She wrinkled her nose. 'Not that I'm particularly interested in discussing Matthew Landley impregnating –'

'All right,' Jess said sharply, and Anna trailed off.

'You're wrong about him,' Jess insisted after a short silence. 'He's actually a really nice guy.'

'Hmm.' Anna reassumed her scepticism. 'Because nice guys are generally in the habit of sleeping with schoolchildren and playing away from home.'

'Can you please keep your voice down?' Jess whispered, sensing that the birdwatchers next to them were suddenly more interested in this conversation than they were in their year lists. That would be a first.

'If you want my honest opinion,' Anna said, which was usually how people phrased it when they knew unequivocally that someone would not, 'I think you're looking for a father figure.'

Jess didn't really want to talk about her dad. 'Because Will's older than me?'

Anna gave an affirmative shrug.

'So is that what you were looking for when you met Simon then?'

Anna snorted. 'Hardly the same. When you met Mr Landley – aged *fifteen* – I think that's exactly what you were

335

looking for. Only the whole thing's gone too far now for you to tell the difference.'

Jess was starting to feel emotionally wrung-out. 'The difference between what?'

'Between someone who's real and someone who's just filling a hole in your life.' Anna paused. 'Don't you think,' she said, more gently now, 'that Zak's the one who's real?'

Thinking this seemed suspiciously like the sort of pop psychology sound bite that Rasleen might impress upon a headstand class, Jess considered Zak, and then she considered Will. 'By real do you mean better?'

'Well, yeah. Real's always better. Zak's offering you a future. What the hell is Matthew Landley offering you?'

Jess rested her gaze on the horizon and the strip of sea glimmering invitingly in the sunlight. And then she shook her head, knowing in that moment that Anna was never going to understand. Because for Jess, it wasn't about what someone had to offer her. It was about who they were.

The cafe was starting to fill up with the lunchtime rush as groups of impatient pensioners hovered, ready to swoop for seats. The midday sun had begun to heat Jess's skin through the glass of the window, making her feel too warm and a little claustrophobic, like she needed to get some air.

Finishing her tea, Anna tipped her head at Jess's chest. 'Is that new?'

Jess frowned and looked down, thinking Anna might be about to start reassessing her solar plexus. 'What?'

'The necklace.'

Jess swallowed. 'Oh. No, it's . . .' She'd not yet shared with Anna the story behind it, and felt suddenly disinclined to do so. 'Just something old that turned up.'

Anna covered Jess's hand with her own. 'Don't be angry

with me, Jess. I'm just trying to look out for you, honestly. Because I really don't want to see you get hurt again.'

'If anyone was going to hurt me, Anna, it would never be Will.'

'No?'

Jess only shook her head as she finished her coffee. Because what she had stopped just short of saying was, *No. I actually think it would be Zak.*

22

Matthew

Friday, 3 June 1994

It was the last Friday night of half-term and Jess was in my living room. This small fact alone was enough to excite me, given that my cottage had been off-limits for us ever since Mrs Parker had enquired about my young visitor, and pulling off either privacy or romance in a public place was about as achievable as you'd think, in that it wasn't.

But for the past few nights, the cottage had been back in play, as Mrs Parker was safely over on the Isle of Skye visiting her daughter and son-in-law. Oh yes. I had been receiving the complete itinerary in handy instalments since March.

The timing was ideal, because for a while now I'd been getting this creepy sensation that Jess and I were being watched. At the beach, in the car, by the harbour . . . I just couldn't shake the feeling.

Only last week, we'd been parked up in a lay-by on an isolated country lane that led only to a farm, when I'd suddenly been struck by this weird sense that if I turned round I would see a face outside, pressed up against my window. I hesitated for a couple of moments, almost afraid to look – but of course, when I did, there was nobody there.

It unsettled me enough, though, to suggest we went for a

walk. I knew I was probably being paranoid, but it still would have felt a bit dim-witted for the two of us to simply carry on sitting there like unsuspecting wildfowl at the start of the shooting season.

The light had started to soften by then and the temperature had dipped. The sensation of open space calmed me down almost instantly, reassured me that I had to be imagining things. Together we picked up the footpath that transected the vast map of fields surrounding us, but after walking for only ten minutes or so, Jess pulled me to a pause.

'Listen.'

The sound of music playing somewhere nearby was drifting our way, spilling like birdsong into the stillness of the early summer air.

A short detour from the path revealed the source of our mystery sound to be a complex of converted barns: we had stumbled, as it happened, upon a wedding reception. The grounds were bordered by a patchy hedge of hawthorn, so Jess and I crouched down together behind it, peeking through the gaps in the foliage. The area of lawn and patio surrounding the barns was filled with wedding guests, most of them young, all of them drunkenly exultant. The bride and groom were in the midst of the assembled crowd, and a vast glimmering web of fairy lights hung suspended between the trees over everyone's heads. Among the branches, strings of paper lanterns were becoming moons in an arboreal galaxy as the light began to fade. A barbecue glowed from the other side of the lawn, and waiters clad in black were gliding about with trays of drinks.

It was a remarkable scene, out there in the middle of nowhere, so Jess and I simply sat together at the edge of our hayfield and watched it all, mesmerized. As dusk began to descend, the lights became even more celestial, a miniature milky way that swayed and glowed on the breeze between the branches.

It must have been getting late, because a blanket of cold had sunk over the hay meadow and Jess was starting to shiver. I took off my jacket and slipped it across her shoulders, and she shuffled in between my legs with her back to me, leaning on my chest, head against my collarbone. And as we sat there like that together, I'd occasionally move to brush the hair from her face, or plant kisses on the crown of her head as her hand made dreamy sweeping circles over my leg. It was the most magical, perfect pause – just Jessica and me, drinking in the music and the lights and the intoxicating buzz of chatter and laughter close by.

I realized then how I knew I truly loved her. I'd never once taken her to a restaurant, or the opera, or a hotel, or any of those other places that were supposed to prove you loved somebody – yet here we were, in the rapidly cooling air of a hay meadow on a Saturday night, and we were both as happy as it was possible to be. Even just to feel her breathe against my chest sent contentment spreading through me in a way I couldn't explain.

'Look at them,' Jess murmured, squeezing my hand as we watched the bride and groom twirling round together to the music. 'They seem so happy.'

I looked at her, not them. 'What about you, Jess?' I asked her quietly. 'Do you think you'll get married one day?'

She tipped her head back to look up at me and nodded – crediting me, to my relief, with the requisite emotional capacity to have a slightly more heartfelt marriage proposal up my sleeve than that. 'Definitely.'

'Okay,' I murmured, my mouth against her hair. 'So how would you do your wedding?'

She only needed to think about it for a second. 'Just like

this. I'd want all my favourite songs, and my friends, and a barbecue.' Then she looked up at me again and smiled. 'And you,' she added. 'I'd quite like you to be there too.'

I let out a short laugh. 'Ha! Thank you. Guest of honour?'

'Something like that,' she murmured dreamily.

We carried on watching the dancing for a few more seconds, before she turned her face up towards me again. 'You know, before I met you I wasn't sure I'd ever want to get married.'

'How come?' I asked her, though I probably could have had a decent stab at a guess.

A small frown made her forehead crumple. 'My dad and my mum were so unhappy.' She paused, and the frown lifted. 'But now I've changed my mind.'

I felt a strong compulsion then to ask her if she'd ever thought about starting a family, but I resisted on the basis that she was still so young. I couldn't deny it was something that had been on my mind a lot lately – I was growing increasingly anxious to make a proper commitment to her, for us to finally become a legitimate couple. I'd been thinking about her suggestion in Venice that we could move to Italy, and I sometimes found myself picturing our future together in a tumbledown Italian estate, wild-haired blonde children running around, dogs scampering loose as we worked our way through the carafe of red wine on our crumbling veranda, watching the sun set over the hills. I thought perhaps I'd get a job teaching English or hook up with my father's family and make my long-awaited debut in alabaster.

Or maybe we'd keep it simple and just stay in Norfolk, emerging safely on the other side of Jessica's final years at Hadley Hall unscathed.

I wanted all of that – or any of it. I wanted to plan and be excited and look forward to whatever was coming next.

'So what about the future?' I asked her. 'What do you want, Jess?'

'To be with you,' she said. 'I want what everyone wants. A husband, children. I want to be a famous chef. I want to write recipe books, own a restaurant. Get a Michelin star.'

Not everyone wants that, I thought to myself. *You're different, Jess. You've got something about you that none of the others have.*

'You'll do all of that,' I told her, entirely confident that this was true. 'I know you will.'

Pretty soon after that, it became clear that the mother of all firework displays was about to make an unexpected appearance from somewhere behind our little patch of hedge. Forced to flee, we streaked back across the hayfield hand in hand, a thunderous explosion of colour and gunpowder chasing us down, almost but not quite catching us.

After all my paranoia about being watched, I was relieved that Friday night to be safely in my cottage surrounded by four relatively solid walls. I might even have been feeling pretty relaxed, had I not been in the process of marking maths workbooks at the time, identical graph paper with red covers that were all emblazoned with the Hadley Hall crest.

Ad astra per aspera.

To the stars through difficulty.

Jess was stretched out on my sofa, The Smiths were on the stereo, and tonight all the curtains were firmly closed. Our evening so far had been nothing short of ordinary, but then that was sort of the point. I knew that spending time with me felt like something of an escape to Jess (though I was confident it wasn't *just* about that). I was protecting her, giving her a bit of sodding headspace. Wasn't that the point of a relationship – to shield the other person from all the problems life has to throw at them?

'Come on then,' she was teasing me, 'if you're not going to give me an A-plus now, I'm never going to get one.'

I looked down at her workbook. It was actually pretty impressive, possibly even worthy of the A grade she so badly craved. Her marks had been nudging upwards over the past few months, and I knew how hard she'd been trying. Anyone would think the girl had been sleeping with her maths teacher.

I pretended to think it over before eventually shaking my head. 'You're right,' I said, striking a thick line of pencil across the page before adding a D-minus for effect (I'd rub it out later). 'You're never going to get one.'

She must have already known she'd done a cracking job with it because she grabbed a nearby cushion with a squeal of mock outrage and lobbed it neatly at my head. It missed and knocked over her bunch of carnations, which she had arranged as elegantly as possible in a jam jar.

The jam jar stayed intact but a vast pool of flower water soaked quickly into the carpet. I couldn't have cared less. Jess was genuinely incapable of doing anything to piss me off. She really was perfect – patient, sweet, funny, thoughtful. I wasn't even sure she had a bad bone in her body. Whenever we were together, we just had a great time.

And I wanted all that to continue. In fact, I wanted to be Jessica's boyfriend much more than I wanted to be her teacher, which was why I had decided to leave Hadley Hall at the end of the school year. If we were going to be together, that was the only way it could happen. But I was constrained by my notice period: to be free by the summer, I had to see Mackenzie on Monday.

So I had written out my resignation. It was already in my bag, tightly sealed in a thick white envelope, ready to go.

Jess was panicking about the water on the carpet as if it was some sort of omen that our relationship was doomed. I'd learned that she was pretty big on things like omens and fate – drivel I felt convinced must have come directly from her mother, or her chubby sister, or possibly that weird religious studies supply teacher for whom religion seemed mostly to revolve around telling everybody she was agnostic and hanging dreamcatchers from classroom window frames when she thought no one was looking.

Jess disappeared into the kitchen to fetch a tea towel and then got down on her hands and knees, desperately mopping at the wet patch. 'It's going to stain.'

'Jess – I rent,' I said, in an effort to regain her attention. 'Seriously, it couldn't matter less. The carpet's been here since the seventies. And anyway – I need to talk to you.'

She rocked back on her haunches and looked up at me. 'That doesn't sound good.'

'No, it is. It's really good. But I don't know how you're going to take it.'

She swallowed. 'Okay.'

'I . . . I want to be your boyfriend. Properly.'

She blinked owlish grey eyes at me. 'But you already are.'

'No, like, make it official. I want to stop hiding, looking over my shoulder, panicking every time the phone rings.'

She stared at me, well aware of and (to her credit) normally unfazed by my occasional outbursts of paranoid behaviour. 'But we can't. Not until I'm sixteen, and even then –'

'I'm leaving,' I said quickly, cutting her off. 'I'm leaving Hadley. I've written my resignation letter and I'm speaking to Mackenzie first thing Monday morning.'

344

She stared at me. 'What?' she breathed.

'I've been thinking about it for ages, Jess. I want to be with you.'

'But you love teaching!' She looked for a moment as if she might cry — and not from happiness either, which threw me off a bit. 'You can't leave a job you love because of me. What would you do?'

'Well,' I said carefully, 'I was thinking about what you said in Venice. Maybe after your sixteenth birthday, we could go to Italy. I could do some teaching. Or get in on all that alabaster.'

Jess's jaw sort of flapped at me, like it was completely independent of her face. 'Get in on all that what?'

Maybe moving to Italy was the stuff of fantasies, maybe it wasn't. And Jess was right. I did love teaching — and Hadley too, come to that. But no matter where we ended up, I knew there were things I wouldn't miss. Like the staffroom, with its bitchy politics and crappy coffee that tasted and looked as I imagined tarmac would taste and look if it was scraped from a hot road and whizzed up in a food processor. I wouldn't miss the endless altercations with Lorraine Wecks over who was supposed to sit where in bloody sodding assembly. I wouldn't miss the feeling of Sonia glaring at me if I dared to open my mouth in the Monday-morning staff meeting. And I definitely wouldn't miss having to catch my breath with panic whenever I saw Mackenzie striding purposefully towards me down the corridor, half expecting him to slam me up against a wall by my neck and say, *I know your dirty little secret, you filthy fucking pervert.* I had nightmares about this exact scenario maybe two or three times a week, from which I always woke up drenched unattractively in sweat. Sometimes, I even dreamed that Mackenzie was the one with his face pressed up against my car window.

Much of Hadley's ethos focused firmly around letting the girls know there was a world out there – Mackenzie was a staunch believer in education being as much about shaping outlook as it was about instilling facts, and I totally bought into that. Since getting together with Jess, I'd found myself spending more and more of my time running on about it in class as we paused between the problems I'd chalked up on the board, hoping that at least some of what I said might resonate. But I was beginning to realize that perhaps it was time for me to start following my own advice.

Because I was ready to feel alive. I was ready to go with gut instinct. I was ready to stop feeling like Sonia Laird's icy glare was right behind me everywhere I went – fuck it, for all I knew, *she* was the one with her face pressed up against my window.

Oh yes. I was definitely ready to kiss all of that goodbye.

Since Venice, I had gone out of my way to avoid Sonia. I only went into the staffroom if I knew she wouldn't be in there, and I'd memorized her timetable in order to steer clear of any possible corridor clashes. She had tried to corner Jess on her own a few times recently – asking her to stay after class and glaze her bread, enter into pointless discussion on the best way to avoid a sagging soufflé, that sort of thing – but Jess, far more intelligent than Sonia would ever be, always had some excuse to hand about having a bus to catch, or being on her period, and so far it had worked.

But even more pressing to my mind than handing in my notice, pissing on Sonia's bonfire or even just doing something a bit exciting, was my desire to simply be with Jess. I hadn't been able to stop thinking about the two of us spending a few incredible years in Italy, getting married, one day starting a family. I knew what kind of future we could have – it was there for the taking – and it excited me. I could trip out on the thought of that like a hippy with a pocketful of acid tabs.

Jess was still sitting in the middle of the carpet, wet tea towel in hand, carnations slotted back into the empty jam jar. They looked like a slightly sorry prop from the school play – and as its leading lady, Jess appeared to be lost for words.

So I got down from the table and joined her, taking her free hand in mine as I continued to enthuse. 'You could get a job in a restaurant, and then maybe after a couple of years we could come back here and open that trattoria,' I said. 'We could ship in the wine barrels. We'd be free, Jess.'

'But . . . I can't leave my mum.' The little sparks of excitement that had flared momentarily in her eyes began to fizzle miserably.

I was never going to be Jess's mum's biggest fan, but I was willing to make a small concession for the fact that she was flesh and blood. 'Well, we could come back and visit.'

'What about my GCSEs?' she said quietly. 'My dad really wanted me to get A-levels at Hadley and go to university. It was his dream.'

This I suspected to have come straight from the mouth of her mother: the same woman who couldn't even get out of bed in the morning until she'd knocked back a double gin. Who was so out of it every night that she would frequently wet the bed like a baby. Who had taught her own daughters by example how to crush diazepam into vodka if they wanted a quick and easy way to pass out.

'Your dad would want you to be happy,' I told her then, meaning it. I was sure I was right. What father wouldn't? Being dead didn't make too much of a difference on that front. 'And university . . . well, it might not be for you, anyway. What about catering college or cookery school? There's

347

places in Italy you can do that.' Yes, there were – I'd done the research during several recent lunch hours, hunched over piles of gap-year books in the school library, pretending I was all about the maths.

'You really think I could?' She hesitated for just a moment. There was something about any discussion featuring Jess's mum that always seemed to tip her temporarily into uncertainty.

'Yes,' I said firmly, and I knew I wasn't lying. If there was ever a girl who had the potential to really make something of her life, it was Jess. 'Do you want to do this, Jess? Because if you do, we will, and it'll be perfect.' And then I didn't say anything else because, actually, I didn't want to persuade her. I wanted her to want it like I did.

She looked up at me without saying anything further for what seemed like a full minute. 'Yes,' she breathed eventually. 'Let's do it, Mr L. Let's go to Italy together.'

And after that we simply stared at one another for a while, holding hands and breathing in sync as we both absorbed the magnitude of what we had agreed to do. It felt as if we were readying ourselves to step off the edge of something, like we were counting down to jump with no real way of knowing who or what would break our fall.

Finally, seeming to nudge herself back to reality, Jess sighed. 'I should go. I told my mum I'd be back by ten.'

Well, people probably told her mum things all the time, I resisted the urge to point out – like to steer clear of mixing alcohol with prescription drugs, for example. And look how much attention she paid to that.

As Jess began to cast her eyes around the room for her stuff, I suddenly remembered something. 'Hey, I nearly forgot.'

'Forgot what?'

'Sorry it's taken me so long, but . . .' I reached under the dining table and passed her a gift-wrapped bundle. 'I wrote down what they were but I lost the piece of paper. Found it in a pocket last week.'

She looked bemused. 'What's this?'

'Open it.'

Inside the parcel were three hard-backed books: *Delia Smith's Christmas*, *White Heat* by Marco Pierre White and – most relevant perhaps – Antonio Carluccio's *Passion for Pasta*.

'They were the ones your aunt took back at Christmas.'

She stared at the books for longer than I'd expected, and for a moment I thought she was working out how to tell me that somebody else had already replaced them. But when she finally looked at me, her grey eyes were spilling tears. 'Why would you do this for me?'

'Because I love you,' I said, because I did.

She crept across to me and as she tipped her head up, putting her lips to mine, I felt the dampness of her cheek against my own. 'Thank you so much. I love them. I love you, Mr L.'

'Call me Matthew,' I mumbled into her mouth as I kissed her more passionately than I'd probably ever kissed her before. 'Call me Matthew.' And then I lifted her on to the table and sat her squarely on top of everyone else's maths books, where we fucked each other harder and faster than even I had thought possible.

Several hours later, in the middle of the night, I woke up: *BANG*.

It was dark outside, and I wasn't quite sure why I'd jumped. I wasn't having a nightmare, as far as I could tell: there were no immediate looming visions of Mackenzie or Sonia Laird or pitchfork-wielding child-protection campaigners in my head. But the bedroom, the house and the street were all eerily still; I was alone; and it was freaking me out.

I decided to go and get a glass of water, because that was what I did at school when the girls in my class were having hysterics about boys or periods or prime numbers, and it usually helped me to clear my head.

As I reached the living room and started to make my way to the kitchen, I got the bizarre sensation again that I was being watched. I turned round, almost on auto-pilot, just to prove to myself that I was being a prime twat, never mind prime numbers, and virtually succumbed to cardiac arrest right there on the spot.

Sonia Laird was sitting bolt upright on my sofa like a sodding fright-night waxwork.

'JESUS!'

She didn't say anything for a moment or two. She just sat there, completely motionless (apart from her red lips, which were twitching slightly, as if it amused her to sit there and watch me momentarily spreadeagled against the living-room wall in my pants. Which it probably did).

'What the *fuck*, Sonia!' Even I was surprised by how quickly my fear turned to hands-down rage. 'How the fuck did you get in?'

'This is Norfolk, Matthew,' she said, with a roll of the eyes. 'Nobody locks their doors in Norfolk.'

I thought about telling her that was probably because they didn't know there were red-haired lunatics like Sonia out there on the loose, trying doors. You only had to look at her to know it was worth a dead-bolt or two.

'Nice pants,' she said then, raising an eyebrow and nodding in the direction of my crotch.

For some reason, this pissed me off almost as much as the fact that she was in my living room in the first place. 'WHAT

THE FUCK DO YOU WANT, SONIA?' I shouted. 'Tell me now or I call the police!'

Sonia laughed then, like this was the funniest thing she'd heard in a long time – which didn't exactly surprise me, given that she had the approximate wit of an invertebrate on tranquillizers. Slowly, she raised one of her freakishly long index fingers and rested it against her lips. I could imagine those sculpted scarlet fingernails scraping marks into skin, gouging out eyes. They were evil fingers.

'Sssssh. I don't think you *really* want the police round here. Do you?'

I knew then that she knew – and that this time, it wasn't guesswork. Even Sonia wouldn't have had the nerve to break into my house in the middle of the night unless she had a hefty file of evidence that she could lob at my head like the killer Molotov cocktail we both knew it to be.

She'd got my attention then. Folding her arms, she fixed me with a triumphant stare that was probably not dissimilar to the one I had used when I was taking the piss out of her tits in Venice.

'Well, well, Mr Landley. Quite the smooth operator, aren't you? Shagging a schoolgirl.'

'You need to shut up now, Sonia,' I growled at her, concentrating really hard on not marching over to the sofa and slapping her self-satisfied little face.

'Or what?'

I was reluctant to issue her with death threats straight away. I wanted to hear what she had to say first. 'Just tell me what you want,' I said steadily. I had to play it cool, appear calm, call her bluff. I'd watched *Columbo* enough times to know that, for God's sake.

'I've been following you.' She let out a sigh, flicked her

hair back over one shoulder and crossed her cankles smugly. 'You and Jessica Hart. Everywhere.'

There was an ominous silence.

I didn't for one minute doubt what she was saying. For weeks I'd felt as if we were being watched; now, it all made sense.

'That's right.' She smiled again, and I realized then that this was the moment she'd been waiting for. 'I knew what you were up to, so I've been following you, and I've got the photos to prove it.' She bent over, giving me a gratuitous view straight down her top that nearly made me gag, and reached into the tacky red handbag at her feet. She pulled out a camera, a little point-and-shoot.

Feeling my stomach flip clumsily, I took a step towards her. 'Give that to me,' I growled.

She laughed again. 'How rude! Weren't you brought up to ask nicely, Mr Landley?'

It was becoming obvious that Sonia was not going to be obliging in the manner of a cat caught defecating on my lawn, in that if I shouted at her loudly enough, she might piss off. Still, I had to try and shut this whole thing down as quickly as possible, so that I could get her the fuck out of my house and buy myself some time to think.

'Sonia,' I said, my voice shaking like I was trying to talk a loaded gun from her hand, 'give me the camera. Now.'

She smiled again. 'Or what?'

'Trust me when I say you don't want to find out.'

Sonia eyed me levelly. 'If you touch me,' she said, 'I'll scream blue bloody murder.'

I didn't doubt it, actually. I'd heard Sonia singing in assembly and though she couldn't hold a tune to save her life, she had lungs like a town crier's.

'So if you don't want the police to find out exactly what

you've been up to, *Matthew*,' she continued, like I was so pathetic that even my name didn't warrant taking seriously, 'you'll stay exactly where you are.'

It hit me then, like a violent smack to the nuts, that she was about to blackmail me. She was going to use those photos to get what she wanted. Of course – why else would she have taken them?

At this point, my ongoing tactic seemed to consist of playing along begrudgingly until an escape route became apparent. Admittedly this was not exactly a watertight plan to exonerate myself, but I had nothing else. She'd caught me way off guard, as evidenced by the fact that I was standing in front of her wearing only my pants. 'Okay, Sonia. You win. You've got me.' Despite myself, I couldn't resist giving her a sarcastic little round of applause. 'So what the fuck do you want?'

She smiled again. 'Ooh,' she crooned, 'now you're asking.'

'Don't fuck about, Sonia,' I said, my voice quivering dangerously. Somewhere in the back of my mind, I was naively thinking she might just say *money*, and I tried desperately to recall how much I had in my savings account. I'd been earmarking it for a flat deposit (or – why not? – maybe a down payment on a little trattoria), but if it meant getting Sonia the fuck out of my house, she was welcome to take the lot.

But Sonia wasn't talking about money. Instead, she was twirling a ringlet of red hair around her index finger and smiling the nastiest little smile I'd ever seen. 'Weren't you paying attention, Mr Landley? I already told you. I want you to ask nicely.'

I swallowed. Clearly, the answer was no – I hadn't been paying attention, which given that I was half naked in the middle of a blackmail situation, wasn't a great start. 'What?'

'I want you to say you're sorry,' she said, speaking very steadily, her green eyes flashing with her newly assumed power. 'You're going to tell me you're sorry for treating me like shit all these months. You're going to apologize for dismissing me and making me out to be an idiot in front of all your stupid fucking friends. You're going to beg my forgiveness for looking at me every day as if I'm something you've trodden in.'

But you are, Sonia. You're as horrible as the very worst kind of excrement.

I swallowed and said nothing. I was starting to sweat lightly. I had wanted to put a stop to this, not play her game – but I was beginning to realize they were going to end up being the same thing.

I wondered briefly again if I dared to try and get that camera off her, but then I envisioned the strength of her scream, like an off-key foghorn in the early-morning silence of North Norfolk – a place where you couldn't so much as buy a pint of milk without opening yourself up to a game of Chinese sodding whispers – and decided, with a resigned stab of mortification, that I didn't.

'That's right.' Sonia was fingering the camera meaningfully. 'Say you're sorry, and you get your sordid little reel of film.'

Briefly, I considered the conversation that I actually wanted to have with her. My opener would have been a polite enquiry as to the state of her mental health followed by a series of little newsflashes – *she* was the one who thought it was normal behaviour to keep hitting on me even though she had a boyfriend, then throw indignant little fits around like hand grenades when it didn't achieve the desired result. *She* was the one who had turned up like a prostitute on my doorstep wearing nothing but Christmas-themed underwear, demanding to be seduced. *She* was the one who kept persuading the rest of the staffroom to help her drag out our tiresome little tug-of-war, in which I hadn't even been a willing participant to begin with. The thought of apologizing to this woman – who since the day I set foot inside Hadley Hall had been about as easy to please as a tethered pit bull – repulsed me; but then I looked back at the camera in her hand, and I knew I had no choice.

If sorry is all she wants, just swallow your pride and play along. Think of Jess. Just do it.

I forced my mouth to form the words. 'I'm sorry.' I felt like I was gagging on a particularly repulsive foodstuff, like undercooked egg or a forkful of mollusc. Dry and at a higher pitch than was strictly acceptable, it didn't even sound like my own voice, but Sonia didn't seem to mind. In fact, she looked positively gleeful.

'*Are* you?' she said, folding her arms, enjoying every second. 'How sorry, Mr Landley?'

I should have known that it wouldn't be as simple as just saying the words and booting her off my property, but still I clung to the idea that if I just played along, I could get hold of that camera and regain the upper hand. I could always pour salt into her tea on Monday morning, let her car tyres down at lunchtime, accidentally trip her up as she walked back from supervising detention. The potential for inflicting a long, slow campaign of needling revenge was infinite, I told myself. *Infinite.*

So I swallowed. 'Really sorry.'

'Yeah?'

I nodded. My mouth was annoyingly dry. *Okay, you've got what you wanted. Now just hand over the fucking camera.*

Sonia shook her head and made a sarcastic little tutting noise. I wanted to punch the sound right out of her. 'You're going to have to *show* me how sorry you are, I'm afraid. Saying the words – well, that's just not going to cut it.'

My heart thudded helplessly. 'What?'

She smiled again, and spoke slowly, relishing every word as if it tasted delicious. 'Yeah. Get down on your fucking knees and beg me for forgiveness.'

'Come on, Sonia.' My words came out like I'd dry-heaved them up. 'You've got what you wanted.'

'Oh no, I haven't, Mr Landley – not yet.' She let out a little laugh. 'Don't worry, nobody's looking! Or did you want your sexual exploits with a *child* made public knowledge by Monday morning?' She waved the camera gleefully from side to side.

I made a groaning sound that was supposed to indicate no.

'Then you had better get on your knees right now.' With that, she stood up in front of me and crossed her arms, waiting.

So, I'm ashamed to say, I did it. I got down on my knees right there on the carpet in my own living room and let her make me beg her like a dog, three times, for her forgiveness, apologize for ignoring her, tell her she was beautiful – and all the while she towered over me, snapping away with her nasty little camera.

It must have only lasted a minute or so, but the grinding humiliation was such that it felt more like days. When she finally permitted me to get up off the floor, I experienced a minor head rush, sweating, feeling faint and needing air.

Get it together, you pathetic fucking loser.

'So give me the camera,' I rasped, holding out my hand, failing to meet her eye. In an attempt to preserve my dignity on an internal level at least, I attempted to recall all the things I had promised myself I would do to her when we got

356

back to school on Monday. *Car tyres, salt . . . what was the other thing?*

Sonia laughed shrilly then, smashing my naive illusion of closure like a soprano shattering glass. 'Oh, Matthew,' she said, making a big show of sliding the camera tauntingly away into her handbag. 'You didn't think I was actually going to hand this over, did you?'

The realization of my own stupidity struck me in the stomach with the approximate force of a wrecking ball. I struggled to focus. I thought for a moment that I might have to grab her by the hair and neatly knock her face against my living-room wall.

'Sonia,' I said, my voice shaking dangerously, 'you got what you wanted. Now give me the fucking camera.' I couldn't let her walk away with it, I just couldn't. I even put out my hand, a last vestige of hope.

'Oh no, Mr Landley.' She patted her handbag and – evidently sensing my panic and the related possibility I might be about to do something rash – began to edge backwards towards the front door. 'This is staying with me. In case you ever decide to start behaving like a cunt towards me again.' Her eyes sparkled with greedy delight at the prospect of forever having a hold over me. 'But thank you for being so game.' She started laughing. 'That was absolutely priceless.' She offered up a jaunty little wave, waggling those poisonous red fingernails, before finally leaving.

I sank straight back on to my knees, hanging my head right down towards the carpet like I was about to be sick.

I knew then that it was over. I knew then that we were going to have to leave.

23

Saturday evening, and a fine mist of pre-thunder drizzle was trying and failing to disperse some of the humidity that had slithered eastward from the mid-Atlantic via Wolverhampton last week to hang selfishly around like a hot fog ever since. Jess was at work in the small unit she rented near Carafe, preparing salted cod fishcakes for a lunch party the following day. She paused when she heard car tyres, ripping off her vinyl gloves and quickly rinsing her hands, hoping it might be Will.

Through the glass panel of the front door, only an enormous bunch of flowers was visible. As she hesitated, Zak's head slid out sideways from behind a purple chrysanthemum.

Her heart flexed slightly. Not Will. For one reason or another (one being Natalie, the other being Charlotte), she hadn't seen him since that night out on the marsh, and she was missing him.

She opened the door. 'Do chrysanthemums even come in that colour?' was all she could think of to say as she pushed a damp strand of hair from her face, already strangely resentful of the fact that Zak would probably be expecting her to gasp and swoon under the enormity of his gesture. She noticed, somewhat ungenerously, that the bouquet contained no carnations.

He stepped past her, swiping the flowers against her chest and smothering her whites in powdery yellow pollen, possibly deliberately. Oddly, she noticed, the blooms barely carried a scent.

'You're welcome,' he said, making a big deal of offloading the bouquet into the sink in the manner of a harassed executive forced to shoehorn the funeral of an ancient relative in between a Canary Wharf lunch meeting and after-work cocktails in the West End. He glanced at Jess's iPod. 'Oh, okay. Now it all makes sense.'

The music was Ani DiFranco, Zak's least favourite singer ever – mostly because she was politically minded and an advocate of feminism, and Zak was definitely neither.

'What all makes sense?'

'The twitchy suffragette act. I can spot it a mile off.'

Jess sighed. 'It's not an act, Zak, I'm just busy.'

He pushed a hand through his hair, a small gesture that indicated he was already struggling to preserve his own patience – though he managed to style it out with a smile. 'Well, that's a relief. Since I've only just turned up, I'd have thought that even you would find it hard to be pissed off with me already, Jess.' He checked his watch to make his point, then leaned back against the work surface to observe her.

'Well, give it ten minutes,' she mumbled, failing to look at him, feeling suddenly and stupidly self-conscious in her stained whites, clogs and hairnet. She tried to forget the times he'd turned up here unannounced and they'd had sex against the sink, and once on top of a chopping board where she'd been rolling pastry for an apple pie. Zak had thought it hilarious that the following morning she was still emitting a tiny fog of flour from her knickers; Jess was more annoyed that the pastry had gone to waste. They'd done it in the cold store once too, a sort of thrill-thing that she secretly worried fell somewhere on the same spectrum as erotic asphyxiation – but in the end she had been so paranoid that the door was going to shut on them, condemning them to a long and horrible death by hypothermia, that she couldn't really get into it. That evening had concluded with Zak roaring back off down the A11, playing Eminem at top volume and making repeated calls to her mobile for the sole purpose of ranting at her for spoiling a great weekend.

'Well, I must say, you look beautiful,' he said now. 'How many girls can pull off a hairnet and clogs?'

She attempted a smile but it didn't come as easily as it once might have. 'I need to finish off these fishcakes.'

'Hmm. I wondered what the smell was.' He wrinkled his nose, then shrugged and wandered over to the fridge. 'Any wine?' He stuck his head into it optimistically, like he was half hoping it might turn out to have a false back leading to a magical world of lonely supermodels, Carlsberg on tap and a rolling cull on poor people.

'Sorry,' she told him. 'Only Amontillado sherry.'

'Does it contain alcohol?'

She paused. 'Yes, Zak. It's sherry.'

'That'll do then.' He followed her gaze to the cupboard on the right of the cooker hood, opened it and extracted the sherry bottle. He removed the half-screw half-cork with his teeth and spat it into the sink before throwing back his head and taking a long, hard glug like he was drinking orange juice straight from the carton. 'Oh, baby,' he declared as he eventually came up for air, and she wasn't sure if he meant her or the sherry.

'So, Jess,' he said then, lowering his head to meet her eye. 'This is no good. How come we haven't seen each other for two weeks?'

Jess pulled on a fresh pair of gloves and resumed shaping. The mixture itself was simple – just salt cod, potato and a touch of white bread – but the magic came in the hot sauce accompaniment. Moulding the little patties, sticky and damp against her fingertips like potter's clay, should have been a therapeutic and creative process, but this particular client was insistent on everything being uniform. A long-time sufferer of OCD, he had recently sent a meal back at Burnham Manor because it wasn't arranged with *quite* the right level of symmetry on the plate. And that was after he'd called in advance to request it.

'You know why,' she said mildly. There'd been back-to-back work commitments on both sides – Jess was moving into her busiest time of year, and Zak had cancelled on her last week when a colleague asked to swap shifts. This had disappointed her more than it might usually have done, because at that point, she'd already made her decision.

She had to – *had to* – end it.

She'd realized too late that Zak needed to be with a girl who wanted everything he had to offer. He was simply one of those guys who was all about the package – for the right girl an unbelievable catch, exceptional enough on paper even to cancel out the worst of his faults. To a different girl, perhaps, Zak's good looks and passion, amusing anecdotes and undoubted charisma would probably make it matter less that he was quick-tempered, possessive, and apparently above keeping things casual yet with a version of commitment that could loosely be described as setting out his position and refusing to budge.

It was funny, in a way, because Jess was beginning to realize that the girl Zak really wanted was probably a lot like Octavia – a woman whose territory was more mews house than marsh, who cared about postcodes, who craved cars with added horsepower and credit cards with no spending limit. Who would kill for a pair of designer shoes, even if they were two sizes too small. The reality, Jess knew, was that Zak had probably been happy with Octavia, right up until the moment he'd discovered her with his brother at the theatre, wobbling away on top of a cistern.

His natural reaction to all the operatic unsavouriness, of course, had been to seek out Octavia's opposite, so that he might have a chance at least of avoiding an encore. And he had been the antithesis of Jess's usual type too. When they'd eventually stumbled upon each other, they both believed this strategy to have led them to a rare find – a gem to be joyfully plucked from the muddy aftermath of a divorce or series of disastrous dates. But in fact, she realized now, all that had just been the novelty of newness, which had carried them as far as their one-year anniversary before dumping them rather unceremoniously straight back in the mud they had come from.

Perhaps if Jess had moved to London when he'd first suggested it she might have discovered all this sooner, but the distance had enabled her to conveniently dip out of reality several times a month. It wasn't even to do with Will, in the end. It really was all about Zak.

Jess turned a fistful of fishcake mix over between her palms, rolling it into a ball before flattening it gently with the heel of her hand against a peppered mound of organic white flour. And although it went against every one of her principles, she knew she would now have to crack out the pastry cutter. Just the idea of it made her wince. She took a deep breath, shook some flour over it and bore down on her lovely, irregular fishcake. The act of popping it from the cutter was like making a child colour inside the lines, she thought. *Takes all the beauty out of it.*

They said nothing else for a few more moments, the only sound Ani's voice, sublime against the silence of the room. Eventually Jess moved the fishcake carefully to one side and scooped her next handful of mixture from the bowl, at which Zak jumped impatiently off the counter, still clutching the sherry bottle by its neck like he'd been swigging from it since noon.

'Right, come on. Can't you leave that until the morning?'

'Er, no?'

'Okay,' he said, oddly agreeable. 'I'm going to come back later and pick you up.'

She hesitated. 'Where are we going?'

'The beach house. I want to stare at you over dinner.'

He couldn't be more different to Will, the man who had waited seventeen years to present her with a necklace because he was worried about appearing cheesy. Zak, on the other hand, lived for cheese. He was probably planning champagne and candlelight. He was probably planning oysters. Hell – he was probably planning lobster.

She agreed to meet him later for one reason: she was going to finish it. Tonight she was going to end it with her charming practitioner of emergency medicine, once and for all.

'I hope you're hungry. I fancied lobster.'

Kicking off her flip-flops, Jess stepped on to the icy polished stone of Zak's vast hallway. The space smelt of vanilla oil and musk – a comforting, homely scent that was slightly at odds with the person she knew Zak to be. There were flowers too, and mood lighting, which made Jess feel a bit like she'd wandered barefoot into a five-star boutique hotel or exclusive wedding venue. She wouldn't have been surprised to see a butler step out coolly from behind the coat stand to offer her a glass of something chilled. Or maybe complimentary slippers.

'Oysters to start,' Zak added.

Of course.

The beach house was inverted, which meant the bedrooms were downstairs and the living space was on top. It was better that way, he'd told her before, if you had a view.

She followed him up the stairs, conscious that her bare feet, still warm from the heat of the day, might be leaving an inelegant trail of damp patches behind her as she walked.

The exterior of the house, perched just behind the sand dunes overlooking the beach, was what architects would hail a triumph and locals would call an eyesore. A combination of steel and glass, its design was all very self-storage warehouse, the only nod to its stunning coastal location an occasional window mimicking a porthole – hardly enough to appease the neighbours. But the interior was easier to like, with its clean lines, muted palettes and plush textures. The ceilings were low, and the place felt surprisingly cosy where she'd initially expected draughts, sharp edges and acres of cold, hard flooring.

Upstairs, the vast open-plan living space was designed to dazzle. The far wall, which was made entirely of glass, came on hinges, and Zak had opened it up to reveal an oak-decked balcony boasting a dramatic vista over the North Norfolk coastline. Tonight, the view was even enhanced by a blood-red sunset, complete with the sound of the sea gently pulsing as it worked the shoreline below. The setting couldn't have been more perfect if Zak had ordered it in.

He was dressed smartly for the occasion in a sharp grey shirt – sleeves folded carefully to the elbows – and pressed black trousers, though his feet were bare. The table on the balcony was laid for dinner, an elaborate display of crystal and white linen, red roses, a candelabra and champagne on ice.

Jess hesitated, wondering if she should just tell him now and get it over with; but before she could say anything, he was murmuring, 'Take a pew, beautiful,' and pulling out an oversized cushioned rattan chair in shades of cream and chocolate that would have been far better suited to a beach club cabana in Marbella. It was big enough for two, really, and as she sat, she instinctively tucked up her feet underneath her.

The view was stunning. Wisps of cloud were strewn across the sunset like they'd been scattered deftly over it by hand, and the sea had turned flamingo-pink.

Zak flicked the remote on the sound system. It took her a couple of moments to place the music, elegant trumpet jazz, and she felt him watching for her reaction.

'Christian Scott?' she guessed.

'I remember you saying you liked him,' he replied smoothly. Removing the champagne bottle from the chiller, he popped the cork, dripping fat beads of condensation on to the tablecloth as he filled their glasses.

She nodded. She had mentioned it, she remembered now, on the very first night she'd met him at that wedding reception in Holkham, when she'd been drunkenly and ungraciously criticizing the playlist for being a bit too heavy on the Billy Joel. By the time she'd started reeling off a list of her own favourite musicians, she could have sworn he'd zoned out – so she was surprised to discover now that, actually, he'd been listening to every word.

He raised his glass then, and waited for her to do the same. 'To us,' he suggested.

She hesitated, but he went ahead and chinked her glass

anyway, so she let it slide and they both drank. The champagne was dry and creamy, a pale shimmering gold, and it made a beautiful buzz as it settled softly in her stomach.

She could feel Zak's gaze trained steadily upon her. A slight breeze tickled the hair at her face and she brushed it back.

'You're looking very brown,' he observed. 'It suits you.'

'Thanks,' she said. She wanted to make a comment about his nose seeming better now, but she thought she could detect on it the very faintest traces of concealer, which she suspected he might get defensive about.

'I love your dress too. You look stunning.'

Jess had deliberately chosen a dress she thought might not be to Zak's taste – a wispy creation of loud, clashing colours in a particularly bold geometry. It was long enough, thankfully, to cover the large brown smudge that remained on her thigh – the blueprint of a faded bruise which she now suspected might never fully disappear; a mark, like the scar across her palm, that would always remind her of Will. She enjoyed the way the dress set off her tan but it was the sort of outfit that would normally make Zak wince, in the way that most people winced at girls with their knickers on show falling out of nightclubs.

Not knowing quite how to begin what she wanted to say, she looked down at her hands, gripping the cold stem of the champagne flute. 'Look, Zak, all of this . . . the music and the champagne and –'

'You don't like it?' he said with a smile, as if this was inconceivable.

'Well,' she said carefully, 'it's just that lately I've been thinking that –'

'I want us to start again, baby,' he said quickly, cutting her off. 'I want you to come and live with me in London. *Vena vivir conmigo.*'

'Zak.' She shook her head slowly. 'We've been through this.'

He leaned forward, setting his drink down on the table. The flames from the candelabra were reflected like fireflies against his glass and in his eyes. 'Then let's go through it again. I'm serious, Jess. I'm sick of you being here and me being there, all this to-ing and fro-ing.'

The to-ing and fro-ing didn't just apply to their geographical locations, she thought. Was he forgetting their frequent bickering, their fundamental differences, their general inability to make it through a weekend without falling out in some way?

She looked away from him and out across the sea, taking another sip of champagne to buy herself some time, the bubbles gently rushing her bloodstream. The strength was running out of the sun and into the water, streaking it pink and orange like someone had swilled paintbrushes in it.

Zak misinterpreted her silence then in a way that only he could. 'It doesn't make sense for me to move to Norfolk, Jess. It never did.'

Jess concluded silently that he was definitely right about that.

'Debbie told me she's selling your house. So you're going to have to find somewhere else to live anyway. This is the perfect opportunity to make a fresh start.'

Bloody Debbie.

For the past few days, Jess had been attempting to put all her worries about the enforced relocation to the back of her mind, finding gin, Portishead and fashioning small effigies of Debbie from tin foil before crushing them with her thumb to be quite soothing.

'Look, my job is here,' she insisted. 'I've worked really hard to build up my client list. I couldn't just move to London, even if I wanted to. And really, Zak, that's the point, because the thing is –'

He smiled condescendingly, raising a hand. 'Jess, don't get me wrong, but this is Norfolk. A great weekend bolthole but hardly a booming economy.'

'I *think* we've touched on this before, Zak, but generally it's the weekend boltholes that obliterate local economies in the first place. Just a thought.'

He smiled serenely, completely unfazed, like he had in mind some complex fiscal theory to completely disprove her argument that she would never be able to grasp. 'Look, you keep saying your work is what's keeping you here.' He shrugged, like it couldn't be simpler. 'Fine, you've got clients, but your profit margin's an embarrassment, frankly. Move in with me, I'll get you into NW3 and you'll triple your turnover in the space of a week.'

'Don't talk in postcodes, Zak. Please. It means nothing to people outside of London and it's really annoying.' She took a brief swig from her glass and tried to calm down.

Why was he getting to her so much? *Why am I even having this argument?*

'Okay,' he said, with a slow smile like her anger was somehow, inexplicably, charming him, 'I'll get you into the *best neighbourhood* in London and you'll make a fucking fortune. Does *that* mean something?'

A long time ago, it might have done. She might once have been able to picture herself catering private parties for crowds of Magic Circle lawyers in houses with chandeliers for lampshades and five floors instead of two.

It might once have excited her to think about wiping clean all her bills, about waltzing into Starbucks for a *Venti* and not having to pay for it with a fistful of coppers, about spoiling her nieces with fabulous birthday presents. But so much had changed since then, and she knew now that Zak's little postcode-based fantasy couldn't have mattered to her less.

'Well,' she said, looking down at her champagne as Christian Scott's trumpet called out to her in hot, breathy blasts from the living room, 'I think you're asking me for all the wrong reasons. You're asking me because I'm about to be made homeless. And probably because you shared a long car journey with my sister two weeks ago and she put the idea into your head.'

'Bullshit,' he said straight away. 'I'm asking you because I love you. *Estoy enamorado de ti.*'

Jess replaced the urge to speak with another sip of champagne. He had said it to her before, but never like this, facing her almost-sober across a table without the crutch of being able to disguise what he'd just said with sex or the final drink of a long bender. She stared at him and felt strangely crushed, disappointed, like he'd taken significant words and squeezed all the meaning out of them. Because she didn't believe that he did love her, not really. Zak was a man who fell in love with concepts, with the idea of himself as the star of his own complicated TV drama. That was how he was able to detach himself so easily from the daily horrors he witnessed in the A & E department of a London hospital – because other people were simply the supporting cast, the cameos, the women-with-prams. He, Zak, was the star of the show, and if it suited the screenplay on this particular warm night in June to tell her he loved her, then fuck it – why the hell not?

Dusk was looming. The sea continued to gently move, expanding then collapsing like the motion of deep breathing as it began to fall asleep.

'You know, your sister is of the opinion that you're madly in love with me,' Zak said then, which was his way of prompting Jess to confirm it. 'She told me that.'

Jess blinked. 'Zak, this is going to sound harsh, but Debbie has her own little agenda in life. Always has done. She's probably imagining that if I move in with you, it'll somehow make her richer by association.'

'Financially?'

'No, spiritually . . . yes, of course financially. Debbie is obsessed with money.'

A soft breeze picked up then, travelling in quick gasps across the balcony and making the skin on her arms tighten slightly.

'We could have an amazing life together, you and me, Jess. If you want I could take a break from medicine. I've been thinking of doing that anyway. Christ – you wouldn't even have to work, if you didn't want to.'

It made her angry, almost, that after all this time, he still didn't know her at all. *You've got me all wrong. That's not what I want from life.*

'And you'd bring Smudge, of course. He'd like the roof terrace, don't you think?'

'No, he could never live in a city,' Jess mumbled. 'He's a border collie, not a shih-tzu.'

Zak frowned. 'What's the difference?'

She stared at him. 'Did you just say, "What's the difference"?'

'Er, yeah. Let's just say I feel about dogs the way you feel about high heels.' He slugged back more champagne and met her eye. 'I can take them or leave them.'

She swallowed and looked down. 'Okay, Zak.'

'Is that, *Okay, Zak, I'll move in with you*?'

'No,' she said firmly, to avoid any further confusion.

He beamed as if she'd just said yes and leaned forward to top up her glass. 'Oh, we can work on that, baby.' He set the bottle back into the chiller and grinned, bizarrely convinced that he was making headway. 'Hungry yet?'

It seemed mean-spirited to say no, but the thought of oysters and lobster was making her feel slightly queasy. Maybe because she'd been drinking on an empty stomach; maybe because it seemed a bit like the culinary equivalent to serving her up some scratchy red lingerie and expecting her to thank him for it.

'The oysters are ready and I've got a chef on standby to cook up the lobster linguine.'

She stared at him. 'You're not serious. Here?'

'Why wouldn't I be serious? Thought you might enjoy being catered for, for a change.'

This was embarrassing. 'Oh,' she stuttered. 'Who is it?'

'Who – the chef?'

'Yes. Is he local? Do I know him?' *Please say no. Please say no.*

'No, he's from London. Friend of an acquaintance. Paying him a small fucking fortune.'

Relief that he wasn't a local competitor was swiftly replaced by a creeping sense of mortification. 'Well, where is he?'

'I told you, he's on standby. He's downstairs in the games room playing *Grand Theft Auto*.'

'Wow.' She'd been asked to do a few strange things during her private catering career – dress up as a Tudor queen, speak only in French using pre-determined phrases, cook fillet steak as a one-off for a pair of committed vegetarians who hadn't touched meat in twelve years – but she'd never before been locked away in someone's third living room with a video game, waiting to be summoned.

'I know.' Zak picked up his phone. 'Shall I call him, tell him to come up?'

'Let's have the oysters first,' she suggested, hoping to delay the inevitable. She was quickly starting to realize that she should never have come, that by even agreeing to dinner with Zak tonight, she had given him the wrong impression.

'Okay. Wait there.' Zak put down his glass and disappeared.

Jess sat up, setting her feet back down on the floor and taking a long slug of champagne as she attempted to allow Christian Scott to drown out the noise in her mind.

'So, I've been meaning to tell you,' Zak said then, returning with a white china platter heaped with ice, lemons and oysters in shells. He moved the candelabra aside to make room for it. There was already a finger bowl ready and waiting, the red head of an open rose floating prettily on top of the water. He set the platter on the table and then sat back down. 'I finally remembered how I know your friend Will Greene.'

Jess's heart did a small somersault as Zak leaned forward and plucked an oyster from the ice. A couple of cubes rolled off as he did so, skidding from the edge of the table and shattering messily on the decking. He ignored them, lifted the shell to his lips and sucked, before flinging it down with a clatter on his plate.

'Well, go on,' he said, turning his attention to her. 'Dig in.'

Jess hesitated. The name Steve Robbins was making panicked laps of her mind like a startled bird. Could Zak have come across him? Had Mr Robbins somehow managed to track Matthew down?

'Go on,' Zak urged her, more sharply this time. The expression on his face had darkened slightly.

Reluctantly, she lifted one of the shells from the platter and sucked the oyster from it, allowing it to slip down her gullet without so much as tasting it, though she did feel its icy sliminess. She mashed her lips together before chasing it down with champagne.

'Good girl,' Zak murmured, pressing her leg with his foot beneath the table. 'Now, what were we saying? Oh yes, Mr Greene. Our man of mystery with the quick fists.'

Jess moved her leg away. Zak leaned back in his chair and smiled, like it pleased him to make her uncomfortable. 'God, baby, you look all flushed and nervous. Stop fidgeting.'

The dusk had almost enveloped them, the water now strangely still. She looked away from him, out across the sea, and attempted to ignore the heat of his stare. 'Don't call me that, Zak,' she whispered.

He gave a short, dismissive laugh, swallowed another oyster and flung the shell down on to his plate. 'So, this Will character. You know, it was bugging me, Jess. I *knew* him, but I couldn't say where from. Something about his face was just so . . . familiar.'

Jess braced herself.

'And then the other day, I had this patient . . .' Zak took a swig of champagne and smacked his lips together. 'He'd tried to kill himself, actually. Chased down a few packets of paracetamol with five years' worth of vodka in the space of five minutes.'

Jess didn't interrupt him to ask if the poor guy had made it. She half suspected the story would turn out to be figurative anyway.

'*Apparently*, his wife had caught him with a load of questionable images on his laptop.'

Jess felt her entire body tighten, like he'd trapped her in a vice and was slowly inching it shut.

'Most of the pictures were of children,' he said matter-of-factly. 'She'd called the police.'

'What's your point, Zak?' Jess asked, her voice small. She felt suddenly cold, like his story had brought with it an easterly wind.

'Well, it jogged a memory.' He picked up his napkin and dabbed at his mouth. 'Involving that idiot Will Greene. Isn't that fascinating?'

She said nothing.

'Three years ago, when I was working at a different hospital, I treated an attempted suicide. Very similar. Pills. Vodka. Last-minute change of heart. Waste of everyone's time.' He sipped his champagne and regarded her steadily. 'Anyway, I had a colleague check the records. Monday, ninth of June, 2008. Guess what his name was?'

Jess felt the colour slowly sink from her face. It would have been Will's fortieth birthday.

Zak's stare gradually hardened. 'His name was Will Greene.'

She swallowed and looked down into her glass. It briefly occurred to her that she had never once shared champagne with Zak when it felt like a celebration of anything – and tonight was beginning to feel increasingly like a last supper. 'You're not supposed to do that, Zak,' she managed to say eventually, though even as she spoke, she wasn't sure her voice was loud enough to be heard.

'He'd stuck in my mind, you see, because the nurses said that while he was coming round he kept saying this girl's name, over and over. Wouldn't shut up about her apparently. Anyway, eventually one of them asked who this bloody girl

374

was that he kept gabbling about. Do you want to know what he said?'

Jess shook her head. She felt as if she might self-combust at any moment.

'He said it was a girl he'd sexually assaulted, a *child*, and he kept saying he couldn't live with it any more.' He leaned back in his chair. 'He's done time, Jess. Your friend's a convicted sex offender.'

For a moment, she forgot to breathe.

'The fucking idiot couldn't remember he'd said anything when he woke up the next morning. But everyone else did.' He leaned forward, his eyes brimming with malice. 'So there you go. This guy I keep seeing you with is a *convicted paedophile*.' He drove his index finger on to the table for emphasis, just in case his words weren't enough. 'Admitted it himself. How do you feel about that?'

Finally, she permitted herself to exhale.

'Well?' He was waiting for her answer.

She mumbled something incoherent.

'He was fucking pathetic, Jess, honestly. Miserable cunt – wobbling and crying and spewing up all over himself. He was trying to keep the whole thing a secret from his girlfriend too, that was the best bit. I mean – *Hello? You're a PAEDOPHILE.*'

Zak had started to go a bit red in the face, like he did when he was talking about religious fanatics or people he went to school with who now had more money than he did.

'Was she there?' Jess whispered. 'His girlfriend?'

'Was she fuck. They'd had a steaming row and she'd fucked off with the kid, he reckoned. Refused to let us call her. Refused to let us call anyone. Pathetic.' He shook his head, visibly attempting to soothe his own hatred with another swig of champagne. And then he set down his glass and fixed her with a steely gaze. 'You know, I had this crazy little theory about you and him.'

Jess went very still.

'I had this theory that you'd shagged each other. Had a one-night stand or a little fling.'

Breathe. Breathe.

He paused. 'I mean, if you'd done that . . . *ugh*. You'd feel dirty now, wouldn't you? That would just be . . . well, it would be pretty disgusting, wouldn't it?'

'Okay, Zak,' she said, finally biting.

He held up his hands, all innocence. 'What? Just looking out for you, *cariño*.'

'Can we drop it now?'

His eyes narrowed. 'You know how much I hate a liar, Jess. Octavia was a liar. I would hate to think you've been lying to me too.'

She held the urge to speak in her mouth.

'Thank me if you like,' he said then, throwing her a sarcastic little nod. 'For saving you from someone like that. It's decent of me, I know.'

'Drop it now, Zak. I'm serious.'

There was a pause. Finally, he was finished toying with her. 'All right, Jess,' he said. 'I'll drop it, if you promise never to see him again.' He swigged from his glass. 'And while we're at it, I'll make you a little promise of my own. If he comes anywhere near you again, I'll see to it that his legs get snapped in half and everybody finds out about his grubby little secret. So, do we have a deal?'

She shut her eyes briefly, and the tears began to fall.

'Oh, and Jess? I really do think you should consider moving to London with me.'

She swallowed, hardly able to form the words, unable to look at him as she spoke. 'Or what?'

He leaned forward and plucked another oyster from the pile of ice. It was dribbling now, melting along with Jess's brief illusion – if she'd ever really had it – that she might have been able to finish things with Zak tonight.

Leaning back in his chair and tipping the oyster down his throat, Zak swallowed, then shone her a winning smile. 'You must remind me to tell you what happened to my brother just before he left for San Francisco.' He fired a wink at her. 'Better not while we're eating though. Come on, baby. Have some more.'

As midnight approached he tried to kiss her, and for a couple of moments she let him before pulling away. The feeling of his lips on hers made her stomach clench, the scent of gutted shellfish filling her nostrils. Zak's breath smelt rankly of parsley and garlic, the remnants of their lobster dish.

He waited for her explanation, eyebrows raised, carefully cultivated threats at his fingertips. She had to tread carefully, she knew that.

'I just need some time to think,' she said, swallowing. 'About London. I think I want to do it . . . I just . . . I need to be sure. Can you give me a few days?'

Though he had one arm locked round her, even Zak wasn't quite animal enough to try and force her into bed. She had to trust him on that front at least.

He was chewing it over. There was not a lot else he could do at this stage. 'Fine,' he said eventually. 'I'm working tomorrow anyway. But I'll be back on Friday. You can tell me what you've decided then.' He fixed her with his gaze. 'Though I'm pretty sure I know what your answer will be. I'll have the champagne ready and waiting.'

*

Twenty minutes later, she was climbing into a taxi, shutting her eyes against the thought of Zak standing there outside the house, watching her depart as the car swept away down the length of the drive.

I have to warn him. I have to warn Will.

24

They were sitting together in the car outside the locked gates to Hadley Hall. Will had turned silently off the road and down the long poplar-lined driveway, coming to a gentle halt just in front of the school crest.

Ad astra per aspera.

To the stars through difficulty.

'Not quite . . . sure why we're here,' he said, as if the car had located the school and parked neatly up of its own accord.

'I think your subconscious took over.'

'Yeah.' He rubbed his chin with one hand, looked across at her and smiled. The bruise on his face had more or less vanished now, save for some traces of yellow along the edge of his jawline. 'Although I have to admit I was hoping I could rely on you to stop me doing something stupid. Like – oh, I don't know – driving back to the scene of the crime with you in the passenger seat.'

She laughed. 'Sorry. Directions aren't really my strong point.'

Neither, it had transpired, was finding the courage to somehow tell Will what had happened at the beach house before Zak returned at the end of the week, tapping his watch and demanding a decision.

Jess knew that for Will, panic wasn't so much an inclination as something that was hard-wired into his muscle fibre. If she told him now about Zak, she felt sure he would bolt back to London with his girlfriend and daughter as fast as a Mafia defector fleeing hand-delivered body parts. And she didn't think she could deal with being abruptly parted from him all over again.

Which was probably why she was having trouble forcing the words to leave her mouth. It felt as if she'd been working them over and over on her tongue for days, like they were fish bones at a dinner party and she was waiting for the right moment to cause a fiasco by spitting them out.

'Was it hard to get away?' she asked him now, meaning from Natalie. The question tasted duplicitous, sly. She hated the sound of the words.

'Not too bad,' he said. 'Had to feign a craving for a particular type of beer.' He shrugged, but heavily, in a way that suggested the deceit was starting to get to him.

But then he took her hand, and after two weeks of only sporadic contact by text and the occasional hasty call, his touch made her feel like a tiny acrobat was doing backflips somewhere deep inside her belly.

Jess stared straight ahead out of the windscreen towards the main school hall, an imposing example of high-Victorian architecture sitting at the top end of a sweeping green lawn, the grandeur and beauty of which she'd never appreciated as a pupil, of course. It was lit up against the black of the night sky like a great ship twinkling out at sea.

'It *is* stunning,' she said now.

'Yeah. Coffee was fucking diabolical though.'

She laughed. 'That's your abiding memory of teaching here?'

'Well, no,' he said, looking at her meaningfully, 'but I doubt the amazing architecture is yours of being a pupil, is it?'

'Not exactly.'

A brief silence followed.

'Let's go in,' she said.

He turned his head to look across at her. 'What? It sounded like you just said, "Let's go in."'

She laughed. 'I did. Come on, it'll be fun.'

'Fun like a long-overdue drinking session or fun like inspecting my own toenails for fungal ingrowth?'

She thought about it. 'We could reminisce.'

'Oh, Jess, now you're just toying with me.'

She opened the passenger door and stepped out into the quiet warmth of the night. Across the wide expanse of lawn, Hadley Hall was floodlit and majestic in the manner of a luxury wedding venue. In fact there had been talk a few years ago of turning it into one – a bit of extra income for the school at weekends – but then the trustees got scared about creating dual purpose literature and confusing their Russian feeder schools, and the whole thing got shelved. Jess leaned back down into the car. 'Are you coming?'

'I might wait here. Looks like a one-man kind of a job.'

'Don't you think your subconscious brought you here for a reason?'

'If it did, that reason wasn't breaking and entering.'

'We won't go *inside*. Just walk around the grounds.'

'They have twenty-four-hour security. CCTV. Strangely enough, I don't fancy another spell in prison, Jess, it didn't really agree with me the first time round.'

She thought about it. 'Okay. Do you mind if I go? I won't be long. Just want to . . . have a look round.'

'Not at all. I'll treat myself to Radio 4. If I'm lucky I might catch *Book at Bedtime*.'

She smiled, shut the door softly and walked across to the low brick wall skirting the school's perimeter. Wooden signs threatening trespassers with prosecution were planted along its length like sentries, no doubt to ward off ex-pupils and disgraced teachers in mind of breaking and entering for a quick trip down memory lane.

Having scaled the wall, Jess stuck to the far edge of the dew-soaked lawn, which was mowed meticulously into stripes, following the line of the shingle driveway. She was careful to keep the hall to her left, so she wouldn't illuminate herself in the glow thrown off by the building's elaborate uplighting.

Then, from somewhere behind her, she heard a car door slam, and a few moments later he was at her side, grabbing her hand.

'Oh, hello,' she said, turning and smiling at him. 'What was the book at bedtime?'

'*The Bell Jar*,' he said. 'As a member of the patriarchy, I was made to feel quite unwelcome.'

'Oh. Well, they might do the *Witches of Eastwick* tomorrow for balance.'

'Updike?'

She nodded, privately impressed. 'A little different to Plath.'

'I'll listen out for it.' He fell into step with her across the grass. 'Just so you're aware, this really isn't very good for my anxiety levels. I try to stay at the averse end of the risk spectrum these days.'

She thought about it. 'Like, no smoking, five-a-day, keeping criminal activity to a minimum?'

'Exactly.'

'Well, this can be the only criminal activity you engage in this year, if you like.'

'I'll hold you to that. Though there does seem to be a pattern emerging here.'

'What's that?'

'Of you being the common denominator whenever I'm caught breaking the law.'

She laughed. 'Ah, that's sweet. Some maths-speak to make up for the Plath. Do you feel better now?'

He grinned. 'Yeah, much. Thanks.'

They walked a few paces further.

'Hey, Jess – let me ask you something.'

'Go on.'

'Do people ever talk about me when you're around? I mean, do you ever overhear anything or get strange looks?'

Jess thought about it. 'Yes, sometimes. Not very often. Hardly at all now, actually. It was worse back then, straight after it happened.'

He seemed to be mulling something over. 'It's just that I was out with Charlotte the other day, walking down the road to the playing field, and . . . there was this woman. She was on our side, but she crossed over when she saw us.'

'Okay . . .'

'The strange thing is, she was staring at me the whole time. Properly staring, like she knew exactly who I was. And it was almost to the point where I would have said something, but Charlotte was with me. Anyway, I carried on walking, but then I glanced back over my shoulder and I swear she'd just taken a picture.'

Jess felt her heart begin to thump. Had Zak started spreading rumours?

'It was creepy. I even picked Charlotte up and carried her, I was that weirded-out. Spent the rest of the night waiting for Natalie to get a strange phone call or for someone to knock on the front door.'

'What did she look like – the woman?'

'Hard to say. She had sunglasses on. Average height, non

descript clothes. Almost too non descript, though – and absolutely enormous hair. If I didn't know Sonia was dead, I'd have sworn it was her in disguise.'

Jess felt her chest stiffen with fear. She shook her head, trying to override it. 'Maybe she thought you were some-one else.'

'Yeah,' he said. 'Like Matthew Landley, circa 1994.'

She took his hand, wanting to reassure him but knowing she'd have to follow it up with a conversation about Zak. She swallowed, promising herself she would do it as soon as they had finished their impromptu little tour of the school.

They were approaching the far end of the hall and the cluster of buildings to its right, where the driveway fed into the large shingle car park. She used to scan the cars in it every day, feeling her heart thump with disappointment if she couldn't see Matthew's.

Will grabbed her hand and steered her along the paved footpath that transected the shingle. 'We don't want to crunch,' he whispered.

Another minute passed, and they were almost in line with the back of the hall. The tennis courts lay dead ahead and to the left of them was the school playground, encircled by buildings housing the design and tech workshops, lecture theatre and music school. To their right was the drama stu-dio, surrounded by the same shiny-leaved shrubbery as it had been almost eighteen years ago.

'Wow,' said Will. 'Talk about a head-fuck. Being back here . . . it's really, really weird.'

'God, it is,' she breathed. 'I can just picture you striding about in your cowboy boots . . .'

'. . . Sonia Laird boring holes into my brain . . .'

'. . . making all the girls swoon,' she teased.

There was a pause. They reached the side of the drama

384

studio and came to a halt. Around them, the air was as calm as something sleeping, not a whisper of wind to disturb them.

Jess looked across to the shrubbery. 'Let's go in.'

'In where?'

'Secret footpath,' she reminded him, and started walking, leading him down the side of the studio. Although still in existence, the footpath was no longer visible – it was completely overgrown by vast shocks of bold green laurel, and they had to force stiff clumps of foliage apart to make progress. Eventually they reached their little wooden bench, diseased now with creeping green moss and blue-grey lichen, completely encased in shrubbery.

Will snapped a couple of branches to make room for them to sit. 'Poor old Peggy,' he said, reading from the little bronze plaque, blackened up from the years of weather and solitude. 'She loved this place and now she's got even less of a view than she had before. And she's neglected her personal hygiene a bit.'

Jess smiled. 'Well, at least we're here to keep her company.'

'I think we're the only ones who ever were. Hey, we should look her up, now we've got Wikipedia. Who was Peggy? What terrible crime against tap dancing led her to end up dumped and unloved in the middle of a laurel bush?'

'Hadley Hall love triangle?'

He feigned outrage. 'Not at Hadley. *Never* at Hadley.'

They settled down against Peggy's inscription, their little hideout carrying the intense aroma of rich soil and green leaves. Tipping her head back, Jess could see a smattering of stars decorating the dark sky. They looked as if they had been shaken across the canvas of it like glitter.

'It's beautiful,' Will remarked quietly. 'You know, I'm

quite the amateur star-gazer these days, Jess. Turns out insomnia and cloudless nights are perfect partners.'

Recalling his comment in the cafe about craving outside space, Jess was struck by an image of him alone across the years, sitting out the dark in London parks. And then she remembered how carefree he used to be, and the futility of it all tugged at her somewhere deep inside.

'The last time we sat here, I was trying to finish with you, I think,' Will said then, into the still of the night air. 'Before it had even begun. I had a speech prepared and everything.'

She shut her eyes, attempting to remember what he'd said to her. 'Your opener was, "Saturday night was a mistake, Jess."' She dropped her voice into baritone to imitate him.

He laughed. 'Surely I was more creative than that?'

'No, you definitely weren't. I remember laughing heartlessly at you when you said it.'

'That sounds about right.' He smiled.

A few moments of silence ensued.

I have to tell him. I have to warn him about Zak.

She frowned. 'Look, Will, I need to tell you something.'

He looked across at her. 'Something-like-herpes or something-like-you-don't-think-we-should-do-this-any-more?'

She smiled. 'Well, which would you prefer?'

'Herpes,' he said, without missing a beat. 'Definitely, herpes. Go on. Please. Hit me with the full extent of your various undisclosed STDs.'

'Zak . . . still wants me to move to London with him,' she said, and then tried to work out how to say what she needed to say next.

He nodded. 'And what do you want?'

She hesitated. Somewhere in the distance, she could hear the swish of a car passing by on the road. The sound of it was strangely comforting, a little reminder that nobody knew they were here. The lack of scrutiny felt luxurious, something intoxicating she could happily have drunk.

He looked away from her then, up to the scattering of stars in the sky, and decided not to wait for her answer. 'Okay, look. I'm aware that I have no right *at all* to say this, but I really hope you don't.'

'Move in with him?'

'Think about it, move in with him – any of it.'

She waited for him to elaborate, wondering at what point she should stop him.

'He just doesn't strike me as a very nice guy. And I know that's coming from me, so you can laugh and disregard everything I say, but –'

'Oh, I will,' she said. 'I mean, you're the worst.'

He stuck an elbow softly into her ribs. 'Listen, Jess – I'm sure he's okay, but I don't think you should be with someone who's only okay, who'll do because he's got a house and you haven't. I think you should be with someone who really and truly loves you.'

Someone who really and truly loves me – like you? she desperately wanted to ask him, but she didn't, because deep down she was afraid of what his answer would be. Instead she said, 'Well, I always think principles are great, provided you can afford them at the time.' *He's blackmailing me, Will.*

He shook his head. 'Okay, that's just bullshit. For the purposes of nothing else but preserving your dignity, I am telling you that in this instance you can afford them, okay? In fact, I shall personally go out and purchase some lovely principles for you. Just . . . leave it with me. I'll think of something, I promise.'

She swallowed, thinking maybe she'd try a different angle.

'Will . . . have you ever felt . . . on the edge? Like you wanted to just . . . end it all?'

He frowned at her. 'What?'

'No! Not me. I just wondered if you've ever . . .' She trailed off, hoping he might choose this moment to tell her about the overdose, and then she could tell him about Zak.

'Are you thinking about your mum?'

'What? No.' She hardly ever allowed herself to think about her mother.

'Is being here bringing back memories?'

'No,' she said. 'Not like that.'

From somewhere in the trees behind them, the gentle call of a tawny owl drifted through the air.

'I blame myself,' he said quietly. 'For what happened with your mum.'

Jess swallowed. 'Don't,' she said. 'You know what she was like.'

'But the whole thing – it must have tipped her over the edge.'

He was right, she supposed, but it was hardly his fault. By the end, her mother had been so riddled with addictions and demons that she barely knew which way was up on the vodka bottle.

'I think she wanted to go,' she said, feeling an unexpected sting of emotion in her throat. 'She was looking for reasons, Will. She was tired of . . .'

The tawny owl called out again, a pleading song in the stillness.

'Of what?'

In the end, it had been simple, really. 'Of living.'

Will looked down at his hands and frowned. 'Why do you always want to make me feel better about everything, Jess?'

'Would it help if I made you feel bad instead?'

'Well, it wouldn't help me, but it might help you. You should try it sometime.'

'God, why?' she said then, into the cool gloom of the darkness. 'I love you.'

There was a long pause before he spoke again, and when he did, he picked through his words carefully, like he was weaving around broken glass with no shoes on. 'We need to figure this whole thing out, don't we?'

I need to tell you about Zak. Just let me find the right words.

But she couldn't find a way to begin. 'Any ideas?' she ended up asking him weakly.

'None. You?'

She shook her head. 'Zero.'

'Excellent. Well, that's a good start, then.'

She offered him a smile and he took it, his eyes grateful. She was happy to enjoy the fantasy for a few minutes longer that they would somehow find a way to be together.

'Maybe if I go away and think about it, and you go away and think about it,' he suggested, 'between us we might actually come up with something.'

There was a brief moment of contemplation, and then she remembered. 'Oh, I got you a birthday present,' she said, reaching into the pocket of her jacket and handing it to him.

He smiled. 'Thanks, Jess, but I don't think you'll be able to top the last one you gave me,' he said softly. And then he looked down at the gift-wrapped package and shook his head, like he was her teacher all over again and she'd just presented him with her latest attempt at trigonometry. 'Hang on though. A CD. This could be good – your music collection's got some gems.

She smiled back at him as he unwrapped it.

He laughed. '*The Best of UB40*. Thanks, Jess.'

'Well, you didn't seem overly familiar with their work, so . . .'

He reached up and gently brushed a strand of hair from her face. 'And thanks for your birthday text, too.'

'Oh. No problem.'

She'd wanted him to know she was thinking of him, and after hovering guiltily over the 'send' button for a while she'd eventually persuaded herself that a single text was harmless in the same way that alcoholics tell themselves half a pint at lunchtime never hurt anyone, when what they're actually thinking is that they'd quite like to just crack on with a massive three-day bender.

In the end he'd responded only with *Thank you* and a solitary *x*, presumably (understandably) to be deleted from his sent box straight away. She could appreciate that blowing virtual kisses on his birthday to the girl he ran over might be tricky to explain.

'Sorry if my reply was a bit – you know. Brief. I tend to mark my birthdays now by getting absolutely shit-faced.' He half smiled. 'Luckily Natalie thinks I've just got a pathological fear of middle age. Avoids getting me cards with any reference to scaling hills or counting candles. If she knew the real reason . . .'

Thinking sadly of Will's fortieth, and how Zak had laughed about him being wheeled into A & E with half-digested paracetamol all over his face, Jess decided that she finally felt ready to say what she needed to say. And once she'd done that, perhaps she would carry on talking and finally make her confession, get it over with. Unearth the little grub of guilt that had been writhing like a maggot inside her since the day he ran her over.

But as she started to speak, so did he, and he hadn't

seemed to hear her. 'I should get going. There's only so long you can legitimately claim to have spent in Tesco at this time of night.'

She nodded, but inside she had shrunk slightly. 'Especially with lichen on your T-shirt,' she pointed out.

He twisted round, pulling the fabric to reveal where it had rubbed bright green against his shoulder.

'Not sure how I'm going to explain that one. There isn't too much randomly exposed lichen in my local Tesco.' He turned to her. 'Hey, I have an idea.'

She waited.

'Something nice we can do for Peggy. She deserves it after all these years.'

So between them they carried Peggy out, hulking her across the damp grass and towards the line of poplars, with the idea that at least she would be able to enjoy the grand vista of the sweeping lawn and hall as opposed to the arse end of a laurel bush.

But as they approached the halfway point, they heard voices, and then footsteps – both of which sounded as if they were mid-sprint – followed by the jolting beam of a torch light. They set down the bench and turned to see two portly security guards streaking surprisingly rapidly towards them.

'Bollocks,' Will breathed. 'Run.'

So they did, abandoning Peggy where she was. It wasn't a bad spot – halfway across the lawn at the edge of the main driveway. At least she'd have a bit more social interaction.

Will was quick, and Jess fitter than she'd thought. It must have been all her hikes across the salt marsh with Smudge, who himself was something of a fast mover. They were leaving the security men for dust.

'Go, go, go!' Will shouted at her as soon as it became clear they would outrun them. He started laughing then, which set her off too, and she began to lose ground; but it didn't matter, because they were approaching the low wall of the boundary.

Will scrambled over it first, and then, breathing hard, turned round and extended his hand, bright green from where it had been gripping the bench. 'Come on, Daley Thompson.'

She laughed and grabbed it. He hauled her over in one quick movement and, landing safely, she glanced back over her shoulder, her heart hammering, breathing hard. 'Shit, they're still coming.' She bent down briefly to let her diaphragm recover from the unscheduled sprint, resting her hands on her knees.

Will swiftly flicked the lock to the car. 'Well, this is probably the most excitement they've had all year.'

Afterwards, as he was dropping her back off at the cottage, Jess turned to him and said, 'Will, I really need to tell you something.'

He frowned. 'What's up?'

A long silence.

Just tell him. Tell him now.

She'd been mentally collating all the words she would need, attempting to assemble them into some sort of order, but just as she finally started to speak, Will's phone began to buzz.

Fuck it.

He glanced at the screen. 'I'll call her back.'

Okay, enough now. Just come out with it. Time's running out.

'Will, I really have to tell you something. I've been trying to tell you all night and I keep fucking it up . . .'

He looked concerned. 'What's wrong?'

The phone cut off. Jess took a breath to speak – and then it started to buzz again.

'Sorry,' he said, frowning. 'I should probably get that. Natalie's not normally one for repeat ringing. If she can't get hold of me the first time round she usually just likes to cut my bollocks off after the fact.' He tapped the screen. 'Hello?'

From where she was sitting, Jess could hear Natalie's voice erupting from the phone, frantic, gabbling, like a cassette tape on fast-forward.

'I've been in Tesco,' Will said, in answer to something. His voice sounded hollow, fearful. 'My phone was in the car.'

More gabbling. More. More.

Jess watched Will as he listened, his face tightening up with disbelief.

'Okay, where are you?'

Gabble. Gabble.

Suddenly: 'Okay, Natalie, I get it! JUST TELL ME WHERE YOU ARE!'

A last eruption of noise, and then silence. Will tapped the phone and turned straight away to Jess, but he was looking almost through her.

'Charlotte's eaten peanut. It's serious. I need to go.'

Jess was propped up in bed with a bowl on her lap and Smudge snoozing soundly on her arm, the tip of his nose a comforting damp warmth against her skin. After Will had dropped her off she'd felt the urgent need for comfort food, so at midnight had found herself in the kitchen whipping up a black cherry clafoutis, a sweet sort of toad-in-the-hole – clouds of pillowy yellow batter and liberal scatterings of fat violet cherries, which she'd finished off with a plentiful dousing of vanilla bean custard. Outside, it had begun to rain, gentle patters on the windowpane that along with the sugar from her pudding had finally lulled her into a state of half-dazed calm.

By one a.m. she had heard nothing, but all she could do was wait for him to contact her. It was too risky to call him – there was no way of knowing what had happened since he'd dropped her off. She felt consumed by guilt: while they'd been messing about dragging Peggy across the lawn at Hadley Hall, Will's seven-year-old had been – potentially – close to death.

So she called Anna, aware that disturbing her friend's ovaries mid-sleep was not a decision to be taken lightly, but too desperate for reassurance to resist.

Anna picked up after only two rings, and Jess knew immediately that something wasn't right. 'Anna? Are you okay?'

'I'm . . . I started my period.' It was clear she was crying from the lurch of her voice as she forced out the words.

Staring straight ahead at the rain-spattered glass of her windowpane, Jess wondered what she could possibly say that would even come close to touching what Anna was going through.

'I was two days late and I thought . . . I thought . . .'

'Oh, Anna,' Jess whispered, her eyes filling up as she pictured her friend's excitement, the bated breath, the barely daring to move for fear of shattering the future she longed for – followed by the abrupt arrival of the heart-wrenching moment she'd been dreading and the subsequent plunge into bitter, raging despair.

'I'm actually starting to think . . . that this is never going to happen for us.'

'No, Anna,' Jess said straight away, 'you know you've still got lots of options –'

'Don't, Jess,' Anna snapped. 'Don't talk to me about test tubes, or adoption, or Simon fucking some other girl so that she can do the job I'm supposed to do, okay?'

'Okay,' Jess said quickly. 'Okay, I won't, I promise.'

There was a long silence, both girls breathing hard as they tried to contain their emotions.

'So, come on,' Anna relented eventually. 'You don't normally ring me this late unless Philippe's called a lock-in.'

Jess couldn't face filling her in on Zak's ultimatum and having to fend off a raft of practical suggestions, all of which would undoubtedly involve Will high-tailing it back to London and Zak conveniently transpiring to be less of an arsehole than everybody had first thought. So instead she told her about Charlotte. To her credit, Anna listened without digging at Will, and together they ran through various scenarios – Charlotte okay, Charlotte brain-damaged, Charlotte dead. And then they decided between them that Charlotte had to be okay, mainly because Natalie carried an adrenaline pen everywhere with her in the manner of a disaffected youth with a flick knife.

'Jess. Can I ask you something?'

'Of course.'

'What happens when Matthew and Natalie finish doing up that house?'

'What do you mean?'

'I mean, do you seriously think he's going to leave her and stay here with you? You really believe he's going to stand back and watch as she just . . . takes his daughter back to London?'

Instead of replying, Jess took another mouthful of clafoutis, ashamed that she still found it easier to focus on wanting

395

Will for herself – as she'd been able to all those years ago – than dwell on the fact that there were other people now who wanted him too.

Against her arm, Smudge shifted sleepily and let out a long, satisfied sigh.

'Come on, Jess,' Anna coaxed. 'I mean, even you know the chances of that happening are – well, they're more or less zero.'

'I just . . . I don't think he really loves Natalie,' she said then, almost desperately. 'And I do think he loves me.'

'Do you?' Anna said pointedly, openly sceptical in the manner of Debbie attending a church wedding.

'Well,' Jess said, popping a small balloon of batter with the edge of her spoon and watching it deflate, 'he said, "We need to figure this whole thing out."'

'Oh, well in that case, it's completely irrefutable.'

'I really want you to stop hating him. He's a nice guy, Anna.'

'Yeah, real stand-up. He's proved that time and time again.'

'We've all got our faults,' Jess murmured, staring down at her final irregular wedge of clafoutis, half submerged by a custard snowdrift.

There was a pause, and Jess suspected Anna was thinking that Rasleen – with her smear-free lifestyle, ability to balance indefinitely on one hand and stoic abstinence from any solid foodstuff excepting maybe steamed pak choi – was in fact as close to perfect as any of them were going to get.

'So tell me this, Jess. If Will makes you so happy, why do you sound like you want to cry whenever you talk about him?'

Jess reached down and stroked Smudge's ears. His little

head was smooth and warm. 'I don't.' It was a lie, of course – she was trying not to cry at this very moment – but she wasn't sure if that was because she was thinking about Will, Charlotte or Zak. Pondering on any one of them for too long came with varying degrees of melancholic side effect.

'Oh, really?' Anna countered. 'Then tell me what you're doing right now.'

'Right now?' Jess repeated, pausing to survey the mound of batter and cherries that was halfway to her mouth on a spoon.

'Yes.'

'Pudding,' she admitted.

'See, this is what I mean,' Anna said sternly. 'You need to look after yourself more. That means cutting out all the junk food and it definitely means cutting out Matthew Landley.'

'Clafoutis isn't junk food,' Jess objected, thinking that Anna was starting to sound a bit like Zak, albeit with added zen. 'I made it from scratch.'

'And Matthew?'

'No comment,' Jess mumbled, if only in response to Anna's interrogative tone.

Anna tutted disapprovingly, which wasn't too much of a surprise given that she'd recently expressed allegiance to the idea that keeping things to yourself gave you cancer, as well as a whole host of other health complaints that probably stretched as far as excess hair growth and athlete's foot.

'Okay, Jess. Look, I'm coming round tomorrow morning. Eight o'clock. I need to talk to you about something.'

'Something else?' Jess said, momentarily thrown by the notion that they might be capable of having a conversation based on a topic other than the human reproductive system or Will. *How did it come to this?* 'Are you bringing Simon?'

'Nope,' Anna said, 'but I'll bring coffee.'

Jess scraped round the edge of the bowl as quietly as she could. 'I'll need it, if you're coming at eight. Smudge might have to let you in.'

The dog opened one almond-shaped eye in response to his name, then promptly shut it again.

'Stop thinking about him now, okay?' Anna said softly. 'Go to sleep, Jess. Matthew Landley's not worth it.'

'Actually, that's where you're wrong. Because I think he is.'

25

Matthew

Sunday, 5 June 1994

We fled the scene of the crime – our exit path the grey and
shitty A3, our destination Portsmouth (equally grey, even
more shitty. I knew: I'd been there on a field trip before I
started teaching at a private school). The windscreen wipers
were on double time. I'd never witnessed a thunderstorm
quite like it.

After Sonia had played her winning hand, our only real
choice had been to cut and run. The tide had risen quickly,
without warning, and now we needed to make snap decisions and only hope we wouldn't drown in the process.

'Holy fuck,' Jess kept saying. She was fidgeting like she'd
eaten a load of crack by mistake and swearing as if she'd only
just realized. She didn't seem to be able to stop her mouth
from moving. 'Holy fuck.'

'Are you saying "holy fuck" because of the rain or because
you've changed your mind?' I had to ask her eventually as
we passed our first sign for the ferry terminal. I'd been putting off the question for as long as I dared. The thought of
turning round and heading back through the rain to the
Sonia-infested snake-pit of North Norfolk quite honestly
scared the shit out of me, but if it was what Jess really wanted,
I was prepared to do it.

I'd not yet told her exactly what had gone on between me

and Sonia in my living room on Friday night. I had informed her that Miss Laird was armed and dangerous, menacingly poised to take me down with her fail-safe artillery of photographs and blackmail, but that was about the extent of the intel I was willing to share at that point. Supplying the pertinent details of me in the prayer position wearing only my pants was unlikely to inspire her to sleep with me again, I knew that much.

To my relief, Jess grabbed my hand. 'I swear when I'm excited, Mr L.' She turned to look at me, and her expression melted into what I could only interpret as love. 'You know that.'

I do know that. She was right, of course. Jess was always right.

'And the rain is kind of cool,' she added, just in case it had momentarily slipped my mind that she was fifteen years old.

It had actually been Jess's idea to flee. That wasn't to say I hadn't started fantasizing about pitching up at my relatives' Tuscan alabaster estate almost as soon as Sonia had shut my front door behind her (failing, I'd noted with some bitterness, to break her ankle again on her way out). But I had been too afraid to suggest it – because suddenly the idea of it threatened to sully us somehow, to make what we were doing seem slightly grubby. Moving to Italy to build a life for ourselves after she'd turned sixteen was one thing; scarpering illegally across international borders with her while she was still underage felt worryingly close to sex trafficking.

But I also knew Sonia well enough to realize that we didn't have a choice. She was unlikely to keep her mouth shut or her horrible little roll of film a secret for much longer than forty-eight hours. I had guessed from the immediate lack of law enforcement in my living room that her plan was to wait until I'd arrived at school on Monday before calling them in, nicely timed so that I could be handcuffed and shoved into a police car in full view of parents, staff and pupils – herself and Jess included. And there it would be: |the perfect opportunity for her to catch my eye one last time and let me know she'd won with a final little fuck-you wave, before I was driven straight off to Norwich police station to be charged with multiple counts of God-knows-what.

I had been trying to work out what to do, pacing backwards and forwards across the living room like my television had broken and I was waiting to hear who'd won the World Cup. Fortunately Jess had popped over to Anna's, so she hadn't been there to witness me pounding out the miles on my carpet. But what I didn't know at that point was exactly what she'd popped over there for: the key to the Baxter family's Spanish villa, high up in the Picos mountains.

'What the fuck is this?' I asked her, two seconds after she'd slapped the key into my palm and told me what it was. I shook my head. 'Sorry. I mean ... how did you get this?'

'I took it.' She shrugged, like that was explanation enough, which it wasn't.

'You haven't told anyone?'

'Of course not. I know where they keep the key.' She gave me a quiet beam of pride then, which made me feel a bit like Fagin debriefing returning child pickpockets.

Given the choice, Italy would have been my preferred location of criminal stronghold, but even I could appreciate that having not seen any of my father's family since before I hit double figures, it might be a tad presumptuous to turn up now with a teenage girl on my arm and an international manhunt on my tail. Plus, we apparently had a ready-made hideout waiting for us in the Picos. Jess assured me that the Baxters had no plans to return to their Spanish villa until Christmas – so it was sitting there empty, practically begging to be squatted in.

I had procrastinated on it for the sum total of about fourteen minutes before relenting and admitting that the villa was our best – or possibly only – option. Jess simply nodded and smiled, like, *Well, duh*. She was the very epitome of calm while I was flapping and flustering about like a duck being chased by a dog.

'You really think it'll be okay?' I asked her, referring to the unauthorized occupation of the Baxters' villa but realizing too late that it sounded like I meant our plan overall. It should have been me masterminding logistics and issuing all the relevant reassurances, not Jess.

Then again, Jess having the capacity to think on her feet hadn't really come as a surprise. I'd seen her self-confidence blossom in the months we'd been together. Not that I was about to try and claim all the credit for that, but I sure as hell wasn't giving any to her mother or sister.

Jess replied by smiling possibly the calmest smile I'd ever seen, deflecting my anxiety with perfection by saying, 'Let's go to Spain, Mr L.' It was exactly the same technique I employed in my maths classes whenever I needed to stem a flow of meaningless questions and get everyone just to focus on the task in hand.

Still. Thieving the key to someone else's holiday home so we could break the law in private made me feel highly uncomfortable. But I knew I had run out of time to waste on thinking about it.

*

'You know Anna's parents have a wine cellar?' Jess was saying now. She'd been to stay in the Picos with the whole Baxter family last summer, which at least gave me some basic level of reassurance that we weren't heading for a fictional log cabin hidden away in the depths of some fairy-tale forest. This was despite the fact that Jess had drawn me a map of the place this morning that seemed unlikely to relate to anywhere on planet earth, let alone in Europe.

'The wine came with the villa,' she continued, 'but they're teetotal.'

In my view, a bunch of teetotals sitting on an unused wine cellar were no better than OAPs with their life savings stashed underneath their mattresses: there was a certain smugness to their untouched plenty that rendered pilfering almost defensible. What's more, I had a feeling I was about to enter a period of my life where the term *teetotal* would become about as relevant as the words *law* and *abiding*.

Jess had discovered Blur's *Modern Life is Rubbish* in the glovebox and was jiggling her knees up and down completely out of time to the music, attempting to disperse nervous energy. The uneven rhythm of the rain on the windscreen was adding an odd syncopation to the music, distracting me. There was too much going on at once.

Currently, my concentration was divided between the road ahead of us (cars, pile-ups, lane closures), slip roads (traffic-slash-undercover police lying in wait) and the rear-view mirror (serious crime squad in hot pursuit). The level of steady focus required of me represented a strange release from the stress of the previous night, which I had mostly spent jolting bolt upright in bed every time a car drove past the cottage. Given that my bedroom looked out over a B-road, this had occurred frequently enough for me to give up after a couple of hours and head downstairs in my boxer shorts to consume as much of last year's Christmas haul as possible – the stupidly expensive single malt from my dad, as yet unopened because I really wasn't much of a whisky drinker, and Katy's thoughtless airport gesture of rolled-in-China Cuban cigars. Fuck it, why not? Who knew when I would be coming back – if at all – and I certainly wasn't planning to risk an encounter with customs in Santander by packing a vast stash of alcohol or tobacco-based goods into the bottom of my sports bag. So I unearthed an old Christmas cassette tape just to complete the picture and sat there in the dark, drinking, smoking and listening to my favourite festive hits, thankful that Jess was not around to witness quite how tragic I could be when pushed. I think deep down I was quietly saying goodbye to my little cottage, my life and probably – thinking about it now – my freedom.

Our passage appeared so far to have gone undetected, but I couldn't quite bring myself to relax yet. I was saving that for Spain. Until I was somewhere high up in the Picos, having avoided any unscheduled detours to local police stations en route, I had to focus and get us there in one piece, under the radar.

I turned my head and watched Jess in profile for a couple of seconds. Her face was tipped up, her chin raised slightly; she was listening to the music and humming, atonal as always. She was also sporting a brand new haircut, courtesy of her ham-fisted pervert boyfriend and a pair of blunt scissors. I had been close to tears as I'd hacked into it that morning in the manner of a seasoned child abductor – and it had pained me that afterwards she'd scooped it all quickly off the floor and stuffed it methodically into a carrier bag without so much as passing comment on her wonky fringe, like she was subjected to this sort of deranged behaviour every day of the week. (Then again, Jess's own mother was a woman who had once drunk a shot glass of bleach because she'd run out of vodka, so it was little wonder really that the impromptu haircut had failed to faze her.)

I had debated doing something similar myself – shaving my head perhaps, ridding my chin entirely of facial hair for the first time since I was sixteen – but something had stopped me. It wasn't fear, exactly, but a sense that I might need to save that particular form of disguise for when I really needed it.

Packing for my new life had quite literally consisted of chucking some randomly selected clothing into a bag before dousing down my cottage with wet wipes like a petty thief in training, a feeble attempt to remove all traces of my underage girlfriend. I'd hoped as I was doing this that I would never be forced to commit any form of violent crime, primarily because I would be embarrassingly inept at covering up the evidence.

I'd wavered for a moment over tipping all the loose change from my giant plastic whisky bottle into a carrier bag and taking it along for the ride as well. The collection had been mounting up for years, and it seemed prudent in a way to arm myself with as much cash as possible if I was about to go on the run. But the reality was that a Spanish bank clerk was likely to be singularly unimpressed by having to count out a Safeway bag full of English pennies, so with some reluctance, I left the bottle untouched in my bedroom. One day, I thought, I'd use all that spare change to get Jessica something nice.

I did throw the little copper statue into my bag, though, along with the necklace I'd bought for Jess but had never given her. Maybe, with the help of some sunshine, relaxation and contraband wine, I would finally work up the nerve.

Or maybe I would go one better and buy her a ring. The thought made my stomach skip.

26

'Tired?' Anna asked Jess from the opposite side of Jess's kitchen table. Dressed in a pale blue vest top and white yoga pants, Anna was cradling a cup of raspberry leaf tea – looking about as alert herself, Jess thought, as someone who'd just donated their adrenal glands to medical research.

'No, I'm fine,' Jess lied, thinking this all felt a bit like competitive wellbeing, before sipping from the takeaway coffee Anna had brought round and promptly burning her tongue. Anna herself seemed resolutely to be resisting the use of artificial stimulants and had even declined a slice of Jess's home-made yoghurt cake, explaining that dairy facilitated inflammation in the gut and inhibited her ability to carry out one-legged king pigeon poses in particular.

Assuming the pigeon thing to be something Anna routinely did to cleanse her ovaries, Jess hadn't pushed it any further. So she took an oversized bite from her own slab of sponge, and with the smooth, sugary tang that ensued, felt her exhaustion abate slightly.

'How's Charlotte?' Anna asked.

Having not yet heard from Will, Jess had no idea if Charlotte was alive or dead. 'I don't know,' she confessed. 'Haven't heard.'

Anna was massaging Smudge's head in a repetitive circular motion like she was nervous about something. Her skin appeared to be in need of some heavy-duty moisturizer and her hair looked as if it hadn't seen shampoo for a while. She was also thinner than ever, which had the effect of making her nose and ears seem somehow too big for her head. Though Jess could hardly claim to be an expert, angles and bones just didn't seem compatible with falling pregnant, which worried her.

'Are you okay?' she asked, to which the correct answer, if she'd thought about it before she opened her mouth, was clearly no. Nothing had changed since yesterday: Anna was still not pregnant.

When Anna failed to either look up or offer a verbal response, Jess attempted to de-awkward the pause by filling it with the sound of low-level coffee slurping and cake consumption. It worked only to the extent that it muffled the ticking of the clock. Anna wasn't normally one for long silences, which made it slightly unsettling to experience her resolutely going the distance on one.

'Anna?' Jess eventually prodded her beneath the table with her foot, surprised to notice just how little flesh jiggled on Anna's calf as she did so. Her leg felt more like the bony arm of an elderly woman.

Finally, Anna looked up and met her eye. 'Okay.' She exhaled stiffly. 'Yesterday, after ... I realized I wasn't pregnant, Rasleen and I had a heart-to-heart.'

'About?' Jess said, and for some reason she got the feeling that Anna was about to say, 'you'.

'You.'

Jess felt her stomach turn over like someone had reached in there and physically flipped it. Being assessed in absentia by Rasleen felt like being probed without permission, needlessly violated, and the thought of Anna colluding with it brought a shock of indignation to her throat.

'Rasleen thinks there's something stopping me conceiving.'

This was nothing new, which could only mean that Anna

was throwing it into the mix as part of a wider circuitous preamble to something more significant.

'Yoga for fertility is all focused around truth and honesty, Jess.' Looking up, she registered Jess's cool expression, which seemed straight away to put her off maintaining eye contact. 'Look, I've been holding something in, keeping something from you. Anyway, Rasleen thinks it could be at the root of why I can't get pregnant. Who knows if it is? But she asked me to come and talk to you today.'

Anna was speaking like a mediator arriving on-site at a high hedge dispute, as if she had all the pertinent facts stowed away in her leather holdall and she just needed Jess to comply with whatever it was she was about to propose.

But then her face tightened slightly, and Jess was suddenly hit with the uncomfortable feeling that she wasn't going to like what was coming next.

There was a drawn-out pause, punctuated only by Smudge's deep breathing and the gentle howl of a wind gust trapped inside the Aga pipe.

'It was me,' Anna said then. 'I called the police, in 1994. I reported you and Matthew first thing on the Monday morning. It wasn't Miss Laird, it was me. I made the phone call.'

Jess laughed. 'Don't be stupid, Anna.'

Anna looked at her, and both girls knew this was her last opportunity to take it back and say she was joking. She shook her head. 'I'm not.'

Silence. Jess began to feel the truth sinking in like the sharp kick of a well-placed foot in the pit of her stomach. 'What?'

'I knew about you and Mr Landley from the start. I knew you were having an affair.'

'Hold on. You called the police? Not Miss Laird?'

'Yes,' she whispered. 'Anonymously. They never knew it

was me.' Pause. 'I knew where you'd gone – I saw you take the key to the villa.'

Jess floundered. 'You told the police where we were?'

'I didn't say exactly where. I just said . . . the Picos.' Her words seemed to shrivel as she spoke. 'I didn't want you to suspect me.'

'Oh.' Jess's eyes sprang with disbelieving tears. 'Well, I definitely didn't.'

Anna pressed her gaze to the floor.

'Why would you do that?' Jess's voice was tiny now, like it had curled up with shock on being hit with something blunt.

'I hated him,' Anna said, though she sounded more defensive than apologetic. 'You and me, Jess – we were like sisters before Matthew Landley came along. And then you ditched me for him, and you never even told me you were seeing him. He forced you to keep quiet and I hated him for that.'

'But . . . I thought you were my friend.' Jess half spoke half choked, parking for the moment Anna's false assumption that Matthew had been some sort of one-man intimidation racket as opposed to her loving boyfriend. 'And now you're telling me . . . everything that happened was *your fault*?'

'What happened wasn't my fault,' Anna replied, though the way that she said it was almost rehearsed, the result perhaps of drumming it into herself for the past seventeen years. 'Matthew Landley brought it all on himself. You *know* that, Jess.'

Jess stared at her in disbelief. 'If you hadn't called the police, they would never have found us and everything would have been okay. Matthew wouldn't have gone to jail. We might still be together. My mother might still be alive. And my . . . our . . .' But unable to complete her sentence, she allowed the ragged fragment of it simply to hang, exposed and accusatory.

'They'd have found you eventually,' Anna said, avoiding Jess's eye. 'You're crazy if you think they wouldn't have.'

Jess wasn't too sure about that, given the Baxters' little villa was high up in the Picos surrounded by nothing but Picos. They'd taken long enough with a cast-iron tip-off.

Seeming somehow to sense the change in atmosphere, Smudge got up from where he was sitting next to Anna and trotted over to plonk himself down at Jess's feet instead. His fur felt warm against her skin, a tiny comfort as she struggled to grasp what Anna was telling her.

'Matthew Landley changed you, Jess,' Anna said now. 'He turned you into a completely different person. You started lying to everyone. My mum treated you like a daughter, but you still came round to our house and stole the key to our villa. After everything she'd done for you, you risked implicating her in the whole fucking thing.'

'We've been over this,' Jess reminded her, because of course they had. She'd apologized to Christine numerous times in the wake of Matthew's arrest. 'I told the police your mum knew nothing about it. I told them that, straight away.'

There was a sharp pause.

'Dangerous,' Anna enunciated then. 'Matthew was nothing short of dangerous. He deserved to go to prison.'

'He wasn't dangerous. Don't be crazy.'

Anna's whole face became a reproachful glare. 'Well, he got you to drug me in Venice.'

'What?'

'I saw you crush diazepam into my drink. Do you remember, in the hotel room?'

'That was my idea,' Jess said quietly. 'Not Matthew's.'

'I poured it straight back into the bottle while you were in

411

the toilet,' Anna continued, talking over her. 'And then I pretended to pass out. But I followed you into the square, Jess, and I heard him asking you whether his little cocktail plan had worked. I *heard* him.'

There was no point in correcting what Anna had in fact misinterpreted, Jess could see that now, because her best friend was clearly no longer in the market for a two-way conversation.

'Poor Miss Laird was trying to protect you on that trip. She knew what Mr Landley was like.'

'Oh Jesus,' Jess said, pressing an index finger against each temple. 'Don't *poor Miss Laird* her. The woman was completely insane, Anna. She'd been following us, taking pictures of us together. She broke into Matthew's house and threatened him, remember?'

'Don't you think,' Anna replied coolly, 'that if there were photos, they'd have been handed over to the police?'

Jess fumbled in her mind for the fragments of half-information she'd been given. Matthew's lawyer had never seen any photos, had said they'd probably been disregarded at the outset for reasons of quality or similar. She struggled to recall the phrase – *inadmissible evidence.*

'There were never any photos, Jess – Sonia was calling his bluff.' Anna's voice sounded faintly derisive. 'There was nothing on that camera. She suspected you both, but she didn't know for sure.'

Jess remained very still. She felt as if her heart was stretched taut inside a catapult, ready to go *ping* at any second.

'I was the one who was following you,' Anna continued. 'I knew all your hideouts, the places you went together. I saw you at the beach, by the harbour. I even sat in his back garden one night after dark. Someone had to find out what was going on. I knew Miss Laird couldn't do it. She was too scared of Matthew clocking her and making things worse for herself. I mean, he'd already put her in plaster, for God's sake – what else was he capable of?'

What?

Jess blinked and shook her head. 'What?'

'When Sonia broke her ankle.'

'What about it?'

'He pushed her off that step.'

'No, he didn't. Who told you that?'

'Oh, come on. Everyone knows that's what happened.'

'No.' Jess's stomach clenched with indignation. 'Everyone *thought* that's what happened.'

But Anna was clearly not in the mood to pause and rewind. Instead she remained steadfastly focused, speaking in the hushed tones of someone delivering a witness account for true crime television, which was annoying enough for Jess to think that pixelating her face out and adding a bit of voice distortion might in fact have been quite satisfying.

'Sonia went back to the police a few weeks after he did it, to make a formal complaint of assault. But they didn't take her seriously. That's why she was so reluctant to report you both – she was scared about the repercussions if she made accusations she couldn't back up. She was terrified of Matthew. The way he treated her was . . . well, it was verging on sociopathic, Jess.'

Jess said nothing, mostly because this was now becoming bullshit that barely warranted breath. Matthew was about as sociopathic as a serial fundraiser doing sky dives for charity.

'Her only option was to call his bluff, so she did,' Anna declared. 'She made him think she was going to report him, and he fell for it. Fled to Spain at the first sign of trouble, taking you with him. Implicated himself. I always did think he was spineless like that.'

Jess knew that Sonia hadn't been scared of Matthew. It was far more likely that the only reason she'd not been the one to report them that Monday morning in 1994 was because she'd been beaten to it.

'I felt so sorry for her,' Anna said now. 'She was only standing up for what she thought was right. It was her moral duty as a teacher.'

Jess paused, suddenly unsure how Anna had come to be so familiar with the inner workings of Miss Laird's unique psychology. 'Hang on . . . how do you know all this, Anna? About Sonia?'

A brief silence.

'We kept in touch, afterwards.' Anna's eyes had opened very wide by now, the body language shorthand for being entirely beyond reproach. 'We met up occasionally. I went to London sometimes, she came to stay at Beelings. I just thought she did a really brave thing, getting involved like she did. She was a good teacher. I felt sorry for her. It wasn't just your life Matthew destroyed, Jess – there were other people affected too. Sonia ended up teaching at some shitty inner-city comprehensive in London because she was too traumatized to stay at Hadley. She was living in a bedsit. It was tragic.'

Jess recalled Matthew's account of Sonia with her camera in his living room, and of the statement he said she'd given to the police when they were gathering their evidence. For Anna to reveal she had stayed in touch with Sonia after all that was no different to her saying she'd befriended the genius who'd lent her alcoholic mother a shotgun.

'Sonia used to tell me what Mr Landley was *really* like,

Jess. Did you know he used to mess her about when she was dating Darren? He'd lead her on and then reject her, ignore her at school whenever he wasn't in the mood to flirt with her. I mean, come on – why do you think she was at his cottage that night in her underwear? Are you so naive, Jess? Mr Landley was a fucking *snake*.'

'Matthew wasn't a snake,' Jess countered, a truth that felt about as basic to her as the need to breathe. 'He was anything but.'

'It was a gross abuse of his position.'

'So says the law.'

'Since when does the law not count?'

'It does – it does count! Which is why I'm sitting here with you now, Anna, and Matthew's round the corner with Natalie and Charlotte! The law worked – it did everything it was meant to do. You should be pleased about that!'

Anna failed to respond, and then neither of them said anything else for a very long time.

'So now what?' Jess asked Anna eventually. 'Now you've dropped your little bombshell, you're going to scuttle off back to Thornham to stand on your head and absolve yourself of all responsibility? How very karmic of you.'

Anna took a steadying breath. 'Rasleen did warn me that you might reject my truth, Jess, but I've offered it to you. That's all I can do.'

'Well, I must say I appreciate having your truth shoved down my throat, Anna. Shame it's made me feel like I want to throw up.'

Anna looked away from her and down into her cooling cup of raspberry leaf tea.

'So what happens next? You fall pregnant?' Jess clicked her fingers. 'Just like that?'

'Well,' Anna said, seeming oddly surprised that Jess would

be so heartless as to bring that into the equation, 'of course I hope so.'

Jess swallowed back a glut of fierce tears. 'Why didn't you just do what most people do, Anna, and take some time out to relax instead? Book yourself a holiday somewhere hot? It might have had the same result in the end. But hey – what would I know?'

Anna waited for a couple of seconds. 'But of course you would, Jess,' she spat. 'Of course you would fucking know. Who the fuck are we pretending for now?' Suddenly animated, she swept an arm dramatically around the empty kitchen.

The meaning behind her words was so brutal, so unexpected, that it struck Jess almost physically – as if Anna had whipped out something sharp without warning and plunged it very deliberately into Jess's gut.

Anna began to discharge accusations then, rapid-fire in quick succession like they were bullets. 'It's not fucking fair, Jess. Do you know how hard it is for me to go through this month after month – to look you in the eye and ignore the fucking great elephant in the corner of the room? You chose to throw away the one thing I want most in the world. So you tell me, Jess, how is that fair? TELL ME HOW THAT'S FAIR!'

She gasped for breath, her face pink and furious, clenched up with the outrage of injustice like a child in the grip of a violent and unstoppable tantrum.

Jess was so stunned by Anna's outburst that she could barely form the words. 'I think I stopped believing in fair a long time ago, Anna.'

After Matthew's arrest, Jess had been taken straight to her aunt's flat in Dalston, where the artfully minimal square footage would only serve to aggravate already-precarious relations between Jess and her aunt, mother and sister over the following thirteen months. The totalitarian regime they imposed on Jess in the wake of the scandal should really have been punishment enough – but then her secret was discovered by nosy Debbie when it was a mere five weeks old, only minutes after Jess had learned of it herself. Suspecting something was up, her sister had until that point been conducting a crude and unsubtle style of investigation that essentially amounted to bursting through the bathroom door whenever Jess was in there, and staring meaningfully at her stomach whenever she wasn't. So in a way it had seemed inevitable that Debbie should clock the pregnancy test by the sink one night while Jess perched numbly on the toilet – upon which Debbie snatched it up and rushed breathlessly into the living room with it like she was carrying fistfuls of dynamite. Triumphant, she threw down the lit fuse of her sister's pregnancy, complete with her spite-laced informant's commentary, before making a hasty retreat to the kitchen to observe the ensuing explosion. The row was indeed so forceful that a neighbour ended up calling the police, upon which Jess was shooed outside to shiver and sob on the balcony wearing only a T-shirt while her mother and aunt assured the nice men from the Met that they'd both just had a bit too much to drink. The nice men from the Met stayed for exactly the length of time required to verify this – approximately twenty seconds – before legging it off up the Balls Pond Road without looking back.

That night marked the start of seven long days of agony for Jess, during which she was relentlessly and mercilessly ground down by the adults until she finally reached the point of miserably believing she had no choice. It had been a team effort – coordinated, deadly and, ultimately, effective.

Matthew would be locked away for years, they'd told her. A decade, probably more, once the court had considered all the counts of sex offences, on top of child abduction. He was about to become a convicted paedophile, blighted for the rest of his life with no hope of ever returning to normality – and banned, of course, from ever coming near Jess again. He didn't love her, that much was clear: what man gets a fifteen-year-old pregnant in circumstances like this? It was utterly abhorrent. And where would Jess go, what would she do? Because if she chose to keep this child she could forget about staying in Dalston or Norfolk. And she needn't think that Anna's mother would be willing to take her in, either – Mrs Baxter was still furious about Jess thieving the key to their villa, contaminating the place with her sordid affair. So where was she planning to go? Did she want to end up homeless, on drugs? What would her father say if he could see her now – no prospect of GCSEs, pregnant at fifteen? And then came the emotional blackmail, powerful as a poison dart. If the authorities were – by some chance – to discover she was pregnant, it could add years to the already weighty sentence Matthew would surely receive. *Years.*

So eventually, dutifully, Jess attended an assessment at a private clinic, accompanied by her aunt. And after that, she had only seven more days to get used to the idea, to prepare her goodbye to the blossoming little bump in her belly.

The night before returning to the clinic, Jess stayed up until late and left the flat after dark. She only went as far as the estate's now-empty playground, standing close to the railings and watching the swings move in the breeze, the roundabout creaking sadly. She thought about Matthew, wretched and oblivious in his prison cell, and wondered whether he was thinking about her too.

I'm sorry, she whispered to the vision of him in her mind. *Please forgive me. I don't know what I'm doing. But I'm trying to do the right thing. Please don't hate me.*

And then she put her hand against her stomach and let the tears fall, because maybe in a different life, in a world far away from this one, the three of them could have been a family.

But not in this life. *Not in this life.*

After that, she quietly made her way back upstairs to the flat to eat cottage pie for the fourth night running (her aunt being bulk cooking's most loyal disciple) and watch Debbie having a major meltdown over BSE contaminants in beef.

Jess and her aunt walked the ten short minutes to the clinic the following day, journeying back to the flat by taxi just a few hours later. Her aunt had never been one for the lexicon of reassurance, but she did offer Jess some advice to the tune of never discussing the abortion with anyone, ever again.

Two more years passed before Jess had amassed the requisite self-belief to verbalize her anguish and defy her aunt's instruction. Over the past twelve months they'd been back in Norfolk, the three of them living together in a new cottage while Debbie studied to re-take her failed A levels and Jess made a half-hearted stab at her GCSEs. Their mother simply continued with her own unique practice of failing to be a parent, as determined a student of this particular discipline as either of her daughters were of theirs.

But the night before seeing fit to remove her own face with a shotgun, her mother made the mistake of picking a fight with Jess about Matthew, prompting Jess to pick one back about the baby. This inflamed a row unlike any they'd had before, which somehow culminated in Jess backed up against the fridge defending herself with a bread knife while

Debbie screamed hysterically down the phone at the police, who seemed coincidentally reluctant to attend a night-shift domestic that was kicking off at the same time as a Euro '96 football match.

'Rasleen told me I should be honest with you about how I really feel,' Anna was saying now. 'And how I really feel is that . . . maybe you're the wrong person to see me through this.'

'You told her?' Jess stared at Anna. 'You told Linda about Matthew and the baby?'

Anna gaped at her, as if it hadn't even crossed her mind that this should count as betrayal. 'I had to tell her, Jess. You and me, we never talk about it, but it kills me every day that you chose to give up the one thing I want the most! It tears me up inside!'

'It tears you up inside,' Jess repeated numbly.

'Yes,' Anna said, but she wavered as she caught the expression on Jess's face. 'It does.' She trailed off.

Jess nodded. 'Do you want to know what tears me up inside?'

At this, Anna said nothing. Instead, she shut her eyes and mouth, a quiet act of bracing herself against what was coming next.

'It tears me up inside,' Jess said, her voice lurching clumsily outwards in lumps as she struggled not to break down, 'that every year on 12 March is the day I should be celebrating a birthday. That by now, I'd have a sixteen-year-old son or daughter.' Her breath became a hot shudder in her chest. 'You know, I think about . . . what they might look like. Whether they'd have Matthew's height or my eyes, or if they'd be good at sport, or if they'd have inherited his stupid sense of humour. I think about what it would feel like to see them smile. I think about giving them a hug.' She stared at her friend, wide-eyed and stark with helplessness. 'But do you want to know what really kills me, Anna? That they have a living, breathing half-sister. She's it, Anna. Charlotte should have belonged to *me and Matthew*.'

Across the table, Anna put her face in her hands; and together, but apart, the two girls finally began to weep.

'And the worst part is, it's all my fault. It's not Matthew's fault – it's mine. He wasn't there to stop it. I should have been stronger. It was my turn to fight.'

From behind the screen of her fingers, Anna shook her head, unable to reply.

'I owed it to him, Anna! It was his baby too! He loved me, and he would have loved the baby, and if he'd known what was happening he would have been *screaming* at me to fight them but . . . I didn't. You want guilt, Anna? Walking away from that clinic is guilt. Seeing you fail to get pregnant over and over again every month is guilt. Looking Will in the face and knowing what I did on his behalf is FUCKING GUILT.'

There followed a silence as stunned as if someone had been punched. It seemed for a while that it might never end, that neither of them would ever speak again.

Eventually Anna found her voice. But it sounded weak and pitiful, an empty attempt to urgently back-pedal. 'I know they ground you down, Jess, after Spain. I know you probably didn't have a choice. I was only just saying that I'm finding it hard to be around you . . .'

'Well, you know what? I find it hard to be around you too, sometimes, Anna. I find it hard to hold your hand and listen to how desperately you want to be pregnant, praying that it might happen for you without selfishly wanting to turn back the clock for myself. I find it hard to know that Will is such a fantastic father that all Natalie wants to do is pop out more of his babies left, right and centre. But worst of all, I find it hard to look Will in the eye without wondering what his face would do if I told him the truth.'

'Well, maybe you *should* tell him,' Anna urged. 'Because you need to move on, Jess – you're living in the past.'

Jess shook her head. 'I love him so much, Anna. If I told him now, after all this time, it would kill him. It would kill me.'

'If you really love him, Jess, as much as you say you do, you'd tell him. Because right now, everything between you is based on lies. It's just fantasy, without a future.'

'It would kill him, Anna,' she repeated.

Anna looked almost blank, like she didn't understand.

Jess finally let her have it. 'Don't you get it, Anna? Matthew and me – we were supposed to be together! That's the way it was SUPPOSED TO BE! But you and my mother and my aunt – you took all that away from us, even though you were the ones who were meant to love me the most!'

Anna made a choking sound, like she'd sampled Jess's point of view and found it to taste utterly vile. 'I can't *believe* you're blaming me. That you still can't see Matthew Landley for what he really is.'

'What is he?' Jess exploded. 'What does he do to me that's SO BAD, Anna? I mean, come on – I really, really want to know!'

The two girls locked eyes for just a moment, and then Anna looked down in the direction of Jess's right hand. 'Well,' she said, breathing evenly, 'you ended up with that fucking ugly scar for one.'

Jess swallowed hard. She couldn't have felt more shocked if Anna had spat in her face. 'Ouch,' she managed eventually.

There was a pause. 'Well, you asked,' Anna said uncomfortably.

Without saying anything more, Jess got up and headed to the front door, put her fucking ugly scar against the handle and shoved it open as wide as it would go.

'Get out.'

It all happened so quickly – it could only have been ten seconds, possibly less – and on a day when her head felt less like a wet sandbag she might have been quicker to react.

At that moment, a cat streaked across Jess's front lawn in the direction of the road, and Smudge bounded through the open door after it.

The cat made it safely to the opposite pavement, but Smudge did not.

27

'Are you ready?'

Jess nodded numbly. She was standing in a white, windowless room that smelt of antiseptic and dog biscuits, stroking Smudge's damaged ears, gently massaging his silken fur over and over with her fingers. He'd already been sedated, and his breathing was laboured, as if he was sleeping by the fire on a winter's night, his paws on the edge of the rug and his eyes squeezed contentedly shut, tail on standby to wag if she said his name or got up to make a drink.

'He doesn't know what's happening,' the vet said kindly. 'I promise. He'll just go quietly to sleep.'

Jess tried to recall the last time that Smudge's trusting brown eyes had blinked up at her, the last time she'd looked back into them and smiled. Had it been in the kitchen, when he had moved so loyally from Anna's side to hers?

She smiled faintly as she remembered teaching him to give her a paw, to roll over, to fetch his favourite toy – a battered old ring made from plastic that was supposed to resemble a doughnut. She thought of the miles they'd walked side by side, the nights they'd spent stretched out together on the sofa watching the sheepdog trials on television, the way that he would lick her hand and nudge her gently with the damp tip of his nose, as if to let her know that he would always be there.

She had once read somewhere that during a dog's final moments, it was kindest to act normally, as if today was just like any other day and tomorrow would start as it always did, with a long, lazy walk followed by breakfast in the back garden, soaking up the sun. She wondered now if the person who wrote that had ever lost their dog in this way – if they themselves had ever tried not to shake as they drew a hand across the warm fur of their loyal companion for the very last time.

She nodded, and as the vet applied the needle, Jess shut her eyes. She kept her fingers against Smudge's ears, fondling them steadily, hoping he could somehow feel her there.

When she opened her eyes again, she was just in time to see his paws flex slightly as his little chest made one tired, final breath, and then he was still.

Jess leaned forward and buried her face against his warm neck, inhaling his familiar smell.

'I love you,' she whispered into his fur, her voice thick with grief and desperate tears. 'Be good, okay?'

28

'Will?'

'Jess? What's wrong?'

She couldn't quite bring herself to say the words. 'How's Charlotte?' she asked him.

He exhaled. 'Fine. Natalie panicked. The needle on the adrenaline pen bent. But she was quick-thinking enough to shove a load of antihistamines down her neck, thank God. She spent the night in hospital, but she's okay.'

'That's great,' Jess said, but her voice broke as she spoke. Hot tears escaped down her cheeks, but tonight there was no calm neck to bury her face against, no bundle of warm fur on her toes. There was just an empty space on the floorboards where Smudge used to be.

'Jess? What is it?'

'Smudge was hit by a car.'

Will waited, presumably for her to say that it was a close shave, but he was okay.

'He was put to sleep this morning.'

'Oh my God.' He sounded almost breathless, his voice tight, like her news had winded him. 'Jess, I'm so sorry.'

'He was with me every day,' she said, the pain becoming almost physical. 'I don't know what to do now.' She wanted to reach into the phone and grab his hand. 'Can you come over?'

There was a long silence.

'I can't leave Charlotte.' He spoke like it was tearing him in two to say it. 'I'm so sorry, Jess. But I can't leave her, not tonight.'

She felt an uncomfortable wave of grief and bitterness rising up inside her then, and for a couple of moments she didn't trust herself to speak.

'Friday?' he asked her, sounding nearly as distraught as she was. 'I'll try and call . . .'

A vision of Zak taking a claw hammer to Will's kneecaps loomed large and ominous in her mind. 'Will, I need to tell you something . . .'

'Bollocks,' he said, almost under his breath. 'Natalie's looking for me. I've got to go.'

'I love you,' she said, but it was too late. The tone of the dead line cut right through her, as harsh and unbearable as the noise of squealing brakes.

29

Matthew

Thursday, 9 June 1994

As soon as we'd disembarked at Santander, I made the conscious decision to try and forget my former life. We were virtually fugitives now, and Matthew Landley was gone – at least for the foreseeable future. Rather than dwell on the enormity of this fact, I attempted to embrace the idea that I could completely reinvent myself, free as I now was to become someone brand new – but, of course, that concept only really held appeal if you didn't much like the person you were to begin with. I'd thought about it, and the only thing about myself I was desperate to change – other than my feet, and my propensity to blink like a nerd when I was tired – was the fact that I was the sort of guy who could sleep with a fifteen-year-old schoolgirl. But that wasn't something I had plans to stop doing any time soon.

As it turned out, forgetting was easy in the Picos. Compact and (at some point in ancient history) whitewashed, our little hideout was just ramshackle enough to be romantic and for it not to really matter if we spilt coffee or red wine on the floor; but not so run-down that we were afraid to open cupboards for fear of disturbing vermin or flush the toilet in case the septic tank exploded. The villa was perched neighbour-less on one sharp, green slope of a lush Cantabrian mountain; most days, the only sound that could be heard was the soaring swish of raptor wings against the vibrant blue of a Spanish sky.

Each morning, the sun would flare and throb, and the scent of citrus would rise in the garden. Jess would pluck fat yellow lemons from the trees, and together we'd squeeze out the juice by hand, adding chunks of brick-hard sugar from an ancient packet we'd found in the kitchen. The resulting concoction was still so sharp that it made my tongue shrink on contact, but it definitely outdid any shop-bought lemonade I'd ever drunk.

And, of course, we raided the wine cellar on our very first night. Pulling bottles from dirt-encrusted racks by torchlight and brushing layers of dust from the labels, we made a big deal of pretending to examine and assess them before finally admitting to one another that, actually, we couldn't care less what was what because as far as we could both tell, and in the absence of an expert to advise us otherwise, wine was pretty much always going to be just wine.

'Plus they were never going to drink it anyway. I doubt they even knew what was down here in the first place,' Jess said.

I was a big fan of this theory too, but the teacher in me felt forced to point out that it fell roughly on a par with siphoning loose change from the piggy banks of children on the basis that they'd failed to maintain an accurate running total.

Over the next few days, since we had very little to do except stretch out on the patio in the sun, Jess's skin slowly turned a beautiful shade of freckled sun-kissed brown, and her hair crept a couple of tones blonder. I'd look over at her as we lay there holding hands and swigging lemonade, and think about how lucky I was to have found her all those months ago, albeit at the back of my maths class and heading straight for a D-grade in her GCSE. She'd talked more since arriving in Spain than I'd ever heard her talk before, about our dream of Italy, and wanting to finally arrange some proper help for her mum when we got back to England, and what was the point of pi anyway, and did I think that Mr Michaels was happy? And I just shut my eyes and listened to her and thought that if I never had to go back to England for the rest of my life it would be too sodding soon.

There was no phone to the villa, and no means of accessing newspapers, unless I actually wanted to go out and buy one, which I definitely did not. Jess occasionally wondered out loud what was going on back home, and more than once expressed concern for her mum. Quite honestly I was of the private opinion that her teenage daughter fleeing the country should have been her mother's big fat cue to quit the muscle relaxants and stop using gin as a substitute for breakfast cereal, but I assured her that all we had to do was wait a week or so for the inevitable shit-storm back in England to subside. After that, I said, we could perhaps think about a safe way of getting a message to her – although whether she would be able to tear herself away from daytime television for long enough to pay attention to it was anybody's guess.

I knew – of course I did – that it was unrealistic and naive to feel invincible, and occasionally my father popped up unhelpfully in my subconscious to remind me that pride comes before a fall and blah, blah, blah; but as the minutes, hours and days ticked past and no Spanish sirens came hurtling up the mountainside, I felt increasingly confident that nobody was going to find us. Perhaps we really could hide out here until September and Jess's sixteenth birthday, surviving on our strange little diet of home-made lemonade, plain pasta and somebody else's wine collection. Or maybe in a few weeks we'd move on to Italy. I began to imagine that my fantasy of a family and a life in the sun with Jess could really, incredibly, be just a train ride away.

Occasionally I'd indulge in a minor daydream about what might be happening back at Hadley Hall, happily picturing the look on Sonia's face when she found out that I'd pissed all over her nasty little plan to have me arrested. I imagined her bitching noisily about us to Lorraine Wecks, blabbing on and on about it to Mackenzie, moaning to the National Union of Teachers – all of whom were powerless to act, mainly because we were holed up in the middle of a Spanish mountain range and nobody had a fucking clue where we were.

Nobody, that is, unless you were counting the CNP, Interpol, the UK Immigration Service and the British Embassy in Madrid.

Late that afternoon, I heard the crunch of car tyres against gravel (the police were evidently wise to the use of sirens in an area where if somebody so much as sneezed it was audible from several hillsides away). Ironically enough, it was my birthday, and we were celebrating by soaking up the last of the sun and drinking our latest batch of lemonade, alternately wincing and mumbling to one another about perhaps daring to venture out for a paella supper.

Paella supper my arse.

Years later, I can still clearly picture Jess as she was that afternoon, flat on her back in her pink bikini top and cut-off denim shorts, a pair of plastic sunglasses clamped across her face – a clumsy attempt at glamour. I realized with some sadness that she looked disturbingly like a child on her first ever foreign holiday, which in hindsight probably didn't do a lot to endear me to the Spanish authorities.

'Jess,' I said softly, squeezing her hand.

Whenever I had permitted myself to think about how this moment might feel, I had assumed a fireball of terror or similar would spontaneously erupt in my gut – after which I could only hope I'd be man enough not to run off screaming and hurl myself from the nearest rocky outcrop. So it was something of a pleasant surprise to realize that, now the time had finally come, I felt utterly calm. Stupidly calm – as calm as only someone slightly high on sex and sunshine can be. I didn't even come close to having an aneurysm.

I reached across and took her sweet face between my hands for the last time. 'I love you,' I whispered as her eyes filled up and she understood what was happening.

'No,' she said simply as she started to sob. 'No.'

And then there was a lapse of approximately five seconds before everything went crazy, with the police springing out of their cars to corner me like I was a puma escaped from a zoo, spray cans trained on my face and pistols on my shins. Some people were screaming in Spanish and some of us in English as they tried to lure Jess away from me and towards their cars, as if I had my arm round her neck and a gun to her head. Her reluctance to obey them by leaving my side seemed to throw them off a bit, and in the end I wouldn't have been surprised if they'd had to whip out a lasso to finish the whole thing off.

True to form, Jess used those final five seconds productively by kissing me for the last time and pushing something desperately into my hand. It was my birthday present, I realized, a bracelet woven in black leather. She must have bought it from the roadside with a snatched peseta note when we stopped for petrol en route to our perfect little hideout.

432

I only just had time to get it round my wrist before they slapped the handcuffs on.

I turned to look at her as they shoved me roughly on to the rear seat of the police car, hands behind my back in the cuffs, and a lot tighter than they needed to be. A female police officer had her arm round Jess's shoulders, and they'd made her put on a weird blue shirt to hide the bikini, as if I was some sort of gangmaster who'd been forcing her to wander about semi-naked for my own entertainment.

She'd been crying so hard the whole time that the skin around her eyes was red, and as the police car started up, she began to sob hysterically all over again. The flashing blue light, which was ready to announce the triumph of my capture all the way back down the mountainside, was reflected against her beautiful brown skin.

I shouted it out. I didn't care. 'I love you, Jess.' I thought about maybe giving it a go in Spanish too, but the police didn't look as if they were going to wait around patiently while I fucked up my syntax.

Jess sobbed harder, beside herself – so hard that, to my dismay, she was unable to form words.

'Wait for me, okay?'

But before she could even attempt to answer, they had slammed the car door shut rather unceremoniously against the side of my head. It hurt like fuck, and burst my naive little bubble of happiness like a Mexican taking a baseball bat to a papier-mâché donkey.

30

Zak's incoming text crash-landed amongst a flurry of others from Anna, all variations on a theme – to please stop ignoring her calls, to at least text with news on Smudge, to answer the sodding door. Flicking over those, and with some trepidation, Jess opened the one from Zak.

It simply read: *Happy Friday, baby! So is it two cases of champagne for your welcome-to-London party, or three?*

She rolled back over into the pillow and shut her eyes. *As far as I'm concerned you can buy fifty*, she thought to herself, *and shove the whole bloody lot of them up your arse.*

She had no idea what she was going to do about Zak, but this much she did know: she was categorically *not* going to move to an overdeveloped mews house in Belsize Park with a four-by-four in the garage, a cleaner whom everybody referred to as a maid, self-cleaning glass where all the ceilings were supposed to be and fewer interior walls than a distribution warehouse. Added to which, she would far rather go and drown herself on the salt marsh than be made to celebrate her enforced relocation with the aid of twenty-quid-a-glass champagne, a pretentious buffet of hummus-on-things and lots of smoothed-out affected wankers called Glen who were big in pharmaceutical sales and still thought that being mildly pissed was sufficient justification for manhandling the arses of passing females.

Her time had finally run out, but she knew what she was going to do. She was going to fight. And she was going to fight for Will.

*

En route to Carafe for bread mid-morning, having struggled against the impulse to grab Smudge's lead from the coat hook and whistle him to her side, Jess made the surprising discovery of Will on her front doorstep. She wondered at first if he'd been there all night – such was his spaced-out demeanour – but he claimed she hadn't responded to his knocking, which was weird, because she hadn't heard a thing.

He looked almost formal in dark brown jeans and a long-sleeved shirt, like they had some sort of appointment, and his behaviour was odd. Moving awkwardly, he wasn't relaxed at all, and did nothing for a few moments but rub his chin and fail to look at her. He seemed stiff too, like he'd come straight off the weights bench in his garage.

But he was lovely as ever: tall, brown, kind. He smelt faintly of baby shampoo – the scent of early childhood, safety and happiness.

They were running out of time, though. Zak's nasty little clock was ticking – she was all too aware of that.

Standing there in the middle of the room with his head almost touching the beams, Will allowed his gaze to rest on her; and his expression was so sad, it almost made her heart break.

'I'm really sorry about Smudge, Jess.'

Just the sound of his name made the tears rise. 'Oh, don't,' she pleaded, afraid that if they talked about him, she might start to cry and never stop. 'I can't talk about it. I really can't, I'm sorry . . .'

'Oh, hey, don't,' he said, but he didn't make a move towards her. 'I'm sorry. We don't have to talk about it.'

They stood there for a couple of moments, just regarding each other. Will looked as if he had something he wanted to say but no words to say it with.

'Are you okay?' she asked him. 'You seem a bit . . .'

What was left of his smile flattened then, before disappearing completely. 'Actually, I'm not, Jess. I've got something I need to tell you.'

She swallowed. *Good, because I've got something I need to tell you too. Something I should have told you seventeen years ago.*

But the words simply wouldn't form. So she just stared weakly at him, her mouth dry, and nodded. 'Something-like-herpes or something-like-you-don't-think-we-should-do-this-any-more?' she managed eventually.

There was a long silence before he said, 'Something like I don't think we should do this any more.'

She stared at him. For some stupid reason, she hadn't been expecting him to say that at all. She had been expecting him to choose option C. Whatever the fuck option C was.

'What?' she said, her voice weak but her heart thumping fast as if she'd just been mugged.

'Natalie's pregnant.'

Feeling her chest clench, she blinked fiercely. It took her a few moments to recall the art of speech. 'Oh,' was all she could think of to say. If he had whipped out a cricket bat and swung it into her stomach she could not have felt more stunned or more wounded.

'So we're moving back to London next week.'

She's what? You're what? When? What?

'What . . . what about the house?' *What happened to staying until September?*

There was a long pause. 'Well, Natalie tells me the building work's ahead of schedule.'

'Oh,' she said, with a single bewildered nod.

He shut his eyes for a moment as if he couldn't bear to see her looking at him. 'What happened with Charlotte the other night made me realize how much I love her, Jess.'

Does he mean Charlotte or Natalie?

'Do you mean Charlotte or Natalie?'

He didn't answer her straight away, making her wait for the one response that should have come easily. 'Both, of course,' he said eventually. 'I love both of them, very much.'

'Oh, right,' she said, struggling for a moment to digest this particular thunderbolt. 'Sorry to ask. I must have misunderstood, before.'

He hung his head then, like he was completely exhausted. 'What's been happening with us, Jess . . . it's just fantasy. It's not real.'

The tears stung. 'What? Will! I don't believe you . . .' She stepped towards him, grabbing his hand. It felt limp and cool, like he wasn't even in there. 'Look – I could come to London,' she said, her mind and voice moving quickly as if she was first on the scene at a road traffic accident and was desperately trying to stop him from slipping into a coma. 'I could come, and we could see what happens. You're just scared, you're just panicking . . .'

And then she met his eye, and he shook his head slowly, and she felt despair like she had never felt before. Not in Spain. Not with her mother. Not even when she was stroking Smudge's head and whispering her goodbyes.

Her gaze fell in exasperation, and as it did, she realized that there was something missing from round his wrist.

'You're not wearing your bracelet,' she observed sadly. And then, her voice smaller, 'Did it break?'

He swallowed and said nothing, which she took to mean he had removed it out of respect for his freshly pregnant girlfriend.

She sensed things were coming to an end. 'You can choose me,' she said desperately, squeezing his hand, her voice spun with the tiniest, most delicate thread of hope.

437

He shook his head. 'No. I can't.' He sounded like it physically pained him to speak, like someone had their hand pressed very firmly against his windpipe.

Jess met his eye, trying desperately to save him from the long lifetime of dumb slumber he seemed determined now to enter. 'It doesn't have to be like this, Will.'

'I think,' he said, almost talking over her, 'you should go out and find a good guy.'

Please don't.

'Someone who can give you what you need. Just please promise me that. If there's nothing else to say, at least tell me that you're going to find yourself a really good guy.'

She smiled at him. 'Well, actually,' she whispered, her eyes full of tears, 'I think I've already found him.'

Incredibly, he missed it completely. 'You mean Zak?' he said, his voice shaking slightly. 'Yeah – you could probably have a good life with him, Jess. Move to London, give it a go.'

She could hardly believe what she was hearing. 'You told me the other day that I should be with someone who really and truly loves me,' she said, incredulous.

He swallowed. 'Well, I probably got it wrong about him. I mean, he's a bloody doctor, after all. How bad can he really be? You should give it some thought, at least.'

She was starting to feel dizzy, like she needed to rest her head. 'Please don't. You're actually making it worse. Which is amazing, because it was pretty bad already.'

He met her eye then and despite his words he looked as if he could happily have stuck himself in the chest with her sharpest Swiss fillet knife. 'Well, didn't anyone tell you, Jess? I specialize in wanker. It's the only thing I'm really fucking good at.'

There followed a long silence during which Jess attempted

to imagine never seeing him again, to realize that he was ending it now, today. He must have decided, as Anna would say, that everything between them was just fantasy without a future.

And she knew then that if he was leaving, if she might never actually see him again, she had to tell him. She could no longer justify keeping it from him, if not having the courage had ever been justifiable in the first place.

She thought back to his words on the marsh that night. 'It should have been us, Mr L.' Her voice was a fierce twist of emotion. 'It should have been us, with the marriage and the baby and the perfect fucking life.'

Painfully, incrementally, the expression on his face began to change – as if she had taken something very sharp and was winding it steadily into his abdomen. And she knew then that he knew.

Somehow, without her even having to say the words, he knew.

Almost straight away, she started to cry, because the reality of telling him was so much harder than she'd even imagined. She had to force her mouth to release the words, to let them scatter into the room like tiny prisoners on the run, determined to wreak havoc after so much time inside. 'I've got something I need to say. If this is it – if you're really leaving, I need to tell you something I should have told you seventeen years ago.'

He had become almost entirely motionless, like he was hoping that if he stayed very still, her words might somehow fail to find him.

'I was pregnant, Matthew.'

The gaze of his green eyes remained unflinching against her face. And then he slowly shook his head and mouthed the single word, *Don't*.

439

But she couldn't comply; she had to continue. She had kept it from him for too long. He deserved to know the truth about what she'd done.

'I'm so sorry.' She could hardly summon the breath to say it. 'I had an abortion. I'm so sorry. It was a mistake. I didn't know what else to do.'

It was a few more seconds before his face completely broke in half. 'Oh, no.' Tears pooled rapidly in his eyes as he covered his mouth with his hands. 'Please don't, Jess.'

Her own tears began to fall now too. 'I'm so sorry. I wish I hadn't. Please know how much I wish that.'

He put his hands up then to hide his face and silently shook his head, begging her with his whole body to stop.

'I thought it would make everything worse,' Jess said, painstakingly transferring her regrets from heart to mouth. 'They told me you were going to get years. I thought we wouldn't ever be allowed to see each other again.'

She had realized long ago that hindsight was caustic like acid, corroding excuses over time until all that was left was a toxic mess where reason and judgement used to be.

'It was the biggest mistake of my life,' she continued, hating the sound of her own voice as she was sure Will now did too. 'I regret it every single day.'

Will took his hands away from his face, and the sight of him failing to fight his tears made her crumple up inside. 'How could you not tell me, Jess?' His voice was raw with devastation and disbelief. 'How could you not *tell me this*?'

Seventeen years of dread was too quickly becoming reality. The realization that everything was about to change irreversibly came at her as brutally as iced water being shoved down her neck, and for a moment she was forced to catch her breath. 'I couldn't,' she finally managed. 'The social workers –'

'Not then.' He shook his head, cheeks freshly wet with tears. 'Now. For these past few weeks? I've been so happy just to know you again, Jess, and all along . . .'

Her voice, when it arrived to meet his, was tiny. 'I'd only just found you. I didn't want you to leave again.'

Why could she not say a single thing that sounded even slightly defensible? Perhaps, she realized, because none of it actually was.

Will swallowed, nodding several times in quick succession in that way people did when they were trying really hard not to say what they were thinking. 'Wow. Okay.'

'But you're leaving now,' she finished quietly. 'I might never see you again, and I couldn't let you go and not tell you.'

There followed a silence so dark she could almost see it.

'FUCK,' he shouted then, his voice a swift punch against the unyielding cruelty of her honesty. 'HOW THE FUCK CAN THIS BE HAPPENING?'

And then he turned away from her, leaning over and resting both his hands on the mantelpiece, an involuntary act of despair. Jess stood very still and looked at his back, wishing she could offer him even a solitary sentence that didn't sound feeble and pathetic the moment it left her mouth.

'So tell me now,' he said eventually, without turning round.

She forced herself to form the words. 'I found out . . . five weeks after Spain. Debbie told my mum and my aunt – they were furious, they didn't want me to go through with it. They threatened to go to the police . . . I didn't know what to do.'

'How many weeks?'

'Nearly seven.'

A pause. 'July.'

441

She nodded, which was stupid because he still had his back to her.

'I wish . . . I could turn the clock back, Will. I just – I need you to know that.'

He didn't move or speak.

'I don't have a single excuse,' she continued.

'You don't need one, Jessica,' he said into the fireplace, cutting her off. 'You were fifteen.'

Neither of them moved for a few more seconds.

'Please don't hate me,' she breathed, her final desperate plea to him, because that was the only thing in the world that she wanted now. He could walk away, go and rebuild his life with Natalie, be a father to two wonderful children – the same life the law had never wanted for her and Matthew. But Jess knew that if his lasting memory of her was coloured by contempt, she would not be able to live with it.

'I don't hate you, Jess,' Will said then, his head hanging right down towards the floorboards. He let out a guttural groan. 'Don't you get it? I still love you.'

And there they were: words that should have been happy, possibly even life-changing. Yet all Jess could do was watch them go by, carried away on a tide they'd both missed.

Because it was too late for them to love one another now. For the briefest of moments they had been hand in hand on the same little patch of their past, and now they were divided once again.

Eventually Will straightened up and faced her, and from across the room she could see that he was fighting the urge to step into the space between them, to reach out and take her hand.

'So, look,' he said, his agony as visible as an open wound. 'I think we've firmly established that I've fucked up your life in every way imaginable.'

She shook her head at him, muted now by grief.

'And I should tell you that I'm really sorry. I'm more sorry for that than I can put into words, Jess.'

Finally, she had to speak. 'Please stop saying sorry. I wish you wouldn't. Please.'

He looked her in the eyes, and she felt his confusion and anguish as if it was her own. 'What should I say instead, Jess? That I wish more than anything you'd made a different choice? That if you had, we might be together right now – married, kids, living somewhere fucking spectacular? That I wish you could have found a way to tell me – to somehow let me know? That if you had, I would have begged you like a selfish bastard to keep the baby, because I would have loved the *bones* of you – both of you – for the rest of my life?'

She shook her head again, releasing a thick rush of hot tears.

His voice was raised now, strung out with pain. 'But I can't tell you any of that, Jess, because it's not fair! It's not fair! You were fifteen years old!'

There followed a long, agonizing pause, broken only by the sound of Will's tormented breathing as Jess fought the urge to sink to her knees and sob.

Eventually he managed to speak again, his voice steadier. 'I was the lowlife who got you pregnant, and you were the one who had to deal with it. And that's why I'm sorry.'

There was time, she hoped, for one final attempt to absolve him. 'Don't say that,' she whispered through her tears, though it sounded more like a shudder than a sentence. 'Please. You were the best thing that ever happened to me.'

He flinched slightly as she said it, as if her words had cleaved open some tiny part of him deep inside, a sharp incision he could feel but not see. Only the shake of his jaw gave him away – the rest of his face he succeeded in holding precariously together, though it was threatening to fall apart on him at any moment.

'Actually,' he said after a few moments' pause, 'I think I was probably the worst. You know – all things considered.'

He moved past her then towards the front door, only pausing briefly to touch her shoulder with his hand, like they were distant dysfunctional relatives having a moment, or colleagues calling it quits after a bout in the boardroom.

And just like that, he was gone.

A few moments later, there came the sound of his car pulling away from the kerb. She listened numbly to it from where she was standing motionless in the middle of the living room, like she'd just borne witness to a suicide-by-shotgun.

It had a similar effect, in the end, because she had an overwhelming urge to lean over and throw up all over her shoes.

31

Will

Friday, 17 June 2011

That is the thing about doctors of emergency medicine. They really know which bits of your neck to press on to make you feel like you're about to suffocate. They also know what body parts are the best for kicking so that nobody knows you've been on the receiving end of a really good pounding.

I'd never seen his friends before – I assumed they were from London. It was funny, in a way: they looked as if they hung out at Ascot in their spare time and they spoke like Old Etonians, but they punched like they came from Walthamstow.

Anyway, after I'd been half throttled and beaten into submission (which was how they finally got me to confess to having run Jess over with my car), Zak deposited me on the sofa in his weird upside-down warehouse-style beach house and made me repeat the little script he'd prepared for me, word for word. Clearly a details man, he'd thought of everything, right down to a phantom pregnancy for Natalie.

He managed to make me feel like I didn't have a choice about the whole thing by threatening to have me framed for further sex offences. He had a consultant friend, apparently, who was more than happy to claim he had 'suspicions' about the way I was behaving around my daughter at the hospital following her anaphylactic attack (fast-tracked, too, if any of them got wind of me telling Jess about this particularly vile brand of bullshit).

'Nice touch,' I muttered, when he dropped that one in.

'Well, don't be a dick about it, Will,' Zak said, as if we were arguing over a car-parking space and I was frankly being wholly unreasonable. 'We all have our flaws, don't we? Yours is, you like to have sex with schoolgirls. Mine is, I get very angry when people lie to me.'

'Yeah,' I managed, though as I spoke I was starting to suspect that my ribcage was no longer fully intact, 'I'm getting that bit.'

Privately, I was pleased that he had called me Will. It felt like a small victory. He thought he was sodding Poirot but he'd failed to dig down beyond even the most basic of details.

It turned out that Zak and I had met before, at his old place of work, where I'd apparently blabbed about my conviction in between rounds of upchucking. Zak claimed that he never forgot a face, which was annoying because neither did I, except when I'd drunk my own body weight in vodka and punched through the recommended limit on white-label paracetamol. Happily, though, our hospital encounter happened long before Jess had the distinct misfortune of bumping into him under a portico in Holkham park, so her name – and therefore my real one – appeared to have passed him by.

This was of some comfort to me as they dumped me back outside Carnation Close, rolling me out of the four-by-four in the manner of Latin American drugs barons. Jess and I would always have what came before, and nobody – not even Dr Zak Foster – could take that away from us.

I just needed time to think. I could sort this whole mess out, I was sure of that. I'd always thought of myself as a bit of a pessimist, but where Jess Hart was concerned, I could in fact rival the most nauseating of carol singers with my levels of inner cheer.

For now though, to buy time, I would have to go along with Zak's plan. It would be brutal, but I'd do it.

I would go and see her at once, just like he'd said.

32

Jess's head had been pounding since the moment Will
walked out, so eventually she opted to manufacture her own
brand of analgesic by way of some ancient diazepam and a
brand-new bottle of gin, resourceful in the manner of an
agoraphobic making supper from couscous and a gravy
cube.

Five missed calls from Anna and a text from Debbie to
say an offer had been made on the cottage only accelerated
her descent towards gin oblivion, but no sooner had she
arrived there than her haze began to be obliterated by waves
of crippling stomach pain. Suspecting this to be the down-
side of mixing different toxin groups in large quantities, Jess
thought momentarily about calling Anna back – if only to
demand an explanation again for why she'd done what she
did – but she swiftly became swamped with remorse once
more over Smudge, and Will, and the baby. There were easier ways to make herself feel worse than she did already.

Like, maybe she'd go down to the beach and cast free her
things, watch them get carried away on the water. Smudge's
name tag from his collar. Those designer shoes from Zak
that would probably result in broken bones if she ever
attempted to walk in them. Will's necklace. She could do it
all now – the tide would be high.

And while she was at it, she would try very hard to lose
the chattering sound inside her mind too, because it was
really starting to irritate her. It was mechanically repeating
just one thing, over and over again.

Natalie's pregnant. Natalie's pregnant.

'What?' said a male voice.

She definitely recognized the touched-with-amusement scoff. She was sure that she'd heard it somewhere before – maybe when she'd been trying to speak in Spanish and failing to correctly conjugate her verbs. And then she realized that, without noticing, she'd managed to pick up a call from Zak.

Her hand was shaking like the phone was on vibrate. She hadn't even heard it ring. 'Yes,' she said, swallowing back tears and staring blankly at the trinkets on the mantelpiece, the ones that Will had so admired the first time he'd been here. When had he first been here? She could hardly remember. 'What is it, Zak?' At least, that was how it sounded in her head. Zak had a different perspective, specifically that she was slurring incoherently like a tramp on a park bench.

'I've got stomach ache,' she told him then, sadly. At which point she hung her head, dropped the phone and noisily discharged vomit all over her knees.

'Stay there, baby. I'm coming to get you.'

Zak was supposed to be waiting in for the delivery of a cast-iron chimenea that would allegedly add ambience to his devoid-of-life garden, and was insisting on bringing Jess back to the beach house with him so he wouldn't miss his time slot and end up having to pay £200 to collect it himself from Solihull or similar.

He'd brought along a specially designed hospital-issue vomit bag, which he looped around her neck before helping her into the four-by-four. Jess felt momentarily inclined to make a dash for the open road, but something about the way that Zak was having to angle her into the car head first while her eyes rolled and her mouth produced strange noises made

449

her think that perhaps an impromptu run was a touch ambitious.

The sick bag came complete with a drawstring and reinforced gusset, but that didn't stop Zak from hitting the handbrake and ejecting her from the vehicle as soon as she began to heave again. He was clearly a bit paranoid about vomit fumes pervading the car's leather interior trim of his Range Rover, in the manner of a taxi driver on the graveyard shift over-zealously chucking people out of his Vauxhall Insignia the minute they asked if he wouldn't mind opening the window.

Once she'd finished throwing up, Jess found herself weeping weakly into the verge, the pattern of Zak's flashing hazard lights adding an unfortunate end-of-disco feel to being sick on all fours in the middle of the pavement. She started telling Zak about Smudge, but she realized that she was crying more loudly than she was talking, so she abandoned the effort and then couldn't find a way to stop sobbing, let alone get to her feet.

By the time Zak had scooped her up, wiped her down, put her back in the car and attached a fresh bag round her neck, she was beginning to think that, on the plus side, today was unlikely to get much worse.

Slumped on the sofa with her head in a bucket, Jess wished Zak would take a short intermission from his lecture about stomach linings and delayed-onset multiple organ failure to hold her hair back for her. They'd established an hour ago that she hadn't taken anywhere near the required quantity of assorted toxins to cause any real damage, and she'd already assured him she wasn't attempting an overdose, merely anaesthesia.

'Fuck,' she groaned as the room bulged and slid about, a

sensation that wasn't much improved by Zak chiding away in her ear. 'Fuck.'

'And what the hell are you doing stockpiling diazepam anyway?'

My mother shot herself in the face and I found her, she wanted to say to him. *They give you a lifetime's supply of tranquillizers when that happens.*

'Just leave me alone,' she whimpered, dipping her head to retch once more, wishing that Zak would for once cooperate and turn out to be a stockbroker or a Rolls-Royce salesman as opposed to a bloody A & E doctor.

He paused then, probably thinking she was approaching contrition. 'Look, I wouldn't normally recommend this, but I think you could do with a coffee. It might perk you up a bit. You look exhausted.'

Just the mention of something as foul as fresh coffee was enough to elicit another bitter stream of vomit from Jess's gullet. As she heaved, the violence of her physical reaction reminded her without warning of morning sickness, and she was besieged by grief all over again.

Zak made a sound like he'd just seen a flasher in a park. 'Urrrgh, Jess, that is grim.'

'You don't have to stand there and watch,' she gasped, stomach acid running down her chin. She groped wildly to her left for tissues.

'I've got to keep an eye on you,' he admonished. 'If I let you in the bathroom you'll probably never come out again.'

Another sour river of sharp bile rose. Her head thumped like her brain was trying to make an escape, like it was hammering on the inside of her skull, trying to tell her something.

'This is exactly why we're going to London, Jess,' Zak was

saying. 'You need to sort yourself out. I mean, look at the state of you. You're a mess.'

He seemed as smug to see her like this as if he'd mixed up her little cocktail of gin and diazepam himself.

Trying not to remember how he'd goaded her over Will, and resisting the urge to ask him why he'd bought a second home here if he thought the place was so crappy, Jess concentrated on aiming her surging stream of puke in the right direction. Finally, it subsided, and she sat breathless and shivering, her arms round the bucket in the same way as she used to wrap them round the dog. She began to cry, but was still too woozy to think lucidly about Smudge – all she knew was that she missed him, and she wanted his head on her lap as opposed to Zak's self-satisfaction in her face.

Sensing her lack of desire to engage in a debate on her various shortcomings, Zak buggered off to clatter about in the kitchen with his over-engineered coffee machine. 'I know a removals guy,' he called through to her after a few moments, 'who can do all your stuff. He's good. He won't break your piano.'

Zak had a habit of seeing as selling points what most people would think of as standard service, which frequently made Jess feel indignant in the manner of a budget airline passenger.

Before she could respond, there was a noise from the kitchen that sounded like he'd dropped a full bag of coffee beans. 'Fuck,' she heard him exclaim. Then louder: '*Fuck* it.'

Something compelled her to stand up and wobble slowly over to the kitchen, where she saw him lifting his foot in hesitant distaste like a cat attempting to navigate a puddle. He'd somehow managed to fling a giant bag of frozen peas all over the room.

It was odd. They'd clearly been defrosting for a while,

because most of them were neon green and soft enough that he'd already mashed a fair portion of them into the soles of his socks.

Looking up, he registered her presence with a wince of irritation. 'Go away, Jess,' he said sharply. 'I'll clean this up.'

She nodded. 'What were you doing with them?'

He paused for longer than seemed natural. 'I was going to make soup.'

'Soup?'

'Yeah, as in . . . pea soup.'

Zak was no chef. He barely knew how to reheat soup, never mind make it from scratch. He was also not a man known for storing value bags of anything in his freezer, let alone choosing it as the base ingredient for impromptu home-made soup in the middle of summer.

None of this made any sense.

'Soup for what?' she asked him with a frown.

'To eat! Go away, Jess.'

As he spoke, he reached over to pick up a sopping wet tea towel from the sideboard, tossing it quickly into the sink as if he was trying to conceal the evidence of something.

'Jess, please just go and sit down while I clear this up,' he said, as if she was a toddler he'd just caught flinging biscuits around his house.

So she sat back down on the sofa and listened to him faffing about locating errant peas, cursing and slamming things like this was all the cleaner's fault for being off-duty. And she wondered again why the hell he would be making pea soup, desperate all the while for her head to clear so she could work out what was going on.

She leaned back and shut her eyes. Five or ten minutes later, Zak emerged with the coffee and no socks on. She took the cup from him, although she wanted it even less now than she had before, and as he passed it to her she noticed that his knuckles were the colour of pulped strawberries.

She was about to say, *Jesus, Zak, what did you punch?* but something stopped her. Her brain was slowly starting to grind into action, halting and juddering as it tried to move forward in a way that was not dissimilar to Debbie attempting to drive a car that came with gears.

Zak perched on the edge of the coffee table and waited for Jess to be appreciative, so she took a sip from her cup. Predictably, it made her stomach recoil, which meant she'd have to tip the rest of it on to his yucca while he wasn't looking.

'You made the right decision, *cariño*,' he told her then, watching her steadily, and she knew he wasn't talking about the coffee.

She didn't bother pointing out that there hadn't really been a decision on offer, because Debbie had already sold her cottage and Zak had been threatening to break Will's legs. The intended outcome wasn't too hard for anyone with a basic grasp of how blackmail worked – which was everybody – to decipher.

But she knew it was easier to let Zak think he'd won.

The smile he shot her was laced with triumph. 'Sleep this off tonight. We'll go to London first thing in the morning. I'll get my guy to bring over the rest of your stuff next week.'

Then he put a hand on her leg, but – entirely out of instinct – she jerked away from him.

There was a tense pause.

'You need a shower,' he said eventually. 'You smell like a Saturday-night stomach pumping.' And then he got up and left the room, presumably to fetch her a towel (or, if he really wanted to hammer his point home, a mirror), and it was then that Jess registered something solid on the floor, underneath her bare foot where she'd jolted it backwards.

The object was dark, half hidden under the edge of the sofa. She bent over shakily and picked it up.

It was Will's bracelet, broken once again at the glue join.

The feel of the leather against her fingers as she stared down at it and recalled the colour of Zak's knuckles brought a fresh tide of nausea to her throat. This time, she was careful to miss the bucket, and on Will's behalf left her mark indelibly in tones of bile and jaundice all over Zak's made-to-measure bamboo silk rug that had always been, in hindsight, a very vulnerable shade of cream.

Jess gained some minor satisfaction from watching Zak gabbling and swearing in Spanish, crawling about on his hands and knees and rubbing at her puke with toilet paper, turning his knuckles from red to orange. He had his phone on hands-free to the emergency rug people, who seemed to be saying that the earliest they could come out would be next Monday and under no circumstances should he attempt to rub the stain.

The following morning, Jess waited outside the front door of the beach house for Zak, having showered, Alka-Seltzered and ingested vast quantities of aspirin and caffeine for breakfast. The chimenea was outside in the back garden looking bizarre, the cleaner had promised to locate all the remaining peas before they rotted, and now they were locking up and preparing to head to London. Jess breathed in the smell of the salt air for the last time.

'This is the best thing for us,' Zak said to her as they walked across the gravel together towards the waiting car.

She nodded. 'I'm sure you're right.'

He bent down and delivered a kiss to her cheek. 'Baby, I'm always right.' And then, with a smile, he opened the car door.

Will's bracelet, at least, was safe. As Zak turned up the music and pulled out of the driveway, Jess slid her left hand into her pocket and let her fingertips rest on the snapped scrap of leather, just so she could feel it there.

33

Will

Saturday, 3 December 2016

Twenty-three years ago this weekend, a girl tapped on my back door in the middle of a snowstorm, asking to be let in. And now, I had returned to North Norfolk with a plan to do the same.

As if to mark the occasion, the snow was back.

I'd heard about a great little Italian trattoria that had opened up close to the coast. It was getting rave reviews and, by all accounts, the chef had talent. I was keen to try it, find out what all the fuss was about.

La Piccola Trattoria was tucked away near to Carafe, the French wine bar. From the not insubstantial amount of time I'd committed to online research, I already knew the restaurant would be snug and intimate, its tables crammed closely together, the ambience cast in candlelight. It had a reputation as somewhere special, and you generally had to book ahead. On a night like tonight, I was expecting it to be packed out.

But as I crunched up towards the entrance, heart pounding, snow in my hair, the place looked eerily still. The lights were on, but . . . anyway. I cupped my hands and pressed my face against the front door, peering through the glass.

It was at this point that someone thought it would be an intelligent move to tug the door open sharply from the inside. I stumbled forward, forced to grab on to the door handle to stop myself from falling over and braining myself on the flagstones. The momentum sent the door swinging forcefully round on its hinges with me still attached, gripping on to the handle with my arms straight and knees bent like I was learning to waterski.

'Oh my God! I'm so sorry! Are you okay?'

It was a young waiter with plentiful facial acne and a voice that was probably a third of the way to breaking.

'Yeah,' I said, straightening up and clearing my throat, as if I routinely entered rooms like I was auditioning (badly) for an action film. 'I'm okay.'

'That would have been a mistake,' the boy said, passing me a menu as if he hadn't just nearly killed me. 'We've only had five covers tonight.'

I shook out the collar of my woollen coat, sending snowflakes drifting down on to the flagstones. 'Snowstorm,' I said, stamping my feet on the coir mat.

'Yup,' the boy replied. 'You can sit where you like. We're really quiet.'

He wasn't joking, and there wasn't even any sappy faux-Italian music being piped in from behind the bar to fill the void. (Personally, I considered this to be a good thing – in my mind, authentic trattorias relied on their clientele to provide the sound system. Tonight being the exception, obviously. The only noise we could hear right now was the drip of gathering snowmelt in an outside gutter.)

Disconcerting silences aside, the room itself was impressive: a single-storey converted barn that had all the irregular features preserved, like the bowing end wall and wonky ceiling beams. The tables were styled with red-and-white checked tablecloths, glassware sparkling in the candlelight, and I was pleased to see a row of wine barrels lining the far edge of the room. I smiled, raising an imaginary toast to Brett in my mind, before attempting to refocus on what it was I had come here to do.

'Actually,' I said, swallowing, my heartbeat gathering pace, 'I was hoping to see Jess Hart.'

'Oh,' the waiter said, looking slightly flustered. 'I'm afraid she's not working tonight.'

His words were like water to the little blaze of hope that had so far been keeping me warm. 'Oh. Okay.'

'Was she expecting you?'

I shook my head. 'No. I wanted to surprise her.' A thought occurred to me. 'Would you happen to know if she's at home?'

'Sir, I'm sorry, but I can't give you her home address,' the boy said gravely, like I'd just pulled on a knee-length mac and whipped out a pair of night-vision goggles.

'It's okay, don't worry,' I told him, handing back the menu as I prepared to leave. 'I've already got her address.'

'Would you like to buy some arrabiata sauce while you're here?' the boy asked me, suddenly uplifted by the opportunity to do some cross-selling.

'Er, no,' I told him. 'But thanks.'

'*Aperitivo? Antipasto?*'

'*No, grazie. Sei stato molto utile,*' I muttered, hoping that might shut him up. It did. But then I had an idea. 'Actually,' I said, 'I'll take a bottle of champagne.'

He sold me a bottle for forty-five quid, so I gave him fifty and told him to keep the change. I didn't have a clue if the stuff was good or bad, but it came with gold foil round its neck and a bottle shape that said *this sparkles*, so as far as I was concerned, it was perfect for the job.

I pulled up my collar and strode out again into the cold, cradling the bottle against my chest to guard against a smash if I slipped on ice, crunching the five minutes or so it took me to get to Jess's cottage.

I knew some of the detail. We'd exchanged a couple of texts soon after Natalie and I had fled back to London, and shortly before Christmas Jess had written me an email. Her plan, it transpired, had been to bide her time with Zak until the inevitable happened – which was that living on top of each other in a poky terrace masquerading as a mews house worth a couple of million quid had finally served to underscore their fundamental differences, to the point where even Zak was forced to stop pretending they didn't exist. Only a short time after that, he'd been fortuitously required to assess the hip injury of a semi-famous lads' mag model who had toppled off her high heels while staggering out of a nightclub close to his hospital. Ever the committed professional, Zak had popped back to see her at the end of his shift, whereupon she'd handed him the latest edition of *Maxim* and he promptly forgot he wasn't single. Just a few weeks later, Jess had packed up and moved back to Norfolk, renting her cottage again from the buy-to-let investor who'd bought it from her sister.

She'd posted my bracelet back to me too, having discovered it lying underneath Zak's sofa after my pounding, which was how she'd managed to work out what he'd done.

Jess also informed me that Anna Baxter had finally confessed to being the architect of our demise all those years ago, which wasn't entirely surprising, given that I'd always felt about as comfortable in her presence as a pacifist ringside at a boxing match. Unsurprisingly, the news had not been received well by Jess – but since then, the two of them had managed to meet up for a few tentative discussions, so I assumed a reconciliation would be on the cards at some point. (Several months after Jess's email, Anna began to unnerve me once again by cropping up in various media outlets as some sort of clean-living fertility guru with a book to promote, having recently become a mother to triplets. I'd seen her in the *Guardian* and the *Mail*, and twice on breakfast television – but thankfully she'd not yet used the opportunity of national airtime to out me as a convicted sex offender. Though never say never.)

But the best bit about Jess's email was the part where she modestly related to me the news of her own success. She'd worked hard to secure sufficient funding to open her own restaurant from some investors she'd met during her brief stint catering in the Hampstead area. She said she hoped I'd visit as soon as it was open and tell her what I thought of the food.

And then she apologized to me again about the baby. *I hope that one day you'll forgive me*, she wrote, *but I really would understand if you feel you can't.*

She'd sent me that email at about three a.m. one Saturday morning. I was awake too, suffering from my usual insomnia and staring out at the stars from the window of my attic room in Chiswick. So I'd emailed her back by return because I didn't want her feeling needlessly guilty for a second longer than necessary. I told her I loved her and always had, and that I would never blame her for what happened. There was only one person who should be shouldering the full weight of that responsibility, I insisted, and that was me.

I also opted to clarify, in case she hadn't already worked it out, that Natalie wasn't pregnant, and that Zak's little *Sopranos*-style mob threats were the only reason I'd been forced to pretend otherwise that morning at her cottage.

It took me a long time to decide how to sign off that email to her. Eventually I opted to say simply that I wouldn't be back for a while, as we were putting our holiday home on the market (Natalie having been shamelessly seduced by the valuations she'd requested on a whim soon after we'd finished the renovations). I told Jess I hoped she would find happiness – I'd wanted to give her the chance to move on from me, have the opportunity to meet someone special who could commit to her in the way she truly deserved. I knew I had to step back – as I had tried so hard to do over all the years that had gone before – and let her recover from the heartache I had brought her.

Ironically enough, it was Natalie's distinct lack of pregnancy that had eventually inspired her to leave me. My replacement's name was Henry (inventive nickname: Henners, which basically told you everything you needed to know). He was something very big in financial auditing and the only man I knew who wore his real hair like it was a wig. Apparently, at the time he met Natalie he'd been desperate for children, having missed out the first time round with a wife who turned out to be chronically frigid. Natalie naturally saw this as an enormous selling point, so Henners moved into our house in Chiswick while I moved into a box room in Wembley with a selection of people from various jurisdictions of Europe. As it turned out, Henners was not one for wasting time, because Natalie was now five months pregnant, less than a year after they'd first met. Thankfully, it seemed that Charlotte was more excited than the rest of us put together.

Henry was okay, even though he wore deck shoes at the weekends and bought his shirts from a taylor. He'd managed to talk me into letting him pay for Charlotte to attend private school as a day pupil, where she was just nearing the end of her first term. She loved it there, and she was thriving – I could see that for myself.

Somewhat generously, given the extortionate fees, Henry had also let me go to Charlotte's first parents' evening in his place, which had been quite entertaining – mainly because it took me back to Hadley and my very last parents' evening as a teacher. Just as we'd been about to start, I'd happened upon Josh and Steve in a cloakroom, illicitly off their faces on the lager they'd managed to smuggle past Mackenzie, which – combined with the fact that as Hadley's IT technician, Steve was not even supposed to be there – had led me swiftly to the conclusion that Josh's job was well and truly on the line. I'd spent most of the evening trying to coax the pair of them unseen out of a fire exit between my various appointments, while insisting solemnly to Mackenzie whenever I bumped into him that Josh had been looking decidedly peaky earlier in the day.

I'd understood back then what a child's school days meant to their parents, and I understood it even better now – because to see Charlotte in her uniform, flushed from a hockey game or beaming at me because she'd just attended her first ever flute lesson, brought a swell of pride to my chest every single time.

Helpfully, Charlotte attending school had also freed me up to get a job, since I now had rent to pay. So I'd started delivering flowers for a living, which was actually okay, because in general it seemed that people were pretty happy to be presented with a bunch of flowers they hadn't been expecting. Sometimes they would open the little card before they signed for them too, and then I'd get the back story. And I loved to listen – it was the best part of my day, to hear those stories.

Wembley wasn't bad. It was the right side of the river for seeing Charlotte and I'd also learned a lot about Andorra from my new housemate Vincent, who kept me in cheap booze and didn't seem to mind when I drunkenly referred to him as Vinnie.

Jess's cottage was swathed in darkness but all the downstairs lights were on, so I could see in. Everything looked exactly the same as it had the last time I'd been there, right down to the fairy lights that were strung around the fireplace, lighting up the brickwork like contented little glow-worms.

There was no sight of anyone inside, but her car was parked out the front. She was home.

I needed to take five minutes, because I was shaking, and not from the cold. So I brushed some snow from the low stone wall on the opposite side of the road from Jess's cottage, and took a seat. My jeans soaked instantly through to my boxers, but I figured that once I was in Jess's living room I could angle my backside to the open fireplace while I was talking to her, and hopefully speed up the drying process.

I'd been months building up to this moment. It was my first time back in Norfolk since Natalie and I had left a little over five years ago. In my mind I had committed to staying with Natalie until Charlotte was at least sixteen, but then Henners pitched up in his Porsche Cayenne, which threw me slightly (and not in a horsepower kind of way). Because, four years earlier than expected, I was finally free to think that, maybe, now could be the right time for me and Jess.

I'd conducted some basic research from Vinnie's laptop, which had told me that her surname was still the same; and I hadn't found any references to a live-in boyfriend mixed in with all those restaurant reviews either, so after everything had settled down with Natalie and my life seemed to have arrived back on an even keel, I decided to make the trip.

I would never find anyone else like Jess, that much was clear to me. I'd loved her from the very beginning, and that

464

was really it. Because for the rest of my life, whether in my head or by my side, I just knew she would always be there.

What I'd felt for her had invariably seemed – to my mind at least – like the simplest thing in the world. It was – for reasons I had finally come to respect – everyone else who had made it all so very complicated.

I didn't have a plan at all beyond knocking on her front door. I'd stood here enough times over the years to know that if there was one girl with the ability to render me instantly amnesic, it was Jess.

My heart was pummelling urgently against my chest cavity and my throat had closed up to the point where I predicted falsetto upon opening my mouth. But then I pictured her face when she saw me on her doorstep with a bottle of champagne, and it made me smile.

This is it.

I crossed the road and made my way along the front path, mind spinning, heart hammering; but as I reached the door, I happened to glance through the living-room window at the very last moment. What I saw brought me to a halt-cum-skid, and I only narrowly avoided smashing the champagne bottle on the ice at my feet.

There was someone inside, and it wasn't Jess. It was a guy.

He was medium height and slightly pudgy, with blond hair in need of a trim and cheeks the shade of ruddy you get after coming indoors from chopping logs. Even in my state of half-shock I remembered to play the push-him-over game: *what would he do if you pushed him over?* My guess was that he'd look a bit upset, dust himself down and then hold up his hands and apologize for something he hadn't started.

I exhaled, probably out loud. She'd found him. She'd found her Good Guy.

The snow whirled around me. The wind was whipping

up and I was freezing. I knew I had to either knock or leave, but I couldn't move. I simply stood out there in the pitch black, watching.

And then, like a vision, she was there, creeping up slowly behind him. I gripped on to the champagne bottle, transfixed by the sight of her slipping slender hands around his slightly plump waist and delivering a kiss against his neck, upon which he gently turned to kiss her back. His lips met the crown of her head, and she looked for a moment angelic, her hair shimmering blonde in the light and falling in natural waves across her shoulders. She was beautiful, I thought to myself for the millionth time. She was exactly how I remembered.

I retreated quietly to the wall across the road, sitting back down without pausing to brush away the snow. And then I popped the champagne, raising the bottle in a bittersweet toast to Jess. I felt the tug of her proximity as strongly as I felt my own heartbeat, but I knew that this guy wanted her too – and he was the one in her living room, not me.

I smiled to myself, recalling my best memories of her between swigs as the snowstorm picked up. I don't know how long I sat there. It must have been a while, because I was halfway through the bottle and borderline hypothermic by the time the front door opened.

The guy emerged alone. Wearing a thick coat, gloves and hat (some people are sensible), he slipped what I assumed to be a wallet into his pocket. Checking my watch, I realized it was just before closing. He was probably off to get some more wine in before everything shut.

'Red or white?' he called out to her, leaning back into the cottage.

'Surprise me,' I whispered under my breath.

'Surprise me,' I heard her say faintly from inside.

I smiled to myself and took my last swig of champagne as he disappeared down the road in the direction of Carafe.

In ten minutes or so, he'd be back. I knew it was now or never.

Now.

Or never.

I glanced into the cottage again. Jess was standing with her back to the fireplace, holding herself in a hug, maybe for warmth. She had turned towards the window and was staring dreamily out into the blackness, a smile on her beautiful face. I pictured her new boyfriend crunching jauntily up the road to fetch the wine, whistling, oblivious, happy.

And then she lifted her head, and she could have been looking right at me – the shadow of her past, watching her silently there in the dark.

I shook the snow from my shoulders, and got to my feet.

Acknowledgements

Thank you to my amazing agent Rebecca Ritchie, for all your encouragement and support from the outset. Also to Sophie Harris and everybody at Curtis Brown – it's truly been a dream to be part of such a wonderful team.

I would also like to say thank you to my incredible editor Kimberley Atkins, for your constant enthusiasm, insightful editing and so much more. And to Maxine Hitchcock, Sophie Elletson and everybody at Penguin – what a privilege to be working with you all. Thanks also to Karen Whitlock and Cordelia Borchardt.

To my family, friends and colleagues for ongoing support, understanding and excitement on my behalf – thank you.

And finally to Mark. For being there with quiet words of encouragement when I needed them most.

Reading Group Questions

1. Do you think there is a specific moment in the novel where one or more of the characters actively makes a choice to overstep a line? Can it ever be possible to pinpoint a single moment that changes your life for ever?

2. When it comes to relationships, to what extent do you believe age is just a number? In the case of Matthew and Jess, if he had not been her teacher would their relationship still have been inappropriate?

3. Do you see Matthew and Will as separate characters? How has he changed over the years? Do you empathize more with one version of him than the other, and, if so, why?

4. Do you think that Sonia is a character to be pitied? Why do you think she behaves the way she does towards Matthew? Did she genuinely like him, or did she always have another agenda?

5. Discuss the significance of Will's *It can't be night for ever* tattoo. Do you believe that Will feels regret about what happened with Jess, or just regret that they were caught?

6. Why do you think Debbie and Jess have such a hostile relationship? Do you think that Jess' actions in the past are to blame for how they are now? Does Jess need to take more responsibility for what happened?

7. Discuss how mothers and the idea of motherhood is presented in the novel. In what ways can the female characters be seen to be ineffectual role models?

8. How do you feel about Will's treatment of Natalie throughout the novel? Is it fair that she has been lied to without any remorse from her boyfriend?

9. The novel hinges on betrayals. If you were in Jess' position, would you be able to forgive Anna for what she did?

10. At the end of the novel, it's uncertain what will happen next. Do you feel this is a fitting end, given how precarious Will and Jess' relationship has always been, or would you prefer their story to have a more definitive conclusion? What do you think is going to happen next? Is Will going to walk away? Should he?

He just wanted a decent book to read ...

Not too much to ask, is it? It was in 1935 when Allen Lane, Managing Director of Bodley Head Publishers, stood on a platform at Exeter railway station looking for something good to read on his journey back to London. His choice was limited to popular magazines and poor-quality paperbacks – the same choice faced every day by the vast majority of readers, few of whom could afford hardbacks. Lane's disappointment and subsequent anger at the range of books generally available led him to found a company – and change the world.

'We believed in the existence in this country of a vast reading public for intelligent books at a low price, and staked everything on it'
Sir Allen Lane, 1902–1970, founder of Penguin Books

The quality paperback had arrived – and not just in bookshops. Lane was adamant that his Penguins should appear in chain stores and tobacconists, and should cost no more than a packet of cigarettes.

Reading habits (and cigarette prices) have changed since 1935, but Penguin still believes in publishing the best books for everybody to enjoy. We still believe that good design costs no more than bad design, and we still believe that quality books published passionately and responsibly make the world a better place.

So wherever you see the little bird – whether it's on a piece of prize-winning literary fiction or a celebrity autobiography, political tour de force or historical masterpiece, a serial-killer thriller, reference book, world classic or a piece of pure escapism – you can bet that it represents the very best that the genre has to offer.

Whatever you like to read – trust Penguin.